THE SHROUDED PATH

by the same author

IN BITTER CHILL
A DEADLY THAW
A PATIENT FURY

The Shrouded Path

SARAH WARD

FABER & FABER

First published in 2018
by Faber & Faber Ltd
Bloomsbury House
74–77 Great Russell Street
London WC1B 3DA

Typeset by Faber & Faber Ltd
Printed and bound by CPI Group (UK) Ltd, Croydon CR0 4YY

A CIP record for this book
is available from the British Library

ISBN 978-0-571-33241-0

2 4 6 8 10 9 7 5 3 1

For Tony Butler

I

Wednesday, 6 November 1957

The first week of November and Susan was already humming the Twelve Days of Christmas. She needed to get it out of her head before she reached home, as her dad would have no truck with carols until the night before Christmas. His Methodist upbringing had been left far behind as he'd gratefully abandoned the church services and interminable hymns. Some childhood habits are hard to shift, however, and the tradition of the tree going up with the minimum of fuss, and carols put on hold until after tea on Christmas Eve, was a convention from which he refused to budge.

Susan's mum let him have his way, although Susan had recently caught her listening to a festive medley on the Light Programme. *Don't tell your father,* she'd cautioned with her eyes before turning the dial of the wooden console with a snap. The hymn book with its meagre selection of carols had already been taken down from the shelf by Susan's brother and left on top of the upright piano in readiness for their father's heralding in of the festive season. Come seven o'clock, Christmas Eve, the routine would be the same. Their father, after much bother looking for his glasses, would fumble over the keys to pick out a tune barely recognisable from the ones sung throughout December outside the closed front door. For even well-meaning carol singers weren't immune from her father's edict. No Christmas about the house before the 24th. Even on the doorstep.

But carols need to be learnt. Susan, a high alto with a knack for holding a note in the face of her classmates' flat and occasionally sharp pitch, was expected at Wednesday evening choir practice in the hut near the school gates. Warmed by only a three-bar fire, she and the other members of the fourth and fifth forms who were willing to practise in time for the school concert breathed out cold air as their lungs ached and chests heaved with the effort of singing in the damp fug. *Twelve drummers drumming, eleven pipers piping, ten lords a-leaping.*

The tune swirled around her head as she steered her bike through the autumn mist along the thin track that would take her across the bridge to her home on the other side of Bampton. The wheels bumped and squeaked over the uneven path, startling the few birds prepared to stay in the Peak District for the winter. Frost had begun to settle on the fields, giving the landscape a shimmering glow. As the temperature dropped, Susan tightened the ends of her headscarf under her chin, pulling the thin material away from her ears so that she could hear any encroaching sounds. Her thick blazer warmed her body and she dragged the sleeves of her jumper down over her cold palms, which grasped the metal of the handlebars.

Susan kept a wary eye on the fields around her. She'd been told not to come this way ever since her friend, Iris, had seen a man standing in the field far off, completely naked. Iris had rushed back to her house in the street next to Susan's and some of the fathers, Susan's included, had gone in search of the pervert. Of course, he'd gone by the time the men arrived. Disappeared into the mists but not forgotten by the community. Don't go the back way home from choir, she'd been warned. First by her dad and afterwards, more sharply, by her mother, who'd looked like she wanted to expand the conversation into something more meaningful. Susan had hung about in the kitchen but nothing further had been revealed.

When she got home, she'd pretend she hadn't come this way. Would tell her mother that, of course, she'd taken the way up Bampton High Street, cycled behind the cottage hospital and continued along the main road over the railway bridge to the entrance of the new housing estate. However, no matter how quickly she cycled, the fact was that this back way would get her home quicker on a cold November evening, despite the uneven path. The route was a direct line from her school to the back of her estate where she'd have to lift her bike over the chained five-bar gate.

She looked around the chilled landscape but could see nothing through the grey mist. She pinched the bike's tyres to reassure herself that they were rock solid. Any problems and she'd hop on and make a quick getaway, confident she could ride faster than any man, especially a naked one, could run.

In the distance, she could see the stone bridge over the railway line, its graceful arch obscuring the final part of her journey. She put her head down and bumped along the track towards it. Once over the hump, she'd hop onto the saddle and freewheel the rest of the way. *Nine ladies dancing, eight maids a-milking.* Her navy blue skirt snagged against the stubble of the harvested fields. She'd have to brush it off before she reached home or it would be a dead giveaway which way she'd come.

Seven swans a-swimming. As she trundled down onto the bridge, the fog parted for a moment and she checked her watch. Ten past four. Too early for the hourly London train that would slow by the bridge in anticipation of its arrival into Bampton station. On summer days she would sometimes come up and watch the red engine approach and close her eyes as the steam engulfed her, its hot vapour leaving her skin glistening in the sun. Tonight, it would be another twenty minutes before the first hiss of the engine would be heard.

At a sharp sound below, she stopped in alarm and lifted a leg, ready to take flight. She looked down onto the track below her and relaxed. Six figures were clad in grey uniforms. Not the garb of Bampton Secondary Modern for the Eleven Plus failures like herself but of the grammar school. Thick grey gaberdine blazers, pleated skirts over grey ribbed tights, and black berets perched on top of their heads like plumage. *Six geese a-laying*, thought Susan, as she watched them walk towards her. There were six of them too, squawking with annoyance. Susan leant back against the stone pillar. There was less rivalry than between the boys from the different schools but she was outnumbered and afraid of any taunts being directed towards her.

The chatter continued but Susan became aware of an undercurrent of menace. The tone of the words spoken was sharp and bitter. She tried to listen to what was being said but could only make out fragments. 'Better not.' 'Sorry.' 'I said not.' The group passed underneath her and into the tunnel below. She counted them in. *Six geese a-laying, five gold rings. Four calling birds, three French hens, two turtle doves and a—.* The final figure looked up before disappearing into the darkness and Susan shrank back into the mist at the look of malevolence on the girl's face.

It would take them around five minutes to make their way along the tunnel. Long enough for Susan to get on her bike and cycle down the hill the other side and along the path running parallel to the track before it turned sharply away from the line. Susan set off, enjoying none of the whoosh of cold air she normally felt as she plunged down the embankment. The urge to get away was as strong as if the naked man was chasing after her. She pedalled furiously, too hard, because as the incline levelled she felt the chain buckle and slip against her calves. Her legs flailed as she tilted herself off her bike. She upended it and tried to put the chain back on but her frozen fingers wouldn't cooperate in the icy chill. She could hear the sound of the girls as they approached the end of the tunnel. No laughter this time but muted voices and the echoing of feet on the gravel around the tracks.

There was nothing for it but to wheel the bike the ten minutes back to her house, but, if she did that, she would be just in front of the girls; a lone figure in the distance and the thought chilled her. Instead, she shrank back into the undergrowth, pulling the bike with her, and took refuge behind a tree. Down here, near to the track, the mist was churning again. Susan watched as the girls came out in a line. The music had stopped in Susan's head, replaced by a creeping fear. *One, two, three, four, five,* she counted and stopped, waiting for the sixth. No one appeared. She stayed squatting and, as the mist cleared for a moment, looked at the retreating

5

backs and counted again. Five. One of them must still be in the tunnel.

The girls were no longer talking to each other. They continued in silence around the bend and out of her sight. Susan watched them, the pull of home so strong that she wanted to call out for her mother. Instead, checking that none of the girls had doubled back on themselves, she left her bike in the undergrowth and made her way towards the tunnel. The strip lights on the wall were dim but she could see the opening in the far distance. A dark arch filled with hazy light.

Susan entered the space and walked down the side of the track, feeling along the slimy wall with her fingertips and keeping her eyes on the ground. She was holding her breath, expecting the worst, but the anticipated form never materialised.

When she reached the end of the tunnel, Susan crossed over to the other track and walked back towards her bike, switching her attention between the floor and the walls. There was no opening, no corners to hide in. She was alone inside the gloom, although, perhaps, the ghosts of past passengers tried to invade her confused mind. A faint cry or was she imagining it? Her eyes darted around the dank space, looking for something, anything, that would explain the missing figure.

It was nearly dark when she left the tunnel. Without looking back, Susan retrieved her bike and wheeled it along the path, unaware of a lone figure, also in a school uniform, watching her from the embankment. The outline, silhouetted by the low, setting sun, looked like the angel of the railways. By the time she'd reached the bend, the half-past-four train was arriving, its brakes squealing as it slowed into Bampton station, just visible around the corner. Susan veered to the right, away from the track towards the warmth of her mother's steamy kitchen.

The following days were spent in a frenzy of fear as Susan waited for news of a missing schoolgirl that would force her to reveal her own part in witnessing the drama. Nothing. Over the next few weeks, she listened and waited. Returning from choir practice, she always made the trip the long way around and persuaded her dad to buy the bike a new chain that never slipped out of the cogs. Until the day she left Secondary Modern the following year, she never travelled down the path again.

Years passed, then decades. Beeching gave his verdict on the state of England's railways and the line shut down. The old station house became a private residence and the tracks were first left to rust and then removed. Susan left Bampton and returned. All the while, she avoided tunnels. She held her breath on her honeymoon when her new husband drove them through the Brandberg Pass, and refused to take her children on the steam train up to Devil's Bridge one holiday in Wales. It was the joke amongst her grandchildren. Granny doesn't like trains. Finally, the old fear resurfaced and Susan, feeling the familiar dread creeping through her, braced herself for what might come next.

PART ONE

Murder

2

Friday, 27 October 2017

Before the railways, there were canals. Built with less vision but possibly more enterprise. You can drive a steam locomotive up a mountain path but water needs to be harnessed and channelled. The Bampton waterway had never been loved, even at the time of its construction. If people talk about the golden age of canals, Bampton never had one. The canal had, however, served its purpose. Slabs of granite hewn from the nearby quarries had been heaved to the wharf for shipment to London and Liverpool, the stone becoming the foundation of a wealthy industrialist's townhouse or a municipal building to celebrate a city's prosperity.

Mina slowed the canoe and pushed a child's scooter out of the way with her paddle. Now that the rain had returned, a sheet of needles obscured her vision and she'd nearly careered into the metal frame lying partly submerged, one rotating wheel just visible above the waterline. The oar snagged against the handlebars and she jerked it away, the sudden movement causing the canoe to rock slightly. The buoyancy vest gave her comfort but wouldn't save her from deadly bacteria in the stagnant water if she swallowed a mouthful. She steadied herself and made a mental note of the scooter's location. When she got back to the boat, she'd retrieve her phone and call the Canals Trust to clear the obstacle.

'It's a bloody disgrace.'

The sound of a voice so near made her jump. She looked to the bank to find the speaker but saw only a lone dog walker coaxing his puppy out from under a tree, whispering encouragement to the shivering animal. The small dog, frightened of the long grass, resisted so the man scooped it up, placed it inside his jacket and hurried off.

'They're savages. Someone threw a bottle at me the other morning.'

Through the rain, Mina saw another person on the water. A man in a top-of-the-range kayak, its colours too bright on this dull day. As she drifted nearer, she saw he was more a boy, his long beard making him look older than his years. What did they call them? Hipster beards. A hipster in a kayak.

'It's unusual to see scooters in the water these days,' she shouted across to him. 'When I was growing up, this canal was a no-go area. There were all sorts thrown in. Bicycle wheels, old prams. Now it's cleaned up and we're paddling on it.'

He rolled his eyes, not interested in the past. 'It's those pikeys camping up near Hale's End who've probably dumped it,' he shouted back at her and carried on towards Higgs Lock.

Great. A racist hipster. Mina felt tired and depressed, her mood plummeting. *State your position and bugger off,* she thought. *Is that what counts as debate these days?* She picked up her pace and made her way east, away from the boy and the lights of Bampton. Her tired arms settled into a rhythm and she could feel her black mood lighten as the day darkened.

She paddled towards the landmark she used as her late afternoon watershed. This distance was all she would allow herself in the failing light. As she approached the arch of Step Bridge, which was cracked with age and stained with soot and algae, she stopped short of the entrance and steered the canoe so that its tip rested on one of the banks. Tired from the exertion, she sat back slightly as she caught her breath.

The bridge over the canal had probably once been a route for carts coming into Bampton but it was pedestrian only now and empty of people. At dusk, the canal had an eerie character. Dog walkers and cyclists preferred the former railway track, renamed the Topley Trail, for their daily exercise rather than this desolate place despite the money pumped into the area to spruce it up. Mina looked into the blackness of the tunnel, its ripe air occasionally wafting towards her, and was glad that she wouldn't be entering it today.

The towpath was also empty, except for a lone jogger approaching her in the distance. She squinted to make out the gender of the runner. Long legs, probably a man. They were running confidently, covering the ground between them faster than Mina expected. Or perhaps it was a woman because at the top of the runner's head was a mane of blonde hair tied in a ponytail behind a hairband, just as Anna wore it.

Mina dipped her paddle into the water and allowed the canoe to glide away from the bridge. The runner got closer, their gaze directed towards Mina. Now she could see that they weren't running in the way that joggers do, focused on the distance in front of them. Instead, the runner was deliberately making her way towards Mina's canoe. Mina glanced back towards the tunnel where she could take refuge if necessary but, as she was weighing up her options, she saw the gauzy figure coalesce into someone she recognised. The runner didn't wear their hair like Anna. It *was* her neighbour.

Mina's heart contracted. She paddled clumsily towards the opposite bank but there was nowhere to dock and haul herself out. She was in the water about half a metre below ground level, too low to pull herself out of the boat. She clawed at the grass until Anna reached the canoe, her dirty white running shoes at eye level.

'Mina! Your phone's been going and going. Charlie and I were worried so I went onto the boat to retrieve it. The cabin door was open. You don't mind?'

'Did you answer it?'

'No, but look who's been calling.'

Mina saw the single word of the caller ID. Hospital. She'd programmed in the number of her mother's ward. The direct line to the nurses' station by the entrance. The phone used by people who knew her, knew her mum, knew when to call. With shaking fingers, she pressed redial and listened to the tone ring once.

'Oncology.'

'It's Mina Kemp. You've been calling me.' Mina could hear muted laughter in the background. A huddle of nurses joking with each other. The voice on the other end told them to hush and the sound dissipated.

'Mina. I'm sorry about this but your mum's taken a turn for the worse this afternoon. We're still trying to stabilise her and we thought we'd better let you know. Can you come in?'

'But she was all right this morning when I saw her.' Mina

looked up at Anna towering over her, a look of concern on her face.

'There's been a change in her condition. These things do happen. The consultant thought I'd better call you.'

'Is it bad?'

The nurse hesitated. 'I think you should come here as soon as you can.'

3

The open plan office, formerly known as CID HQ and re-named the Detective Room, smelt of stale food and damp wool. Wet hats and gloves had been placed on radiators and umbrellas left open to dry before the evening commute. People had stayed put for lunch, only nipping across the road to buy a sandwich and throwing the remains in the wastepaper bin. Now deserted, the room still held the smell of recently absented bodies. DC Connie Childs was studying the report she'd been putting off all day, keeping a wary eye on DI Matthews who was trying to look comfortable in Sadler's office.

'Getting herself settled in, I see.'

A young constable she didn't recognise slapped a report on a desk opposite her. Connie, who had been thinking the same thing, scowled at him and he scarpered.

Two years after passing her inspector's exams, Matthews had successfully applied for a temporary DI post to cover maternity leave. She saw it as a step towards a permanent position, which was possibly true, but, for Connie, the promotion was bad news. It wasn't that Matthews was being an arse. Far from it. Instead, she was so carefully watching her back that she was demanding that all paperwork was completed on time and constantly checking up on the team.

Connie was bidding for a pair of Whistles boots on eBay,

size four and in a buttery fawn suede that were completely impractical in a Derbyshire autumn and yet irresistible. She'd already been outbid once but every time she took her phone out of her bag to check on progress she was aware of a pair of eyes studying her through the glass partition. She turned a page on her desk calendar to see how long it was before Sadler returned. Good God. He'd only been gone five days. She had all of the following week to get through. Why had he offered Matthews the use of his office while he was away? She wasn't comfortable with it and neither were the team. Aware of Connie's gaze, Matthews stood up and opened the door.

'How are you getting on?' Matthews's glasses were perched on top of her head revealing eyes reddened from tiredness and strain.

'Just examining the details of a deceased person found this week. Everything looks fine but I'm double checking.' Matthews nodded and shut the door. Connie looked down at the file and sighed.

A sudden death the previous day, routine. The woman, Nell Colley, unmarried, had been found sitting upright on her sofa by a neighbour who had let herself in with a spare key when Nell hadn't answered the door. The deceased had been ill with worsening cardiac arrhythmia. She'd been seen by her GP only days earlier, complaining of pain and weakness in her arms. The illness was debilitating, although the neighbour had reported that Nell had been feeling slightly better in the days before her death.

The ambulance service had verified that life was extinct and completed the appropriate form and left it with the next of kin, in this case Nell's neighbour. The neighbour sent a request to the woman's GP to come to the house to provide a death certificate, which he'd done. It had come under the auspices of an 'expected death' and had been dealt with in a textbook way.

No further action, although . . . Connie picked up the file and flicked through it. No, Matthews was getting the wind up her, that was all. There was nothing there. No further action. Connie put the file to one side as DC Jill Mayfield came into the office, shrugging off her mac and hanging it on the coat hook. Rivulets of water dropped onto Connie's dry umbrella. She opened her mouth to protest but thought better of it. It would get wet again soon enough. Mayfield sat down at her desk and rubbed her burgeoning stomach.

'That was a waste of time. A burglary in west Bampton. No fingerprints, no identifying ID on the electronic items taken. You should see the window they got in through. I couldn't have fitted my leg through it let alone the rest of my body, even without my bump. Why do we go to these houses when we know there's nothing we can do?'

Connie nodded over to Matthews.

'Yes, that's true. God, I can't wait for this baby to arrive. I feel like I'm carting around a sack of spuds every time I go anywhere.' She looked at her watch. 'Bloody hell. It's nearly time for me to pick up the kids from the child minder.'

'What did you come back for? You could have gone straight there.'

Mayfield grimaced. 'Need to show my face. Matthews made a snide comment earlier today, something about it being difficult to balance being a detective with a family life.'

'She never did.' Connie's voice dropped. 'That counts as discrimination. What did she say that for?'

'I dunno. Actually, it is a bit funny. She's so meticulous about us doing everything by the book and then she comes out with crap like that. Whatever happened to our flexible working policy? Anyway, what are you up to?'

'Paperwork.' Connie picked up the file and wafted it at Mayfield. 'Non-suspicious death that I'm checking is, well, non-suspicious.'

'And is it?'

'Definitely.'

Mayfield looked up from the computer. 'What's the matter?'

'Nothing. I said it was non-suspicious. Why do you think something's the matter?'

'It's just the way you said it, that's all.'

'You're imagining it. I'm passing it back to Matthews marked no further action.'

Mayfield sighed. 'Fair enough. Have you heard from Sadler?'

'Me? Why would I hear from him? He's on holiday. It's not like we're mates or anything.'

Mayfield shut down the computer, got up and winked at Connie. 'Just going to make a point of saying goodbye.'

Connie watched Mayfield sway over to Sadler's office and stick her head through the door. A murmured conversation and she came back looking confused.

'That was odd. She said I should have gone straight home after the house visit. She's changed her tune. Oh well. No pleasing some people. Do you know we've got someone new starting on Monday?'

'Who?' The force of Connie's reply surprised them both. 'Sorry. I had no idea, that's all.'

Mayfield smiled and winked at Connie. 'It's a guy.'

'So? What's that got to do with anything? I'm done with detectives. Look where it got me last time.'

'Oh well. I suppose *I* can always look. It's one good thing about carting around this lump. It makes you virtually invisible to men. You can gawp as much as you want.'

'And do you?'

'Of course.'

Connie laughed. 'I suppose it's just as well that it's quiet, really.'

'What do you mean?'

'Well, we don't want anything happening while Sadler's away. I mean, a non-suspicious death and a break-in. All's quiet on the Bampton front. Long may it continue.' Her eyes dropped to the file on her desk and she refused to acknowledge the feeling of disquiet that crept over her.

4

There's a smell common to all sick rooms that's impossible to dispel. Mina had learnt that spraying yourself with Estée Lauder's Pleasures not only failed to mask the waft of decay but mingled with it, creating an aroma so cloying that it made her want to gag. Six months earlier, she had been unaware of the practicalities of the hospital room but you learn quickly when you have to. Her mother's diagnosis had been slow but the decline rapid.

Hilary lay in bed with her eyes closed, a slight sheen on her face. Only this morning, she'd been able to sit up a little and tell Mina that she was feeling better. Better as in, I might go home soon. I might not need to go to that nursing home that wasn't a hospital and wasn't a hospice. The something in between for the nearly dying. I might feel well enough to go back to the boat and spend my final days there. As Mina looked down on her mother, that morning seemed a lifetime ago. The hospital was right. Hilary had deteriorated.

'She was all right earlier.'

How many times had Mina said this since she'd arrived? The nurse stirred beside her.

'It does happen, you know. She's very poorly. She has a raised temperature so she's probably picked up an infection. We're going to give her some antibiotics to fight it but we need the results of her blood tests first. What we give her depends on the origin of the problem.'

'An infection from where? She hasn't had many visitors apart from me.'

'This is a hospital. We do our best but . . .'

'Is she comfortable? She's not in any pain, is she?'

'She's settled now but she was very anxious before.'

'Anxious? About what? Anxious to see me?'

Mina's sharp tone did nothing to ruffle the nurse. 'She seemed a bit confused, that's all. The infection combined with the cancer . . .'

There was nothing more to say and, at the sound of a buzzer down the hall, the nurse hurried away. Mina picked up a sponge resting in a dish of water and wiped her mother's cracked lips.

'Are you thirsty?' she whispered.

Without opening her eyes, Hilary nodded.

Mina looked up at the drip that was slowly pushing its nutrients through the thin body. 'I'll give you some more water.'

She dipped the sponge back in the liquid and squeezed drops into Hilary's mouth. 'No more,' her mother croaked and Mina stopped.

'How are you feeling, Mum?'

Hilary's eyes, too large in her face with its translucent skin, opened slightly. Her lips worked, trying to form words.

'Is something the matter?'

Even as she said it, Mina was aware of the absurdity of the question. Of course something was the matter. Her mother, however, took the question at face value, her eyes holding Mina's.

'Scared.' Hilary's voice was hoarse. During a recent operation, the anaesthetist had been too rough pulling out the tube and had slightly damaged her voice box. Nothing in the general scheme of things, but still. More pain on top of all the other.

'Oh Mum.' Mina laid her hand on her mother's arm, feeling the dry, hot skin.

'Strange . . . just . . . doesn't make sense.'

Mina felt the stillness of the hospital room. A closed world where the hubbub of the rest of the ward could be heard distantly through the closed door. 'What do you mean?'

Hilary tried to lift her head, straining with the effort. 'This morning.'

'What happened this morning?'

Hilary shut her eyes briefly with the pain. Mina leant down, feeling the heat from her mother's fever. 'You don't need to talk if it's painful. Just rest.'

A slight shake of the head. 'Strange.' The words came out as dry as parchment. 'So strange to see her.'

'Who? Who've you seen?'

Her mother took a shallow breath. 'Valerie. I've seen Valerie.'

'Valerie? Who's she?'

Her mother's eyes turned towards the plant sitting on the windowsill. Mina had heard of hospitals that banned flowers but, although St Bertram's didn't go that far, it was generally discouraged. Instead, Mina had brought in a huge cyclamen and no one had complained of its presence. A difficult plant to sustain, the white flowers liable to wilt and the leaves to pale and wither. Preserving the plant was a shared effort but her mother couldn't know how much energy Mina put into keeping the cyclamen alive. It was a warped reasoning but Mina held onto it. While the plant survived so would her mother.

'Friend.'

'You've seen your friend. Where? Here in the hospital?'

Her mother's eyes held hers. 'I thought it was a dream.'

'Maybe it wasn't a dream. Perhaps she is here at the hospital.'

Hilary shook her head, so slight a movement it was hard to see. 'Didn't expect to see her. Not real. Like a dream.'

'Oh Mum. We all have strange dreams sometimes. You're on lots of medication. It could have been that.'

Hilary was shaking her head. 'She must hate me.'

'*Hate you!* Why on earth should she hate you?'

Hilary pulled Mina towards her. 'Scared. I'm scared because . . . I . . . I have to tell you. About . . . about Valerie.'

'About your friend, Valerie? What do you need to tell me?'

Her mother's head dropped in frustration.

'Tell me if it's important. I'm listening.'

'I want you to find her and check she's okay.'

'Why wouldn't she be okay?'

A nurse put her head through the door but withdrew when she saw Mina.

'She was here and she shouldn't have been. She was next to me.'

'But I don't understand. I didn't think you had any visitors. How was she next to you?'

'Saw her.'

It was important to her mother. Mina could see that. In the struggle to make herself articulate, Hilary was conveying her desperation. 'You saw Valerie. That's okay, isn't it?'

24

Hilary shook her head.

Mina struggled to make sense of her mother's agitation. 'Your friend Valerie was here and you were surprised to see her. Was it a long time since you'd seen her?'

Hilary looked up and nodded.

'How long was it since you last saw her?'

'School.'

'School?' Mina's voice rose and her mother looked alarmed. 'Sorry.'

Her mother hadn't kept in touch with any classmates. There'd been plenty of work friends in and out of the house over the years but Mina couldn't ever remember her mother talking about her school years, let alone keeping in touch with a friend.

Hilary was trying to raise her head. 'I want . . . I want you to find her. See if she's okay.'

'She lives in Bampton?'

Her mother tried to smile but the rictus that crossed her face made Mina want to pull her head away.

'I don't know. I heard she went away.'

'Okay, well, maybe she was back in the hospital visiting someone and she heard you were here.'

'Can you, can you find her?'

'I can try. What was her last name?'

Hilary scrunched up her eyes. 'Can't remember.'

'You only know her first name?' Mina couldn't keep the note of despair out of her voice. 'Can't you tell me anything else?'

'Cold. Never went back there. Terrible place.'

'You went to a cold place? Here in the Peaks? That's not

narrowing it down much.' Hilary had closed her eyes. Mina leant forward. 'Mum. Did Valerie live in a cold place? Really high up. What about Flash? That's the highest village here, isn't it?'

Hilary was silent. Mina turned her head away from her mother and stared out of the large window that looked down onto the top of a sycamore, its crown a riot of yellow and brown leaves. It was a tree that Mina hated. Introduced into England in the Middle Ages, the little helicopter seeds dispersed everywhere and made her job in the summer a nightmare.

'If you can't remember her last name, how will I find her?'

Mina could feel a well of desperation bubbling up. No last name and a first one that was hardly uncommon for that generation. Valerie. Her mother had opened her eyes again and was looking at her in desperation.

'It's important.'

I shouldn't be promising anything, thought Mina. *Suppose I can't find Valerie. How will I feel afterwards, bound to a promise I couldn't keep?*

'I can try to find her for you. She was here in the hospital so that will help. Is that okay? I'll start looking for Valerie tomorrow.'

Hilary's head dropped to the pillow in relief. 'Need to see if she's okay.'

'You need to see Valerie? Why?'

Hilary closed her eyes. 'Because I thought she was dead.'

5

Detective Inspector Francis Sadler let slip a few weeks before his leave that he'd always fancied visiting West Wales and, from then, it became office fact that this was where he was heading on holiday. There had even been some superfluous Welsh jokes which he'd smiled at and then regretted. In fact, he had no intention of going anywhere, soured by his experience of previous autumn holidays. Damp, chilly weather did nothing to lift his spirits and, after a few days of lie-ins, boredom would set in. By the end of the holiday, he'd be doubting his reasons for being a policeman and brooding over the lack of any relationships on the horizon.

Staying put, he'd discovered the previous year, lightened his mood and smoothed the worries gnawing away at him. Sadler could do nothing about the weather but he felt rooted in the landscape around him. He'd gone along with everyone's assumption that he was heading off on his travels but had, instead, stayed in his house, reading and walking in the Peaks, keeping out of the way of his usual haunts. This year, he was doing the same. He'd ordered a case of wine online and three hardbacks from the independent bookshop struggling to pay its lease over the colder months.

He'd just started the second of the books, a biography of Charlotte Brontë, when there was a knock on the door.

He went to open it, glad of the respite from the tiny print. His neighbour, Clive, stood on the doorstep, a badminton racket dangling from one hand, as rain spat onto his head.

'Do you want to come in?'

'I won't disturb you. I'm just back from the gym and I saw your car at the front. Not at work this week?'

'I'm on holiday. I think the official name is a staycation.'

His neighbour grinned. 'I don't blame you. I could never stand going away myself. Not the best week for it, though.'

Sadler shrugged. 'I don't mind. Are you sure you won't come in?'

'I'll step inside out of the rain.' Clive moved into the porch. 'I noticed you were off at the beginning of the week but I thought you'd want a bit of privacy first. You must be getting bored by now, though. Fancy sharing a bottle of wine one evening? It's been a while.'

'Since my last holiday, I think.'

'I'm not complaining. There are benefits to not seeing your neighbours too often, even ones as congenial as you, Francis. How about tonight?'

'Sounds like a good idea.'

'Would it be all right if I invited a friend too? It's someone I'd like you to meet.' Clive glanced at Sadler's face and laughed. 'Not female. Sorry, I wasn't trying to set you up. I saw one of my old partners today for a game. I'd like you to meet him.'

'There's not a problem, is there?'

'I don't think so but . . . look, maybe I shouldn't have asked. It *is* your holidays.'

'Not at all. I don't have any other plans. Will eight-ish be okay?'

'Perfect. And thanks.' Clive's eyes dropped to the book Sadler was holding in his hands. 'I didn't realise you were a Brontë fan.'

'I can't say I am particularly. I've only recently started it.'

He was so badly read these days that his sister, Camilla, constantly teased him about his preference for Netflix binges over high literature.

'You know there's a Derbyshire connection with Charlotte Brontë?'

'Is there? I'm barely beyond the first chapter but I always associate her with Yorkshire.'

'Well, of course, there's Haworth and that's where all the devotees go, but of the three sisters, it was Charlotte who was the best travelled and who had friendships outside the close family circle. You'll see as you read on a bit.'

'And she came to Derbyshire?'

'Her friend, Ellen Nussey, had a brother who was rector of Hathersage and she used parts of the town as inspiration for fictional places in *Jane Eyre*. Different names, of course, but the buildings from the town are recognisable in the book. It's worth a visit.' Clive turned to brave the rain. 'See you later. I'll provide the wine. I'll even light the fire in your honour. And thanks again.'

After his neighbour had retreated, Sadler stood on the doorstep watching the shower as it increased in ferocity and then eased up. Tonight's problem, if there was one, would be revealed soon enough. However, the pull of the outside was drawing him away from the comfort of his sitting room. He crossed to his bookshelves and took out a guidebook. Hathersage was around a twenty minute drive from Bampton, too far to walk to from his house but as good a place as any to get some fresh air. Sadler put on his walking boots and drove to the town. He parked outside the church, the place that had apparently brought the eldest Brontë sister to Derbyshire, and walked into the graveyard. He was surprised to see a huddle of men in hardhats drinking tea on the path.

'Sorry, mate, the church is shut,' one of the men shouted over to him.

'How long for?'

'It'll be a few months yet. We're improving the lighting.'

'Damn.'

The workman grinned at him. 'You couldn't see anything even if we let you in. All the statues and paintings are covered up. It's not a wasted journey, though. The churchyard's worth a look if you like Robin Hood.'

'Robin Hood?'

'The grave of Little John's here. You know. The tall one in the films. Didn't you know? It's usually what brings tourists to the church. It's over there.' He nodded his head to the left and turned back to his colleagues.

Little John and Robin Hood. Not exactly the literary pilgrimage Sadler had envisaged. He could remember from primary school one of his teachers telling the class about this grave. He hadn't been much interested in the folk tale, preferring cricket and dinosaurs, but still, he remembered hearing about the story of a tall man in Derbyshire.

He followed the path and found a low iron fence next to a yew tree and a stone with a modern inscription. Not much, but something. Touched, he stayed there for a moment. Did it matter whether it was true or not? Someone had cared enough to mark the spot and it was part of the local history.

He left his car outside the church and walked down the steep hill towards the town. Turning into Baulk Lane, he checked the guidebook and followed the public footpath until he came to a house with tall spindly chimneys. Brookfield Manor, the template for Vale Hall in *Jane Eyre*, where the heroine teaches under a false name. It was a large building, made of Derbyshire stone, with an air of genteel wealth. North Lees Hall, further along the path, was more to his taste. It was the inspiration for Mr Rochester's Thornfield Hall, and Charlotte Brontë had even used the family's surname, Eyre, for her heroine. Sadler leant on the wall and studied the crenellated roof. It would have suited Hercule Poirot as a home, he thought. The house's footprint was a perfect square.

'Fancy living there? You'll have to beat me to it.'

Sadler turned, taken by surprise by a woman standing over the hedge opposite him wearing loose dungarees over a bottle-green top. She had a rake in her hands, sweating from recent exertion. 'Sorry, did I startle you? You had a look in your eye that I see often with walkers. Dreams of domestic grandeur.'

'It's an imposing house. A bit big for me, though.'

'That's what I tell myself too. What would I do with all that space?'

'Is it privately owned? They must get sick of people stopping to take a look.'

'It's owned by the Peak Park but they rent it out. There are tenants in at the moment. They take it on with the knowledge that there's a public footpath running alongside the house so they can't complain.'

'You're the gardener?'

31

'How did you guess?' She clutched the rake to her, getting it tangled in her curls that were being unsuccessfully tamed by a headscarf.

'I'm very observant. It's what comes of being a policeman.'

Why did he tell her that? He, who kept his professional life so separate from family and friends.

A shadow crossed her face but she smiled and pointed at the hall. 'It's wonderful, isn't it? I'd give my eye teeth to live there.'

'You don't live on site then?'

She laughed, dimples appearing in her round cheeks. 'I'm not a permanent gardener. It's part of my rounds. They pay me to come here one day a week.' She pointed at her van standing in the drive, which had the name 'The Land Girl' emblazoned on its side. 'That's me. Mina, the land girl.'

'It's a good name.'

'It is, isn't it? My mum thought it up. She's got a much better imagination than me. She loved it when I told her I was working at North Lees Hall too. All those Gothic associations.'

'She's a fan of *Dracula* too.'

Mina tried to stop herself looking pleased. 'You mean my name? I guess so. She just, you know, liked reading.'

'She's not alive?'

There it was again. A flicker of pain as she spoke. 'She's in hospital. No more reading for her, I don't think.'

Very ill then. Discomforted, Sadler turned away. 'It's a busy time of year for you, clearing all the leaves. I'm keeping you from your work.'

'Don't worry. I should be having a break but I'm pushing on so I can leave early. You're the first person I've seen all morning.'

'The path's usually busier?'

'It's wonderful. It brings people from all over the world to Hathersage.'

'The workman at the church said they mainly came to see Little John.'

'*Did* he? Well, I've worked here for three years and I can tell you for every person looking for Little John, there are five who are Brontë fans.'

'That's good to hear.'

'Did you know that there's a local legend that the hall even had a mad woman in the attic? The name of Agnes Ashurst. It's where Charlotte Brontë got the inspiration for the first Mrs Rochester.'

'Is it true?'

Mina shrugged. 'Who's to say? Is it Little John from legend in the grave up at the church? That's the point of legends, isn't it? We don't know.'

'True.' Sadler made to go.

'Listen, can I ask you something?'

He stopped. 'Of course. What is it?'

'I'm just wondering. Oh, I don't know. It's about finding someone. I've been raking and thinking and then I meet you and you say that you're a policeman. Do you believe in serendipity?'

He shook his head. 'No.'

She laughed. 'No. Actually, neither do I. But, anyway, you must sometimes have to find people as part of your job.'

'Occasionally. You want to find someone? Are they missing?'

'No, I don't think so. Not missing but lost. Don't mind me. I'm thinking while I'm talking. It's my worst trait.'

'If you think a crime has been committed . . .'

'Oh, there's no crime. I might need to find someone from decades ago, that's all.'

But lost is an odd way to describe someone, thought Sadler.

'I was wondering how easy it is to look for someone when you only have a first name?'

'Officially, it's going to be quite hard but if you've got the name of a place or a work address you could probably ask around based on first name only.'

'A place?'

'Well, yes. My name's Francis and I've told you I'm a policeman. I might be hard to find on an official document with only those two bits of information but, if you asked around Bampton or went to the station, you'd find someone who could identify me.'

'Right. So I need to ask around?'

'It's just an idea. Is everything all right?'

'Don't mind me. I've got a lot on my plate, that's all. I'll let you get on.'

'Are you sure?'

She nodded and returned to the leaves she was gathering. He carried on down the path, past her van. The Land Girl. The van was old but well cared for. Recently washed, the gold letters of the business name glinted in the low sun. The back doors were open and he could see the tools laid neatly on top of each other. Mina, a woman with a lot on her mind and with a mother sick in hospital. Perhaps he should have asked her for the name of the person she was looking for.

He turned around and she was staring after him. She raised her rake in farewell and he waved back, intrigued at what was clearly preoccupying her.

6

Mina left North Lees Hall thinking about the unsettling man with the cool demeanour and steady gaze. He'd be a good policeman, she suspected. He hadn't appeared surprised by her question, just concerned. What had he said his name was? Francis. She'd wanted to ask him for help there and then but had been struck dumb by the futility of her task. How ridiculous it would have been to ask him to help find her mother's childhood friend when all she had was a first name, Valerie. He had, however, helped. Given her an idea where to start.

She drove around the main square in Bampton, keeping her eye open for a parking space. When a traffic warden came down the street, a few idling cars drifted away, leaving her with a choice of spots. She picked one nearest to the library and went inside the building. She'd rarely used the library since childhood. The horticulture section had been hopelessly out of date, full of texts with black and white photos and old-fashioned advice. Unlike the hospital, however, the library had survived cuts and threatened moves and been refurbished at least twice in Mina's memory. It looked like it needed a third. The front desk was staffed by a lone figure hunched over a book, rubbing out pencil marks. He glanced up at her and then again in surprise.

'Mina? Is that you?'

Mina crossed towards him, not recognising the man in his twenties although he reminded her of the kayaker she'd encountered the other evening. The same sharp cut hair and soft beard. She squinted at the top half of his face, trying to place him.

'It's Joseph. You probably don't remember me but I worked with your mum for years. She introduced me to you in the street about a year ago. How is she?'

Mina winced. 'Not good.'

'I'm sorry to hear that. How's she coping on the boat?'

'She's not coping at all. She's in hospital.'

'Oh no. She loved her houseboat.'

After retiring from the library, Hilary had made radical changes in her life that Mina realised she'd been planning for some time. Always independent, she had gradually stripped her small semi of the furniture and other items she deemed unimportant. Mina had hardly noticed to begin with. Days at college had been augmented with backbreaking work, either at the allotment or at Chatsworth House where she'd got a temporary job staking the tall lupins that graced the borders of the large gardens. Only once had she remarked the house was looking a bit sparse and she found out why on the day her mother handed back her staff pass to the local authority. The house was given to Mina, an advance on her inheritance, and her mother had proudly revealed her new home, the *Evening Star*.

'Can you help me?' Mina looked around, aware of her unkempt appearance and the dark rings staining her T-shirt under her armpits.

'Of course.'

'The thing is, I'm trying to find someone for my mother, a school friend, and all I have is a first name and that they presumably went to Bampton Grammar School in the fifties. That's certainly where my mother went. Are there any records here that might help?'

'Bampton Grammar?' Joseph shook his head. 'We don't have any school records at all. What's the first name?'

'Her friend was called Valerie. That's all I know. What about alumni organisations? Are there any groups connected to the school?'

'Not that I've heard of. The school's still going so you could ask there. Aren't there any friends you can ask?'

'My mother hasn't kept in touch with any of them. Is Carol in?'

'Carol? She's retired too. She left just after your mum, but she wasn't originally from around here anyway.'

'Mum might have mentioned a Valerie to her.'

'Maybe.' Joseph leant against the desk, doodling on a pad in front of him. 'The only information she ever gave me about her personal life was in relation to you. She'd talk a lot about you. She said you'd been born with green fingers.'

Mina felt tears prick behind her eyes. 'Can I have Carol's address?'

Joseph hesitated. 'I can't do that but I can tell her you want to speak to her. Leave your mobile number with me and I'll get her to call you.'

Mina wrote her number on the proffered Post-it, which Joseph inspected. 'I tell you what you could do, though. Why don't you put some notices around town? Something along the lines of "Looking for Valerie. Student at Bampton Grammar in . . ."'

'I don't know. The fifties, I guess.'

'Okay, so, looking for Valerie, a student in Bampton in the nineteen fifties, a friend of Hilary Kemp. Was that her maiden name?'

Mina nodded. 'Yes. She never changed it.'

'So write that and leave your contact details. Put the notices up in the supermarket, Costa, that sort of thing. You know, Valerie might even come forward herself.'

'Mum thinks she's dead.'

'Well, her family then. It's worth a go.'

'Do you know what, that's a good idea.'

'While you're here, why don't you fill in one of these cards and I'll put it on the community noticeboard over there.'

Mina followed his gaze to a large board dotted with cards. 'I can do that?'

'We have to police it something chronic. There's always some chancer wanting to put up a flyer, which is why we've created this system. As long as it's not illegal, if it's related to the community you can fill in the card and we'll display it for you for two weeks. Okay?'

Mina filled in the information in her neat script and handed the card back to Joseph. 'Thanks.'

He smiled back at her. 'Fancy a drink sometime?'

She laughed. 'I'm too old for you.'

He stuck a pin in the card. 'Worth a try.'

*

Ten minutes before closing time, a hand unpinned the notice from the board and studied it closely.

LOOKING FOR VALERIE. PUPIL AT BAMPTON GRAMMAR SCHOOL IN THE 1950s. FRIEND OF HILARY KEMP. CALL MOBILE OR LEAVE A NOTE ON THE EVENING STAR HOUSEBOAT.

Replacing the pin in the board, the hand hesitated for a moment then put the card between the pages of a book and left the library.

7

Having an argument with your partner isn't the best way to start your weekend. Ruth departed to her vintage furniture shop, slamming the front door, leaving Matthews still in her pyjamas, red faced and near tears. Not only was she being an idiot at home but she was aware that she wasn't exactly making herself popular with her team at the station. She couldn't relax enough to get people on her side, but now, when she finally had her chance to prove that she could do a DI role, she wasn't going to ruin her chances by allowing standards to slacken just because Sadler was away.

Alone in the house, she was aware that there was a basket full of washing that needed doing and a layer of dust on the living room table. Their cat, named King William and who had a clear preference for Ruth, marched past her with his nose in the air and departed into the garden with a clatter of the flap. It was the last straw. She left a pile of dried biscuits in his bowl and drove to Bampton station to check everything was okay.

The station was empty except for a few duty officers. The CID sergeant had already telephoned her as asked to say that nothing had come in during the night. He glanced up briefly as she entered the Detective Room, looking put out at her appearance. Matthews sat at Sadler's desk, powered up her laptop and began to go through her checklist again. She heard a heavy tread outside her office followed by a cough and Superintendent Llewellyn put his head through the door.

'I saw you park your car. Everything all right?'

Matthews stood up, annoyed at the red flush she could feel creeping across her face. 'Of course. I've everything under control.'

'I'm sure you have. Don't get too comfortable there. Sadler's back a week on Monday.'

'He said I could use the office.'

'I'm only joking. It's been a quiet week for you, which is probably a good thing. Anything I need to know about?' He looked across the deserted Detective Room. 'What's Connie up to while Sadler's away?'

'I've asked her to look at a sudden death in High Oaks. Nothing suspicious but I want everything checked.'

'Quite right. That'll keep her out of trouble, or, come to think of it, maybe not. What about the new chap who starts on Monday? Peter Dahl.'

'Everything's set up for his arrival.'

'Have you seen the note from Human Resources that I emailed you?'

Feeling on safer ground, Matthews sat down. 'I have. Sadler mentioned something briefly after the interview but it's good to have his exact needs in writing. We'll accommodate him as much as we can, of course.'

'We're going to have to. I'm the one that goes to these bloody flexible working meetings. Keep an eye on it, will you? He's supposed to be very able but I want to see how much his home life becomes a distraction.'

'I'll certainly be monitoring him.'

It came across too harsh and Llewellyn frowned. 'Maybe give him to Connie to chaperone his first week. Despite their disparate backgrounds, I have a feeling those two will like each other.'

'Sounds like a good idea.' Matthews didn't add that if Connie didn't like him, they were all buggered.

Llewellyn was looking at Sadler's unusually tidy desk. 'Sure there's nothing you need a hand with?'

'I promise you. Everything's under control.'

*

The weekend stretched out like a gaping hole for Connie. With few friends and no work on which to legitimately do overtime, she was left with free time to . . . what? The Chinese meal she'd ordered the previous evening was so salty that she'd had to get up three times in the night to drink a glass of water. It left her tired and sluggish and, staring at herself in the bathroom mirror, she winced at her pasty face. Her New Year's resolution had been to get fitter and, now at the end of October, she realised she'd done absolutely zilch.

Her apartment block, a converted warehouse sitting high above the canal, was strangely quiet. In her bedroom, she looked out onto the car park below and could see only her ancient red Clio. She had the building to herself this weekend and the thought depressed her. She opened her wardrobe door, surveyed her running shoes and, after a moment's hesitation, put them on. Now that she'd made up her mind to go for a run, her legs were tingling with the anticipation of exercise. She took the stairs down onto the street and set off down the towpath. Eleven o'clock on a summer's morning and this track would be filled with people and the unlicensed ice cream van that she should really report. Today, it was deserted, the summer visitors an echo of footprints and departed noise that still hung over the canal.

Connie began to run, her legs stretching out on the once familiar path and she could feel her head begin to clear. Her lungs, at first in shock at the enforced activity, settled into a shallow rhythm. When she reached Step Bridge, she turned right onto the Topley Trail, the former railway track. This was busier than the canal path, mainly dog walkers and cyclists who whizzed past her, ringing their bells cheekily. One rider, clearly liking the rear view, turned to look at her from the front but she ignored him, aware of her red face and the enjoyment she was getting from the endorphins that were pumping around her body.

She reached a tunnel and a blast of cold air rushed at her. The underpass was also busy but quieter, people reducing their noise to a hush as they entered the dark space. The lighting was adequate but nothing more, and she wished she'd thought to put in her contact lenses for this stretch. She moved to the side of the tunnel, nearer to the strip lighting, and ran on, grateful when she reached the other side. A woman was trying to coax her young son into the tunnel but his enjoyment of a former railway had come to an abrupt halt at the entrance.

'I don't want to go in.'

'Don't be silly. There's nothing to be scared of.'

The child began to wail as Connie sped on. As she reached the viaduct, the majesty of the industrial revolution revealed in its solid construction and purposeful design, she slowed for a moment and allowed her lungs to take a few deep breaths.

An old woman was sitting on a bench, her walking stick held in knotted hands.

'That's the trouble with running. You miss the beauty of your surroundings.'

'It's all right for you.' Connie leant over and hit her solar plexus. 'If I didn't run, I wouldn't come this way at all. Better seeing the sights from speed than not at all.'

'I suppose. Where are you running to?'

Connie looked at the woman. She was wearing an old-fashioned walker's outfit of corduroy trousers tucked into walking boots and a checked shirt. Where was Connie running to? Good question.

'I'm trying to get some exercise. You?'

'I come down here every day. I get my exercise by hobbling here and watching the world go by.'

'Routine is a good idea. I've left it too long between exercising. This run will kill me.'

'Routine is boring but the Peaks are never dull, I'll give you that. I've seen plenty over the years.'

'Here?' Connie was seized by the desire to keep going. Away from the woman, away from the tunnel.

The woman wheezed with laughter. 'A new broom sweeps clean but the old one knows the corners.'

Connie gave her a puzzled glance and sped on, still hearing the woman's chuckle in her ear.

*

Clive had lit the fire as promised, although the flames were meagre and ashy sparks jumped in the grate. 'I can't get it started. The coal must have got damp sometime. We had those three weeks of non-stop rain in September. It must have been then.'

Sadler looked at the smoking embers. 'Oh, I don't know. It'll take the chill off the evening at least.' He sat in his usual chair as Clive handed him a glass of wine. 'I went up to Hathersage today.'

'Did you? I thought I might have piqued your interest. What did you make of it?'

Unbidden, Sadler thought of the woman with a rake in her hand. 'It's a magnificent house.'

'Which one? North Lees Hall? It's a little gem. I'm good for something then.'

Sadler looked at his neighbour, a widower who missed his old solicitor's practice, still doing a roaring trade despite his retirement. 'Feeling the turn of the seasons?'

Clive shivered. 'Sorry, someone just walked over my grave. I *am* feeling my age.' There was a bang at the front door and he left Sadler to answer it. He returned followed by a man in his late thirties. 'This is Max. We crossed briefly as partners in the practice but he plays a mean game of badminton. Keeps me on my toes.'

Max held out his hand and gripped Sadler's. A masonic shake and bone crushing. Clive handed him a glass of wine and pulled an armchair into the group.

'Sorry about the fire.'

'Don't worry about that. I appreciate you inviting me to drop by.' Despite the handshake, the man appeared to be nervous. He stretched out his legs in front of the fire, trying to relax. 'I've put the kids to bed so I'm in my wife's good books.

She's sitting watching a Bear Grylls programme so she won't miss me.' He looked at Sadler, his gaze direct. 'Thanks for agreeing to see me.'

'You have something you're worried about?' *It's the second time today I'm a confidant*, thought Sadler.

Max's eyes drifted over to Clive's. 'It's probably nothing. I just, well, mentioned it today and Clive suggested that I talk to you. You'd be able to put my mind at rest or know what to do otherwise.'

'It's to do with the solicitor's?'

'Yes, but it's not relating to a client, which is why it's straightforward to talk about. It's to do with a secretary who used to work with us and who died this week. Clive knew her. Her name was Nell Colley.'

'How did she die?' Sadler felt the familiar prickle of interest.

'Well, that's the thing. Natural causes. She had a heart problem, although while she was working with us it wasn't particularly an issue, so I was surprised to hear she'd been ill with it recently.'

'Was she with you long?'

Clive stirred, poking at the fire. 'She was my secretary for years before I retired. When I first started out in practice, they all used to leave to get married. Remember those days?' He eyed his neighbour. 'Probably not.'

Sadler smiled. 'Can't say I do.'

'Well, when I first interviewed Nell Colley, I asked her if she had any marriage plans. I have the grace to blush about it now but I was sick of the bloody women leaving me once they got hitched. What the hell was wrong with being married and working? It wasn't my choice that they left.'

'What did she say?'

'She said she had no boyfriend and, to be fair, she stayed with me for years. Bloody good she was too. I'd have retired sooner myself if it wasn't for her. The pair of us soldiered on until I'd had enough but she wanted to carry on and Max inherited her.'

'She was good?'

Max nodded. 'Excellent as a secretary. Not brilliant with computers but I got someone else to help with that. But she knew the legal procedures inside out. She could have trained as a solicitor herself if she'd wanted to. She was reliable, kept clients happy, chased outstanding documents. Then, one day, she gave her notice.'

'The heart problem?'

'She didn't mention her health at all although she had complained occasionally of chest pains. She came to me in June this year and said it was time for her to leave. She was way past retirement age anyway. She could have left with a pension years ago but she liked working so we kept her on. But, all of a sudden, she decided she wanted to go. She said she had a book in her. Don't we all?'

Sadler grimaced. 'I think I have more than one. Did she start the book?'

'I assume so because I got a call from Nell the other week. It started off as a general chat, catching up with office gossip and so on, and then she steered the conversation onto libel law.'

'Libel?'

'Exactly. She asked me about the law surrounding memoirs and how people are represented in them.'

'What did you say?'

'Well, we were talking really broad terms so I said that, basically, a person could only be sued for libel if they'd written something that could be considered damaging to the person bringing the claim.'

'Did she give any specifics? What she was writing about?'

'Nothing at all except that it was some kind of memoir. It's not my area of expertise but I could certainly have helped a bit if she'd been more specific. If anything, she seemed to be talking very carefully so that I didn't recognise the people involved. I was concerned it wasn't anything to do with the practice and she said definitely not.'

'When was this call?'

'A little under two weeks ago. I've checked my diary and I think it was around Monday or Tuesday the week before last.'

'And she died of natural causes?'

'Apparently so. I visited a neighbour she was friendly with.'

Sadler looked up. The eyes of the two men were on him. Clive's relaxed, confident in his neighbour's abilities, Max's troubled.

'You're worried about the fact she died so soon after the call?'

'It's odd and yet, when Nell put the phone down, she seemed much happier.'

'Then you must have reassured her. How did the conversation end?'

'It was a throwaway comment, but I basically said that one good thing was that you can't libel the dead. She sounded positively chirpy when she put the phone down.'

'You can't libel the dead?'

'Exactly. The comment cheered her up no end, but now Nell's dead and I can't sleep wondering what it was all about.'

8

'I saw her again.'

'Oh Mum.' Mina sat in the seat next to her mother's bed, taking care not to disturb the drip. She'd preferred it when Hilary was in the main ward as she'd been able to talk to the other patients and visitors. Especially on a Sunday, a time of family lunches and shared activities, a hospital can feel the loneliest place in the world. Mina, over the weeks, had developed a loose friendship with some of the other long term patients and their families. Sometimes, when Mina had rushed in from a gardening job, fortified only by endless cups of tea, she'd joined a visiting relative in the hospital canteen for a bowl of soup and a chat. Mutual commiseration.

Since Hilary's delirium, however, they'd moved her to a private room as she'd been shouting in her sleep, scaring the other patients. So now it was just Mina and Hilary, and a stultifying pressure in the room that made Mina's head ache. Hilary's fever hadn't yet abated, although the nurse who came in to check on them said it hadn't worsened. Mina picked up the clipboard on the end of the bed and looked at the figures. Her mother's temperature was still 38.9 degrees.

'She was standing there. She didn't talk to me but she knew who I was.'

'You mean you saw your friend, Valerie, again?'

Hilary nodded.

'You said yesterday you were scared. Are you scared today?'

Hilary closed her eyes. 'Confusing.'

'I know it is. Listen, Mum, you asked me to find her but you need to tell me more. Can you remember where she lived?' Mina remembered the words of the policeman. Find out more information so you can ask around.

'In that cold place. The village. Cold Eaton.'

'Cold Eaton? Where's Cold Eaton? Ah.' A memory cleared. 'I remember. You pass it on the Matlock road. Did Valerie live in Cold Eaton?'

The nod was hardly perceptible but it was there.

'Shouldn't have done it.'

'Done what, Mum?'

'The tunnel and after everything too. The reservoir came rushing in over the village and next she has to deal with the dark. Too much for anyone.'

It was gibberish. Mina leant across to lay her hand on Hilary's forehead and her mother stilled. After a few minutes, she began to snore lightly. Mina got up and went down to the nurses' station near the entrance of the ward.

'Who was my mother's visitor today?'

A male nurse in a white short-sleeved top looked up in surprise. 'I didn't know your mum had a visitor. I didn't see anyone. Did you, Sue?'

A nurse rapidly typing something into a computer looked up and shook her head. 'I don't remember anyone going into see Mrs Kemp. I would have remembered as she's so poorly, it's really only family she should be seeing. Was it a relation?'

'No. She says she saw an old school friend in her room today.'

Sue locked eyes with the male nurse. 'It could be her condition, you know. High temperature can be disorienting. It can even cause hallucinations. It's not uncommon.'

Mina felt the need to defend her mother. 'She seemed pretty sure. She said the woman's name was Valerie.'

'I'm sorry.' The nurse turned back to the screen. 'I'm pretty sure that your mother didn't have a visitor today.'

Mina went back to Hilary who had begun to toss in her sleep, her frail body troubled. Mina put out a hand to steady her but her mother rocked underneath it. Mina leant over and pushed the button by the bed. The male nurse appeared.

'She's really agitated. Is there anything I can do?'

The man came forward and checked the drip. 'She's been like this since yesterday when the fever appeared. We're not really getting on top of things.'

'Is it bad?'

'You know her immune system is weakened by the chemotherapy. Any infection isn't good.'

'She seems to have a lot on her mind. I'm not sure if she's talking nonsense or not.'

'Bit of both, I suppose.' The nurse looked down at Hilary. 'Delirium is like a dream. Part real, part made-up. You must have had a fever as a child.'

'Of course.'

But it hadn't been her mother who had soothed her. Bookish Hilary Kemp, who had shocked her family by having a child by a married man and, refusing his offer of financial support, had brought up Mina by herself. The male figure in Mina's childhood was Hilary's own father, Grumps. Nothing to do with his temperament but Mina's mispronunciation as a toddler, which

51

had delighted him. Grumps he'd stayed until his death fifteen years ago.

She remembered that when she was ill, it was to Grumps' house that she'd gone while her mother went to work. He'd fed her ginger biscuits and flat lemonade, his cure for all types of stomach ailments. Comfort food that she so desperately craved at this moment. *Don't think of him*, she cautioned herself. *Keep yourself together.* She looked down at his daughter, Hilary, who had opened her eyes and was struggling to sit up in her agitation.

'Mum!' She reached down and held the frail body in her arms.

'I *am* scared.'

'There's no need to be. There's nothing to be scared of.'

'Valerie's here. I saw her.'

'That's okay then. If she's been to see you, I'll find her for you and we'll clear up the confusion. She's obviously not dead, is she, if she was here?'

'Oh, she's dead. Grumps told me.'

'Grumps? He knew her?'

'He'd heard that she was dead and wanted to tell me himself before I heard it from anyone else.'

'Maybe he got it wrong, Mum. These things happen.'

'Oh I know he was right because I knew Valerie was already dead.'

'You knew it already?'

'Of course.' Hilary twisted her face to Mina's. 'Because we killed her.'

9

Connie wished she'd had a cigarette that morning before coming into work rather than a few deep puffs on the new vape she'd treated herself to at the weekend. It was a super strong model but even the blast of nicotine had failed to quell her cravings for the real thing. Feeling jittery, she looked in dismay at the folder with Nell Colley's name on it that had been put in the place for the most urgent of cases. Her chair.

'Now what?'

No one else in the office raised their head, clearly occupied with their own bureaucratic workload. At the sound of Matthews opening her door, Connie picked up the file and sat down sharpish, trying to look busy. A man around Connie's age wearing a mismatched jacket and trousers and thick black glasses followed her superior.

'Connie, can I introduce you to your new colleague, DC Peter Dahl? He's starting with us today.'

Connie stood up again and held out her hand. He towered over her. Another tall copper.

'Dahl has transferred to us from the Glossop division. I'd like him to shadow you today, if that's okay?'

'Sure, I mean, of course, but there's not much on at the moment.'

'What about that sudden death I gave you? Nell Colley.'

So it was Matthews who had put the file back on her chair. 'The correct procedure was followed. I've checked the report and the guidance for sudden deaths. Plus the flow chart. There's nothing suspicious about the circumstances so I've labelled it as no further action.'

Matthews frowned. 'Have you been to see the next of kin?'

'No, but one of the officers attending the scene talked to a neighbour. We're going to struggle for any close relatives as Nell Colley was an only child. The neighbour was very friendly with her, though, and thinks she's the legatee of the deceased woman's will. She's prepared to organise the funeral.'

'Go and see her, Connie, and take Dahl with you.'

Connie opened her mouth to protest but Matthews stopped her. 'Got anything better to do?'

Connie glanced over at Dahl who was looking embarrassed. To her surprise, he mouthed 'sorry' over Matthews's shoulder. Connie bent down to pick up her handbag so that neither would see her smile.

'No problem. Shall we go?'

They walked in silence out of the Detective Room and down the long corridor.

'Is it always this quiet?' Dahl sounded relaxed.

'Is that why you transferred? Fancy a bit of peace and quiet? Is it getting hairy up at Glossop?'

He laughed. 'I was supposed to start next month. Due to report to DI Sadler but, because of staffing issues, they asked me to start earlier.'

'Staffing issues?' Connie stopped and stared at him. 'What staffing issues? We don't have a major investigation on at the moment. Unless you count the case of the non-suspicious death. You fancied a change from the Dark Peak?'

Connie took in his pressed jacket and trousers and noted his rumpled shirt. Posh but single, she decided. He'd had his jacket dry cleaned but he'd matched it with the wrong trousers and had no one to iron his shirt.

'I transferred for personal reasons.' He sounded unwilling to give any more information. 'I have family commitments.'

Wrong again. Connie turned and led the way out of the station.

The High Oaks area of Bampton was one of its wealthiest neighbourhoods populated with tall, graceful Victorian houses that were still family homes and well looked after. The houses in Pullen Road were less impressive than those of neighbouring streets but still elegant. Derbyshire granite blending into the landscape and built to last for centuries. Connie drew up outside number 59 and looked over to the sash windows with the curtains neatly drawn and a bunch of flowers sitting inside a Portmeirion vase on the sill.

'Do you think the neighbour put the flowers in afterwards?' asked Dahl.

'That would be an odd thing to do, putting flowers in a dead woman's house. Nell probably bought them herself. The notes said she'd felt a bit better before she died. Let's go inside.'

From an evidence wallet, Connie removed a single key that fitted the front door. The house had a slight antiseptic smell infused with pine, the aroma of cleaning fluids. Dahl sniffed the air. The hall was beautifully decorated but in a dated style, having floorboards of good quality laminate set against wallpaper with large bunches of blue flowers.

'She was found on the sofa in the living room.'

Dahl pushed open a door on the right leading into a room that held a large maroon leather sofa and two armchairs. The antiseptic smell was stronger here. Connie looked around. A remote control was sitting on the coffee table next to the free local paper. The room was neat as a pin, only the scent of the roses trying to vie with that of the cleaning fluid. Connie fingered the petals.

'They're drying out. Not a recent buy then. Shall we have a quick look around the house?'

Dahl went into the kitchen while Connie made her way upstairs. Nell's bedroom was easily identifiable as it was the only room with a bed made up. Connie lifted up the pillows and saw a nightdress folded under one of them. Nell Colley had expected to go to bed that evening. She rifled through the wardrobe and inspected the chest of drawers as she listened to Dahl moving around downstairs. The bedside cabinet was crammed full of medication. Connie picked up a few packets to read the labels: verapamil, atorvastatin. The names meant nothing to her.

'Heart medication.'

The voice in her ear made Connie jump. 'Jesus. Are you trying to give *me* a heart attack? Do you recognise the drugs?'

'This one,' Dahl took the packet out of her hand, 'is a statin. It reduces cholesterol, which causes heart disease. I think the other is a calcium channel blocker. Used to treat high blood pressure.' Dahl flicked through the other packets in the drawer. 'I'm no expert but there doesn't appear to be anything odd there. It looks like Nell Colley took aspirin regularly too, to thin her blood.'

'No expert? You could have fooled me. Let me bag up the medicine so I can show it to Matthews. Anything downstairs?'

Dahl shook his head. 'The doors are all secure. Everything looks fine. Someone has been cleaning, though. There's no trash in the bin. The house has been tidied up after Nell's death. Can I show you something?'

Connie looked up at him. 'What have you found?'

'Take a look at this.' Connie followed Dahl out of the bedroom and down the stairs. In the hall there was an old-fashioned telephone table from the days before hands-free phones. The dark mahogany seat was covered in a regency stripe. Dahl pulled open the drawer and pulled out a black book. 'It's Nell's address book.'

'Anything of interest?'

'A list of addresses, obviously. When someone died, she put a little cross by their name. Look.'

Connie looked to where he was pointing. Next to a name, a small cross.

'You think that means she's dead?'

'Yes. My mother does the same thing.'

Connie picked up the book and leafed through it. 'Quite a few names with crosses next to them. That's not surprising for a woman in her seventies, is it?'

'Did you look at what was on the coffee table?'

'The local paper.'

'It was dated the fifteenth of June.'

'So? She read old copies of the paper. So do I. Well, I take them from the recycling bag into the bath with me to see if there's anything remotely interesting happening in Bampton. There never is.'

'Come and take a look. I flicked through it. See what happens when I get to page twenty.' Dahl turned the pages until he reached one ringed with coffee cup marks. Death notices.

'Oh great. I have an aunt like that. Not happy until she's checked who's died this week.'

'I know people like that too but they check and move on. Look at the ring marks. There are five of them. It's as if she spent time reading them with a cup of tea or whatever. Look at the death notices. How many?'

'Four.'

'Right, and I've checked the names against Nell's address book. Look at this one.'

In Memoriam. Ingrid Neale. Died 10 June 2017. Funeral at Cold Eaton Parish Church. Family flowers only.

'Ingrid Neale. So someone she knew had died. That probably explains her interest.'

'Yes.'

Connie stared at him. 'It's not very exciting, is it?'

He was grinning at her. 'No, but I wanted to show you my investigative skills.'

'I'm impressed, Dahl.'

He looked pleased. 'Are you going to speak to the neighbour who found the body?'

'Of course. I'm not going back to Matthews without examining everything. She's going to triple-check we did this properly.'

Connie pulled the front door behind them and peered through the front window. 'Funny, though, that the neighbour didn't look through the window. I mean, even if you had a key, surely you'd have a look through the window before you let yourself in. According to the report, the neighbour, Janet Goodhew, when she got no answer, used her key to open the front door. She says she didn't see anything until she got into the living room. Why didn't she look through the window?'

Dahl glanced at the next door house where a woman, neatly dressed but shod in slippers, had opened the door and was watching them anxiously. 'Let's ask her, shall we?'

IO

Sunday had been a bitter day. A strong wind began in the morning, sweeping over the canal, which ruled out even a short paddle and Mina had stayed on the boat, brooding and thinking. It was nearly two weeks since she'd slept in her own house, her childhood home, and for the first time, Mina could see why Hilary had chosen to live here. There was a comfort in having so few possessions around you. It gave you time to think and reflect. After a disturbed night, Mina woke with a headache, which was always a bad sign. Regular Nurofen could relieve headaches that came on during the day. If she woke up with one, it was impossible to shift.

She idled in bed, contemplating her plans for the morning, when the boat rocked. A motor cruiser was going too fast down the canal. She heard Charlie next door shouting something she couldn't make out and a word beginning with 'c', which she could. She got up, reached for her diary and considered her next move.

She'd be visiting Hilary again this afternoon. The dreaded night-time phone call hadn't come, and she had a good few hours to get some work in. She switched on the Tassimo machine. In the tiny shower, she washed as quickly as she could, eager to get away. While the coffee was brewing, she stepped off the boat to check the tools in the back of her small van.

Autumn was the time of clearing. Leaves falling from trees needed hoovering up and brown stalks of plants required hacking back ready for the new growth of the spring. Monotonous work but it kept Mina fitter than the summer months of deadheading and mowing lawns. Mina reckoned she'd got as much gardening work from the name of her business as she had from personal recommendation. The Land Girl gave you what it promised. For twenty pounds an hour, you got one girl, trained in horticulture and a willingness to tackle anything your garden threw at her. The name of her business also had a reassuring effect on her older clients who, even if they couldn't remember land girls, certainly knew the reference.

She hadn't a single client in the village of Cold Eaton but she had, she remembered, once been approached by the pub owner who wanted a gardener to mow the lawns and keep the window boxes full of blooms all year round. She'd turned down the job because the landlady had baulked at her charges.

'I have to pay national insurance and tax out of that,' she'd protested but Emily Fenn only wanted to pay the minimum wage and had probably found a local lad to do the work. It was, however, the only introduction into that village that she had.

She set off, waving at Charlie who was checking his boat for damage and muttering under his breath. As she drove down the Matlock road, the rain was pelting onto the windscreen and she nearly missed the sign directing her to Cold Eaton. She had to put her foot on the brake suddenly, causing the driver behind her to lean on his horn.

The road was long and narrow, pitted with potholes and with only a few passing places. *Don't let me meet anyone*, she prayed. She climbed a steep hill and then sharply descended into a village with a sign at its entrance warning drivers to watch their speed. The place had a closed off feel to it. Façades of grey with small, mean windows looking out onto the road. A telephone box was painted not the usual red but a fern green to blend in with the landscape. Finally a sign adorned with a painting of a clipper ship indicated she'd arrived at The Nettle Inn.

Parking to one side, Mina noticed that the window boxes were empty and the gravel leading around the pub was strewn with weeds. The front door was shut and a sign taped onto the rotting wood warned it wouldn't open until half twelve. Mina knocked anyway and a large woman with an old-fashioned pinafore tied around her waist opened the door. She looked too old to be running a pub but the proprietorial way in which she looked Mina up and down made it clear who was in charge.

'We're not open until later.'

'I know. I don't need a drink. I've come about the gardening email you sent me in the spring. I was wondering if you still need the work doing.'

'The Land Girl?'

'You remembered?'

'It's a nice name.' The woman opened the door further. 'You'd better come in. If I remember, we had a conversation and I couldn't afford your rates.'

'To be honest,' Mina lowered her voice, 'I drop my prices at this time of year. People are prepared to let their gardens lapse when they don't have to sit out in them. So I thought I'd visit businesses where it's important to maintain, well, a good impression. Kerb appeal and so on.'

Emily snorted. 'You've seen the weeds then.' She led Mina into the pub where a fat log glowed, spitting out sparks at a mangy dog that was lying on the hearth.

'Your wood's a bit green.'

The woman opened the hatch to the bar and looked over at the logs. 'You're right. Old Malcolm Cox has diddled me again. It happened last October too. He runs short for his orders so gives me wood not seasoned long enough. I've got a pile of the stuff out the back.'

'If you pile them up in a round formation, like the old-style haystacks, it'll speed up the drying process.'

Emily switched on the coffee machine but her stance suggested that she didn't welcome the advice. Her face when she turned, however, was neutral.

'What did you say your name was?'

'I'm Mina. Mina Kemp.'

'Kemp?' She narrowed her eyes. 'You're not from around here, though.'

'Bampton. That's around here, isn't it? Why, does the name mean something to you?'

Emily turned back to the machine. 'Would you like a coffee?'

'I'll have an espresso, if that's okay.' She watched as the woman competently made a coffee using the huge machine. She brought the steaming black liquid over to Mina.

'I could do with a bit of help outside, getting it ready for the winter. What's your minimum rate?'

Mina nearly spat her coffee back into the cup. 'That's certainly direct.'

Emily smiled slightly. 'I can't afford to be anything else. Would you take a tenner an hour?'

Half her usual rate. Mina made a show of considering the offer. 'As long as you don't mind me fitting the hours around my other work.'

'I can only afford five hours a week. Can you make a difference for that?'

Mina caught the edge of a plea. 'Of course. I can do a few hours today, if you like, and come back next week. I'll have your grounds looking spick and span in a couple of weeks. You won't need to keep me on over the winter.'

Emily sipped her own heavily milked coffee. 'I've never been much of a gardener. My grandfather was. I remember a greenhouse out the back groaning with tomatoes. It was a different world then. Shorter opening hours. You actually had a life.'

'You own the pub?'

'It's been in my family for generations. I had aspirations away from this place. I wanted to become a teacher would you believe, but . . . anyway . . . here I am. Worked to death behind the bar with two grown-up children who have no interest in taking it over from me.'

'What will happen, afterwards I mean?'

Emily grimaced. 'That will be for them to decide. I'm staying here until I conk out. Then it'll be their problem. It's a good enough earner if one of them changes their mind and decides to take the pub on.'

'It's a small village. It seems quiet.'

'Tiny but it's just off the Topley Trail. We get walkers through here every day. It's why I invested in the coffee machine. We make more serving coffee and cake than we do pulling the pints these days.'

'Isn't there a school here? That would bring new blood into the village.'

'It closed a while back. They were warning us for years then one day it happened.'

'Why did you change your mind about teaching?'

Emily stood and picked up Mina's empty coffee cup. 'No reason. I changed my mind, that's all. Anyway, you want to start straight away then?'

Mina also stood up and adopted a casual tone. 'I think my mother might have had a childhood friend here, though. She mentioned Cold Eaton. Her friend went by the name of Valerie. Do you know her?'

Emily stiffened and made a show of thinking. 'Valerie? That's a name you don't hear very often. I can't think of any Valerie ever living in the village.'

'Perhaps my mother was mistaken. She seemed so sure too.'

Emily had disappeared into the kitchen. When she came back, she was wiping her hands on her apron. 'What did you say your mother's first name was?'

I'm not sure I did, thought Mina. 'Hilary. Her name's Hilary Kemp.'

Emily stared at Mina. 'I don't remember a Valerie living in Cold Eaton.'

Mina let it go. 'I've got my tools in the back of the van. I'll come back in when I've done, say, three hours.'

'I'll see you at lunchtime.' She looked at the fire and back at Mina, puzzled. As she hurried away, Mina was sure she heard the whisper of the word 'Valerie' being repeated under Emily's breath.

11

Connie and Dahl were asked to leave their shoes in the hall while Nell Colley's neighbour disappeared into the kitchen. Connie noticed that Dahl had a hole in his left sock that he tried to hide by folding the seam beneath his toes. He caught her eye and smirked.

'I'll bin them when I get home.'

They padded through to the living room and Dahl crossed to the window. 'She has a good view of next door's drive. There's not much she won't notice.'

Janet Goodhew came back into the room carrying a tray laden with tea things and a plate of cake. She was flustered, ill at ease at having detectives in her house.

'You knew Ms Colley well?'

'Ms? She wouldn't have liked you calling her that. She pre-ferred "Miss" to the end of her days. Women's lib passed her by. Mind you, I lived next to her for thirty years and called her Nell from day one.'

'You were friendly?'

'She helped me bring up the children. My husband, Frank, was away a lot. He worked for IBM in the early days of computing. He was often in America and he'd bring great presents back for the kids. Stuff you couldn't get then. Now, of course, everyone travels and, anyway, you can buy whatever you need in the shops.'

Dahl pulled a notebook from his jacket pocket. 'She never married?'

'Oh no. She was a spinster, if you see what I mean. I don't think she ever had a boyfriend. I tried to ask her about it once but she changed the subject.'

'She worked?'

'As a secretary in a solicitor's. She loved her job. She carried on until this year when her health started to play up and, anyway, she wanted to write her book.'

'A book?' Dahl looked up from the notes he was making. 'A novel, you mean?'

'Well, a memoir. She'd been meaning to do it for years. It wasn't something she talked about much, in fact she was quite reticent when I asked her for more details, but used to say to me that one day she'd write this book of hers.'

'Has it been published?'

Janet poured the tea, her hand wobbling slightly. 'Oh no. She'd only just started it. A bit of research and I think she'd also put something down on paper because she mentioned that writing was much harder than she thought. Trying to arrange all your memories in the right order.'

Connie looked down at her patterned socks and wondered what propelled people to examine their past in such forensic detail. She'd happily left her old life in Matlock far behind. Her father had remarried and was living in Scotland and there only remained the pinch of the memory of her mother's struggle with alcohol addiction that she rarely allowed herself to dwell on. Was the memoir important?

'Perhaps the fact that she had a life-threatening illness made the writing more pressing,' said Dahl.

'It's funny that, despite talking about writing a book for so long, she'd only just got around to it. That was unusual for Nell. Normally, when she decided to do something, it got done.'

'Life got in the way,' said Connie.

'I suppose so.' Janet looked at them both. 'It doesn't really matter now, does it?'

'A memoir,' Dahl said, his voice encouraging. 'A memoir on her work at the solicitor's?'

'Oh no, I don't think it was that. She never said what it was about but I didn't get the impression it was to do with work.'

'I've checked downstairs in Miss Colley's house. I didn't see any evidence of a laptop.'

'I think she was going to write it out by hand. She wasn't on the internet or anything like that. It was a personal project for her.'

'A personal project,' repeated Connie. Dahl turned towards her slightly and the room fell silent. Connie considered how to articulate the uneasiness that references to the book evoked. Memoirs were important to people who write them, so why was there no evidence of it in the house? 'You've no idea what it was about?'

Janet shook her head. 'She wouldn't tell me anything at all.'

Dahl glanced at Connie and changed tack. 'So Ms, I mean, Nell, she was ill, wasn't she?'

'She had this ongoing thing. Her heart would start fluttering and then beating irregularly. She'd have to sit down. While she was working it had been infrequent, but over the summer it got worse and worse and she was suffering from a heart condition.'

'Her GP signed off the death certificate, I believe. He'd seen her within the last week.'

'Oh, Nell was always at the surgery after she retired. Me, I only go when I'm at death's door, otherwise they get sick of you, don't they? I'm worried that if I go too often they won't take me seriously when there is something properly wrong with me.'

'But there was something seriously wrong with Nell?' Connie watched as the woman flushed slightly under Dahl's scrutiny.

'Well, as I said, she had a heart condition. What did the GP put down as her cause of death?'

'Heart arrhythmia.'

'That's it. I can never pronounce the name properly. A dicky heart. She was always a bit worried she'd go quickly. The hospital consultant warned her that sudden death was a possibility.'

Connie looked down at the sheet of paper she'd retrieved from her bag. 'According to the paramedic, you said you'd spoken to Nell that morning.'

'That's right. I gave her a call on the phone. I asked how she was and she said she was all right. Then, I nipped around at ten to four with a piece of carrot cake I'd baked, and when she didn't answer the door, I let myself in.'

'You had the key on you?'

Janet flushed again. 'She had no downstairs toilet. If she was upstairs it'd take her an age to get down the stairs so I'd let myself in. She never minded. We'd talked about it.'

'You didn't think of looking through the living room window?' asked Dahl.

'No. As I said, I thought she was upstairs but anyway . . .'

'What?'

'Well, I'd have been able to see her from the front door as she always sat in the armchair by the window. She liked to watch people coming and going.'

Connie frowned. 'She was discovered on the sofa.'

'I know that. I found her, didn't I? All I'm saying is that she usually sat in the armchair, which is why I didn't look through the window.'

Dahl leant forward. 'How did she look when you found her?'

'She was dressed. She had her nice silk blouse on and her blue cardigan and a skirt. She was sitting upright on the sofa. I thought . . .'

'Yes?' asked Connie.

'Well, I thought she'd had a funny turn and she'd sat down and then, well, left us.'

Dahl looked up at Connie. 'When you spoke to her on the phone, she didn't say that she was expecting a visitor?'

'She never said a thing, although someone did call.'

'How do you know?'

'I heard her front door go at around half eleven. I didn't look out because there were plenty of people who were in and out of the house. Friends, health visitors.'

'You didn't see who it was?' Connie leant towards Janet. 'You didn't even catch a glimpse of the visitor?'

'I told you. I didn't look. It's not important, is it?'

'It would be interesting to hear who was actually the last

70

person to see her alive. If they didn't raise the alarm, Nell was presumably alive at half past eleven.'

'The GP came after the ambulance and signed the death certificate. I saw him do it. Dr Parsons at the medical centre. He thought she'd died around lunchtime.'

'Did she talk to you about the death of her friend, Ingrid Neale?' asked Dahl. Connie sat back in the sofa, watching him take over the questioning.

'Who?'

'One of her friends died in June. She kept the newspaper with the funeral notice on the coffee table.'

'She never mentioned anything to me. Funny that, she'd normally tell me about that sort of thing.'

'So you don't know why she kept the paper?'

'No. I saw it on the coffee table when I was cleaning after they took the body away but I didn't want to throw anything out, just tidy up.'

'Did she go to a funeral this year? Of a friend, perhaps?'

'I don't think so. She never mentioned it.'

'That's fine.' Dahl put his notebook away. 'I don't think we need to bother you any more.'

'Would you like more cake?'

Connie looked at the piece of carrot cake, probably from the same slab that Janet had baked for Nell Colley. She swallowed. 'I think we'll leave you in peace.'

They walked in silence to the car. Dahl turned back towards the house. 'Worth following up, do you think? Finding out who the visitor was.'

Connie started the engine. 'I think we need to do at least that. There is something odd about the fact we've not found any evidence of the book she was writing.' There it was again, the tug of disquiet. 'I wonder why she was writing a memoir.'

'The dark secrets of Bampton perhaps. You think it's important?'

'I'm not sure. Perhaps it's connected to the funeral notice. Do you know what? I'm glad Matthews put the file back on my chair this morning.'

12

'Are you Mina?'

Mina wished she'd had a chance to get back to the boat and give herself a wash. Two hours of backbreaking weeding before lunch, interrupted by Emily who had brought her a sandwich perhaps to make up for the meagre wages. Emily hadn't been inclined to talk but had again given Mina a puzzled look before retreating behind the bar. Mina lost track of the time in the afternoon and had been forced to rush, throwing her tools in the back of the van and taking the cash Emily handed to her in an envelope.

St Bertram's had been built in the eighties to replace the old cottage hospital that had been deemed no longer fit for purpose. Victorian buildings were out of fashion, modern constructions of glass and concrete were in. The architects, however, had made an attempt to integrate the hospital into the Peak landscape. The building was clad in grey stone and they'd named the place after a local saint who had built his hermitage in nearby Ilam. Or that's what people said. Oral tradition was alive and strong in Derbyshire and the name, at least, had found favour. The hospital itself, however, was unpopular with the old residents of the town who'd been fond of the intimacy of the former cottage hospital and were uninterested in the statistics that proclaimed it a high performing health hub.

Mina stopped in surprise and looked down at a teenage girl dressed in the unmistakable uniform of Bampton Grammar School. A thin V-neck jumper and pleated skirt emphasised her small frame. From her neck hung a nametag with the blank side showing.

'Is everything okay?'

The girl checked to see if anyone was listening. An officious-looking woman with a sash across her body was directing an elderly couple towards the lifts. 'I'm one of the volunteers, a visitor, although St Bertram's calls us patient support.'

'You visit the sick, you mean?'

'Yes. I'm in year nine and we have to do some community work for our Personal and Social Education course.'

Mina's eyes dropped to the lanyard around the girl's neck. The schoolgirl blushed and turned the plastic wallet around. The label identified her as *Catherine Hallows*. Mina took in the thin frame and mousy hair and felt a pang of remorse. You forget what it's like to be fourteen. Or rather you try to forget. The girl stared at a spot to the left of Mina, unable to make eye contact.

'I visited your mum a couple of days ago. I remember her from the library when I was small. She used to help me choose my books. Mum didn't know what was good. She introduced me to Philip Pullman and Harry Potter.'

Mina felt the urge to cry. 'How did you know who I was?'

'She said you were a gardener.' Catherine glanced down at Mina's earth-spattered dungarees.

'Right. Are you visiting Mum then?'

'We get assigned a ward to visit. I was given the ophthalmology department, which is okay but a lot of patients are bandaged up so they can't see you properly and it makes them shy. So I've got time on my hands. I saw your mum being pushed down a corridor in a wheelchair and I followed her back to the ward.'

'When was this?'

'Last week. I've been going every day but they won't let me see her today. They say she's poorly.'

The girl looked distraught and Mina relented. 'Mum's taken a turn for the worse. Didn't they tell you that?'

'They said she wasn't up to any visitors apart from family.' The girl's thin face was pale, unused to the ravages of the sick room. 'She talks about you a lot. She showed me the plant with the white flowers.'

'Cyclamen. It's a cyclamen.'

'Is she okay? She's not—' Catherine's age made her tongue-tied. She looked to Mina for help.

'She's very poorly.' Mina turned to move away.

'I really wanted to see her again. When I visited her, she was very agitated.'

Mina stopped. 'What do you mean?'

'Something had really upset her.'

Oh no, thought Mina. *Don't say she mentioned killing some-one.* 'Did she say what it was?'

'She was a bit upset and rambling a bit. She was trying to tell me something. About—'

'About what?'

'It was all so disjointed. She said something about she couldn't believe it. And I said, "Believe what," but she wouldn't tell me what.'

'Anything else?'

75

Catherine shook her head. 'She talked a bit about a drowned village. I didn't know what she meant. Then I had to run to get help because she kept saying "cutting" and I thought she was in pain. Maybe something was cutting into her.'

'Cutting?'

'That's what she said. Then I remembered that you're a gardener. Maybe she was talking about plants.'

Mina considered the word. Cutting? Why would Hilary be interested in a cutting? It must be part of her delirium. Mina took a step back. 'Look, let me go to her. I'm sorry she's too sick for you to visit her for the moment.'

Mina left Catherine in the lobby. As the din reverberated around her, she looked back at the girl, who was standing very still, following her progress. Mina carried on to the lift at the back of the hospital and waited for it to descend to the ground floor. The oncology department had initially been so difficult to find, tucked in a corner at the back of the hospital, but now Mina could have got there in her sleep. She buzzed the ward for admittance and a male nurse behind a computer let her in without looking up.

'Is everything all right with my mum, Hilary Kemp? Any improvement?'

'I've just popped in to see her and check her drip. She's asleep.'

'How's her pain?'

'We're monitoring it. We have to be careful how much morphine we give her but she appears to be relatively pain free at the moment.'

Mina went into her mother's room and checked the cyclamen. She poured a dash of water from her drinking bottle onto the dry earth and put her rucksack down by her mother's bed. Hilary's breathing was steady but shallow. There was a small heap on the bedside cabinet, pushed to one side and nearly crushed under the weight of a magazine. Mina leant forward to pick it up. It was a rough bouquet of flowers, mainly red campion, picked from one of the hedgerows. It was a nice gesture, left perhaps by Catherine.

Her mother's eyelids flickered and she opened her eyes in consternation.

'It's me.'

Her mother tried to smile. 'Mina.'

'How are you feeling?'

'Tired.'

'You look a bit better than yesterday. Do you want me to put the television on?'

Hilary shook her head. 'There was a girl—'

'That'll have been a visitor called Catherine. That was the other day, though. She hasn't seen you today.'

Hilary frowned in concentration, trying to remember.

'She knows you from the library,' prompted Mina.

Her mother smiled slightly. 'Difficult to see her. The sun was in my eyes.'

Mina looked to the blinds, which were drawn. 'I think she must have left these for you. They're flowers.'

She placed the loose stems into her mother's frail hand. Hilary looked at them for a moment. 'Nice.'

'Mum. Do you remember what you said?'

'I don't remember much. I remember feeling hot.' This was a calmer Hilary, less agitated than Mina had seen her the day before.

'You asked me about someone called Valerie.'

The panic returned to Hilary's eyes. 'Valerie? Valerie who?'

'Mum! Don't you remember? We had a conversation about a Valerie. You were at school together. You thought you saw her at the hospital.'

'Valerie? But Valerie's dead.'

Bloody hell, thought Mina. 'You thought you saw her at the hospital,' she repeated.

Hilary shook her head. Resolute. 'Valerie's dead.'

'That's okay, Mum. Your temperature was really high. Don't worry.' She thought of her stained dungarees and the hard morning's toil. All for nothing. Cold Eaton an unnecessary job she needn't have taken. 'How did she die?' The question was clearly unwelcome. This afternoon, however, Hilary wasn't wracked with guilt, just tired and bad tempered.

'I don't know. I heard from your Grumps that she'd died. It was years ago. We'd lost touch by then. Never mind about that.'

'I thought you wanted me to find her so I went out to Cold Eaton.'

'I don't want to hear about there.' It was as loud as Mina had heard her mother in the last few weeks.

'I thought Valerie might still be living in the village, that's all. I didn't mean to upset you. It was you who mentioned Cold Eaton.'

There was silence.

'You don't want me to find her then?'

'She died.' Hilary was drifting off again. Mina lightly held her wrist. 'Mum, listen, you told that girl Catherine about a cutting. What did you mean?'

But Hilary was asleep. Mina kissed her mother on her cheek and left the room. There was a different nurse at the station.

'She's better today.'

'That's good. She's still very ill but we've got her temperature down a bit.'

'She doesn't remember what we spoke about yesterday. Is that normal?'

'Completely. She'll have been in and out of consciousness yesterday. It can be very confusing when you feel a bit better.'

Mina thought of Hilary and Catherine's anxious face. And that most horrible of words. Cutting.

'I don't want anyone else seeing her apart from me. No visitors. Okay?'

13

Catherine – Three Weeks Earlier

She turned up on the doorstep at midday as promised. She'd had to bunk off the last morning lesson at school, inventing a visit to the doctor and composing a note in her mum's writing. She'd then walked down to the bus stop three streets away from the classroom so no one would notice that she was heading in the direction away from the cluster of Bampton's doctors' surgeries. The person she'd come to see was waiting near the door and it swung open before she'd even had time to lift her hand up to knock.

'It's you. Come in.'

Catherine was ushered into a room where the sunlight revealed particles of dust hanging suspended in the air. She was shown to a chair and left alone, allowing her to take a puff of Ventolin to ease the tightness in her chest. The woman returned with a glass of Coke still fizzing in the glass. Except it wasn't Coke but bitter tasting. Catherine made a face, and placed the glass back on the table with a bang.

'It's dandelion and burdock. Have you never had it before?'

'No. It's awful.'

'It's the taste of the country. It's made from plants that you see around you. Go on. Try another sip.'

Catherine tried again. It was no better but she wanted to please this woman who had picked up her own glass and taken a seat opposite her.

'Does your mum know you're here?'

Catherine shook her head. 'I didn't tell anyone, like you asked.'

'It's for the best. Not everyone likes their secrets on show. We can talk more freely if I know it's just between you and me.'

'Thank you for helping me.'

'You want to know about your family?'

'Mum won't tell me anything and, anyways, it's not her side I want to know about.'

'You don't remember your dad?'

Catherine scratched her arms in embarrassment. 'I remember him a little bit. I remember him laughing and, later, lying in bed for a long time. But it's not only him I'm interested in. It's about my grandmother too. I want to know about her.'

She looked up and was surprised to see an expression of satisfaction on the woman's face. 'Your grandmother? Well, there's a story that you might be sorry to hear. Are you sure you're ready for it?'

14

Connie looked at her watch. Four thirty. Should she make the offer? It was only on a Friday that she allowed herself a drink before seven. Her mother's struggle with alcoholism that had led to her early death had left its mark on Connie. She liked a drink, enjoyed socialising with colleagues, but kept an eye on her intake. Friday was the exception when she'd go out to the pub straight from work. Today, however, a new member of the team had arrived, which should be marked in some way.

'Fancy a glass of wine?'

Dahl looked up. 'I'd love one but I can't.'

'Okay. Another time maybe.' Connie, embarrassed, sank into her chair.

'Is it a regular thing? Drinks after work, I mean.'

'Not really. Just when we fancy it. I thought, given it's your first day and Sadler is away, that we could do something. Matthews is busy sucking up . . . oh forget I said that bit. And as for her . . .'

Connie nodded over to Mayfield, who was once again massaging her enormous bump.

Dahl picked up a file. 'I'm about to finish off things here. Listen, I've been in touch with the GP and social services. None of them visited Nell at the time her neighbour mentioned. So whoever her neighbour heard, it wasn't from her regular visitors.'

'Family?'

'She doesn't have any, remember.'

'Maybe it was someone connected to the book she was writing.'

'The subject of which we don't know.'

Connie groaned. 'I wish Sadler was here. Books are more his thing. He might have an idea who else we could contact.'

Dahl closed the file and put it to one side. 'I've called everyone I can think of. I guess it's the best we can do. We can let Matthews know at the team meeting tomorrow.'

'I'm desperate for a drink.' Mayfield sighed. 'With the last two kids, I went off alcohol completely. Even the thought of it made me sick. This one, I'm craving a glass of red so badly, I think I might take a bottle into the delivery room so I can have a slug straight afterwards.'

'I thought a glass was okay when you were pregnant.' Dahl began to pack his things away.

'The advice changes all the time and suppose something went wrong? I'm thirty-nine. No point taking any chances. Anyway, this one will be my last.'

'You said that last time.' Connie was chuckling as she too got ready to leave.

'Yeah, thanks a lot. If birth control was as simple as saying "not tonight thanks", life would be much simpler.'

Matthews opened the door to see what the laughter was about. 'All okay? You're not going, are you, Connie? You're on shift until six.'

'I wasn't going to leave, I was tidying up.'

Matthews looked at her watch. 'It won't take you an hour and a quarter.'

Furious, Connie sat down and opened up a window on her computer screen. Looking embarrassed, Dahl put on his coat. 'I do need to go. I'm sorry.'

Connie shrugged, still looking at the screen.

'Listen, do you think you'll still fancy a drink after nine?'

Connie looked up. 'What, tonight?'

'Yes, I mean, if it's too late just say but I'm up for a drink later on.'

Connie thought about the takeaway she'd planned. She could have it first and go out later. 'All right. Sounds like a plan. Where do you want to meet?'

'Do you know The Trip to Jerusalem?'

'There?'

'Why, don't you like it?'

'It's just that it's off the beaten track.' A suspicion entered Connie's mind. 'We're not hiding from someone, are we? You don't have a wife you're trying to keep secret?'

Dahl smiled. Unoffended. 'No wife. I'm busy until nine, that's all. Fancy meeting up or not?'

'You're on. I'll get there at five past if you don't mind. I don't fancy sitting on my own in that place.'

In silence, Connie and Mayfield watched him walk out.

'He's quite fanciable.' Mayfield opened a drawer and started to put her stuff away. 'A bit geekish if you like them like that. I think it must be the glasses. But still, fanciable.'

'I'm staying away from relationships in the workplace. Even with the single ones. I simply wanted to offer him a welcome drink. Why do you think he had to rush away?'

Mayfield looked at her watch and sighed. 'The longest hour of the day. I don't know. Maybe he has something on.

He wasn't being particularly mysterious. He just didn't want to tell you what he was up to.'

'Funny, though. Chuck me that file on Dahl's desk.'

Connie reached over and took the buff coloured folder from Mayfield's hand. It was thin, consisting of the death report and a couple of witness statements. She looked at the record of people Dahl had rung. A substantial list mainly of authorities dealing with the elderly plus the woman's GP surgery. He'd taken a highlighter pen and run it over the name of the woman whose funeral notice had so interested Nell. Ingrid Neale.

She wondered why Dahl had highlighted it and what the hell he was doing buggering off at five o'clock anyway.

*

The thin tower of Bampton church came into view as Sadler picked up his pace. The rumbling of his stomach reminded him that he'd forgotten to pack the sandwiches he'd carefully made that morning and which were still sitting on top of his kitchen counter. He'd left Bampton shrouded in mist but the air in the hills was clear and he hadn't wanted to slow his pace by stopping at an indifferent pub. Now, after a day of walking, he decided to reward himself with dinner at the Wilton hotel. The alternative was a pub meal or perhaps the warm sandwiches still in his kitchen. Neither appealed and, as the outline of the grey stone building loomed up at him in the dark, he could feel the rumblings in his stomach increase.

Perhaps his hunger was responsible for the feeling that had followed him around all day. The worry that something undefined was wrong. He'd mulled over Max's comments about Nell Colley and was still undecided what to do next. He didn't want to interrupt his holiday but, if there was an issue, surely it couldn't wait until the following week. He got out his mobile and called Connie's desk number. She answered it immediately. 'Aren't you supposed to be away?'

'I *am* away. Well, sort of.'

'What do you mean sort of?'

'Oh, nothing. What's happening there?'

'Missing us, boss?' Her voice turned smug.

'Something like that.'

'Aren't you going to ask me about Matthews?'

'I'm sure she's doing a great job.'

'She is indeed.' Connie's voice spoke volumes.

'There you are then. So, what's happening?'

'We're investigating burglaries and a possible unexplained death. Nothing specific to worry about but . . .'

'Unexplained death?' Sadler could feel his heart thudding but kept his voice light. 'What's that about?'

'A possible victim who goes by the name of Nell Colley.'

Sadler closed his eyes. *Everything comes full circle*, he thought.

'I'm looking at it with the new guy, Dahl. We're going over it with a fine-tooth comb. Nothing tangible at the moment but we're checking out some things that don't really tally.'

Sadler debated whether to mention the conversation with Max. Finally, he said, 'Will you call me before signing everything off? Nell's name came up in conversation with a neighbour of mine.'

'Really?' Connie sounded curious.

'She was writing a book and was worried about libelling herself.'

'Nell's neighbour mentioned something about a memoir but we haven't found any evidence of her having started it. Funny that you mention it too. You think the subject matter might have been libellous?'

'Nell was concerned about it but no one knows what she was writing about.'

'I wonder. I'll ask Matthews tomorrow if we can do some more digging.'

'Will you keep me informed of progress?'

'Of course.'

After the call disconnected, Sadler switched off his mobile and put it in his pocket, the sense of uneasiness still knotting his stomach.

*

'You will double-lock the door when I go out, won't you?'

'I always do. Why? Are you going out after dinner?' Alice Dahl's voice was calm, careful not to sound too curious.

'I'm nipping up to the pub. The Trip to Jerusalem. It's not far and it's got good mobile coverage. I checked last night when I walked past. If there's a problem, call me.' Dahl carried on peeling the spuds for the roast potatoes.

'I'll be fine, as I told you, and I'll lock the door after you.'

'It's not just tonight, though. I'm talking generally about locking the door when I'm not here. You can deadbolt it from the inside. I can override it with my keys but it's hard to break into.'

'Why the concern? I may be crippled with arthritis but I haven't lost the use of my brain. I know how to lock the door.'

'Sorry. I know.' Dahl dropped the potatoes into the hot goose fat on the tray. They hissed for a moment and then settled, swimming around in the old copper pan his mother had been given as a wedding present. He put the dish into the oven and reached over and started peeling the carrots.

'It's not going to hold you back, is it? Coming here. You were doing so well in Glossop.'

'We've been through this before, Mum. I asked for the transfer to a CID with a better record of working patterns.' *And a better reputation for decent bosses*, he thought. 'Bampton approved the transfer. If they didn't want me they wouldn't have said yes. They're not a charity.'

'And they're fine with you leaving at five some nights?'

'It's flexible working. As long as I put in my hours, I can leave early. Why are you still worried, Mum?'

Alice used her walking sticks to move nearer the stove and Dahl pulled up a stool so his mother could rest on it.

'I never thought it would end up like this. I thought you'd get married. Have kids. I'd carry on working into my sixties. And look where we are. I'm living off my savings and you're here looking after me.'

'We have help.'

'Yes, but you still have to leave work early some days. Does anyone know why?'

Dahl kept his back to her so she couldn't see his face colour slightly. 'I haven't mentioned it to my colleagues.' His thoughts turned to Connie who was clearly one of life's nosy parkers, although in their job this was a strength not a weakness. 'I'm sure they'll get to know in due course.'

'Don't be ashamed of it. I couldn't bear that.'

'Mum.' Dahl turned to her and hugged her close to him. 'I'm not your carer. I just have to help out sometimes. It'll be fine. I promise you, it won't impact on my job.'

'What about when a major investigation comes up? Then what? I remember the hours you put in during that murder case in Hadfield. What if that happens here?'

'We'll manage. The neighbours are good, aren't they? You have friends too. We couldn't rely on them on a regular basis any longer. It was too much to ask. For short term help it will be fine.'

'I could pay someone to come in for extra hours if that would help.'

'Maybe.' Dahl was noncommittal. They were getting no state help as it was. If a major investigation came up, he was damned if his mother would be spending even more of her hard-earned cash.

'What are your colleagues like?'

'They seem nice.'

'Male or female?'

Dahl laughed. 'Mum. I'd never go out with a copper. It's too incestuous.'

'You're going out tonight, though.'

'You don't miss much, do you? It's a drink with a fellow DC. I have a feeling I need her on my side if I'm going to settle into Bampton. She invited me out for a drink so I'm going.'

'Is she nice?'

Dahl thought of Connie, who despite her scepticism of the wisdom of investigating an unsuspicious case had nevertheless diligently done so.

'She *is* nice.' He laughed. 'Actually, she's really nice.' He saw his mother's face. 'As a friend. I want her to tell me more about DI Sadler. He's going to be my boss and I want to make a good impression.'

'There's no need to worry about that. You'll impress them all.'

Dahl gave his mother a final hug. 'You will be careful, won't you? Lock the door when I'm gone and don't leave any windows open.'

'Of course. Why the sudden concern?'

Dahl turned back to the peeling. 'No reason.'

15

Mina gently lowered herself into the canoe and pushed off from the bank. None of her neighbours were up, although the light had broken through the clouds half an hour earlier. A huddle of ducks were sheltering under the edge of the towpath, next to a swan with its head tucked under its wing. Used to her morning exercise, they didn't stir as she glided past towards Higgs Lock.

As she made her way westwards away from Bampton, the water turned dark and brackish. She stayed in the middle of the canal. One morning, a group of hooded boys, the air around them reeking of cannabis, had thrown stones at her as she'd passed a derelict warehouse, shaking her composure. The police had been helpful and, now, occasionally she would see some PCSOs walking this deserted stretch on the lookout for anti-social behaviour.

It was a hazy autumnal morning and Mina used the exercise to clear her mind of the ever constant worry about her mother's illness and the more immediate problem of Hilary's agitation over her childhood friend, Valerie. Had it been the voice of a woman in her delirium? In Mina's dreams, faces sometimes reappeared from the past, but her mother had been frightened. Scared after seeing a woman she had been certain was dead. What had she said? 'Valerie's dead. Grumps told me.' So Hilary had been told of Valerie's death. What was the comment about killing Valerie then? You can't kill someone and not know about it.

Mina reached a tunnel, thankfully one that she was allowed to paddle through according to the canal rules. She had spotted some other canoeists turn around when they reached the entrance, inhibited from creeping into the unknown, but this was the part she most enjoyed. Entering a cocoon and living in the moment. No future and no past. Inside the tunnel, the outside world shrank to a murmur with only the sound of her boat lapping through dimly lit darkness. Although it only took a few minutes to pass through, during that time Mina was aware of a peace she hadn't felt since her mother's revelations. She stopped the canoe at the side of the tunnel for a moment and waited in the darkness, closing her eyes so that the only sensation was the damp on her face and the sound of the slap of water against the brickwork.

With a determined paddle, she set off again and came out into the morning air. In the distance she could hear a whistle, probably from the steam train that meandered up the restored track over the Topley Trail. Mina stopped paddling, trying to make a connection. Cutting, Catherine had said. Wasn't there a railway reference to do with cuttings? Her knowledge of trains was so scant she wasn't sure if she was imagining it. Cutting. Could this be what her mother was talking about?

Back on land and wrapped in one of her mother's over-sized jumpers, Mina heaved a black bin bag into her van and headed towards her own home. In her childhood semi she pulled out clothes from the bag and put them into her washing machine. Her mother made do with handwashing garments bought specifically for the reason that they didn't need ironing. Mina's clothes, which could hardly have been called chic, needed a more robust clean after work. The house was airless after being closed up for so long. Mina moved restlessly around, watering the pot plants, and then went out to the back garden. A dead robin lay on the lawn, pathetically small in the expanse, a victim of the ginger tom next door. She picked up a trowel and buried the bird in one of the borders, next to a mulberry bush.

She checked her mobile again to see if the hospital had tried to contact her. Nothing but a few missed calls from her friend Jo. She sat on a bench, massaging her temples, then went back inside and rang her friend.

An hour later, Jo hugged Mina to her ample bosom and then looked at her critically. 'You've lost weight.' Mina attempted to shrug away but Jo's arms held her. 'You *are* looking after yourself, aren't you?'

Irritated, Mina pulled away. 'Let's find somewhere to eat.'

Bampton was crowded for a drizzly late October morning. She assumed that the town was catering for the residents of the nearby cities of Manchester and Sheffield with nothing better to do on a wet Tuesday than take a run out to the countryside. Even the chip shop was already open and one family with a white terrier in tow were attempting to eat trays of chips while standing under a large black umbrella.

Mina nodded in their direction. 'I want something a bit more comfortable than that. Do you mind if we climb away from the centre of town? There's somewhere I want to try.'

She steered Jo up a steep hill that had them both panting for breath by the time they reached the top. They walked through a car park towards the entrance of a café painted with the familiar Peak District green. The building was a large cavernous space that had been divided into four separate dining areas with big wooden tables and signs asking diners to help themselves to cutlery. It had the air of an upmarket canteen.

'What's this place? I've never been here before.' Jo was looking around her. 'It's nice.'

'Can't you tell? Well, we did rush in, didn't we? If you'd noticed the huge clock hanging off one side, you'd have realised. It's Bampton station, or it was before they shut it down years ago. The line ran outside that window there and you can walk along it all the way into Buxton. It's pretty impressive.'

'I can't see the path.'

'It's behind the trees. I had a look on the map earlier. I've always meant to come up here but . . .'

'But what?'

'I don't know. For some reason I thought it wasn't that nice.'

Jo picked up a menu. 'I didn't know this café existed but I have walked parts of the trail. We can go for a little walk afterwards if you like and I can show you where you can hire a bike. That's the best way to see the old line. You could cycle seven or eight miles until the path peters out.'

'I didn't think it was that interesting. I got the impression it was fairly derelict.'

Jo looked at Mina in astonishment. 'Who on earth told you that? The trail is one of the most beautiful walks you can do without going out into the hills. It's great for the elderly and young kids because no part of it is particularly steep. It's heaving in the summer but you'll largely have it to yourself this time of year. Who said it wasn't worth a visit?'

'My mum. She always said it was a terrible place.'

'Really?' Jo put down the menu and studied the blackboard hanging from the opposite wall with the daily specials. 'Locals often don't realise the value of what they've got. They also, in my experience, never walk anywhere. I bet she's never even gone down the path.'

Mina, thinking of her bookish mum, smiled. 'You're probably right.'

Jo looked across at her. 'You are coping, aren't you? It's a horrible situation to be in. I can't even bear to think about my mum being ill. I like to pretend she's going to live until she's a hundred and fifty.'

'I'm all right. I'm just trying to make sense of a few things. Let's forget about that for the moment. What are you going to eat?'

Jo humphed. 'I'm going to have a baked potato although I'm trying not to have such a carb fest this winter. Still, it's baked potato weather. What about you?'

'Soup for me.'

'I knew it. You're on a diet.'

'I'm not. It's just since Mum's illness my appetite's gone.'

Jo was silent and looked at the table. 'It's a bloody awful way to go. Although I'm not sure there is a good way to die. With my dad it was quick. Mum went to take him a cup of tea in the study and he'd gone. Is that better? Maybe for him but what about the rest of us? I never had the chance to say to him the things that really matter. Have you?'

'It's hard because some days I think I'm about to lose her and others she's, well, not okay, but better.'

'Will you feel you've said everything you need to say, though?'

Mina shrugged. 'I'm not sure. What might be the end for Mum might be the start for me. Does that make sense?'

Jo stood up, purse in hand. 'Not really, but it doesn't have to. It just needs to make sense to you.'

And that, thought Mina, as she watched her friend go to the counter to order the food, *is the heart of the problem. Nothing at the moment makes sense.*

16

So Dahl wasn't a dick. That was good to know. She'd had two glasses of wine and he hadn't pressed another on her. He'd also stuck to two bottled beers and then headed off. They'd talked of Derbyshire, politics and his last big case in that order. When she'd asked why he'd moved to Bampton he'd changed the subject. She'd woken up clear eyed and, for the first time since Sadler's departure for his hols, looking forward to going into work. She sat down at her desk, keeping a wary eye on Matthews. Dahl came into the CID room balancing two coffee cups on top of each other.

'They give you a tray for them if you ask.' Connie wished she'd stopped off on her way in. She'd been planning to get herself settled and then nip out. Now she was sinking under a mountain of paperwork.

'I wasn't planning on getting two when I placed my order so I didn't ask.'

'Need waking up, do you?'

Dahl placed a cup in front of her. 'One of them is for you, actually.'

'Me? How do you know what I like?'

'I saw you drinking from a cup yesterday so I described you to the server and asked if you'd been in yet. She said no and that you liked a skinny latte extra hot.'

Connie reached into her handbag. 'You'd make a great detective. How much do I owe you?'

'Have this one on me. In future we'll go halves.'

'Nice one. Thanks, Dahl.' Connie took a long sip of the hot liquid and bent her head back over her papers. She was aware of Dahl making himself comfortable at DS Palmer's old desk.

'How did you describe me to the barista?'

Dahl laughed. He had another mismatched outfit on. This time a pinstripe jacket made out of linen with trousers also with thin lines threaded through them but of a thicker material.

'Don't you look in the mirror before you leave the house?'

Dahl looked up in surprise. 'What's the matter? Have I got toothpaste on my cheek?'

'Your cheek? I know you wear glasses but that'd be one hell of a miss.'

He threw an empty styrofoam cup at her. 'Go on then. Tell me what's wrong with my appearance.'

'Your trousers don't match your jacket.'

He looked down at himself. 'Don't they? Oh well. The blind man will be pleased to see me, as my mother says.'

Smiling, Connie switched on her computer.

'By the way, do you own a sewing kit?'

'Me?' Connie opened a desk drawer. 'I had one once upon a time. Why?'

'The hem of your trousers is coming undone.'

Connie lifted a leg and swore. 'This is only the second time I've worn them. They're going back to the shop tomorrow.'

Matthews opened her door and came over, irritated by their laughter. 'How did you get on with Nell Colley yesterday?'

98

Connie looked to Dahl. 'The house shows no sign of disturbance and the neighbour's story rings true. We've taken a bag of the deceased's medication. There's quite a lot of it but nothing that appears out of place. I'll check it this morning.'

Matthews looked relieved. 'Do that and then bring me the paperwork to look at.'

'There is one thing.' Matthews stopped at Dahl's voice. 'She did have a visitor on the morning that she died. The neighbour seemed certain of this but we haven't been able to trace them.'

'A friend?' asked Matthews.

'That would be my guess because I've checked all the authorities.'

'Do you think it significant?'

'I don't think so and the GP doesn't appear inclined to inform the coroner. No further action would be my recommendation.' Dahl's voice had an air of authority and Connie was impressed. Not a colleague who would need hand holding then. Instead of the expected relief at his recommendation, Connie felt the twinge of apprehension she had first experienced while looking over the file and again at Nell's house. She sat back in her chair and wondered whether to say something. Matthews, however, was also clearly impressed with Dahl and she, at least, looked relieved.

'Good. Check through the medication then bring me the paperwork.'

Connie watched Matthews shut the door and turned to Dahl. 'We didn't mention the book she was writing. The more I think about it, the odder it is. Even her neighbour thought it was out of character for Nell to want to start something and then prevaricate about it. The memoir must have been about an important moment in her life.'

'That's the point of memoirs. Important for the person writing it but often not that interesting for anyone else.'

'I guess,' said Connie. 'It's strange, though. I spoke to Sadler last night and he'd heard about the death from one of his neighbours. Nell was worried about libelling herself.'

'Did he give any more information?'

'He doesn't have any more details, but what about the funeral notice that Nell was looking at? Perhaps it's connected to her. You circled the name in the notes on your desk.'

Dahl frowned. 'It's unexplained, that's all. The house was clean so she hadn't kept any subsequent local papers. Only the one with Ingrid Neale's name in it.'

Mayfield looked up. 'Ingrid Neale?'

Connie swung around in her chair. 'Yes, why?'

'She died in June. She was an elderly patient who was found dead. Sadler sent me out to look at the death, check everything was all right.'

'Was it in High Oaks?'

'No, not even in Bampton. A sudden death in Cold Eaton. She was definitely called Ingrid Neale. Lived with her sister Monica Neale and Monica's husband. What's her connection with yours?'

'Our deceased kept the funeral notice.'

'Oh,' said Mayfield. 'They probably knew each other.'

Dahl also turned to face Mayfield. 'How did she die?'

'I think it was an asthma attack. I can dig out the file for you, if you like. The correct procedure was followed, I checked. She'd certainly seen her GP that week and he was happy to sign off the death certificate. She was in some dis-comfort. There was even an oxygen tank at the property.'

Dahl continued to stare at Mayfield. 'Who was the doctor who signed off the cause of death?'

'I'll have to look at the file. My memory's not that good.'

They waited for a moment while Mayfield clicked around her computer.

'Here we are. The woman's GP. A Dr Jake Parsons.'

Connie felt her body go cold. 'But that's the same GP as our death.'

Mayfield looked unconcerned. 'There are only three GP practices in Bampton. It's not that significant.' She looked at them both. 'Is it?'

'Can I look at it?' Dahl got up and walked over to her. He leant over her, rapidly skimming through the notes. At one point, he stopped and looked up at Connie.

'She was found sitting on the sofa, fully dressed.'

'So?'

'That's the same situation as Nell Colley.'

'Bloody hell, Dahl, you've got to die somewhere. Why not on the sofa?'

He was shaking his head. 'I've spent longer in uniform than you, I bet. Remember being called to deaths? How many were sitting up?'

'Lots of them.'

He shook his head. 'No they weren't. A few were, certainly, but not lots. If you're feeling ill you go to bed. You don't sit upright on the sofa.'

'You bloody do.'

'You do not.'

Mayfield was watching them both. 'What's the matter?'

Dahl wrote an address down on a notepad and motioned to Connie. 'Let's go, and this time I'll drive.'

17

Mina and Jo began to walk down the old railway path but the pelting rain forced them back into Bampton where they ran to their vehicles. Mina switched on the windscreen wipers and, checking the map on her phone, took the road out towards Cold Eaton. At the junction where she should have turned a sharp left towards the village, however, she carried on half a mile or so until another turning appeared at the bend. It was marked with a brown tourist sign pointing the way to Eaton station.

The road was as narrow as the one to Cold Eaton but filled with potholes. Mina expertly navigated the van between the fissures in the road and the surface turned to gravel in front of a long squat building built in Derbyshire stone. Next to it, a train hissing steam from the top of its engine looked braced to depart. As she got out of the car, admiring the house opposite which was brightened by window boxes full of winter planting, a capped guard looked Mina up and down.

'You've got three minutes to buy a ticket.'

'I'm not travelling, only visiting the office.'

The guard turned his attention to a couple with a young child in a pushchair who was struggling to get out in the excitement. Mina pushed open the door to the ticket office and approached a small group huddled around a computer.

A woman peeled away and came to the counter.

'You're just in time—'

'I'm not getting on the train, thanks. I wanted to ask you about something. About the history of this railway.'

This got the group's attention. They all stared at her, poised to answer.

'I was wondering if someone could give me information about this railway line. It closed down for a bit, didn't it?'

'It's only been going for the last five years. It's volunteers who look after it,' a tall man answered with an air of authority. 'Why were you wanting to know?'

'I live in Bampton and only know about the closed section. You know, the trail where the old track used to be. I remembered that this bit had been reopened and I'm trying to find someone and they mentioned the railway.'

'Who did?'

At the man's abrupt tone, Mina's eyes filled with tears. The woman behind the counter noticed and lifted the hatch. 'Listen, the train's off. I can hear its whistle. It won't be back for an hour. I'll get Jim to look after the counter and I'll make us a brew.'

She steered Mina into the back room and switched on a kettle rimmed with limescale. The cups didn't look particularly clean but the woman gave them a wipe with a piece of kitchen towel.

'I'll make you a restorative cup of tea. I'm Jean, by the way. Don't mind the man who just spoke to you. He's my brother and he's been like that since the day he was born. Awkward. He speaks to everyone like that.'

'You work here?'

'Volunteer, and it's a labour of love. We used to live in the house over the road.'

'The one with the window boxes? I noticed as I was coming down the path.'

'That's the one. Our father was the station master here until 1966 when the railway shut down.'

'What a wonderful place to grow up. Were you sad to leave?'

Jean chuckled. 'I'm older than I look. By that time, I'd already left and was living in Bampton. The family joined me in a house nearby and that was that for us and the railway. Or so we thought.'

'Did you miss it? The station?'

'I did but not as much as Jim. He told me he used to dream about it. I was bringing up kids and, believe me, they don't leave you much time for anything else.'

'When did this part of the line reopen?'

'About five years ago but we'd been campaigning for it since the nineties. When they announced that they were turning the old track line into the Topley Trail, it was a case of now or never. It would have been lost forever to the dog walkers. Have you been down there?'

'Not really. I remember my mother being a bit sniffy about it. Saying something like it wasn't worth a visit.'

'*Did* she?' Jean clicked off the boiled kettle and filled up two cups. 'She's probably never ventured down the path. Some of the locals weren't so keen on the spot but I think it's really beautiful. You said you were interested in the railway.'

'It's my mother. She's not well. I mean, really not well. And she wants me to find a childhood friend of hers who goes by the name of Valerie.'

Jean sat heavily back in her chair, rocking slightly. 'Valerie,' she mused. 'You think she was connected to the railway?'

'My mother's been saying these random words that are confusing. I have the name Valerie and she also mentioned Cold Eaton. That's near here, isn't it?'

'Not far, although there was never any station. You have to walk a mile down the trail. It's a lovely spot. You can cut down to the village if you want to go to the pub. Can't remember the name. Something funny.'

'The Nettle Inn.'

'That's it. Odd place. You think Valerie might have lived in the village?'

'It's possible. That's what Mum was suggesting.'

'Which school did your mum go to?'

'Bampton Grammar. The thing is, the other day, she told one of the hospital visitors about a cutting. I was canoeing this morning and I heard the hiss of the train. Cutting's a railway term, isn't it?'

'Cutting? That's a general word for when a bit of the hill is taken away for the track to run through it.' Jean stirred her tea with a frown on her face. 'Mind you,' she paused for a breath and then shouted, 'Jim!' Her brother appeared at the door looking no friendlier than before. 'Isn't there a place called the Cutting around here?'

'Down towards Bampton. It's the last bridge before the old town station. The road's called Cutting Lane and locals call the bridge the Cutting.'

'I knew it.' Jean's face was triumphant. 'The Cutting. Of course. Why would your mother be talking about that cutting along with someone called Valerie?'

Mina glanced up and saw, with a shock, that Jim's face was pale and he was looking at her with dark brown eyes that held a warning.

'Be careful down there, lass. There are stories attached to the Cutting. Don't go there alone.'

'Stories. What stories?'

Jim was looking at his sister. 'The railway attracts all sorts. There was one story of a man who used to walk around the fields naked, a loner really, wearing only a pair of walking boots.'

'Jim! That was years ago,' protested Jean.

'The lass asked for an example and I gave her one. We tell a lot of tales around here. Just . . . just, be careful.'

18

Manor Grange was a short drive up the slope to the top end of Cold Eaton. The large house was made of White Peak limestone mixed with grit to give it a distinctive grey pallor. High hedgerows, unusual in this windswept part of the country, obscured the view of the house from the main road but, as Dahl swung into the wide gravel drive, Connie could see the house in all its miserable glory.

'I feel we should be using the side entrance,' said Dahl.

'I know what these huge houses are like. Nothing in them but old furniture. Fur coat and no knickers. Don't be overawed by the exterior.'

'I'm not overawed, it's just that I've met the type of people who live in old manor houses.'

The front door opened as they approached, their arrival anticipated. A tall man stood on the threshold, his greying hair brushed back from his face.

'Are you lost?' His manner was pleasant but their presence an irritant. They showed him their ID, which he scanned and then pulled the door so that the hall was obscured.

'We're looking for Monica Neale. Is she in?'

'Monica? What's she done?' Behind his mock guilt, Connie caught a tinge of anxiety.

'Can we come in? We'd just like a quick chat.'

'Of course. Come inside. I'm her husband, Harry.' He led them into a large kitchen with a shrug of apology. 'Hope you don't mind slumming it. It's the only warm room in the house.'

Connie was right about the interior. It was clean with the smell of recently sprayed polish but was bare of furniture if the hall and the glimpse of the living room were anything to go by. An elegant woman was standing by the Aga making a hearty soup. The vegetables had been chopped into tiny cubes and the smell of warming butter assailed Connie's nostrils. Harry's wife was unconcerned by the chill of the house; she'd rolled up the sleeves of her polo neck jumper and was wiping her face with the back of her hand.

As the woman turned towards them, Connie saw that she was older than at first glance. Harry must be in his late fifties and his wife around fifteen years older. *What of it*, she cautioned herself. Monica Neale's face, unadorned with make-up, was lined and still attractive. Harry filled a kettle and placed it on the Aga.

Dahl sat down at the table and, after a moment's hesitation, Connie joined him and took out her notebook. 'We're following up on a few things and we wanted to talk to you about the death of your sister.'

A look of shock crossed Monica's face. 'It's just routine,' Connie hastened to reassure her. 'Your sister, Ingrid, lived here with you?'

Harry glanced across at his wife. 'She owned the house as well as us. It's a complicated arrangement. The house has been in Monica's family for generations but her father only had two daughters and he left the house to both of them in trust. They jointly owned it.'

'And you all lived here together?'

'When Monica and I got married, their parents were already dead and Ingrid was teaching in the States. So we took over the running of the house but always with the knowledge that if Ingrid came back from abroad she would also live here.'

'Sounds unusual,' said Dahl.

Monica Neale tipped the vegetables into the soup pan and carried on stirring. 'Unusual but not difficult. My sister and I were close and we agreed that even if we both married we would share the house. It's big enough.' Her voice was more girlish than Connie had expected. 'As it was, Ingrid never married and she lived in Arizona until she retired at sixty.'

'When she returned home?'

Monica inclined her head in acknowledgement and poured a jug full of water into the pan. 'She shouldn't have returned, of course. Her asthma was bad when we were growing up, which was a shame as she was so sporty. The dry desert air in the States meant she had a much better life than the one she would have had here.'

'She came home, anyway?' asked Dahl.

'She didn't want to grow old in a foreign country. In any case, her health insurers were beginning to become difficult about the treatment. She was able to use the NHS here.'

The boiling kettle hissed and Harry carefully poured hot water into a teapot.

'You have the same surname as your sister? You didn't change it when you got married?'

Harry smiled. 'She didn't need to. I took Monica's surname. She wanted it to continue and I didn't mind. Our two sons have the Neale name.'

'Who was it who found Ingrid?' asked Dahl.

Harry looked up surprised. 'Me, actually. I'd been out repairing part of the drystone wall. If you don't keep on top of these things, they accumulate. It took me longer than I expected. I was out a good five hours and ravenous when I came back.'

'You weren't in, Mrs Neale?' Connie looked to Harry's wife.

'I wasn't. I'd had a call from a friend in the village to say she'd run out of eggs and could I bring her some so I went and, with one thing or another, I was out for about two hours.'

Harry brought them their tea. 'I went into the living room as the house was so quiet and I noticed Ingrid sitting on the sofa. I went over to her and she'd gone.'

'She was having to take oxygen, the report says.'

'There was a console in the living room that she could wheel to her bedroom downstairs at night.' Harry stirred his tea, a pique of irritation in his voice. 'We've been through this, you know. A detective came around to check on everything. A pretty young lass.'

Connie kept a neutral expression at the comment, although she noticed Dahl was looking furious.

'Was she in the chair she normally used in the living room?' asked Dahl, teeth gritted.

'Of course. Why do you ask?'

'We're checking details. Were you expecting something like this?'

'Not particularly but with the chronic asthma she suffered from it was always a possibility. I know she was feeling the effects of the change of seasons recently.'

'It's how she died. Of an asthma attack.' Monica's voice was firm.

Harry looked at his wife with concern. 'That's what Dr Parsons confirmed. We'd had to rush Ingrid to hospital a few days earlier because of respiratory failure. Dr Parsons said her death was connected to that attack.'

'He came to the house and saw the body?'

'Yes, but there was still a post mortem.'

Connie and Dahl looked at each other. 'Ingrid had a post mortem?' Connie repeated.

'Of course. She was ill but we didn't expect her to die. The post mortem confirmed an asthma attack. Is there a problem?'

'Not a problem as such. Your sister's name came up in connection with another investigation,' said Dahl. 'So we're checking the circumstances of Ingrid's death.'

'After all this time? We buried her months ago.'

Connie looked to Dahl. Good question. What were they supposed to say? 'We're just checking on the background to a recent death.'

'From asthma?' asked Monica. She was still standing by the Aga but had moved the pan away from the heat, her attention focused on them.

Connie sidestepped the question. 'Does the name Nell Colley mean anything to you?'

Harry shook his head. 'Never heard of her. Have you, Monica?'

Monica shook her head as well. 'Don't know the name.'

'Are you sure?' asked Connie, keeping her eyes on Monica. The woman nodded.

Connie gulped down the rest of her tea. 'Could I have a quick look at the room?'

'If you want.'

It was Harry who took them into the living room. It was a square elegant room furnished with two small sofas and not much else. 'No TV,' murmured Connie. She turned to Harry. 'Which sofa was she sitting on?'

'This one.' He pointed to the faded brocade sofa with its back to the window. 'She'd been reading a book.'

As they went to the car, Connie turned around and looked back towards the living room. 'It makes sense. It's the sofa that would give the most light. Why shouldn't she be sitting there?'

'If you're feeling breathless, wouldn't it be more natural to be standing up, opening a window? Anything to get air into your lungs.'

'Look, she had a PM. I know Bill Shields, the pathologist. He'll have done the job properly. We should have checked about the PM before we barged in.'

'It must be a dead end. The name Nell Colley meant nothing to Monica.'

Connie opened the car door. 'When I mentioned Nell's name, do you know what Monica did?'

'No, what?'

'She put her hand to her temple. She was trying to hide the twitch on the side of her eye.'

'Are you sure?'

'She couldn't help herself.'

'She never enquired why we were asking, did she? She asked us why we were interested in Ingrid's death but not the connection to Nell.'

'That's nothing unusual. Police have a reputation for not

giving anything away. She probably knew we wouldn't tell her anything.'

They got into the car and watched as the rain continued to fall, its intensity increasing. 'If she knew Nell Colley, why not say so?'

'I don't know but the name definitely meant something to her.'

Dahl sighed. 'It's not much, is it? We've not checked if there have been any complaints about Dr Parsons. Perhaps we should have looked through the files first.'

Connie groaned. 'You're as bad as me. Act first, think later. What a stupid thing to do. I hope to God we haven't messed things up by rushing to interview witnesses.'

'We can easily check when we get back to the office but, given we're out, why not ask Mayfield to look through the computer for us while we drive down to the surgery?'

'Pay him a visit now?'

'Why not?' Dahl switched on the engine. 'The computer search won't take long and we can question him about any sudden deaths he's attended recently. It'll put my mind at rest at least.'

19

The Cutting was initially hard to find. Jim had given no directions, just that the escarpment was at the end of Cutting Lane. However, when Mina reached the stone bridge at the end of the narrow track, there was only a single house standing in its shadow. There was no car park and no obvious access onto the Topley Trail. With a sigh, Mina managed a tight U-turn and followed the directions to a public car park half a mile down the track. Here she was able to park next to a Range Rover with two bikes strapped to the back. The car's occupants were eating sandwiches while the wipers swished in front of them. Feeling braver, Mina got out of the van and pulled on the manky coat she normally kept in the back for emergencies.

The path was well maintained, compressed gravel imprinted with footprints and bicycle tyre tracks. It might have been busy in Bampton but here, much further along the trail, it was deserted. Dotted along the path were signs pointing out geological features, local landmarks and railway remains. She passed an old signal box where the path split in two, one directing her towards Bampton and the other Matlock. She took the left-hand path, making her way back towards the old Bampton station, when a stone bridge loomed up as she rounded the bend. Mina stopped and looked around her.

So this was the Cutting, an old tunnel where the train would have once passed through on its way to Bampton.

She entered the dark space, the dank smell reminding her of the canal bridges. It was lighter inside though, which allowed her to have a look around as she passed through. As she came to the other side, she noticed an iron gate pushed back against the wall. They must lock the tunnel at night, which was just as well. Jim was right. The place did have a strange feel to it. A sense of the past but not one forlornly forgotten. Instead, there was a feeling of oppression still present. Mina passed out of the tunnel and into the cold air. Her mobile reconnected with a signal and beeped a new message. Joseph from the library. She pressed redial and he answered on the first ring.

'I called Carol and passed on your number. She says your mum never spoke about her school friends but she'll happily talk to you anyway. Do you want me to give you her number?'

'I'm out walking at the moment. Can you text it to me?'

'Of course. She has yours anyway so she'll probably call you.'

'Great.'

There was a silence. 'Have you heard from anyone after you filled in the card for our noticeboard?'

'Nothing. Why?'

'That's funny. When I went to look, the card wasn't there.'

'What? Did someone throw it out?'

'That's not very likely. It's me who does all the tidying. Anyway, it was only the other day. Why would someone chuck it?'

'You think someone's removed it? That's good news, surely. They might have something for me.'

'Why not make a note of your number and leave the card there, though? Honestly, people are so weird.'

'Can you do me another one? Can you remember the details?'

'I'm not sure it's allowed but why not. Yours has gone missing. I'll stick another one up for you.'

Mina disconnected the call and looked around her. The path ahead was deserted but, around the bend, she would be nearly at Bampton. She stopped and turned, ready to retrace her steps. Above her, a figure was standing on the bridge looking down. She put her hands over her eyes, trying to bring the outline into focus, but as she stepped towards it, the figure moved away from her and out of her sightline.

Mina looked around and saw a path leading up to the brow of the bridge. With difficulty, she heaved herself up the embankment but the figure was no longer to be seen. There were fields on both sides, one leading towards the town, the other towards a post-war housing development.

Puzzled, Mina trekked back down the Cutting and along the path to her van. The couple in the Range Rover had left, sick of waiting for a break in the weather. There was something wedged underneath her windscreen wipers, a piece of paper rolled into a flat tube to protect it from the rain. She pulled it off, and found no envelope, only a note scrawled on a sheet from a notebook.

LEAVE VALERIE ALONE.

20

Catherine

'I did it.' Catherine couldn't keep the note of triumph out of her voice. 'I left the note on her windscreen. She'll never know it was me. I even wrote it in capital letters.'

The woman opposite picked up the glass full of her foul-smelling drink. She'd accepted that Catherine would never take to dandelion and burdock and given her a glass of orange squash instead. Catherine, however, could still smell the witchy odour of the drink from the other glass.

'It was definitely Mina Kemp?'

'Of course. I went down to the boat to watch her this morning. The address was on the library card that I took. She was dead easy to find. She came out with this bin bag and drove off in her van. So I thought I'd just go back a bit later to see what she was doing. I couldn't follow her.'

'You didn't go into school?'

'I kept thinking about what you told me, so I went down to the Cutting and she was there too. Mina Kemp was at the old railway line.'

'Of course she was there. It was you who told her that Hilary had mentioned the Cutting. It didn't take her long to work it out.'

Catherine went hot and stared at her feet. 'I wanted to see

if Mina knew. I mean, if her mum had told anyone what happened. She didn't know at all. She walked up and down the path looking confused.'

'Of course Hilary never mentioned it. She wasn't stupid. Now, however, Mina is down there doing her own digging into the past.'

'She won't find anything, though, will she?'

The woman leant forward. 'Catherine. It's really important that Mina doesn't find out anything more about what happened down the Cutting. Do you see? Do you want the truth to come out?'

Catherine shook her head. 'Of course not,' she whispered.

The woman dropped her voice to the same level. 'Catherine, will you help me?'

21

At the sight of Dr Jake Parsons, all Connie's suspicions disintegrated. He was young. Very young, perhaps in his late twenties, but he exuded calm confidence. Wearing a checked shirt and black trousers, he would be a reassuringly casual presence for people worried about their array of ailments. He had a boyish face that still held the hint of a tan. He'd fitted them in straight away, the surgery allocating the rest of the morning patients around the other GPs.

'There are quite robust procedures in place for GPs to sign off death certificates. We are, however, still often the first port of call for patients with chronic illnesses who die in their homes.'

'For some reason, I thought the dead would be taken by ambulance to hospital,' said Dahl.

'It's one possibility but, if a patient is clearly dead, a hospital isn't necessarily the place to take them. First, death has to be confirmed and a paramedic who may be familiar with the patient will call the GP. Take Nell Colley, for example. She was known to me and others in the practice as she was often here. The paramedics also knew her as she'd been admitted to hospital with regular arrhythmia attacks. So, we have a sick patient known to two medical services.'

'But only a doctor can confirm that death has taken place.'

'Exactly. Hospital is one option but the other is to call the

GP practice as one of us is probably making our rounds.'

'Can you give us the sequence of events leading to you seeing Nell Colley?'

'From what I remember, I was out doing my rounds when I received a call from the surgery to say that the paramedics had discovered her unresponsive and that death had occurred sometime earlier in the day.'

'You'd seen her that week in the surgery, I believe?'

'And the week before that, I think. Look.' He rotated the computer towards them so that they could see the patient's records. Jake Parsons ran down the list of visits. Around ten visits to the practice over a three month period.

'She was in virtually every week,' commented Connie.

'Well, she had become sick over the spring and was anxious about it. Miss Colley had a heart arrhythmia, which is a common cause of sudden cardiac death. She'd been well until fairly recently and then deteriorated.'

'She was being medicated for it, though, wasn't she?' asked Connie.

'For that and for high blood pressure and cholesterol.'

'You were happy to sign off the certificate?'

'Certainly. I'd seen her that week. She had an erratic pulse and I upped her medication but she was clearly sick.'

'That's enough to issue a certificate?' asked Connie.

'Yes, although if she'd come to the practice and seen any of us, I could have still signed off the death certificate. You just need to prove you've seen a doctor in the surgery in the previous two weeks and we, of course, have her records.'

'She was feeling poorly?' Dahl squinted at the screen to look for the correct entry.

'She was suffering from thumping in her chest, which was making her feel breathless. I increased the dose of her beta blocker slightly.' He looked at them both, concerned. 'There's not a problem, is there?'

'You didn't notice anything else?' asked Connie.

The GP shook his head. 'Like what?'

'Did she mention a book she was writing?' asked Dahl. Connie frowned but kept her eyes on her notepad.

'She didn't say anything about a book.'

'Let's come on to Ingrid Neale.'

'That's slightly longer ago but I do remember the big old house in Cold Eaton.' Jake Parsons turned the computer screen back towards him and found the records of Ingrid Neale.

'Miss Neale I hadn't seen before, but she was an asthmatic who had been hospitalised twice in the last month with breathing difficulties. She had been given doses of steroids on both occasions.'

'But you referred her for a post mortem,' said Dahl.

'I rang my colleague here, Dr Fowley, for advice on both patients. He's a partner and very experienced. He confirmed that there was no need for a PM in the case of Nell Colley but, in the case of Ingrid Neale—'

'Yes?' asked Connie. Alert.

'I remember him making a comment about the location. Cold Eaton. He said it was a miserable place and not where anyone with chronic asthma should be living. Also, as we hadn't seen Ingrid Neale recently, she'd need to be taken to hospital, which I informed the paramedics was the case and then left.'

'Your procedures seem to be fairly robust.'

'There are guidelines after Harold Shipman, and quite right too.' Jake Parsons typed on his keyboard. 'I'm trying to see how many sudden deaths I've attended in the last four months so you can see what normal looks like.'

He ran his finger down the screen. 'One, two . . . five.' He looked up at them. 'Not that many but, as I said, it does happen. Why are you interested in those two in particular?'

'They appear to have known each other. Nell Colley didn't mention the other woman to you?'

'Do you know what, she didn't but she did mention asthma to me. I dismissed it because Miss Colley verged on the hypochondriac and she didn't have asthma. But I'm sure she mentioned something.'

'Can you remember what?' asked Dahl.

'I think she asked if it was common to die of it. I don't really remember. No crime has been committed, has it?'

Connie looked at Dahl. 'I don't think so. We just needed to check up on the two deaths.'

Jake Parsons looked relieved. 'You know what? I think I'll bring this up at the team meeting tomorrow. One of my colleagues can attend the next sudden death.'

Dahl stood up. 'Goes with the job, I suppose. We have that much in common.'

As they left the room, Connie searched in her handbag for a vape. 'That's that then.'

'I suppose.' Dahl looked deep in thought. He smiled across at her. 'Time to move on, I think.'

22

'They still won't let me see her.'

Mina sighed and looked at her watch. After a fractured night, the work of the morning had dragged on interminably. She was desperate to see her mother and talk to her about the Cutting. If Hilary was in a lucid state, now was the time to catch her. Mina's dreams had been infused with dark tunnels and bottomless voids. She had been so spooked that she had forgone her early paddle so that the morning's work had felt painstaking and arduous. She needed to stretch her muscles and clear her head. Instead, she had to confront the decline of her mother after she'd got rid of this girl who was once more pestering her.

'I really would like to see her.' The pleading tone struck a false note. There was an otherness to the girl that would make her a magnet for bullies. Perhaps this was why she was spending so much time in the hospital away from her contemporaries.

'My mother's not up to seeing anyone. Didn't I make myself clear?' Catherine shrank from the harsh tone and Mina immediately felt ashamed. 'Is there anything you want me to say to her?'

The girl opened her mouth to speak but was halted by a sharp 'Catherine' behind her. They both turned and a woman with a clipboard was staring at them.

'What are you doing here, Catherine? It's not your shift today.'

'I wanted to swap.'

'You know that's not allowed.'

Mina used the opportunity to slip away and left them arguing. The lift deposited her outside the oncology unit and, as she pressed the buzzer to be admitted, she saw through the glass a huddle of nurses, not around the station but at the entrance of her mother's room. As the doors opened, she rushed towards them and one nurse broke away. Diane who had nursed Hilary on and off for nearly a year. She came towards Mina.

'Oh I'm so sorry, Mina. We were just about to call you.'

Mina brushed past her and dashed towards her mother's room. The group parted at her approach and she saw her mother in the bed, her face for the first time in months relaxed and serene. She looked from Hilary to the group in shock.

'She's gone?'

Diane nodded.

'But she felt better.'

'We hadn't been able to stabilise her in the last few days. She likely succumbed to an infection. Her temperature was unsteady this morning too. Here's Mr McQuaid now.' The nurse stepped aside as a tall man with a stooped posture entered. He only glanced at her mother but picked up the notes at the bottom of the bed. Mina recognised him as the surgeon who had performed the most recent surgery on Hilary.

The group at the door dispersed at his arrival leaving Mina alone with the consultant. He looked tired. 'It wasn't unexpected although I was hoping to get her into a hospice before this happened. It's a balancing act. The local one won't take any patient until they're in their final stages. It's an art not a science.'

'I don't have any complaints about her treatment here.'

Mr McQuaid gently replaced the notes into the holder. 'I really am sorry.'

'Will there be a post mortem?'

'Your mother had a CT scan this week and, given the metastasis of her cancer and the growth in particular of the tumour on her parietal lobe, we knew her life expectancy was weeks, even days. I don't think a PM is necessary but I'll talk to colleagues first.'

Mina nodded. 'Did she say anything? Before she died, I mean.'

He frowned. 'As I understand, your mother was found dead when the nurse came to administer medication. I can find out when someone last spoke to her if you wish.' He checked the chart again. 'Her temperature was taken this morning before breakfast and was high. I can ask one of the nurses who were on duty to have a chat with you.'

Mina sat down on the chair next to her mother's bed. 'But she was lucid yesterday. I don't understand.'

'Let me see if I can find a nurse for you.'

He left her for a moment and Mina found she couldn't look at her mother's shape in the bed. Instead she looked out of the picture window and watched a woman pushing a young boy in a wheelchair. She turned away from the little boy's gaunt face. At least her mother had lived a full life on her own terms. So why had she a sense of something not completed?

Diane bustled into the room. 'I'm so sorry, Mina.'

'I can't believe it.'

'I saw her before breakfast and she said she was feeling all right but still very weak. And we couldn't get the temperature down. She was sweating so I changed the sheets for her.'

'Was it you who found her?'

Diane shook her head. 'About an hour after, two nurses came to give her medication and she'd already passed away. I called the doctor to confirm she'd gone. It does happen like that. I'm so sorry.'

Mina dug in her rucksack for a tissue and blew her nose. 'She didn't say anything this morning?'

'Very little. I opened the curtains and it was still dark and changed her sheets as she'd soaked them. Later, when the nurses came in to give her medication, they realised she'd passed away.'

'Without warning.' Mina caught sight of the nurse's face. 'Sorry, I didn't mean it in any way. It doesn't matter.'

*

After Mina had left, Diane did the job that her colleagues hated but which always gave her a sense of conclusion with patients she'd nursed for a long time. She began the meticulous process of laying out. She washed Hilary's frail body, pulling gently on the limbs where rigor had begun to set in. When she had finished, she pulled the sheet up over to Hilary's neck and picked up a hairbrush. With light strokes, she arranged Hilary's curls. As she stepped away towards the corner of the room where the drip had been moved to, she slipped slightly and had to hold on to the bed head to steady herself. She squinted at the floor and stooped down and brushed her fingers over the vinyl.

She went out to the ward and checked to see who was the supervisor on duty. Barbara. She breathed a sigh of relief. Barbara would know what to do.

A few minutes later, Barbara was also looking down at the floor. She unfastened the saline bag still draped from the hook and inspected it for a moment. 'Leave this with me.'

23

'Shit.'

Connie looked up in surprise as Matthews opened the door of Sadler's office.

'What's the matter?'

'We've had a call from St Bertram's. Notification of a suspicious death on one of their wards. They've informed the coroner and want us to have a look at the body in situ before it's moved. Can you attend? Dahl, you go with her.'

Connie got her things together, checking her vape was in her handbag. 'Any other information?'

'You need to go to the oncology department. The death was only this morning. I don't have any more details. Can you call me when you're done?'

'We can take my car, if you like. I know a good place to park.' Dahl waved his car keys at her.

The road to St Bertram's was clear and Dahl sped through the town keeping an eye on the speed limit.

'What do you think it is?' Connie was impatient to get going. 'Suspicious death? You don't think it's anything to do with the two we've been looking at?'

Dahl kept his eyes on the road. 'I think we agreed they weren't suspicious. This one, though, must be more serious. They're calling us in straight away.'

'Suspicious in what way? I don't like the sound of that. Hospitals are bad enough places without having a killer in them.'

Dahl glanced at her. 'I heard you had a spell in St Bertram's last year.'

She didn't return his stare but looked down and fiddled with her vape. 'I couldn't wait to get out of there, to be honest. I felt so helpless and now I'm worried what we're going to face.'

'Could be anything. Suspicious could be in terms of medical treatment given, an action by another patient, an external influence. We're not going to be able to guess until we get there.'

'It's got a good reputation. The problem is I only enter the hospital these days when I'm attending a PM. I don't get to see the alive bit, if you see what I mean.'

Dahl grimaced. 'I don't think "the alive bit" is going to be the term to describe what we're about to see.'

*

Bill Shields nodded at Connie as she entered the room. The pathologist appeared to have got even larger than when she'd seen him last.

'Well, I didn't have to go far for this one, did I?'

Still the gallows humour and Connie could feel the disapproval emanating off Dahl. 'This is DC Dahl. He's just joined us from Glossop.'

'*Glossop.*' Bill's voice was full of meaning. 'Hope you weren't wanting a quiet life around here. Bampton has a habit of throwing up its secrets in a nasty way.'

130

'I'm well aware of what Bampton's like.'

Bill took the hint and turned back to the body. 'We have a seventy-five-year-old cancer patient who was found dead this morning. Cause of death was initially prescribed as a respiratory infection with metastatic cancer of the spleen the secondary cause.'

'How long had she been in hospital?' asked Connie.

'Just over a month, although she's been having treatment in this unit for about a year. Arrangements were being made to transfer her to a nursing home, a rehabilitation unit so that she could return home for a period, but she took a turn for the worse this week.'

'But there's a problem?' asked Dahl.

'Come and see.' They both moved towards the bed. A woman with an emaciated body lay on the bed. Connie, feeling nauseous, took a slight step back but bumped into Dahl who was leaning forward.

'I can't see anything.'

'It's not the body that's the problem. At least, that's not what's brought me here.'

Connie looked around. 'What am I supposed to be seeing?'

Dahl was looking at the floor. 'There's something on the tiles.'

Connie realised that Bill was standing to one side of the bed where a pool of thin liquid seeped towards the corner of the room. She moved closer. 'What is it?'

Bill pointed to the drip. 'It's from the bag. A leaking saline drip.'

'Doesn't that happen often?'

'Anything with liquid in is liable to leak. Take a closer look at the bag, though.'

Dahl gloved up his hand and reached out to touch the drip.

'Puncture marks,' he said.

Bill turned, a look of respect on his face. 'Well done. They're only faint but clearly visible.'

Connie looked forward. Two incisions could be seen in the clear plastic almost invisible to the naked eye, tiny tears puckering the bottom of the bag.

Dahl leant closer. 'It was supposed to be saline?'

'And it might yet be. The hospital, however, is on alert for this type of thing after the incident at Stepping Hill.'

'I remember.' Connie looked at the floor again. 'Insulin was injected into some of the drip bags.'

'It can cause a massive hypoglycaemic episode and when a patient is very ill it's often fatal.'

'Are you going to be able to confirm whether there is a drug and, if so, what it is?' asked Dahl.

'From the body, possibly not. Some drugs pass through the system quickly post mortem. We also have a terminally ill patient probably on a cocktail of drugs. A good way to hide a drugs presence would simply be to increase the dose of something the victim is already taking, such as diamorphine. The most accurate method of identifying the drug may well be from the contents of the drip and what is on the floor.'

Connie looked at the dead woman's hand, still bruised from where the cannula had been. 'You think someone might have given this woman drugs to speed up her death? She was terminally ill.'

Bill looked across at them. 'There's some interesting history from the last few days. According to her records, they were having trouble stabilising her recently. It might not just be this drip we need to look into.'

'Who's her next of kin?'

Bill moved away from the body, peeling off his gloves. 'There's a daughter, apparently. She was particularly concerned that her mother didn't have any visitors.'

'Was she?' Dahl was alert. Again Bill shot him an admiring glance.

'Yes. That's interesting, isn't it? I can do the PM tonight and I'll have more information then but it'll be toxicology that will be crucial.'

Dahl went over to the door where a nurse was hovering. 'Can you give us a moment?'

He shut the door behind the retreating figure. 'What about the possibility of interference from other medical staff?'

Bill looked grim. 'That's a possibility too. It could be something innocent. An accidental puncture of the bag. Mistakes do happen. Or—'

'Something deliberate,' finished Connie.

'Yes. Not a mistake but murder.'

24

Numb, Mina drove back to the *Evening Star*. She tried to call Jo, ignoring any qualms she had about using her mobile in the car, but there was no answer. When the ring tone changed to a voicemail message, she disconnected the call. She shouldn't even be behind the wheel. At traffic lights, she saw people drift past who may have well have been ghosts. At the car park beside the wharf, she stumbled out, desperate to get to the safety of the boat. Neither Charlie nor Anna were to be seen and, grateful for the opportunity for solitude, she climbed down the steps and shut and bolted the cabin door.

Feeling chilled, she lit the wood burner, her fingers fumbling over the matches until the paper caught and glowed. She watched the blaze, drawing comfort from the orange sparks. It was the day she'd been both dreading and expecting. She'd refused to think about it, knowing she'd have to face it one day and would cope. Her mother had offered her no advice. They'd never got to the discussion of 'after'. If time had not been on their side, neither had it been rushing away from them. The suddenness was a shock. Mina, now that the moment had arrived, had no idea what to do.

Staring into the flames, faces from the past flitted through her mind. Her grandfather, who had shown her how to plant seeds and more importantly keep them watered so they grew and flourished. The absent father that her mother had refused to speak of. Her mother as a young woman, expression wary, keeping her secrets. Mina closed her eyes and allowed the grief to wash over her.

'Hello! Is anyone there?'

Mina opened her eyes. It wasn't Anna. Someone else from the houseboat community? She went to the hatch and opened it up. Standing on the bank was her mother's old colleague Carol leaning on her bicycle.

'I got the message from Joseph. I know you want a chat and I thought I'd drop by and see if there was anything else to do for your mum while she's in hospital.'

Mina looked across to her van. A thin figure was lurking under one of the tall trees near the water. 'Mum passed away this morning.'

'Oh no.' Carol whitened and her eyes filled with tears. 'I'm so sorry.'

The figure, as if aware of Mina's scrutiny, turned away and retreated up the path. Mina turned her attention back to Carol, feeling the chill from the canal. 'It wasn't a complete shock but I still can't believe it's happened.'

'What terrible timing. I should have got in touch earlier. Is there anything I can do?'

A cold wind swept over them as Mina shook her head. 'I don't think so.'

'You have my number, don't you?' Mina nodded. 'If there's anything you need, anything at all, give me a call. You shouldn't have to do all this yourself.'

'I'll ring if I'm stuck.'

'You'll let me know the funeral arrangements?'

'Of course, but it'll be small.'

'Lots from the library will want to come, though.'

Mina nodded.

'Joseph said you were asking about school friends. That'll be harder because she never mentioned any of them to me.'

'It doesn't really matter now, does it?'

Carol shook her head. 'Of course not. I'll let the library staff know, if that's okay. It'll save you having to make the calls.'

Mina watched her mother's kind friend hop on to her bicycle while wiping tears from her cheek. Carol had cared. People had cared. Perhaps life isn't about wild gestures of grief, but the smaller pinches of being sorry.

As Mina sat back in front of the fire hugging her knees she pulled out her diary from her rucksack and studied her commitments for the rest of the week. Tomorrow, she was due at North Lees Hall and the following day, at Cold Eaton. Surely she could cancel the latter. That particular journey, with its stuttering start, was at an end. Valerie, whoever she had been, would be consigned to the mists of the past. A memory of her mother's that wasn't even that any longer. She would telephone Emily Fenn and say that she would come the following week and complete the clearing up and that would be it.

She put her diary back in her rucksack and leant back. Valerie. *I don't care who you are*, she thought. *You're not important to me.*

Even as she said it, she was aware of the lie in her words. In the cabin gloom, with the water lapping against the boat and the glow of the fire, Mina could hear the past calling out to her, confirming the fear that she'd confided to Jo. This isn't journey's end, it's the beginning.

PART TWO

The Girls

25

Sunday, 13 October 1957

Thunder rumbled across the Peaks, moving in from the east and hanging over the spine of green hills as it met the cold air that had settled over the limestone landscape. On the escarpment facing her, Valerie could see black clouds rolling down the slopes, the darkening sky moving stealthily towards them. As the pressure dropped, electricity imbued the air around them and settled on top of her head. Her hair, which she routinely battled to keep in place under her hat, was beginning to rise from her scalp. Valerie cast a look around the group to check that they hadn't seen her crouching amongst the trees, before thrusting a hand under the brim and scratching her head.

She was desperate to look at her watch, a birthday present that she was careful to keep dry, but the movement might draw attention to the tree under which she was sheltering. Tea would already be on the table. The fruitcake from the Pudding Shop bought specifically for Sunday afternoon had been carefully sliced and the thin cheese sandwiches, crusts removed just like her mother had seen in *Woman's Own*, would be fanned out on the best china. Four o'clock prompt, when her father came in from the garden, her mother would turn off the television and they would sit down for tea. Why hadn't she stayed with them after church? She was supposed to be doing her homework and the excuse she'd concocted to get away sounded, to her own ears, lame. Her mother hadn't minded, though, and approved of the girls sitting in a broken circle. Liked the fact that most of them came from families a fraction above the social rank that Valerie's own occupied.

In the silence, Valerie finally stole a look at her watch. Ten past three. There was still time to rush back afterwards. Her five friends were sitting cross-legged under the great yew tree, planted, it was said by some villagers, around a thousand years ago. Once, it must have been a small sapling rooted ten or so paces from the front of the church door, placed there, according to Valerie's father, to stop cattle trampling over the graves. The poisonous leaves were an incentive to farmers to keep their precious livestock away from the church, although Valerie feared that the dark tree thrived on the nutrients from the graves. She could see the tentacles of its roots, creeping out beneath where they were sitting and stretching towards those ancient corpses crumbled into the soil.

Thunder grumbled again, louder this time. Valerie looked up anxiously at the canopy of the different yew tree under which she was sheltering. Ancient was good, wasn't it? The tree must have withstood thousands of similar tempests and its dense leaves would shelter them until the storm passed. Or perhaps you weren't supposed to stand too near trees during thunderstorms.

'We haven't got long.' In her anxiety, Valerie missed who had spoken but she saw the group shift uneasily at the acknowledgement of time. There were other families waiting, tables laden with jam and cake. The girls made a broken circle under the tree and no attempt had been made to close the gap. They had taken their places as usual, following the same pattern as if an invisible hand was guiding them, as if it had been natural to leave the empty place for the girl who wasn't there. The space gave Valerie hope. There would be forgiveness and a reconciliation and the gap would be closed.

Ingrid picked up one of the thin branches that had fallen from the tree and broke it in half with a snap. She showed the inside of the limb to the other girls and each peered forward looking at the pattern inside the branch, as distinctive as a piece of rock. They had seen it before but it was part of the ritual and still an object of wonder.

'At the centre the heartwood is red, which symbolises our blood sisterhood that we would gladly give our lives to protect.'

Valerie shifted nervously at the girl's ominous tone in the failing light. She'd heard from the vicar one Sunday morning that the red symbolised the blood of Christ. Just like her friend to change it to suit her purposes. The other girls were looking, their eyes round in wonder, enthralled. Ingrid waved the stick around the circle.

'The sapwood encircling the heartwood is white, which represents our purity. Our devotion to the earth and to each other.'

Valerie put her head down. Had she broken the vow of purity? She lifted her head and looked around in fear but no one was paying any attention to her, their disapproval directed at an absence.

'The yew tree was planted in churchyards to ward off evil spirits. It's your help we're invoking.'

Valerie lifted her head as the girl raised the broken shards of the tree. This was a deviation from the normal script. What was she playing at? The gap in the girls, her place, yawned wider and Valerie could feel her head begin to swim. In the distance, she could hear the hiss of an approaching train. If she looked behind her, she'd be able to see the steam belching out over the hill, just visible from this secluded valley.

The girl too had heard the train and she turned slightly, looking over her shoulder. She stayed in the position, not moving, staring at the engine disappearing down the valley. When she faced the group again, she had a smile on her face.

'The tree has spoken. The purity is broken. The punishment has been chosen.'

26

Wednesday, 1 November 2017

The problem with having a brother for a policeman is that you expect him to be on call even when he's on holiday. Camilla tried Sadler's mobile again. She resented the fact she couldn't get hold of him even though she cautioned herself that she was being unreasonable. He'd been warned by HR about the amount of leave he had outstanding and, with the end of the year approaching, it was a case of take it or lose it. It was typical, however, that the very time he was away and out of touch, she needed to get hold of him.

Their mother Ginnie was now in St Bertram's, the best place she could be. A sudden onset of chest pains had revealed fluid around the site of her pacemaker that needed draining. The hospital had admitted her as a precautionary measure and, at her mother's insistence, Camilla hadn't called Sadler. 'He deserves his rest' had been her mother's only comment and, given that the hospital weren't particularly worried, she'd happily gone along with Ginnie's request. Only today, Ginnie would be having the op to drain the fluid and, all being well, she would be coming home tomorrow. Ginnie was still insisting that they leave Sadler in peace but, for once, Camilla was going to overrule her mother. Being under observation in hospital was one thing, an operation another.

Camilla tried Sadler's mobile again. Still switched off. Where had he said he was going? Wales sounded familiar. Cross with the responsibility of coping with their mother on her own, she turned on her sons fighting in the back of the car.

'What's the matter with you? I need to stop at Nana's and check everything's okay. Can't you stop bickering for five minutes?'

She swung the car into the drive, noticing the bins of other houses on the street pulled out onto the pavement. *Damn.*

'Stay here and don't argue,' she cautioned her young sons. 'I'll be two minutes.' She pulled the black wheelie bin onto the pavement and let herself into the fifties semi, frowning at the chill of the interior. Her mother, amply funded by her husband's pension, had enough to live on but insisted on keeping the house at a low chill. Camilla couldn't remember it ever being this cold, however, so she opened the door of the downstairs cloakroom and checked the boiler. The pilot light was visible and the heating was set to come on again in half an hour. How had the house become so cold since this morning's burst of heat?

Camilla poked her head into the front living room but, apart from the usual messy pile of books and newspapers, it looked fine. The dining room was shut up but when Camilla opened it and went inside, the air was warm and dry. She moved to the back of the house and through to the kitchen where a stale smell hung in the air. Checking the fridge, she threw out a few wrinkled vegetables and bagged them up to drop them into the bin outside.

Samuel came through the door hugging himself. 'It's

freezing in here.'

Camilla rounded on him. 'I thought I told you to stay in the car with Ben. Where is he?'

'Still in the car.'

'For God's sake.' Camilla went back into the drive and pulled a teary Ben from the back seat.

'What's happened now?'

'He won't let me play Minecraft. He says it's his turn on the tablet.'

Camilla looked at her defiant son standing on the doorstep trying to look nonchalant. 'Where's your iPad?'

'I left it at home.'

'That's not Ben's problem, is it?' Camilla thought of the still undetected source of the chill. 'Right, both of you get inside the house. I'll put the TV on.'

'But Nana's not got Sky.'

'Then you'll have to find something else to watch, won't you?'

She left her two sons tussling over the remote control and shut the door on them. She went back to the boiler and over-rode the settings, turning on the heating. Back in the kitchen, she poured bleach down the sink and sprayed liberal arcs of air freshener around the room.

She should get her mother a cleaner. When she'd raised the idea, a year or so ago, Ginnie had been adamant that it wasn't necessary and, given her mother's house was considerably tidier than her own, Camilla hadn't forced the issue. The room still kept its chill. She could hear from the roar that the boiler was functioning and, opening the lounge door, she inhaled the welcome scent of her children and warming air. She went back to the still cold kitchen and checked the radiator. The metal was warm but it was failing to heat the room and, as she stood still for a moment, she felt a draught against her neck.

She opened the pantry door and saw that the little window at the back was open. Standing on tiptoe, she tried to pull it shut but it wouldn't give. She peered at the hinge and pulled fruitlessly at the metal.

'Samuel. Can you come here?' she shouted to make herself heard over the sound of the TV set.

A set of trainers squelched along the kitchen lino. 'You all right, Mum?'

'I can't shut this window. If I lift you up, can you have a go?'

A gleam of pride came into Samuel's eyes. 'I'll climb up the shelves.'

'Well, all right, but be careful.' Camilla kept a steadying hand on her son's backside as he made his way up towards the window. He tugged at the window and closed it a fraction.

'Keep going.'

'I can't. It won't shut properly. The metal is all warped.'

'What do you mean warped?'

Samuel hoisted himself up further, one foot against the wall. 'It's bent out of shape. It looks like someone has tried to get in.'

'Are you sure?'

'It's all twisted. You'll be able to see properly from outside. Nana sometimes keeps it open when she's in the house because she says the larder gets smelly with damp but she always shuts it when she goes out.'

'She leaves it open when she's here?'

Ben had appeared at her side. 'It's true. We've hidden in here loads of times and the window's sometimes like that.'

'But when Nana goes out she shuts it,' said Samuel. 'She's taller than you. She pulls it no problem.'

God, my children know more about my mother's habits than I do, thought Camilla. *How long has the window been like that?*

'Is there a burglar in the house?' asked Ben.

Camilla looked down at the anxious face of her younger son. 'Of course not. Look how small the window is. Go back and watch the TV and I'll phone your dad.'

'What about Uncle Francis? He's the policeman. You should call him,' said Ben.

Camilla looked up at the bent window and the narrow gap that could only fit a small child, or perhaps a very thin adult. 'Uncle Francis is definitely the person I need to speak to.'

27

Connie got through the post mortem by breathing in through her mouth and exhaling through her nose, a trick shown to her by an old timer years ago, and by shutting her eyes during the worst bits. Dahl had made a quick call muttering down the handset something about being late home that afternoon. The person on the other end didn't appear to be bothered and the call ended abruptly. They'd made the trip to the warren of Portakabins at the back of the hospital, aware that the bustle of the building would, in all likelihood, soon be augmented by a team of detectives with their professional manner and intrusive questions.

Connie watched in silence as Bill began his ministrations, inspecting every inch of the corpse for puncture marks.

'There's multiple bruising from various sites on her arms where it looks like she's had blood taken. However, I don't see any puncture marks, on the thighs or buttocks for example, to indicate any rogue injections. It wouldn't be the first time I've seen these on a cancer patient.'

'What do you mean by rogue?' Dahl's face was pale, clearly not enjoying the examination any more than Connie.

'Sometimes well-meaning friends and relatives will try a new type of quackery to add to the already vile mix that patients are receiving. It can be administered via injection. They think they're doing good but, at best, it's useless. Anyway, I don't see any evidence of this here.'

'What do people give them?' asked Dahl.

'All sorts. Pain relief, vitamins, amino acids. I even heard of one patient being injected with mistletoe.'

'So if there's something wrong, it'll probably have come through the saline bag?'

'It looks like it. I'm going to take muscle and tissue sample from around the site of the cannula. I'll leave a wide margin. If the drug doesn't show up in bloods, it might be present in the skin samples.'

'Any idea what it could be?' asked Connie.

Bill looked at them over his facemask. 'I'm not psychic. Let's see what the tests show.'

After the PM, Dahl rushed off and Scott, Bill's assistant who was usually good for a chat, was nowhere to be seen. Bill looked preoccupied and didn't offer Connie the chance for a tea or a natter, so she took herself off to the canteen in the main hospital building and sat nursing a cup of coffee. She called Matthews to update and closed her eyes at her colleague's panicked tone.

'It's not looking good. Should we start questioning the nurses?'

'Dahl and I took statements from those on the ward when we arrived. There are quite a few others to interview, though, if tests prove suspicious.'

'How long does Bill think they'll take?'

'If there are raised levels of morphine or insulin in the victim's blood, which Bill's asked them to look for, he should know within a day or so. Full toxicology will take around two weeks. It's the saline bag that will be our focus. We should know within twenty-four hours if anything's been added to the contents.'

'Shit.'

'To be honest, Bill's playing it cool at the moment. Saline drip bags do break occasionally. It might just be an accident.'

'It looked like puncture marks, though?' Matthews asked.

'I could see thin cuts. Bill says that's typical of puncture marks.'

'Have you spoken to the next of kin?'

'There's a daughter, Mina Kemp. She's not answering her phone. I'm about to head to her house, although I've stupidly left my car at the station.'

'Where's Dahl?'

'Gone home.'

The silence from Matthews spoke volumes and Connie rushed to cover for her new colleague. 'Plenty of taxis outside. I'll go first to the address we have for Mina Kemp and, if she's not there, the deceased lived on a houseboat so that'll be my next stop.'

Matthews breathed in sharply. 'Simply tell the victim's daughter that the hospital noticed an anomaly with the drip and asked for a PM on her mother. Don't tell her anything else for the moment. Play it cool but find out if she was administering any drugs to Hilary. See if she had any concerns about her mother's treatment too. There's a wide pool of people who had access to the patient.'

'Okay. Do you want me to report to you tomorrow?'

'No. I want you to call me tonight.'

Connie sighed and disconnected the call. She'd worked closely with Matthews on a previous case and they'd got on well.

Yet there was an air of desperation in her tone, verging on panic. What Connie needed was someone sensible to talk through the day's events. She sat in the canteen for a moment and phoned another number. Switched off. Damn.

*

Sadler stood on top of the hill and surveyed the landscape around him. The grasses had lost the verdant green of the summer and were softening into a pale brown hue that would see them through the autumn until the snow came. It would soon be too cold to walk in the hills. Unlike those occasionally rescued by the mountain air ambulance, Sadler had no desire to walk in frost and ice-covered Peaks. He was well aware of what an enforced sick leave of six weeks due to a broken leg would do both to his career and his mental health. This holiday would be the last of his walks until the spring. In the distance he could see the town of Bampton, the passage of the canal the clearest landmark visible from here. He took his mobile out of his pocket and switched it on. It was often on top of the hills that he had the best reception, the satellite connection unimpeded by steep valleys, buildings or clumps of trees. He saw, with a lurch, that he'd missed four calls from Camilla and he fumbled for her number to return the call.

'Is everything all right?'

'No, it's not. I've been trying to call you.'

'What's the matter?'

'Mum's been in hospital.'

'What? Why didn't you let me know?'

'Francis! I've been trying to call you since this morning.

Why didn't you turn the bloody phone on? I've even sent you emails and text messages.'

'I'm out walking. There's no signal so I keep the phone off. Is she all right?'

'She started having chest pains. They thought it might be a result of fluid around her heart. I've been back and forth to the hospital for the last couple of days but she told me not to call you.'

'Things have got worse?'

'Not especially but she's having a procedure to drain the fluid today.'

'How is she?'

'She's actually all right. She's hopefully coming home tomorrow. She called the ambulance herself and then me.'

'I'll come over.'

'You've not gone away then? Look, I'm at Mum's and visiting hours are finished for the night. Maybe come and see her tomorrow when she's back home. The thing is, it wasn't only about Mum that I need to talk to you.'

'Why? What's the matter?'

'I think someone might have tried to break in today while she was in hospital. There's a window in the larder that she sometimes leaves open. What with the ambulance and everything it was probably left ajar. It looks like it's been forced further open. Someone might have seen the ambulance outside the house and taken their chance. You know what people are like.'

'Did anyone get in?'

'I've had a look around. Her jewellery is still on her dressing table as is some money in the kitchen tin. That's hidden but would have been easy to find if someone was looking. I don't think whoever it was actually got in.'

'Is the window big?'

'It's tiny.'

Sadler sighed. 'It's probably kids. They saw the window open and had a go at getting into the house. The little sods can get in through tiny spaces. It might even have been an adult with a small child as an accomplice.'

'John's coming over to board it up. Do you think I should tell her? I'm going to try to get it replaced before she comes home tomorrow. Do you think I should call the police? Apart from you, that is.'

Sadler smiled but kept the tone out of his voice. 'I think you should nip down the station to report it tomorrow. Or call 111. Sometimes you notice things are missing after the event. It won't do any harm. The main thing is to make sure the house is secure. Sure you don't want me to come around?'

'I really think it's all right. Only—'

'Yes?'

'I think Mum's struggling at the moment and I feel guilty for not noticing it before. The house is okay but only superficially so. It needs a really deep clean. And the garden hasn't been touched since the spring. You remember how particular Mum used to be.'

'We need to get her a cleaner and gardener then. It'll only be a few hours a week. I can pay for it.'

'Are you sure?'

'Of course. Do you know anyone?'

'I'll ask my cleaner if she'll go into Mum's. I don't know any gardeners, though.'

'I can look at that.' Sadler thought of the woman with the green van. 'Leave it with me.'

'It's just . . . you're coming over for the fireworks on Saturday, aren't you? We'll go to the ones in Bampton. When you come over, let's have a chat.'

*

On the fourth attempt, Connie got through.

'Camilla?' Sadler sounded breathless and she could hear wind whistling down the line. In contrast to the overheated hospital, the sounds of outdoors made her desperate to get out of the building and into the autumn afternoon.

'No, boss. It's me, Connie.'

'Is everything all right?'

'I know you're on holiday but I thought you'd want to know we've got a suspicious death.' Connie could feel relief flooding through her. It was Sadler she had needed to speak to. This was the voice of reason she wanted to talk through the day's events with.

'A suspicious death in Bampton?'

'I'm at St Bertram's hospital. We've got a woman with unaccounted-for puncture marks in her saline drip on the oncology ward.'

'Are you sure it's oncology?'

'Of course. I've just been there. Why do you ask?'

Sadler sighed down the line. 'My mother's in there a moment. Cardiac care.'

'It's not your mother, Sadler. We're not even sure it's erate at the moment. I'm just off to see the daughter

154

I'll update you when you get back to work on Monday. I called because . . . actually I don't know why I called.'

'I'm glad you did. The holiday is beginning to drag a little, to be honest, and it's good to know what's happening at the station. What does Bill say?'

'He's noncommittal but there are what appear to be puncture marks in the drip. It's not looking good, to be honest, and I needed to chat to someone about it.'

'Matthews is in charge of the case?'

'She is and I think I'm going to be calling her every five minutes.'

'Matthews is a competent detective, Connie. She'll be excellent at ensuring the early part of the investigation is handled correctly. You're off to see the victim's daughter now, you said.'

'Matthews wants me to play down our suspicions until we know more.'

'That makes sense. Can you come and see me tonight? Afterwards, I mean.'

'You haven't gone to Wales?'

'I'm enjoying the comfort of my own home, which is where I'm headed. You did the right thing calling me and I'd like an update tonight.'

'Why? What's the urgency? Because of your mum?'

The silence stretched on for so long, Connie had to check the call hadn't been disconnected. Only the whistling of the wind reassured her that Sadler was still on the line. When he spoke, his tone was brisk and professional.

'I want you to tell me where you got to with the sudden death of Nell Colley.'

28

The *Evening Star* had been Hilary's pride and joy. It was painted a deep bottle green set against a red trim and when Mina first saw the boat it had reminded her of a train carriage, although her mother had looked annoyed and told her not to be so stupid. The move onto water had been both a blessing and a curse. A narrowboat isn't the safest place to be when you're unsteady on your feet but, at the same time, the small community had kept an eye out for Hilary, cooking her meals when she was too nauseous to feed herself and popping in to check on her welfare.

With the move to the boat, her mother had also divested herself of the friends that she'd made over the years. There had been people in and out of the house from university and from work all through Mina's childhood but Hilary had stopped seeing them. With the exception of Mina, she had shed people from her life. Mina had never stopped to think about her mother's lack of contact with school friends. It would have been natural for Hilary to have kept in touch with at least one or two of them given that, apart from a three year stint at Leeds University, Hilary had always lived in Bampton. Yet none of her mother's friends were from either her childhood or teenage years.

Mina's mind was full of her mother's fears and, in Hilary's

home, the sense of dread invoked uneasy images. She couldn't get Hilary's last words to her out of her mind. What could her mother have been involved in?

Mina went onto the deck, desperate for some of the cold evening air to relieve the pressure of her aching head.

'How's your mum?' Charlie, Anna's partner, was watering the plants on the roof of their boat, his face buried in the mass of leaves as he struggled to reach the earth. He looked up and caught sight of Mina's face.

'Oh no.'

Mina glanced at the clouds gathering overhead. They hung ominously over the lock, heavy with moisture.

'I need to get away for a bit. Would you keep an eye on the boat? I'm going to pack a few things and stay elsewhere.'

'Of course.' Charlie looked concerned. 'Anna is out. Will you wait until she gets back? She'll want to see you're okay.'

'I'll be around for a short while.'

Mina descended back inside. The interior was less majestic than the outside but imbued with a homely charm. She looked around the room and, in her exhaustion, made a decision. Even though she'd warned herself of the dangers of making a promise that she couldn't keep, she'd nevertheless told Hilary that she would find Valerie. It must have been one of the last words Hilary had heard from Mina and she would keep her promise, wherever it led her. She would find Valerie and check that she was okay.

Mina lifted up the seat of one of the sofas and rooted around amongst the bits and pieces Hilary kept there. Her mother's sparse lifestyle meant that there were few personal items, just a file with the essential certificates and paperwork. Mina flicked through the documents, stopping briefly to read her own birth certificate, and then put them back in the seat. Mina moved on to the bookcase and there, shoved into one corner, was a photo album. Not the one stuffed full of pictures of Mina as a baby but the blue leather book from Hilary's own childhood.

It was a relic of time past. Black and white photos gummed with corner stickers onto thick grey paper. Most of the pages were missing a photo or two, lost over the course of time. Mina carefully turned the pages. They were roughly chronological, starting when Hilary had been given a brownie camera for her twelfth birthday. It was one of the few stories about her childhood that she'd shared with Mina. How she'd asked for a new satchel because the strap of her old one had worn away to a sliver. Her father had played a joke on her and given her first the strap. A replacement one, she'd thought. Well, fair enough. They hadn't much money and a new strap was better than nothing at all. Then had come the second part of the present. Not a satchel as Hilary had requested but something much nicer wrapped in a brown leather box. A camera, black and square. She had celebrated by taking a picture of her two tabby cats, their heads together, eyes wide for the camera.

Here was the photo. One animal leaning slightly towards the other who had its eyes closed in contentment. Two cats, long dead, and yet the affection of the photographer for her subjects leaped decades. Mina turned the pages. There were her grandparents looking improbably young, Grumps wearing braces over a flannel shirt. Another was of her grandmother standing in the middle of a vegetable patch next to a row of runner beans. She was beaming broadly into the camera, but wasn't it Grumps who had been the gardener? It must be him behind the camera. She stopped at a page that held a single photo of a group of girls.

There were five of them, standing together in front of a building made of Derbyshire stone. A barn possibly or the side of a house. Although the picture was black and white, a combination of the light behind the girls and their clothes suggested that it was a summer snap. Mina squinted at the image, searching for her mother, but none of the girls bore any relation to how Hilary would have looked as a teenager. Hilary must have taken the photo of her friends with her camera and put it into the album.

Mina took the photo over to a lamp to examine the five girls more closely. They all looked around the same age, probably fourteen or fifteen, and were dressed for a game of tennis. One of the girls, second from right, was wearing a high-necked cardigan, buttoned at the top and open at the sides. She was carrying a picnic basket and a magazine under her arms. Less sporty than the others perhaps, she looked dressed to watch a game from the sidelines. The other girls had an air of hauteur and advantage. Two of them were looking away from the camera, the stiffness of their postures suggesting that deliberate attitude of nonchalance. The girl resting against the wall was facing the camera but looking behind the photographer. Only the girl on the far left was looking sullenly into the lens.

Mina turned over the photo and saw in faint pencil marks the word 'GIVEN'. Mina stared at the writing. GIVEN? It had a vaguely biblical feel to it. What had these girls been given? Youth, definitely, and possibly privilege. She turned over the photo again and looked at the girl standing in the middle of the group. The shorts she was wearing were wide and high, a

159

daring piece of clothing for nineteen fifties Bampton.

Mina slid the photo between the pages of her diary. She flicked through the rest of the album but found no more featuring teenage girls. She did, however, find a picture of her mother sitting at a desk, a standard school photo of the time. Hilary's girlish curls hung down from a side parting but her mouth bore traces of lipstick. Possibly the pale frosted variety her mother wore in the mid-seventies, an old-fashioned colour that she had refused to update. Hilary's eyes were large and unknowing. If not beautiful, she had a freshness of innocence.

Mina removed this photo from its hinges and checked to see if anything was written on the back. Nothing. She slid it into her diary to join the first and put the book into her rucksack. The rest of the album consisted of family photos and holiday snaps. Mina checked to see if she could recognise any locations. One looked like it had been taken on Bampton High Street, as the form of the buildings was familiar. There was nothing recognisable as Cold Eaton.

Only as she turned the page did Mina spot a picture of her mother that made her go cold. Hilary was about nineteen, posing in front of a dark stone building. Her mother had written 'Leeds 1961' onto the page beneath the photo. It was a picture of Hilary at university staring unsmiling into the camera, her hand clasping the side of her flared skirt.

There were a few years between the first image and the second but the innocence had gone to be replaced by a dark knowledge in her young eyes. Mina shut the album and leant back against the sofa, thinking. What had happened in the intervening years?

29

Camilla watched as John hit the final nail into the wooden board he'd fixed across the window. The larder was plunged into gloom, illuminated only by a faint light from a bare bulb speckled with flies, and the smell of cinnamon and pickling vinegar pervaded the space. John was a reassuring presence. Tall like her brother but more solid. Unlike Sadler, he was also good at practical tasks.

'Will it be secure?'

Her husband slotted his fingers over the top of the panel and pulled. It buckled and then held. 'It'll do for the minute. What did the window guy say?'

'I gave him the measurements over the phone and he thinks he's got something in stock that will fit. He's coming out tomorrow morning to try it.'

John was carefully placing the tools back into his case. 'It'll be all right until then. They won't get through that panel without making an almighty row. Just tell the neighbours to keep an eye on things. Do they know Ginnie's in hospital?'

'I don't think so, otherwise they'd have put out the bin for her. Suppose whoever tried to break in comes back, though? Mum's due to be discharged tomorrow. What if we come back and find they've managed to get back in?'

John shut the case and looked at her. 'Are you all right? You're not normally like this. Remember when we were burgled? You called the police and started peeling potatoes for the tea.'

'It's not my house, though, is it, and, oh I don't know, maybe I got more of a shock than I realised when she was admitted. I'm suddenly aware of how vulnerable she is.'

John put an arm around her shoulder and pulled her towards him. 'Look, if you're worried, why don't you stay here? Leave the porch light on. You don't go to bed until late so they'll know someone is here. Tomorrow the window will be fixed, and make sure it's one with a lock on.'

'Really? Are you okay with that? Putting the kids to bed and so on.'

His face took on an expression of mock hurt. 'Thanks a lot. I have done it before, you know.'

'Had Ben started school then?'

'All right, all right. It's been a few years. Seriously, it'll be fine.' He raised his voice. 'Hey guys, fancy a pizza and a boys' night in with your dad?'

Ben came charging through the kitchen door. 'Oh yeah, with dough balls.'

Samuel followed him, looking concerned. 'What about Mum?'

'I need to stay here and get a few things together before your nan gets home.'

'I can stay with you.'

Touched, Camilla shook her head. 'Don't worry – I'll be fine. It's nothing to do with the window. There are a few things I want to get sorted before Nana leaves hospital. I'll be back tomorrow afternoon to pick you up from school. Your dad will take you in the morning.'

'We can have dough balls,' said Ben jumping up towards his brother.

Samuel looked unconvinced. 'Are you sure you'll be all right, Mum?'

Camilla waved her mobile at him. 'I'll call you before you go to bed, okay? Let you know that I'm fine.'

'But in the night?'

'There's nothing to worry about, I promise.'

As they were leaving, John kissed her. 'Don't worry. That window is small. I think they tried and then realised the futility of it. If you hear anything that bothers you, though, turn on all the lights and call me.'

After her family had gone, Camilla, for something to do, took out a bottle of bleach and wiped down every surface in the kitchen and then mopped the floor. When she'd finished, she peeled off her gloves and jumped in the shower, trying to wash herself under the meagre water that spurted from the calcified head. *We've neglected Mum*, she realised. *She's so bloody independent, we've let her get on with things. Both of us. Me because of the kids and Francis because of his job. Mum's got old and we've not realised.*

She towelled herself dry and made a note to get some descaler the following day to sort out her mother's bathroom. She pulled out one of Ginnie's nighties from a drawer. Made of lemon cotton embellished with broderie anglaise, it wasn't as hideous as she had anticipated but it depressed Camilla looking in the mirror. She had her mother's flat chest and large feet and it was a premonition of what she'd look like when she was seventy-five. She glanced at the clock. Just gone seven, hours to fill before bed, but the nightdress would do while she washed her clothes so they were clean for the following day.

She bundled up the dirty laundry. Hardly enough for a wash so she opened Ginnie's wicker basket and pulled out the contents. There wasn't much. Underwear, a pair of stretchy trousers and a dark green polo neck jumper. Camilla added them to the pile, noticing that the jumper had a darker patch down one side. She picked it up and studied the stain, which had made the fabric stiffen. She went into the bathroom and put the fabric under the tap. The water ran a red hue that gradually turned pink. Camilla stared at it, trying to make sense. Had her mother fallen and hurt herself when her pacemaker began to leak? She'd not mentioned an accident or blood to Camilla. Still frowning, Camilla put everything into the machine and switched it on. Waiting for the cycle to run its course, she wandered around the house, the nightdress billowing around her. She found a cardigan of her mother's and put it over her while she watered the plants and pulled off the brown leaves.

She left Ginnie's room until last. The bed was made, with a Welsh blanket completely covering the duvet and pillows underneath. Camilla slipped a hot water bottle underneath the covers to air the sheets before her mother's return. She sat on the bed and glanced around the large room. Her mother had moved to the semi after their father's death so the house held no memories for her children. The furniture she'd decided to keep had been cherished pieces. The tall wardrobe must have been unfashionable when it had been bought in the late sixties. History is often damning to the decade that immediately precedes it but the fifties had produced solid teak furniture that had smelt divine when she had hidden inside it during games with Francis as a child.

Camilla went over to the wardrobe and opened it, marvelling at the small space that had seemed so cavernous to her when she was young. Her mother had always been untidy and the clothes hung in a muddle of hangers. She shut the doors and went back to the bed. As she sat down, she felt a crunch underneath the bedclothes. Camilla pulled back the covers, and revealed a pale blue envelope. The front was blank. If it had been addressed to her mother, she might have baulked at opening the envelope, but, curious, she lifted up the flap and pulled out the contents.

It was a blue sheet of paper. An invitation to a tea dance at 3 p.m. on Friday, 8 June. Pale blue paper with faded old-fashioned type. Doors open at 2.45 p.m. Prize for the best boy and girl dancer. Camilla turned it over. Nothing on the back, no address. She squinted at it. Odd, why no address? Perhaps it was a regular location, so no need to put that information on the flyer. Her mother must have been going through her things. It dated back from at least the sixties, possibly before. Tea dances? It didn't sound much like Ginnie. Political activism and the Women's Institute but tea dances? Camilla put the paper back into the envelope.

She thought about leaving it on the bedside table but her instinct was to return the envelope to its hiding place. Her mother had made up the bed and then slipped the note under the bedclothes intending to return to it after her trip to the hospital. Making a decision, Camilla slipped the envelope back where she had found it and went to the spare bedroom to make up the bed.

30

'Is this some kind of joke?'

The detective appeared at the side of the boat as Mina was heaving her mother's old carpetbag onto the wharf. It contained all the clean clothes she possessed along with the two photos she'd found and tucked into her diary. As the woman asked Mina questions about her mother's death, she felt herself pale and then tremble with misery. She was seized with an overwhelming urge to throw DC Connie Childs into the dank canal. They were about the same height but Mina was easily three stones heavier than the detective. Connie had a haunted look, dark shadows ringing each eye, although she also had a raw air of authority that refused to quake in the face of Mina's anger.

'There isn't anything to worry about at this stage. It's routine when we have a few outstanding questions.'

'Questions? What do you mean by that?'

'We need to check a few things in the context of your mother's death. You went to see her yesterday?'

'At around six o'clock.'

'And she was asleep?'

'Yes, but her breathing was regular, which was good news. I waited a few minutes in case she woke up and then left. She was fast asleep and peaceful.'

'She wasn't always calm?'

Mina picked up her bag, and moved towards her van. 'Not always. If she'd been agitated, I'd have waited because when she started to shout in her sleep she woke herself up. There was no sign of that at all.'

'You work as a gardener? That can't be easy. Fitting in the jobs around hospital visits.'

Mina frowned. 'Most of my clients knew Mum was ill and the arrangements were that I'd turn up on the given day but the time was flexible. It was hard in the summer as I had so much work but it'd been easier recently.'

'That's tough. There's only you, no other family?'

'Just me. I have friends who are supportive, though.'

The detective smiled slightly. 'Did your mother ever talk about alternative medication? Perhaps adding to the conventional treatment she was getting.'

Mina stared at Connie. 'Mum? She put her trust completely in the doctors. She wasn't into complementary medicine. She called it snake oil.'

'So she wouldn't have asked you or someone else to augment her treatment?'

'Me? What are you suggesting?'

'I'm just asking you a question.'

'Why? Detectives don't normally visit grieving relatives. What's the matter?'

Connie took a deep breath. 'We've noticed a slight anomaly with the drip by your mother's bed and we're checking it out. It's probably nothing to worry about but we need to check. Did you notice it at all during your last visit?'

'The drip? I was always careful when sitting near her in

case I accidentally knocked it. I wouldn't have gone near the thing.'

The detective let out a long sigh. 'I'm sorry, I know these questions must be painful for you. One more thing, was your mother worried or agitated about anything in particular before she died?'

Mina hesitated. 'In terms of her illness she knew her time was limited and she was as fatalistic as you can be about these things. She had, however, become ill in the last few days. She'd started to be very anxious and thought someone was in her room. They were hallucinations but frightening for her.'

'Is this normal? With the treatment she'd been given?'

'I don't know. What's normal? The hospital was concerned and so was I. We didn't know what was causing it.'

Connie's dark eyes were on her and Mina felt the urge to spill out the story of Valerie. *My mother was obsessed with a girl from the past who she thought she'd killed.* That would give the detective something to think about, but surely she owed it to Hilary to keep the confession secret for the moment. *I can't,* she thought, *I can't share this just yet. First, I want the chance to figure out what happened myself.*

'Your mother didn't express concern about anyone in particular?'

Mina shook her head. 'No. Mum didn't mention anyone at all.'

31

Sadler spent the late afternoon walking up Chelmorton Low, keen to see the round barrows that stood on the brow of the hill. They'd been desecrated by wall builders and Iron Age enthusiasts, infamous for tampering with many of the ancient graves standing in the Peaks. Early archaeology, some called it, but Sadler would have preferred the bones of his ancient ancestors to have remained in situ. Sadler's cottage was freezing when he returned to it. He'd switched off the heating, his mother's parsimony continuing down the generations, and the house was icy cold. He flicked a switch and the living room gradually began to warm. His stomach rumbled and he opened a packet of digestive biscuits to stop the noise. After Connie had gone he'd cook himself a meal with something from the freezer. A steak, perhaps.

He wondered how Matthews would take his early return to work. He'd called Llewellyn from the car and let him know he'd heard about the death. Had he imagined the note of relief in his boss's voice? Wait and see, they'd agreed, but from Llewellyn's tone, it didn't sound like it would be Matthews heading up an investigation.

An arc of light swept across his window and he saw Connie's car pulling into the space next to his. He opened the front door and went into the kitchen to put on the kettle. He heard her footsteps approach and the sound of her shutting the door behind her.

'I am glad to see you.'

Sadler smiled into the mugs he was filling with steaming water. 'Matthews is very competent. It doesn't sound like you had much on.'

'Well, we might do now, although, I dunno. It seems a bit of smoke and mirrors, if that makes sense.'

'What's the deceased's name?'

'Hilary Kemp.'

'Kemp?'

'Yes, why?' Connie took her vape out of her handbag, sucked on it and then exhaled with a groan of satisfaction.

'What's the daughter called?'

'Mina. Why? Do you know her?'

'I met her last week while she was working. I was going to offer her some work on Mum's garden.'

'Well, that's not going to make any difference, is it? To be honest, I don't think she's even a suspect.'

'I think not, Connie. Better for you to have told me now before I employed her. Anyway, that aside, you think foul play is likely?'

Connie blew at her tea. 'It's possible, isn't it? It wouldn't be the first time it had happened in a hospital.'

'You've questioned staff?'

'As far as we can when we don't really know what we're dealing with. Dahl, the new DS, and I took statements from the hospital employees who were there, but there was an early morning shift that we need to speak to.'

'Probably worth waiting until the results of the PM.

What did Mina say?'

'She says she didn't notice anything and that her mother definitely wouldn't have asked for any drugs on top of what she was given. She trusted her doctors with her treatment.'

'So at this stage she's a witness rather than a suspect. That's helpful. It wouldn't be the first time a family member has given death a helping hand.' Sadler put his cup down, feeling the need for something stronger. 'Do you want a glass of wine instead?'

'Yes, but I'm also hungry. I can't dunk my digestives in red wine, can I? Anyway, I'm driving.'

'I can cook something and walk you back afterwards. Come and talk to me while I'm cooking.'

'Sounds like a plan.' She followed him into the kitchen and poured the rest of the tea down the sink. 'Funny, though. I did get the impression she had something on her mind.'

'Her mother died this morning.'

'Yes, true. Thanks for that, I'm not completely thick. Look, I'm not brilliant at reading people although I do know what grief feels like. I'm getting mixed signals from Mina, which is why . . .' Connie looked embarrassed. 'I'll be glad to have you back.'

'I'm pleased I've been missed.' Sadler kept his voice light. 'Tell me about Nell Colley.'

'It's such a strange case. During our enquiries we discovered another death, a few months earlier, that she appears to have taken an interest in.'

'In June?'

Connie looked at him in surprise. 'How did you guess?'

'Max, her former boss, said she handed in her notice then.'

Sadler took two steaks out of the freezer and put them into the microwave to thaw. 'Who was it who died?'

'A woman called Ingrid Neale. Lived in Cold Eaton. I went up to interview the family with Dahl. She lived with her sister, Monica, and her brother-in-law.'

'Did Ingrid know Nell?'

'According to Monica they didn't, but I'm not sure she was telling the truth. Nell had been looking at the death notice in the local paper and Ingrid Neale's address was in her book. The death had some significance for her.'

'It's a link of sorts, isn't it? You were right to follow it up and interview Ingrid's family even if you feel it hasn't got you very far. What about cause of death?'

'It's just odd. Both women were found sitting upright on the sofa and both had chronic conditions. A heart problem in Nell's case and asthma in Ingrid Neale's. The same GP signed off the death certificates, a Dr Parsons, but Dahl and I went to see him and we reckon he's completely on the level. Plus, Bill did the PM on Ingrid and he's not likely to miss anything.'

'Dahl. How's he getting on?'

'He's all right, actually. A bit of a geek but all right. He's worried about meeting you.'

'Me?' Sadler swung around. 'Why's he worried about me?'

'Your reputation goes before you.'

'If you think he's all right, I trust your judgement.'

Connie looked flattered. 'What do you think about the deaths, though? Nell Colley had a visitor the morning she died that we haven't been able to trace. Ingrid Neale was on her own in the house as the other occupants were out.'

Sadler began to slice onions into a frying pan. 'Was Hilary Kemp found upright, and dressed?'

Connie sighed. 'Of course not. She was in her hospital bed.'

'So there's nothing to link the three deaths whatsoever.'

'You think it's nothing?'

Sadler was silent for a moment, thinking. 'I don't know. Nell's death was mentioned to me in a legal context. She was concerned about being sued for libel regarding the memoir she was writing.'

'You said. I've got an odd feeling about that memoir, although it's hard to articulate. On the one hand, Dahl and I looked through the house and we didn't see any evidence of her having started the book, which is odd if it's important to her. However, it looks like she might have started the research even though she was very sick. I'd love to know what she was planning to write.'

'You've not found anything at all? No matter how secretive someone is, if they're planning on writing about their life they must have left traces somewhere.'

'I know. Dahl and I had a good look around the house. The trouble is that all resources are now focused on Hilary Kemp so I can't realistically go back and dig deeper into Nell's life. It feels, though, like something half-finished.'

'We might yet uncover a connection. Hilary Kemp's death is being investigated. Let's see what the tests show up.' He kept his voice calm, stirring the onions. 'Dr Parsons wasn't Hilary Kemp's GP as well, was he?'

Connie, in the process of taking a huge gulp of wine, stopped the glass at her lips. 'Oh God, I didn't ask. She'd been in hospital a month so I didn't even think of the GP.'

Sadler didn't turn to her but Connie could sense him weighing up his words. 'I know in the last case you went with your instinct and it led you into all sorts of trouble.'

'That's putting it mildly.'

'It's also your greatest strength. If you think the memoir is important then it probably is. It's whether it has an impact on the case that will affect whether it becomes a priority in the investigation, but don't doubt your instinct if you feel it's an avenue worth exploring.'

'You think I'm doubting myself?'

Sadler poured some of the wine from his glass into the pan to make a glaze. 'I'm looking forward to meeting Dahl. He comes highly recommended from Glossop. Don't let him make the decisions for you, though. If you think there's a connection between the deaths, then you should find it.'

32

Emily Fenn looked astonished to see Mina, her eyes darting from Mina's face to her overnight bag and back again.

'I need to stay the night. Possibly a few more. Do you have a spare room?'

Emily turned to a board on the side of the bar and picked up a key with a huge brass fob attached to it. 'Follow me.'

She led Mina up steep wooden stairs to a large room that looked out onto the front road. She walked over to the curtains and drew them across the window with a sharp tug. Out of the corner of her eyes, Mina could see Emily was taking in her dishevelled appearance. 'It'll be quiet here, despite the road. It's not on top of the bar, you see. I shut at eleven sharp anyway but you can hear the noise from below in some of the other rooms. This is the quietest.'

'Is there a bathroom?'

'It's shared but you're the only one here so it belongs to you. It's two doors down. You'll find it comfortable enough.' She paused for a moment. 'What's happened?'

'It's Mum. She's gone.' Mina could feel her legs begin to shake underneath her and she reached out a hand, holding on to the bedpost to steady herself.

Emily nodded. 'Bad. Comes to us all, but bad. Have you eaten?'

Mina's stomach contracted at the thought of food. 'I couldn't.'

'Come down if you feel up to it. The soup is homemade. There's a lot to do around a death. You need to eat.'

When Emily had gone, Mina sat on the bed and looked around the large, homely room. A candlewick bedspread, soft and comforting, the covered sheets and blankets reminding Mina of her childhood. She opened her bag, took out her pyjamas and put them under the pillow. She left her wash bag on the bedside table and went to the window. There was a street lamp outside the pub throwing a strong yellow glow onto the car park. She hoped it was turned off sometime during the evening. She drew the curtains and listened, hearing only the faint sound of laughter from the bar below.

She descended the stairs and entered the room. Emily pointed at a small round table near the fire with a reserved sign on it. Despite her off-hand demeanour, her landlady must have had a sensitive eye for where a single female diner might like to sit. The table was in the main lounge next to the fire but tucked slightly into a recess giving an illusion of privacy. Two chairs were at the table, one turned slightly away from the room towards the fire, the other facing the other diners. Again, Mina had the choice of being as sociable as she wished. She took the chair facing the room. No one was paying her any notice, although a woman at the table next to her looked up and smiled.

Emily came over and put a small glass of brandy in front of Mina. 'Just the one but it's good for shock. The soup will be along in a minute. That's best enjoyed with a glass of water.'

176

Mina looked at the brandy. 'I can't get a mobile signal. Is there anywhere I can make a call?'

'The village box is outside. You need a credit card, though. It doesn't take change any more. Or you can use my phone in the back if it's local.'

'I'll go outside. Thanks.' Picking up her bag, Mina left her diary on the table and a scarf on the chair to show that they were taken. As soon as she entered the night air, a gust of wind blew her to one side almost knocking her off her feet. She made it to the phone box and pulled open the stiff door. Inside it was clean but with a musty smell. After inputting the card number, it instructed her to dial the number required. Her fingers fumbled over the unfamiliar buttons but the tone changed to a ringing one and then came the voice she'd been waiting for.

'Mina. Where the hell are you calling from? What's this number 01629?'

'I'm in a place called Cold Eaton. Do you know it?'

'I've heard of it. Why are you there?'

'Mum's gone.'

'Gone. You mean—. Oh Mina.'

'Listen, will you do me a favour? I need to sort something out.'

'Anything.'

'Will you go to my house? You'll find the key on the top shelf of the garden shed. The combination lock for the shed is 1122. Go into my house and bring me more clothes. I'm staying at the only pub in the village, The Nettle Inn, and I'll probably be here a while. The other thing is . . .'

'What?'

'If anyone contacts you, please don't tell them where I am. I'm tired and upset and I need some time by myself.'

'Mina. Is everything all right? You don't sound yourself.'

'I need to think, that's all, and I can't do it in Bampton. Need to get away for a bit. You do understand, don't you?'

'Of course I do. Ring me if you need anything, won't you?'

Mina put the clunky phone back in its cradle and braved the wind back into the bar, which had continued to fill in her absence. Her table was still empty and, as she squeezed back into her chair, the woman from the next table leant across.

'A few people had their eye on it but me and the landlady saw them off.'

'Thanks, that's much appreciated.' Mina shrugged off her coat.

'I think the last lot would have argued the toss with me but one look at the landlady was enough.'

Mina laughed and picked up the brandy glass. 'I wouldn't like to get on the wrong side of her, that's for sure.'

'You're local?'

'Not really. You?'

'I'm from Devon. We're staying up at a cottage at the top end of the village. There's a family wedding tomorrow. You don't know your landlady very well?'

'No. Why?'

'It's just, well, when she put down your soup bowl, she had a look through the book you left there.'

'My diary? But that's private. Why was she going through my things?' Mina looked across at Emily who was pulling at a beer pump, her strong arms making the task look effortless. For a woman in her seventies she emanated robust health. It was hard to believe she was around the same age as Hilary, who had shrunk with illness. Mina could feel panic rising in her chest. 'What business is it of hers what's in my diary?'

'Don't worry. It's the same in every country village. They like to know each other's business.'

Mina picked up her diary and hunted for the photos she'd slipped between the pages. They were still in place, decades of secrets nestled between smudged pages of countless gardening tasks. She put her diary in her bag. Despite Emily's gruff kindness, there was something else going on that Mina couldn't grasp. Did she have an enemy in the place she'd come to escape the confusion of her mother's death? There was the note left on the windscreen of her van that suggested someone was watching her movements. Someone who didn't want her asking about Valerie. Could her landlady have left the message for her at the Cutting?

Emily caught her eye and it was Mina who was the first to drop her gaze. *I have nowhere I feel safe*, she thought.

33

Sadler was back at work after an early morning call from Llewellyn summoning him to the station to lead the investigation into suspected tampering with medical equipment at St Bertram's hospital. No one in the Detective Room looked like they had slept well. Sadler was standing in front of the team, going through the sequence of events that had led to the discovery of incisions in Hilary Kemp's drip. He looked tired, his face drawn. Matthews was sitting next to him, trying to hide the fact that she was pissed off even though she knew she only had temporary occupation of his office. Mayfield had announced to all and sundry when she'd walked in that morning that the baby had been kicking her all night and she hadn't had a wink of sleep. Connie glanced over to Dahl, who was trying to stifle a yawn. Which left her, who never slept well anyway. So a team of exhausted detectives. Not a great start to Thursday morning.

Sadler looked at a piece of paper that had been handed to him by Llewellyn. 'So, the PM was done late yesterday and has proved inconclusive. The victim had metastatic cancer but, given the presence of liquid from the saline drip, Bill has held off issuing a death certificate. We're still awaiting toxicology on both body tissue and blood from the PM plus an analysis of the contents of the drip. However . . .' Sadler

lifted up the paper. 'I've had the results of the forensic examination of the bag that took place last night. There was a small
V-shaped cut to the rubber septum of the resealable bung and
two puncture holes to the inner membrane of the bung.'

'Bloody hell,' said Connie.

'The holes are consistent with the punctures made by a
hypodermic needle.' Sadler looked around the room. 'While
we need to know what drug was used, and I'm hoping to hear
that today, the forensic scientist's view is that the saline drip
has been tampered with. Which is where we'll start.'

'This could be a huge operation,' said Matthews. 'It took
ages before they found the person responsible for adding
drugs to the drips in Stepping Hill. Manchester Met were
tied up for months.'

'I'm asking for extra resources, which will be particularly
necessary when we find what was injected into the bag as it will
involve trawling through patient records, access to drug storage
rooms and so on. However, we can start with the patient, Hilary Kemp. I'd like to focus on interviewing nurses and auxiliary
staff. Anyone who had access to the room yesterday morning,
even if they weren't supposed to be there.'

'Including visitors?'

'We'll need a list of people from outside but Hilary died before the first visiting hours so I think it's unlikely we're looking
for a member of the public at this moment. The drip, according
to the records, was changed around 8.30 a.m. when the nurse
noticed it was empty. So we have a small gap in time between
8.30 and 11.15 a.m. when Hilary's body was discovered.'

'What will the hospital feel about us being there?' asked
Connie.

'The oncology department were extremely quick in notifying us of a problem. They have a reputation for efficiency. You'll need to be discreet but I'll ask them to turn over a room in the hospital to interview staff.'

'What about the daughter, Mina Kemp?' asked Dahl.

'I met her by chance last week. I don't suppose it matters but I want it put on record I have met her in a personal capacity. At the moment, given she wasn't at the hospital, she's being treated as a grieving next of kin and I suggest we bear this in mind. We'll reinterview her when we have the results from toxicology.'

As the meeting drew to a close, Connie picked up her bag to go back to her desk.

'Connie and Dahl. Can you come in here for a moment?'

They looked at each other and followed Sadler into his office. He sat down heavily in his chair and pulled out the familiar file on Nell Colley.

'The focus is, for the moment, on the death of Hilary Kemp. However, Connie updated me on the investigations you've conducted on the deaths of Nell Colley and Ingrid Neale. Can you see any similarities at all to those cases?'

Dahl frowned. 'There may be a connection to St Bertram's. Ingrid Neale had been hospitalised with an asthma attack earlier in the week that she died.'

'What about Nell?' asked Sadler.

Connie looked at Dahl. 'She had a chronic condition. I don't remember any note being made about St Bertram's.'

'The nature of their illnesses was completely different. Hilary was terminally ill, Nell and Ingrid only chronically so,' said Dahl.

'Does that make a difference?' asked Connie, surprised to see a flush growing under Dahl's skin.

'They were just old and sick, not dying.' His voice was curt and Connie felt as if someone had pinched her.

Sadler leant back in his chair and considered. 'Leaving out Hilary Kemp, you were prepared to conclude that the deaths weren't suspicious, merely odd?'

'Not odd,' Dahl clarified. 'Unusual.'

'Right.' Sadler looked at his watch. 'I want one of you to look again at Nell Colley and Ingrid Neale. In depth. Check if they went to St Bertram's and any other link between them. In particular, see if you can find a link with Hilary Kemp.'

'You think something's up?'

'I'm not sure but I want this avenue explored. When Connie described the two cases to me, it reminded me of Harold Shipman's victims.'

'The GP mentioned Shipman. He said procedures had been tightened after that case,' said Connie.

'Interesting, although I suspect GPs are at pains to show how things have moved on since then. What was unusual about Shipman's victims, what made their deaths so strange, is that they were sitting upright on the sofas fully dressed when they were found. This isn't normal in death. If you're poorly, you often don't get dressed and you tend to stay in your bedroom. Or, if you are in the living room, it looks like a sick room.'

Connie glanced at Dahl. 'You said something similar the other day. I didn't make the connection then. Shipman was able to enter his victims' homes unnoticed because he paid them impromptu visits outside the hours he normally visited.'

'Exactly,' said Sadler. 'You've followed that up. You went to see Dr Parsons and he has given a convincing explanation for the procedure following both the deaths.'

'But he or someone else she was expecting could have called at her house outside normal visiting hours. That's quite a risk, isn't it?'

'If the deaths are connected, and it's only a very loose if, then we need to see who might have had a legitimate reason for visiting the two women in their homes and Hilary Kemp in hospital. St Bertram's could be the link. Dahl, you go to the hospital and help with the interviews. I'd like you to keep an eye on things bearing in mind what we've discussed. Look for any mention of those two names. Connie, I want you to stay here and look into links between these women. Study their backgrounds and see what you can find.' He paused. 'I don't want a Shipman in Bampton.'

34

Mina came down to the smell of cooking bacon. The plate put in front of her had two thick rashers, their edges curling up at the sides. A squat sausage and a fried egg with a soft yolk filled the plate. Emily hadn't even asked her if she wanted breakfast but Mina's stomach rumbled with hunger. She picked up a slice of thin toast sitting in a silver rack in the middle of the table, contemplated it for a moment, and took a tentative bite.

The previous evening, after taking a hot shower that had been unexpectedly powerful, she'd put on her pyjamas and dropped off to sleep. She'd expected vivid dreams but the soft mattress had enveloped her until she was woken by the sound of bottles clanking from an early morning beer delivery. As she'd emerged from the depths of the bed, the reality of her loss hit her again and all she wanted to do was climb back into the warm sheets and lie in the darkness. Instead, she'd dragged herself out of bed, checked her photos were still in the diary and then trudged down to breakfast.

Cold Eaton had a livelier feel than the previous time she'd visited. People were up and about, getting into cars and talking on the pavement. An air of anticipation. Emily was dressed for a day outside, an old Barbour jacket covering her round body. 'How are you feeling?'

'I'm not sure. It was a struggle to get out of bed.'

'I'm not surprised, but you did the right thing getting up anyway. What are you up to today?'

'I don't know. Nothing, I suppose.'

'Nothing's the worst thing you could do. Why not go out and get some fresh air?'

'Around the village?'

'Why not?' Emily picked up Mina's uneaten cooked breakfast. 'The air's bracing enough. It'll stop you feeling maudlin.'

'I suppose so. I've got some leaflets in the back of the van that I could post through letterboxes as I go around. I might pick up some work in the future.'

Emily looked put out, Mina's plans perhaps not tallying with the actions of a grieving daughter. *I'll mourn in my own way*, thought Mina.

'There's plenty of houses that need a spruce up around here, that's true,' Emily said, finally.

'Are you open today?'

'Of course. Oh I see.' Emily looked down at her clothes. 'I'm going up to help Harry Neale collect the wood for the bonfire night. He's put out a call for people to give him a hand.'

'Bonfire?'

'It's a big thing here. I'm surprised you haven't heard of it.'

'The Cold Eaton bonfire? It rings a bell but we never really celebrated Guy Fawkes.'

'Catholic, are you?'

Mina laughed. 'No. My mum didn't like the celebrations. She thought it was gruesome burning a man on top of a fire. We never went to any bonfires.'

'It *is* gruesome.' Mina turned at the note of satisfaction in

Emily's voice but she had disappeared into the kitchen. She came back with two cups of dark black liquid. 'Coffee.' She put the cups on the table and reached into her pocket then placed something in the window of the pub.

'Good God, what's that?' Mina bent forward for a closer look. It was a tiny doll, dressed in black on top of a wooden structure. Leaning forward, Mina could see that it was an effigy of a man on top of a pile of sticks.

Emily grinned at her. 'Good, isn't it? I made it when I was a teenager and I bring it out every year.'

Mina leant further forward to look closely at the model. It was beautifully made and looked so delicate that it might disintegrate to the touch. Yet Emily had been carrying it around in her pocket.

'It's beautiful.' Mina looked across at solid Emily with her red hands cupping her hot coffee. 'You made it?'

Emily acknowledged the compliment with an incline of her head. Twigs had been bunched together in a heap to resemble a bonfire. But the young Emily hadn't glued them together because, if she had, the structure would have disintegrated by now. Instead she'd threaded wire around the sticks, tying them together so that the copper thread became part of the structure, glinting in the low morning sun. The tiny Guy was even more intricate. He'd been fashioned a small pinstripe suit, every detail perfect down to the stitched collar over a white shirt.

'He's properly dressed. Like an old-fashioned businessman. What made you choose those clothes?'

Emily smiled. 'Just what people liked to wear in the fifties, except one of the villagers who went the other way.'

'What do you mean the other way?'

'Oh, never mind that. Some's so proud of the skin they're born with they don't want to wear any clothes. Do you want to see how I made the buttons on the jacket?' Emily pulled at one of the black orbs and pulled out a pin. 'See?'

Mina recoiled. 'It's like a voodoo doll.'

Two spots of colour appeared in Emily's cheeks. 'It's nothing of the sort. It's a way of making sure everything stays intact.'

'I'm amazed it's lasted so long. It's almost magical that it's still so complete.'

'It comes out every year and it'll be back in its box by Monday morning.'

Mina stirred her coffee. 'The bonfire is on Sunday?'

'Of course. We always have it on the fifth, whatever day of the week it is. None of this nearest Saturday business. It's easier when it's at the weekend, though, as building the bloody thing is exhausting.'

'I'm sure.'

Emily looked out of the window. 'They'll be ringing the bells on the Sunday to say that the church service is over. The villagers will go from there to the Neales' field and take the wood that we've collected today and start assembling the bonfire.'

'Don't they usually do that a few days before? Letting the sticks dry in situ.'

Emily pursed her lips and gave Mina an odd look. 'A few years back some kids built a den inside. We nearly burnt the blighters alive. So now the sticks are gathered one side of the field and kept dry with a cover. We assemble the bonfire on the day.'

188

'I might stay until then. Will there be fireworks?'

'There'll be some.' Emily's tone was grudging. 'We like to do things the traditional way here. A Catherine wheel or two. We don't want to frighten the animals with loud bangs.'

'I don't want to go if it's full of tourists.'

'At this time of year? It's locals, although you will get a smattering of visitors there.'

'I'll think about it. It depends how I feel. I'm not sure I'm up to crowds of people at the moment.' Mina stood up to go, opening her rucksack to check she had everything she needed. The photos had fallen out of the pages of her diary and into the sticky mess at the bottom of her bag. Mina retrieved them and, as she wiped the image of her mother against her scarf to remove the fluff, she heard Emily take a sharp intake of breath and exhale again slowly. Mina looked up in surprise.

'What is it?'

Emily's eyes had moved onto the other photo that Mina was grasping in her hands. 'Black and white photos. That takes me back.'

Emily's expression made Mina want to thrust the images back into the safety of her rucksack. Her landlady's face was a mixture of curiosity and apprehension. 'Can I look?'

Mina hesitated but handed over the picture of Hilary. Emily only glanced at it, her eyes still on the other, which Mina passed to her as well.

'It's of some of Mum's friends.' She watched as a flush of red crept up Emily's face. 'Is everything all right?'

Emily handed back the pictures and wiped her hands on her skirt. 'I need to be going.'

'Do you recognise anyone?'

But Emily was off. 'I can't stay here nattering, I need to get working. Be careful who you show those pictures to.'

35

If Camilla had stopped for a moment to look around her in the foyer of St Bertram's, she'd have noticed a teenage girl, small for her age with a name badge twisted around her neck, crying into the shoulder of an older woman. Camilla, however, barely noticed her surroundings as she made her way to the cardiac care unit. She found her mother in the busy ward sitting with her overnight bag on the made bed, ready to go home.

'Are you okay? I'm not late, am I? I told you I'd get here around eleven.'

Ginnie turned, lost in thought, and shook her head as if to rid herself of unwanted images. 'Sorry. I was miles away.'

Camilla dropped her handbag and reached out to touch her mother. 'You're not anxious about leaving, are you? Your consultant said you didn't need to be here any more.'

Ginnie grimaced. 'I can't wait to get back to my own things. Is the house okay?'

Camilla opened the bedside cupboard to check if there was anything left inside, hiding her face from Ginnie. 'The window in the pantry broke. I think it must have been left open when you came into hospital. The man came out to fix it this morning.'

Ginnie sounded concerned. 'I wasn't burgled, was I?'

'Everything's as it was. It was probably the wind the other morning. It's all fixed now.'

Camilla looked up at her mother, who was frowning. 'Can we go? I want to check the house.'

'Of course. Don't lift your bag, I'll carry it. Is there anyone you want to say goodbye to?'

'I just want to go.' Her mother's voice held an unfamiliar flatness to it.

'You've been discharged, I just need to let the nurse know we're leaving.'

Camilla's mother sat back down on the bed. 'I'll wait.'

A blonde nurse was looking at a clipboard at the entrance, her hair pulled back into a folded plait, reminiscent of one of Alfred Hitchcock's heroines.

'I've come to take Mrs Sadler home.'

The nurse looked up, distracted. 'I've given her all her medication. She's put it into her overnight bag. I checked she knew what she had to take. There are three types of tablets. Two you take morning and evening with food. One just in the morning. Do you want me to go through it again? Mrs Sadler seemed to take it in all right.'

Camilla thought of her grumpy, intelligent mother and suppressed a smile. 'I'm sure she'll be fine.'

'Are you driving her home?'

'Yes, and I can stay with her for a few hours until I pick my kids up from school.'

The nurse smiled slightly. 'I think getting home will do her the world of good. She can't wait to leave.'

'It's not you,' Camilla rushed to reassure the young woman. 'She's not a brilliant patient.'

'I'm not taking it personally,' she said, turning back to the clipboard.

Camilla's mother was still sitting on the bed. 'Can we go out the back way?'

'What do you mean the back way? There's only one entrance to this ward. What's the matter?'

Ginnie folded her arms. 'I don't want to make a nuisance of myself, that's all.'

Camilla picked up her mother's bag and guided Ginnie up by the elbow. 'There's only one way out. We won't stop if you don't want to, we'll just say goodbye to whoever's there as we leave.'

Now that she was on her feet, Ginnie was clearly desperate to get moving. Her strides were longer than Camilla's and as she reached the front of the ward, she tugged fruitlessly at the double doors.

'You need to press the green button at the side,' the blonde nurse shouted over to her.

Without looking backwards, Ginnie slapped her hand against the protruding button and left the ward.

Camilla caught up with her at the lift, panting slightly because of the weight of the bag. 'Mum,' she hissed. 'What's the matter with you?'

'I just want to get out of here.'

'I understand but there was no need to rush out like that.' A horrible thought entered her mind. 'They didn't mistreat you, did they?'

'Of course not.' Ginnie looked her daughter in the eye. 'Of course they didn't mistreat me.'

'Then what's the matter?'

Her mother's mouth settled into a thin line. 'I want to check my home is okay.'

*

Back at the house, as Camilla made a pot of tea, her mother inspected the new window. 'It was bent, you say.'

'Well, warped. I think it had been left open when you were taken in and the wind caught it. The new one matches perfectly, doesn't it?'

'Have you checked if anyone got in?'

'Mum! I told you, everything's intact. Why don't you check yourself? Everything's okay. Your jewellery, the money you keep in the tin on the shelf. Look . . .'

Camilla pulled down the old Fox's biscuit tin and opened it. Five ten pound notes lay loosely nestled inside. Her mother's emergency stash. 'It would have been easy to find if someone had got in.'

She heard her mother climb the stairs and move into her bedroom at the back of the house. She could hear Ginnie opening the top drawer of her dressing room table and then shutting it. *Should I ask her about the blood on her jumper?* thought Camilla. There were more creaks of the floorboards as her mother moved around the room. Finally Ginnie descended the stairs and came back into the kitchen.

'Nothing seems to have been taken,' she admitted. She moved to the front room and Camilla heard her groan as she sank into the high-backed chair next to the strong reading lamp.

'Can I get you a sandwich?'

Ginnie looked defeated and something else besides. Puzzled. No, not puzzled. She looked like she was trying to make sense of something. 'I'm not hungry. I can prepare something later. Is there bread?'

'Bread and cheese. And salad vegetables. Let me take your things upstairs.'

Camilla lifted her mother's overnight bag and took it up to the bedroom. Her mother's search must have been cursory as the room was pristine. Camilla placed the bag on the bed. Listening for any movement from her mother, she slipped her hand under the duvet and slid it across the sheets. They were cold to the touch and there was nothing to impede the sweep of her hand. The envelope had gone.

36

Mina counted the houses in Cold Eaton as she delivered the leaflets. Twenty-nine. A hotch potch of buildings along the narrow road which she discovered led to an imposing grey house, presumably the old manor. She could hear laughter coming from the field where the bonfire was taking place on Sunday. Unlike many of the other houses in the village, the manor house had an iron post box next to the front door. Grateful for an obvious place to drop her leaflet, she posted it through the slot.

Gazing up a narrow private track, she hesitated, unsure if it led anywhere. She chanced it and saw a small white house almost obscured by ivy creeping up its front. She opened the creaking gate and looked around for somewhere to drop her flyer.

'Having trouble finding where to put them?' A man sitting on a stone bench next to the gate took the leaflet out of her hand and studied it.

'Does no one in this village have a letterbox in the door?'

The man grunted. He was tiny. His thin legs, poking out of khaki shorts, were tanned despite the weather. 'We do things differently here. Some of those doors are ancient. You're looking for gardening work?'

'Anything outside that'll see me through the winter.'

He looked her up and down. 'Can you cut a hedge?'

'Of course.'

'No of course about it. One lad I had last year made a complete mess of it.'

Mina took a step back. 'I'm a trained gardener. I use a petrol hedge trimmer and I can even cope with people watching me as I do it.'

The man considered her, scratching his leg. 'Okay. Come back next week and start on the side. You can't do much damage there. If I don't like it, we'll part with no hard feelings.'

'Okay. Great.'

'I hear Emily Fenn's paying you a tenner an hour.' Mina swore under her breath and the man looked at her. 'The Fenns are renowned for being tight as mustard. I'll give you fifteen, all right? If you can cut a hedge properly, you'll deserve it.'

Mina reached into her pocket for her phone. 'What's your name?'

'Malcolm Cox.'

'The wood man?'

'That's me. Who mentioned my name?' His voice was filled with suspicion.

'Emily said you'd supplied her with wood.'

'Oh, did she? She was probably moaning about it being green. She leaves it under that manky shed of hers instead of outdoors and then moans at me when it's damp come autumn. I'm not a conjuror. If you want dry wood, you need to stack it properly.'

'Like an old-fashioned haystack.'

'Exactly.' He stood up, his face level with Mina's. 'It's what we always say in Cold Eaton, although I don't think I've ever heard a young one repeat it. Well, you know about wood. I'll see if you can cut a hedge next Wednesday.'

'I'm staying at the pub until Monday at least. I want to get some work around here. Do you know who cuts the grass in the churchyard?'

'I do. I'm still fit enough for that. I just can't get on a ladder. You been into the churchyard?'

'No, I mean, churches aren't really my thing.'

'There's a medieval yew there. It's worth a visit. They say it bleeds when death comes to the village.'

'Bleeds?'

He stepped backwards, dismissing her. 'It's an old story. It's simply sap from the branches. Forget I said it.'

Mina left him and made her way back down the slope. At the church, a rickety moss-covered gate opened onto a long path that led to a stone porch. She looked at the half-mown grass. Had Malcolm left the job unfinished? She went through the gate and up to the porch, which displayed a rota for readers and church cleaning. Mina moved to the large oak door and turned the iron ring.

There was a smell of damp and dust and something else that Mina couldn't describe but which brought out a feeling of longing in her. Centuries of history that reminded her of the thousands of people who had passed through these doors over the years. The furnishings were nothing special, minimalist and drab offset by a ripped and stained carpet. There wouldn't have been much to interest a church historian here. Toys were scattered in one corner and, again, had an air of dinge about them. Someone's unloved castoffs. Mina wandered idly around the pews and, at the sound of a gust of wind, zipped up her coat and went back outside.

The churchyard had been divided into three segments. At the top of the slope the grass was high, covering most of the graves so that they could be barely seen. Further down, the grass looked like it had been mown for winter but there was still an unkempt feel to the area. It was only at the bottom, in a patch near the road, that the graves looked cared for with plants and flowers in jars. Did Malcolm have his own methods for mowing the lawn?

'It's deliberate.'

The voice made Mina jump and she wheeled around. A man in his late fifties stood in front of her wearing a green waxed jacket and a black felted cap.

'Saw you looking at the churchyard. It's deliberate how it's managed. At the top, the oldest part of the churchyard, it's been allowed to return to the wild. There are no relatives to visit the graves and some of them need repair. So it's managed so that wildlife is undisturbed.'

'It fits in with the landscape. Wild and messy. And the middle bit?'

'That's semi-managed. It's mown twice a year but other than that it's left, again to encourage wildlife to use it as their home. Then, of course, the more recent graves are well tended and family still come. It's looked after and mown on a regular basis.' He looked her up and down. 'You're the gardener at the pub?'

Another one. 'You don't miss much.'

'This is a small village. Do you know this place well?'

There was a note in his voice that caused Mina to frown. 'No. I'm new here. I'm taking any job I can get at this time of year.'

'Of course, of course. I'm Harry Neale. The bonfire will be in my field on Sunday.'

'I put a leaflet through your letter box just now.'

'Did you? It's all hands to the pump today getting the wood together. There's usually some knocking about here. I need to collect it as some of the villagers are superstitious about taking wood from the churchyard.'

'But you're not?'

He shrugged. 'It's holy ground so it'll do more good than harm, surely.'

'What about the yew?'

He looked away. 'Even I draw the line at the yew tree. Well, I might see you on Sunday then.' He turned to walk off and, as he did so, glanced down at the grave she was standing next to. His face dropped and he gave her a curious look.

Mina waited until he'd gone out of the gate and looked down to see the name on the grave. Valerie Grace Hallows.

37

Catherine

They sat in that fusty, little-used room dotted with remnants of a past life. On the sideboard, a faded colour photo was framed in cheap embossed plastic showing a couple in dated wedding clothes. The groom was wearing thick black glasses and a black suit with wide trouser legs. The bodice of the bride's dress had two stiff peaks where her breasts jutted out. Catherine didn't like to stare too long at the photo so instead took a sip of her drink while the woman opposite leant back in her chair, her eyes shut.

'I get so tired these days.'

Catherine also got tired from the confused images racing through her head but she didn't dare say it to this woman. Instead, she sat and waited. The church bell rang out and Catherine looked at her watch in alarm.

'I'll have to go soon. I need to make the lesson after lunch. Mrs Gordon's strict and will report me if I'm not there.'

The woman opposite counted the bell chimes striking the hour. 'Nine, ten, eleven. One of those bells in the tower came from the drowned village. Did you know?'

'Drowned village? Where's that?'

The woman shrugged. 'It doesn't matter.' She looked across

to Catherine. 'But you've heard of it before?'

Catherine flushed and looked down at her skirt. 'The woman I visit in hospital mentioned it. The drowned village, I mean. Why did she do that?'

'She talked about the village, did she? And what did she say?'

'Nothing that made sense.'

'But enough.'

The menace in the woman's voice made Catherine look up. 'Is it over?'

She didn't mean the bells and the woman understood this. There was a short silence except for the sound of the woman opening a drawer. 'I want you to look at this.'

She handed Catherine a leaflet. 'Mina's moved into the village. There's no reason for her to be here unless it's to discover our secrets. It could still all come out.'

Catherine stared at the flyer. It was printed in the colours of mud and sludge green. Across the top were the words 'The Land Girl'. 'Why? Why is she here?'

'She's still trying to find out.' The woman leant forward. 'She can't do that. You do understand, don't you? She can't find out. Do you want the shame brought on your family too?'

Catherine shook her head. 'No. No, I don't want that.'

'Do you have the key?'

Catherine frowned. 'What key?'

'The one to the room upstairs. I need to take that from you.'

'Upstairs? Oh, you mean this.' Catherine reached over to her school blazer and dug into the pockets. 'Is this what you want?'

38

Connie was in a bad temper and Dahl hesitated before approaching her. She was at her desk, managing to scowl and look sorry for herself at the same time. Connie clearly didn't relish being given the job of sifting through computer records that was the bread and butter of detective work. It was she, however, who pointed out they'd rushed to interview Monica in Cold Eaton without first checking whether her sister, Ingrid, had had a post mortem after the fatal asthma attack. Here was the opportunity to slow down a bit and find a strong connection between the three women, if there was one. He had his coat on and car keys in his hand, ready to go back to St Bertram's. He'd thought it wise to say goodbye to Connie but, after one glance at her face, he regretted the impulse. He tried to placate her, aware that his words were falling on deaf ears.

'It's what we want, isn't it? We're being guarded in our observations because we don't know each other very well but we're both wary of how Ingrid Kemp and Nell Colley died. Here's our chance to prove it.'

'By sitting in an office, sifting through paperwork? I want to be out there with you interviewing staff. The death of Hilary Kemp is our main focus because we've got evidence of foul play. Investigating her death will help us connect the other two.'

'Yes, but we've a cast of hundreds as potential suspects and the incident room there is fully staffed. The case might be a priority but the trail is stone cold. I envy you concentrating on those records. I'm going to be spending all day interviewing medical staff whose attitudes will range from terrified to outraged. It's the innocent ones who look most guilty in these situations. If we've a pathological killer in our midst he'll be the most relaxed of them all.'

'He?' Connie looked up.

'Just a turn of phrase. I'm simply pointing out it'll be a complete pain assembling all the testimonies.'

'Want to swap?' asked Connie but Dahl shook his head.

'Sadler must have had a reason behind allocating the tasks.'

Connie snorted and turned back to the files on her desk. 'Hilary Kemp had a different GP so we can put Dr Parsons to one side for the moment unless we have evidence he was at St Bertram's yesterday. Enjoy yourself,' she muttered.

Dahl walked out of the building glad to leave Connie's sour mood and the strains of working with Matthews. St Bertram's had that unusual atmosphere so specific to hospitals, the entrance a mix of bustling activity and unhealthy lassitude. People either had somewhere to go or were killing time. The police personnel had been delivered in unmarked vehicles and were busy working in an allocated room on the eighth floor. The room was subdued when he entered it, the detectives aware that they were dealing with a potential murderer of the vulnerable.

To one side, he heard a hospital porter describing taking Hilary for a scan and her confused ramblings. Dahl sat in a chair that he'd pulled from behind a table and listened for a moment.

'It was Valerie this and Valerie that. I just let her carry on. I waited while she had the imaging and, afterwards, on the way back to the ward she started on about the drowning of the village up at Derwent. This Valerie was originally from up that way, I think I managed to work out. Funny how your mind wanders.'

Derwent. Dahl thought he could take his mother up to the reservoir sometime before the winter set in. It had an interesting enough history and his mother would like the escape from the confines of her house. Near the window, Bill Shields was sitting in one of the chairs, rotating slowly, deep in thought.

'Dr Shields?'

'Ah, the young Dahl. How are you getting on with Connie?'

Dahl took off his coat. 'She seems to like me, which, I suspect, helps.'

The statement seemed to cheer Bill up. 'Does she? Well, Connie has always had excellent taste.'

'Are you helping out?'

Bill rotated away from him. 'Am I helping out? Well, I'm trying not to get in the way, we can say that.'

Dahl sat down opposite him. 'It's upset you?'

Bill stopped moving. 'St Bertram's is my hospital. Oh, I know you lot only get to see me in my scrubs in the pathology department or at the Christmas do if your boss remembers to invite me, but I have a life away from police work. I don't only deal with the suspicious deaths, I look at the unexplained. Patients where the cause of death is clear but confirmation is needed anyway. I look at bodies where doctors are trying to advance medical knowledge and want me to try to work out the progression of the illness. It's looking to the future not just to the past. What I'm trying to say is that there is a whole part of my work you never see. I belong to this hospital.'

'You heard the official findings that the drip had been cut?'

Bill nodded and stood up. 'And so we wait for the results to see what was added to a solution that was supposed to help Hilary Kemp in her final hours, not hasten her end.'

'We're hoping for it today but it might take a little longer.'

'A problem for you certainly but, for me, it's almost irrelevant. The damage was already done when the needle entered the drip. Anyway, I think I'd better make myself scarce.'

'Can I ask you something?'

Bill turned around. 'Go on.'

'Do you ever hear of instances where you should have done a post mortem but it was never referred to you?'

Bill shrugged. 'There's often some debate about when one should be performed. In hospital we sometimes chat about the practicalities of doing a medical PM and I can be involved in the decision making process, but, often, the decision is made without me.'

'What about where the coroner should have been involved?'

'That's—' Bill stopped. 'What are you saying?'

'It's just a query.' Dahl sized up the pathologist. He was a rotund man, probably not long off retirement age, with an air of world weariness about him. Bill was staring at him aghast.

'Don't tell me there's more than one?'

*

Connie was boss-eyed from staring at endless files. The three women had little in common except that they lived within five miles of each other and were about the same age, born in a seven month period between October 1941 and April 1942. If Connie's calculations were right, this meant they would have all been in the same year at school.

She picked up the phone and called the number she had for Mina Kemp. It went straight onto voicemail and she left a message. She tried Mina's landline but the phone just rang out and she put the receiver down in frustration and, looking around her, sneaked out of the office, feeling like a fugitive.

The *Evening Star* had a closed feel to it. The windows were shuttered and a rope was tied across the entrance to the boat. Connie rapped on a window but, receiving no reply, returned to her car and went to the other address she had for Mina, a smart semi in Lower Bampton with a sumptuous front garden.

There was no answer to Connie's knock but from behind the glass she saw a shadow come down the stairs and hesitate for a moment. The door opened and a large woman with a flush of colour in her cheeks appeared. Connie showed her warrant card.

'Do I have the right house? I'm looking for Mina Kemp.'

'It's just she's not here at the moment.'

'And you are . . .'

'Sorry. I'm her friend, Jo.' Connie's eyes dropped to the black holdall the woman held in her left hand. 'She asked me to pick up some clothes.'

'She's staying with you?'

'No. Umm, I don't really know where she is. She's asked me

to pick up some stuff and she'll call to say where she's staying.'

'She's run off then.'

Connie's tone alarmed the woman. 'She's not run off. She's—'

'What?'

'Look, she had to get away for a few days.'

Connie's face darkened. 'If you know where she is, you'd better tell me.'

Jo dropped the bag, defeated. 'She's staying at The Nettle Inn in Cold Eaton. I don't think she's working today.'

'Right.' *Cold bloody Eaton*, thought Connie. *What's she doing there?*

In a temper, Connie drove towards the village, keeping an eye on her speed. Mina's van was in the car park but when Connie tried the side door of the pub it was shut. A pub that adhered to the old-style closing hours. Great. She peered inside the van but could see nothing.

'Did you want me?' Mina was standing on the road with an armful of leaflets. Her expression was one more of distance than guilt.

Connie straightened. 'I've been trying to find you at your various addresses. Your friend Jo didn't want to tell me where you were. Why the secrecy?'

Mina paled. 'My mother's just died. I needed to get away, that's all. Do you have any more news for me?'

Annoyed, Connie shifted, feeling the need for a ciga-rette. 'I don't have anything else to tell you other than we're checking the circumstances of your mother's death. There is something else I wanted to ask you, though. Can you tell me where Hilary went to school?'

Mina put her leaflets into her bag and made a show of closing it. 'Why do you want to know?'

'Something has come up and I need to go back to your mother's childhood to check for a link.'

'She went to St Paul's junior school, I think, and then on to Bampton Grammar. That's all I know, I'm afraid.'

'And does the name Ingrid Neale mean anything to you?'

Mina looked confused. 'Ingrid Neale. Who's she?'

'It doesn't matter.'

'I met a Harry Neale just now in the churchyard. Are they related?'

'Harry and his wife, Monica, live in the manor house at the top of the village. Ingrid was Monica's sister. You definitely don't recognise any of those names in relation to your mother?'

Mina shook her head.

'What about a Nell Colley?'

'I don't know these people. Why are they important?'

Connie didn't reply but a glance at Mina's face revealed bewilderment and, she thought, fear. 'How was your mother in the days before she died?'

Mina turned away. 'I told you, she was a bit agitated and confused.'

'Confused?'

'Yes, you know. Disoriented.'

'Did the medical staff know why?'

'I pressed them but they didn't really give me an answer.'

'There were no other visitors apart from you?'

'No, well, only the girl.'

'Which girl?' asked Connie.

'She was one of the official visitors. They're called patient support, apparently. She saw me the other day and said she'd been visiting Mum.'

Connie took out her notebook. 'When you say girl, how old do you mean?'

'She said she was in year nine but I don't really know what that means. She looked around fourteen.'

'And she visited your mother?'

'She said she did.' Mina looked unwilling to continue the conversation. 'I think Mum remembered it but her memory wasn't great towards the end.'

'Did she go regularly to the ward?'

'I don't think so, although I think she'd spent time with Mum in the last couple of weeks. I really need to tell her Mum's dead. She was concerned.'

'They had become close?'

'Not particularly but Mum did talk to her.'

'Name?'

'Um. Catherine Hallows. It was on her name badge. Only . . .' Mina looked back to the church. 'Hallows. That's funny.'

'What's funny?'

Mina shook her head. 'It doesn't matter. It's a Derbyshire name, isn't it?'

'We'll need to talk to her.' Connie looked across at Mina and was surprised to see a look of relief cross her face. Mina, despite her neutral tone and cautious words, didn't want the girl missed from the list of interviewees. Connie turned to go. 'You won't go away without telling us, will you?'

Mina shook her head. 'I needed to get away, that's all.'

She stopped, thinking something over. 'Listen. What did Ingrid Neale and Nell Colley look like?'

Connie tried to keep the look of surprise off her face. 'I don't have up to date photos at the moment. It's a good point. I'll see if they've arrived at the station. I've met Ingrid's sister, though and, if they were alike, she was tall and slim.'

Mina hesitated. 'I have a photo of Mum's friends. Do you want to see it?' She rummaged in her bag and pulled out a photo, which she handed to Connie. 'It was amongst my mum's stuff. I don't know who any of them are.'

Five girls were lined up ready for a tennis game. They were styled in the fashions of the fifties, rigid hair and fitted sports clothes.

'None of them's my mother. I assume she took the snap. I was hoping to identify the others.'

'That,' said Connie, pointing to the girl second from the left, 'must be Ingrid Neale. She looks just like her sister, Monica.' Inside, she could feel the roar of excitement. It was a link. Mina, however, was looking perturbed.

'Who is she? Why did you mention her name?'

Connie didn't answer but squinted at the girl in the photo. She had Monica's hauteur and gave off a similar air of discontent. 'I'm going to need a copy of this. One of the girls might also be Nell Colley. I can show it to her neighbour.'

Mina looked alarmed. 'That photo is important to me. Can I have it back?'

Connie hesitated. 'I need to check the other girls in the photo.'

'But it belongs to me and you won't even tell me what this is all about. You can't just take it.'

Connie looked at Mina's grief-marked face and relented. 'Tell you what, let me take a photo of it with my phone. That'll do me for the moment and I can show it to my boss, DI Sadler. I'd like a physical copy as soon as possible.'

'If I drop by my house, I can scan it into my computer and send you a copy tomorrow.'

Connie focused the phone camera on the photo. As she pressed the button, a call came through from Matthews, who was probably wondering where she was. Connie, distracted, managed to both fudge the shot and decline the call from her colleague.

'Damn. I'm going to need to return this call, I'm afraid.' The hazy snap would have to do for the moment. 'Don't lose it, will you? Send me a scanned copy as soon as you can.'

39

Mina hiked back up the hill towards the manor house brooding over the village. Thank God Connie hadn't insisted on taking the photo. The thought of giving it up had made Mina feel sick but it had clarified the thought that had been niggling away at her since she arrived in Cold Eaton. This was a village with secrets that it wouldn't give up easily and yet might lead her to an understanding of her mother's final fears. At last, she'd been given the name of someone who might be able to help her understand her mother more. Monica Neale.

The Neale house was a huge grey square that could have been made graceful by the addition of tall windows but instead had been built with thin narrow strips of glass pushed to the outer fringes of the building. Harry Neale stood at the threshold, his green waxed jacket filthy with damp clods of mud from the wood gathering.

'It's the land girl.' Harry Neale had lost some of his heartiness from the churchyard and he looked over his shoulder into the shadows of the house. 'I've looked at your leaflet. You'd have your work cut out with my plot. And I can't afford to pay you.'

'I wanted a quick chat with your wife, if that's okay. About my mum who I think used to spend time here.'

Harry hesitated and opened the door. 'You'd better come

in.' He led her into a large kitchen and pulled out a chair. 'So you want me to ask Monica about your mother?'

'She's not here?'

'Upstairs, I think.' There was a pause. 'She's not feeling that well, otherwise I'd call her down.'

'Maybe you could ask her when you have a chance. My mother's name was Hilary Kemp. I'd like to know if she remembers her.'

'Of course.' He looked to the Aga but didn't offer her a cup of tea. 'I ought to be getting back to the fields. Was there anything else?'

'When we met before in the churchyard—'

'I haven't forgotten.' He sounded amused. 'Walking amongst the graves. Not everyone's choice of an afternoon stroll.'

'It was actually quite comforting. The thing is, I saw some-one who I think my mother also knew. Valerie Grace Hallows.'

'But she's dead. Oh, I see. You saw her gravestone. Well, what of it?'

'Did you know her?'

Mina saw him hesitate. 'No. She died before I moved to Cold Eaton. She was a friend of Monica's.'

'It looks like she died young.'

'She took her own life, I think.'

Mina stared at Harry in dismay. 'She killed herself? What happened?'

'She'd just had a child. A son. They thought she was suffer-ing from postnatal depression. She'd taken too many of her Valium tablets, although the coroner, if I understand rightly, recorded an open verdict.'

'Then she might not have killed herself. There must have been some element of doubt.'

'I don't think that was the reason for the verdict. It's a common conclusion for suicides when there's no note. It's kinder on the family to say they don't really know if it was intentional.'

'She lived in Cold Eaton?'

'No. Up at Hallows Hill.'

'Hallows Hill?'

He looked at her. 'Name not to your liking? They hung poachers up there centuries ago. They reckon at one time the family name was actually Gallows and someone last century changed it to Hallows. Not much there now except Hallows Farm and a couple of cottages. Why are you so interested in the family?'

'I heard the name spoken by someone.'

'By who?' They both jumped at the voice that interrupted them from behind. Mina swung around to get a better look at the woman who had spoken. She was tall and thin with wiry grey hair that hinted at a natural auburn colour. Her lined face looked strained with illness. She came into the room and filled the kettle at the side of the Aga. 'Who talked about the Hallows?'

Mina looked at the woman's severe face and felt the need to protect her mother. Should she reveal Hilary's identity?

'My mother mentioned a name in passing, that's all, and I made the connection in the churchyard.'

'Your mother?'

'You might have known her. Mum was called Hilary Kemp.'

'Hilary?' At the tone of familiarity, Mina frowned. 'You

look like your mum. Same curly hair.'

'You remember her?'

'She was a few years older than me but I certainly remember your mother.'

'And the woman in the churchyard, Valerie Grace Hallows?'

'And her,' confirmed Monica Neale.

'What was she like?'

'She was, well, she was one of the Hallows. She was older than me too, a friend of my sister's really, but I tried to help after she had the baby and was struggling.'

'So you know the family well?'

'Not really, although I still pop up there occasionally. The son's gone too. It's just Lorna Hallows and her daughter Catherine.'

'Catherine, of course.'

'You know Catherine then?'

Mina used the table to steady herself. 'I met her at the hospital. My mum died there on Wednesday.'

Monica glanced across at her husband. 'She died? How?'

'She had cancer.'

'Oh.' The voice sounded neutral but, as she shifted in her seat, Mina saw the woman's hands shaking as she tipped hot water into the teapot. She moved around to face them, leaning back against the Aga. A pose Mina had seen before.

'You said you remembered my mother. She was friends with your sister, wasn't she?'

'She was one of Ingrid's friends. She'd come to the village from Bampton, I think. I don't really remember.'

'Can I show you this?' Mina handed over the photo and Monica scanned it briefly. 'You remember them?'

'I recognise some of them.'

Mina looked at the five girls and pointed at the second girl on the left. 'So this is Ingrid. Which one is Valerie Hallows?'

Monica stared at Mina for a moment and smiled. 'Ahh.' She bent over the photo and pointed at the thin, proud girl on the left. 'Here.'

'That's Valerie Hallows?'

There was a glimmer of humour in Monica's expression. 'That's right.'

'Do you know what "GIVEN" refers to?'

'Given?'

Mina turned over the photo. 'See.'

The woman's eyes were on Mina. 'GIVEN. It must be a code.'

'A code?'

Monica looked at the picture and Mina had the impression she was laughing. 'Valerie Hallows. So that's where you are.' She handed back the photo to Mina. 'Good luck.'

40

For a brand new building, the architects had managed to imbue the corridors with the institutional feel common to all hospitals. As he looked for somewhere to quell the nauseous feeling in his stomach, Dahl's senses were assaulted by the clank of trolleys carting patients in and out of the lifts, the unmistakable smell of disinfectant and vomit, and the disorienting effect of walking past yards of blank white walls. Detectives in the temporary incident room were finishing statements from all staff associated with Oncology B, the ward where Hilary had been nursed, and the question was whether to extend the interviews to other wards. Not his decision, thank God.

Dahl found the canteen full of reassuringly healthy snacks and chose a fruit bar and a packet of plain crisps that would soothe his stomach and strong coffee that probably wouldn't. Back on the fourth floor, and heading back to the interview room, he passed a second set of lifts. The doors opened and deposited a confused-looking Connie.

'Looking for me?'

'Bloody hell. This hospital is like a maze. How the hell do you find your way around?'

'You get used to it.'

She looked longingly at his coffee and he passed it to her. 'You sure?'

'It's my third today. I was just stretching my legs and trying to find something to settle my stomach.'

'What's the matter?'

'All these interviews. Have you heard how sick the patients are in this ward? It's upsetting listening to the day to day tasks of the people who work in here and then asking them if they suspect any of their colleagues, or, more unlikely, any of the other patients, of trying to help Hilary towards the end.'

'Anything come up?'

'Nothing that helps finger the culprit. Hilary was unusually agitated before her death. Staff put it down to an imbalance of medication but it could well have been symptoms of an overdose.'

'You think the drip had been tampered with more than once?'

'It's possible. She seemed to be talking about a childhood friend a lot called Valerie. The daughter reassured her it was a hallucination. Funny.'

'What's funny?'

'Hilary talked to one of the porters about the drowned village underneath the Ladybower reservoir. It related to Valerie. The nurse said Hilary was grasping his sleeve the whole time. I've no idea why. It's strange how the mind plays tricks.'

'Grasping at his sleeve? Then she must have been desperate to tell him something. I don't see any significance in relation to the Ladybower reservoir, though, do you?'

'I'm struggling to make sense of anything. It's bothering me that we're looking into the potential deaths of older people. Their lives aren't any less valuable because their time left on earth was limited.'

Connie looked at him. Surprised. 'No one's saying that.'

'I suppose not but would the deaths of Ingrid Neale and Nell Colley have been investigated more thoroughly if they had been younger?'

Connie hesitated as if she wanted to say something. She changed her mind and looked contrite. 'I appreciate it's hard. Maybe I shouldn't have been so moody this morning because I was stuck at my desk.'

'Moody? You?'

She glared at him, and then laughed. 'Cheers for this anyway.' She took a swig. 'Listen. Two bits of news. First of all I've found a link. Hilary Kemp knew Ingrid Neale as a teenager. There's a photo that Mina has of a group of them taken from Hilary's album.'

'That's good, isn't it? It proves a connection beyond the ad in the newspaper.'

'It's a solid link, which is great, but I think we need more. I also need to track down one of the patient support staff. Apparently, Hilary Kemp was being visited by a girl called Catherine Hallows.'

'She must be the killer with a surname like that.'

'This is no time for jokes, Dahl. I'm going to track down the supervisor but I wanted to check you hadn't interviewed her first.'

'That name's not come up in the list of visitors. I've just been through the list and I'm sure I'd remember a name like that. She definitely saw Hilary Kemp?'

'According to the daughter, she did.'

'Right.' Dahl looked around. 'I'll come with you.'

As they descended in the lift, Dahl looked at Connie standing with her back to the mirror. Her dark shoulder-length hair was tied back in a ponytail but didn't look like it had seen a brush that morning. Her face was bare of make-up, although it looked like she'd put on lipstick and at some point smudged it off. He thought of his elegant mother and wondered what she would make of Connie. The lift stopped at every floor on its descent so that it was crammed by the time it reached the ground floor.

'Pooh. There was someone in there with a serious body odour issue.' Connie looked like she was going to be sick.

'Want me to buy you some mints?'

'Let's get the interview done so that I can leave. The boss wants us back tonight anyway for a meeting to see where we've got to.'

They approached a cheerful woman wearing a sash across her body.

'I'm looking to find one of your regular hospital visitors called Catherine Hallows.'

'Cathy? I don't think she's in today. Let me check the roster.' The woman consulted a clipboard. 'She's not due in until Monday.'

'Monday?' Connie showed the woman her police ID and a look of concern crossed her face. 'Everything's all right, isn't it?'

'We'd like to ask her a few questions about the patients she's been visiting.'

'There haven't been any complaints, have there? I interviewed Cathy myself and I took up references from the school.'

'Does she have the freedom to visit any patient?'

The woman was shocked. 'Not at all. She's given a specific ward, ophthalmology in Cathy's case, and a list of patients who've indicated they're happy to be visited by patient support. She can't just go around visiting people willy nilly.'

'Any idea why she was visiting a patient in the oncology ward?'

The woman opened her mouth and shut it again. 'No idea. Has something happened?'

'Why do you say that?'

'It's, well, she seemed a bit upset earlier this week.'

'Upset? When was this?'

'I'm not sure. Yesterday, or maybe the day before. I remember thinking that maybe she was a bit young for this. It can be difficult to get away from the work. Is that the problem?'

Dahl shrank from the hope in the woman's eyes.

'Don't mention anything to her when you see her. We'll come back then. How old is Catherine?'

'Fourteen.'

They moved away from the desk towards the entrance. 'Think we should call her in for interview before Monday?' asked Connie.

'I'm not sure. All she's done is visit the patient but it didn't come up in any of the nurses' statements. They were specifically asked to identify anyone who had been in the room that morning. They were assiduous. They mentioned cleaners, breakfast staff, someone who wanted an early visit and was turned away, even a lost patient looking for the dentistry department. Why would anyone forget a schoolgirl?'

'Then she didn't visit Hilary on Wednesday unless she managed to slip past staff.'

'She'd have needed to go past the front desk. It's possible but not likely.' Dahl looked at his watch. 'We can bring it up at the team meeting. I think Sadler will be more excited about your link to Ingrid Neale, although God knows where that leaves us.'

'Funny.' Connie slung her cup in the recycling bin. 'The name Hallows clearly rang a bell with Mina Kemp. She's a difficult person to read given she's in the early stages of grief but the name meant something to her. I'm going to follow it up. Mina may well know more than she's telling us.'

41

'I saw a grave when I was delivering leaflets yesterday.'

'Did you?' Emily was distracted, doing a stocktake ready for the expected business from the bonfire on Sunday. 'The dead don't normally need their lawn mowing.'

'The name written on the stone was Valerie Grace Hallows.' Mina took a deep breath. 'Did you know her?'

A bottle dropped from Emily's hands and she went after it on hands and knees. After retrieving it, she stood up and faced Mina, hands on hips. 'The Hallows? They're a strange lot. Live up on Hallows Farm. Miserable place. If you think we're isolated here then you want to see there. Why are you interested in the grave, anyway?'

'My mum mentioned her. I thought she might have been one of the girls in the photo you looked at yesterday morning.' Emily bent down, continuing to count the bottles. Mina could feel her eyes beginning to fill with tears. 'Well, was she?'

Emily didn't turn at the wobble in Mina's voice but stopped counting the drinks in the cabinet. 'I don't remember.'

'Why are you being like this?' Mina felt the tears spill over her lids and down her cheeks. She hunted in her pockets for a tissue. 'It's a simple question. I'm just asking you who was in the photo.'

Emily stood up and finally looked at Mina. 'It was a long

time ago and these things are best left alone. You're grieving your mum. Why rake up the past?'

'Because I think it's important,' she said, dropping her soaking tissue and using her sleeve instead to wipe her face. 'Was it you who left the message on my van at the Cutting?'

'Message? What message?'

Distraught, Mina gathered up her things and hurried outside. Struggling to find a mobile signal, she resorted to the large map of Derbyshire she kept underneath her driver's seat. Hallows Farm was two miles out of Cold Eaton, accessed via a road that wound up a steep hill. From the map it looked more like a hamlet than a village, merely a small cluster of houses around a farm.

The van bounced out of Cold Eaton but as soon as it began to climb, the engine growled and the clutch squealed as Mina progressed down the gears. Bought second-hand five years ago, it was showing signs of its age. Perhaps she could afford a new one with the money Hilary would be leaving her. She would make sure it was the same colour with identical lettering. It would just be less of a faff getting around the Peaks. At the brow of the hill, she passed three small cottages, two of which looked shut up, probably holiday lets closed for the season. A painted sign next to a five-bar gate announced she was at Hallows Farm and the track leading to the house looked decent enough, more suited to a four by four but without any perilous-looking potholes. She was wrong. About halfway down, the track deteriorated and the van lurched to one side and stayed there.

Mina got out of the van. There didn't appear to be any damage done but one wheel had sunk into the pothole. She'd need a push to get out of it and here was an excuse as good as any to knock on the door. She set off down the track and a dog barked as it picked up her approach.

'Hello!'

No one answered her call and Mina was relieved to see that the dog was chained up although he was straining on the leash, his barks reverberating around the yard. She went up to the front door and banged on it hard with her fist. The door remained shut and, as she looked around her, Mina realised that there were no other vehicles on the drive. Whoever owned the farm was out. She made her way back down the drive, past her van and came out onto the road.

'Is everything all right?' A woman was standing in the doorway of the only cottage that looked inhabited.

'I've got my van stuck in one of the potholes on the drive to the farm. I need a push.'

'Hold on.' The woman retreated. 'Gerry!' Moments later, a man appeared pulling a jumper over his head.

'What's the problem?'

'The lady's van's stuck on the Hallows' drive.'

'Let me have a look.' He followed Mina up the drive, trying to damp down his tousled hair. 'It's a bloody mess this path. I keep telling them to fix it. I even offered them some gravel to put in the holes.'

'I'm well and truly stuck.'

He leant under the van to look at the wheel. 'No damage done. I think I'll push you from the front if you can hop in and put the gears in reverse.'

Mina slid into the driver's seat and started the engine. Gerry expertly rocked the van until it was out of the hole then, standing to her side, shouted instructions so she was able to back up down the track. She wound down her window to thank him.

'Who was it you were wanting to see?'

'I was looking for the girl, Catherine.'

'Catherine? It's a Friday, she'll either be at school or wandering around somewhere.' He looked across to the woman. 'She's looking for Cathy, Mum.' The woman shrugged and went back inside. 'Wasn't Lorna in the house?' he asked.

'I don't think so. Her car wasn't there.'

'It sounds like they're both out. Can I give them a message?'

'I'm not sure. Well, if you don't mind. I just wanted to thank Catherine for visiting my mum in hospital. She died this week and, well, I wanted to let her know too.'

'Died?' He looked across at the closed door of his mother's house. 'Maybe I should let Lorna know and get her to tell Cathy. Cathy's only young. It's hard getting news like that.'

'I'm staying down at the village at the moment, if she wants to talk to me. I've a room at The Nettle Inn.'

'I'll let them know.' He moved away, keen to get back to the warmth of the house.

'Can I ask you something?' she shouted after him. 'Is she related to the Valerie Hallows buried in Cold Eaton?'

'Who?' He peered closer at her. 'Oh, yes. Why do you ask?'

'I saw the grave, that's all, and I made the connection.'

'All the Hallows are from up around here. Cold Eaton's where they go to get buried. There aren't many Hallows left now.' He glanced at her and saw Mina flinch at his words. 'I'm sorry to hear about your mum. I'll be sure to let Lorna know so that she can tell Catherine.'

'You will tell Lorna, though, I can speak to Catherine if it helps.'

'I'll do that. Be careful about asking about the grave, though. Catherine is currently obsessed with her ancestors. Last year it was the history of the gallows here, this year it's her family.'

'The gallows?' Mina couldn't keep the horror out of her voice.

'They used to hang poachers on that low you can see over there. Some say there's been some ghostly sightings and Catherine wanted to know all the stories about the place. I was more than happy to oblige.'

'You haven't seen a ghost yourself?'

'Of course not but there is a strange energy up here. Then Lorna came around and asked me not to tell any more stories as Catherine couldn't sleep at night.'

'And now she's asking about her family.'

Gerry turned to go. 'Teenagers are a mystery to me.' He made a grimace. 'As I said, perhaps it'd be better not to ask about the grave.'

42

It was late on Friday evening. The team dispersed after their meeting but both Dahl and Connie gravitated towards Sadler's office. Connie made to shut the door but Sadler shook his head.

'Get Matthews in here too.'

'But—' Connie caught sight of Sadler's face and went in search of Matthews who was putting on her coat.

'We're having a wash-up in Sadler's office. Do you want to come?'

'Me?' Matthews took off her coat and replaced it on the hanger.

Connie was shocked to see tears in Matthews's eyes. 'Is everything all right?'

'I just thought I'd shot my bolt again. Story of my life.'

Ashamed, Connie couldn't look at her. 'You've got your own way of doing things, that's all.'

A Chinese takeaway arrived and Sadler cleared his desk so they could spread the foil containers across it. Connie expected Dahl to make an excuse to leave early but he was tucking into the fried rice as if he hadn't eaten for days.

Sadler drummed his chopsticks on his desk. 'No news yet on the saline drip. I've no idea what's taking them so long. But we have six nursing staff on Oncology B ward who had access to Hilary Kemp on Wednesday morning. We also have the breakfast team. No visitors but various other hospital personnel, such as dieticians, who passed through the ward that morning.'

'Plus we have someone of interest, Catherine Hallows, the teenage hospital visitor identified by Mina Kemp,' said Dahl, shovelling rice into his mouth. 'I can't say if she visited that morning, though.'

Connie took a swig from her can of Coke. 'I think it's an important line of enquiry that we need to explore. Catherine visited Hilary in hospital in the week before her death but appears to have done so without other hospital staff noticing. This is a girl who can access hospital rooms undetected. It's also interesting that Mina gave the impression of wanting me to check out Catherine, although I'm not sure why she was so interested.'

'She's fourteen so a responsible adult will need to be present when we interview her. We're planning to go back to the hospital on Monday,' said Dahl.

'How is Mina?' asked Sadler.

'She's grieving and very protective over her mother, which is natural. I also get the impression she's holding things back but it's hard to identify anything specific.'

Sadler nodded. 'I think it's possibly significant that Mina is worried about Catherine in some way. Surely, though, a schoolgirl isn't going to have the means to get hold of drugs.'

'It's unlikely but not impossible,' said Matthews. 'We've not identified any reason why she would want to harm Hilary Kemp either.'

'Should we look into this?' asked Connie. 'I can do some

digging into the family, although Mina doesn't think the girl was able to see Hilary in the last few days of her life. Mina specifically asked that only she be given access to her mother.'

'Interesting that Catherine was still trying to talk to Hilary, though,' pointed out Matthews.

'Shall I take this forward?' asked Connie.

'Please.' Sadler put down his chopsticks. 'In the meantime, we have St Bertram's on heightened security, which won't be immediately evident to visitors over the weekend. We're keeping the news contained. I briefed the comms team today and there's been no sniff of it in any media outlets. Let's try to keep it that way this weekend at least.'

'You don't want us to put any overtime in?' asked Connie, desperate to avoid a lonely weekend.

Sadler shook his head. 'Not for the moment. I need those toxicology results. A tampered drip is one thing. I want to know if it contributed to her death.'

Connie sighed and threw her carton in the bin. 'That's it, I'm done.'

'What about the connection to Nell Colley and Ingrid Neale?' asked Matthews. 'According to Connie we now know that Hilary knew Ingrid.'

'What about Nell?' asked Dahl.

Connie sighed. 'The photo I took on my phone is shit.' She reached into her handbag and passed it to Dahl. She could see him squinting at it. 'I should have taken the original photo off Mina, but she said she'd found it amongst her mother's things so it was hard to demand it from a grieving relative without going into the specifics of our suspicions.'

'I can't even see their faces, just five blurry figures.'

'I know. I was taking the photo and the phone rang. Mina said she'd email me a scan of the photo today.' Irritated, Connie took back the phone.

Sadler began to neatly stack the containers in the paper bag that came with the delivery. 'Ingrid Neale's death is going to be very difficult to reopen. She was cremated so there are no remains to subject to toxicology tests. I've talked to Bill who's checked his PM reports. Ingrid had inflammation on her lungs consistent with death from an asthma attack. There's also no evidence she received any visitors on the day she died. It wouldn't be considered suspicious if we hadn't identified a link with Nell Colley.'

'You think Nell's death *is* suspicious?' asked Dahl.

'I don't know.' Sadler looked at the remains of the food. 'Have we found out any information on the book she was writing?'

'Mayfield looked through her bank accounts,' said Connie, 'searching for any proof of a laptop purchase because we didn't find one at the property. She'd have to write her book on something. Her neighbour thought she might have intended to write the memoir out longhand but we didn't find any evidence of this. Or perhaps she hadn't yet started it.'

'Possibly the latter, according to her neighbour. Remember she was surprised that Nell kept putting it off,' said Dahl.

'I know but surely she must have written some kind of notes as she was arranging her ideas. We have two witnesses who confirm that Nell was writing the memoir. The solicitor you met and Nell's neighbour. So where's the evidence of it?'

'Perhaps a laptop was bought years ago and has been stolen?' said Matthews.

'If it's been stolen where's everything else? Notes, research material and so on.'

They looked at each other in silence and Dahl shrugged. 'I had a good look downstairs.'

'A memoir.' Matthews leant back in her seat. 'Why would you put off writing a memoir you'd decided to start?'

'Because it was painful,' said Connie.

'Precisely,' said Matthews. 'If it's to do with her childhood perhaps Ingrid was involved.'

'Nell could also be another of the girls in the photo,' said Connie. 'Once I get that photo I'll show it to Janet Goodhew. She should be able to recognise her neighbour as a teenager.'

'Can we officially declare the other two cases suspicious?' asked Matthews.

'I'm going to think about it over the weekend,' said Sadler.

'But there's a link.' Connie's voice rose. 'It's too much coincidence. Dahl and I are looking into two deaths and we find a link with a third confirmed suspicious death.'

'On Monday I'll talk to Llewellyn.' Sadler's voice was firm. 'Matthews, you're duty DI this weekend, aren't you?' Matthews nodded. 'Call me if anything comes up. I need to spend time going over the case.'

'Nell's memoir might hold the key.' Matthews neatly folded up her foil container and added it to the bag. 'That's a book I'd like to read.'

43

Falling leaves from the large trees lining the streets of High Oaks had created a mulch of slippery foliage on the pavements that was, officially, the local authority's problem. However, one of Mina's regular clients had a front garden directly underneath one of the trees. Mina would happily have stayed in the cocoon she'd created in Cold Eaton but Professor Davey had other ideas. He'd left three messages on her mobile, pleading with her to clear the leaves from his lawn. Every autumn was torture for this avid gardener and he stood on his front step, his face a visage of agony.

'Will it affect the spring bulbs?'

Mina sighed. The same question every year. 'It shouldn't do. I'll hoover the leaves up in no time.'

'Can't you do it by hand? There's less chance of damaging the plants underneath.'

'I'm not so sure about that. The air won't touch the stems if I use the machine. It's a tried and tested method.'

She passed Professor Davey the end of her extension lead and she could hear it being plugged in down the hall. Mina had never once been inside the house despite this being the third autumn where they'd had the debate on whether she should be clearing leaves by hand. He was clearly a man who valued his privacy, a young fogey if that was the right word.

For Professor Davey, despite his academic achievements, was barely forty and an expert on the Romans in Derbyshire, unusual plants and keeping his house away from prying eyes.

Mina tested the garden hoover and, putting it on its lowest setting, began with the leaves on the small patch of grass near the bay window. She was aware of him standing watching her and turned her back on him. Once the grass was done, she moved to the side bed, carefully hoovering around each plant. When she had removed the majority of the leaves, she retrieved her rake and began on the hard to reach bits. She looked up at the professor. He nodded at a woman who was passing along the pavement and retreated into the house.

After she was done, she sat in her van and typed the name that Connie had mentioned to her into her phone. *Nell Colley.* An address came up on 192.com from the electoral register but it was behind a paywall. Mina took her debit card from her wallet and paid for ten credits to reveal an address in one of the nearby streets.

Outside the house on Pullen Road, she hesitated for a moment. The garden was well kept and empty of leaves. Someone had clearly been doing some gardening, possibly the woman dressed in a dark blue mac and a red bobble hat pulled down over her ears who was picking up rubbish from the pavement.

Mina wound down the window. 'Is this where Nell Colley lived?'

The woman looked up, her face red from exertion. 'It is. Did you know her?'

'My mum did.'

'You know she passed away?'

Mina nodded.

'I'm still reeling a bit from it, to be honest. Did I let your mum know? I'm Janet. I wrote to those whose names I found in her address book.'

Mina shook her head. 'My mother died recently. I don't think she was in touch with Nell.'

'Oh no. How did you find out about Nell then?'

'I saw it in the paper,' Mina lied. 'I've just started looking for some school friends of Mum's. She might have been able to help me.'

'I'm sorry, love.'

'You didn't know Nell from school?'

'Me? I've lived in Bampton nearly forty years but I wasn't brought up here.'

Mina switched off the engine. 'Did Nell have any old friends she saw or spoke about?'

The woman considered. 'Not that I remember.'

'If I showed you an old photo, do you think you'd recognise Nell?'

If Janet was surprised, she didn't show it. Mina reached into the back of her van and pulled out the two photos. She handed over the first and the woman brightened. 'Is that your mum? What a lovely photo. I remember having one done exactly the same when I was at school.'

Janet handed the photo back to Mina and took the other one. She squinted at the image, her face brightening. 'Here she is. Nell.' She pointed at the girl on the furthest right, her face in profile. She was the tallest of the girls by a few inches, her fair hair curling over her shoulders. Janet turned the photo over.

'GIVEN. What a funny thing to write. Given what? Maybe

it's not "given", it's initials. They stand for something like, I don't know, the girls' names. G.I.V.E.N. Look at the end. N for Nell.'

'What? Let me have a look.' Mina took the photo off Janet and looked at it. GIVEN. 'They've moved some of the letters around. The girl on the left is Valerie. You don't recognise any of the others? This one here, second from the left, is Ingrid.'

'I don't recognise anyone except Nell. She would have been tickled to have seen herself in those photos. I don't ever remember her mentioning school. She really kept herself to herself over the years. I'd have loved to show it to her.'

Mina studied the tall girl with her body turned away from the camera. Nell had clearly done all right in life. High Oaks was a wealthy neighbourhood, well out of the reach of most Peak residents. 'Did she have a happy life?'

Janet shrugged. 'I suppose so. She worked in the solicitor's in town. She never married but she seemed, well, happy, I suppose. Good luck with sorting everything out with your mum. You might want to print that picture of her at school on the funeral leaflet. Best to remember them like that. In better days.'

'At school, you mean?'

'Exactly. I mean, it's a time of innocence, isn't it? Things are never the same again.'

44

Camilla entered the dining room carrying a huge Le Creuset casserole dish, placed it in the middle of the table and took off the lid with a 'ta da'. Ben clapped as steam engulfed them and lifted up his plate while Samuel issued a long, overdramatic groan.

'I can't eat anything. I'm not hungry.'

Ben looked at his mother with sly eyes. 'He had three toffee apples at the fireworks.'

Their father reached over and picked up the serving spoon. 'You need to eat something properly, Sam, or you'll be sick. Give me your dish.' John put a spoonful of beef casserole onto Sam's plate. 'Are you sure Nana didn't fancy coming over?'

Camilla looked at Sadler. 'I did try to persuade her but she said she wanted to get home. A Saturday night in November, it's not really surprising. It was chilly out and she was determined to come but I got the impression that it took it out of her. How did she seem to you, Francis?'

Sadler took the spoon from John and dug into the stew. 'She seemed fine, although I've not really had a chance to talk to her properly since she was in hospital. She had a couple of visitors when I went to see her at home.'

'That's not a surprise. I've never met anyone with so many

friends.' John looked at the siblings. 'Neither of you have taken after her.'

'They were a lifesaver with Dad. He was always at the architecture practice or on site. Mum relied on friends to babysit, have a social life of her own.' She rounded on her husband. 'I *have* friends.'

He smirked. 'Not like your mother. That house is like a bus terminus sometimes, people going in and out.'

'Did you report the broken window?' asked Sadler.

'I rang 111 like you suggested. They took the details and gave me an incident number. It all felt a bit pointless given that nothing was taken.' Camilla looked at the children and mouthed 'later' to Sadler.

After dinner had finished, marred only by a spat between the two children over who had left the most on their plate, John took them into the living room and switched on the TV. Sadler began to stack the plates and carried them through to the kitchen. 'What was it you wanted to tell me about Mum?'

Camilla opened the dishwasher. 'When I stayed the night at Mum's, there was a leaflet under her bedclothes.'

'A leaflet?'

'Well, not a leaflet. I don't know what you call it. A flyer maybe. It was advertising a tea dance.'

'Mum's started going to tea dances? That's nothing strange. She'll try anything once. One of her friends has probably asked her along.'

'Not for now.' Camilla wiped her hands on a cloth and faced him. 'I wouldn't mind that, although it's not really Mum's thing, is it? There was a date on the flyer, June, but no year. Nineteen fifties or sixties, I'd say.'

'Do you think she'd been having a clearout?'

'I don't know. I'd never seen it before, not that it means anything, but what was it doing in her bed?'

'Good question. If you don't think it was there accidentally, and it doesn't sound like it, she must have been hiding it there.'

Camilla relaxed slightly and gave him a hug, putting her face against his chest. 'Do you know what I like about you, Francis? You always take me seriously. It was the same when you were a little boy. You listened to what I had to say even though you were five years younger than me.'

Sadler put his arms around his sister. 'It sounds strange. Mother's never been particularly secretive, has she?'

'Not really. Even stranger is the fact that after I brought her home from hospital, she went upstairs to get herself settled and when I went into the bedroom after she'd come back down, the leaflet had gone.'

'She'd gone into the room to retrieve it.'

'Exactly. The thing is, I also found a jumper in the laundry basket that I think had blood on it.'

'Blood? Maybe she'd fallen before and not told us.'

'You think that might be it?'

'I don't know. It's a possibility, I suppose. Was she injured when she went into hospital?'

'She never said anything and I'm sure the hospital would have told me. It must have been from, I don't know, earlier that day or perhaps the day before.'

'Why don't you ask her?'

'Just like that?' Camilla pulled away. 'Do you think she'll give me an honest answer?'

'Why not? There could be an innocent explanation for both the leaflet and the stain. She might have cut herself in the kitchen, for example. That would account for the blood.'

'Will you ask her?'

'Me?' Sadler stared at Camilla. 'She's more likely to open up to you, isn't she? Why on earth do you think she'd talk to me?'

'Oh, I don't know. Forget I asked.'

*

Sadler walked back from Camilla's house in the cold Bampton night with the sulphuric smell still hanging in the air from the celebrations. A group of teenagers were throwing bangers at each other near the canal but scarpered at his approach. As he neared his cottage, he saw a van parked next to Clive's sports car, the lettering on the side familiar. He went over to it and rapped on the window. 'Mina?'

She wound down the window. 'You were right. You were easy to find.'

'Go on. Tell me how you did it.'

'I had your first name and the fact that you're a detective. Your colleague that I met this week, DC Childs, said her boss was called Sadler. I typed Francis Sadler into 192.com and this address came up.'

'How did you know it was the right one?'

'I didn't. I've just been sitting here waiting for someone to come home. I nearly gave up, especially when those kids started acting up. I had visions of one of them losing an eye or ending up in the canal. I nearly drove away. I don't think I could face any more trouble.'

'You're not in trouble, Mina. Unless there's something you want to tell me.'

She looked up at him, her usual competence fighting with a glimmer of fear he could see in her face.

'Do you want to come in?'

She got out of the van and followed him into his house. Sadler, for the first time he could remember, was conscious of the shabbiness of his furnishings. Old pieces, some of them given to him by his mother when she'd downsized. At least it was tidy. Just.

'This is nice.' He'd expected her to look at his bookcases, but instead she made her way to his windowsill and picked up an orchid, given to him by Camilla for his birthday, which was now looking sorry for itself. She picked up the pot and presented it to him. 'Chuck it. It's beyond saving.'

Sadler laughed and took it off her. 'Take a seat.'

She sat down and picked at the arms of the sofa. 'It took me ages to pluck up courage to come and see you, and now I'm here, I don't know where to start.'

He put the plant next to the front door and came back, sitting opposite her. 'You've spoken to my colleague, Connie. Is that why you're here, for more details on your mother's death?'

Mina nodded. 'I guess so. I don't understand what's going on.'

'Neither do we, right at this moment. We do, however, suspect your mother's drip may have been tampered with.'

'You're not even sure of that?'

'The bag shows signs of damage. That's all I can tell you because it's all we know. It may yet be an accident and may have no bearing on your mother's death.' He checked her reaction. She was attentive, but behind that he thought he detected a hint of relief. 'I hear you're having a short stint away from your house.'

'Well—'

'You're not a suspect but we do need to be able to get hold of you.'

'To be honest I'm staying in Cold Eaton. Your detective found me there. Connie.'

'Cold Eaton. That's an unusual place to be.'

'I'm staying at the pub, The Nettle Inn. I needed some space.' She paused, unwilling to continue.

'Is everything else okay? I remember you saying something about trying to find someone. Connie says you have a photograph of your mother as a teenager.'

'I think I've found out the names of a couple of the girls. Connie was right. One of them is Ingrid Neale and I found out today another was Nell Colley.'

'Nell Colley. Are you sure?'

'According to her neighbour, it was definitely a young Nell in the photo.'

'And you said when I met you at North Lees Hall that you were looking for someone else.'

'Oh that. It was nothing really. Valerie has died.'

'Died?' Sadler couldn't keep the concern out of his voice. 'When did she die?'

'In 1963.'

'Oh.'

'You don't need to worry about Valerie. Valerie is long dead.' She looked out of the window. 'Perhaps I should be going.'

'I can make some coffee, if you like. You've only just arrived.'

Mina, however, having satisfied herself that Sadler had no more information he could give her, looked anxious to leave. He walked her to the van and watched her depart. *Valerie is long dead.* Sadler repeated the words to himself. *Why does that phrase sound so ominous?*

45

Mina arrived in time to watch the ceremonial lighting of the fire. A listless Sunday, where images of the past had jostled for attention, had convinced her that tomorrow she should pick up her work and get back into a routine. The police investigation would proceed at its own course and Valerie, it seemed, was lost to the mists of time. A flaming torch, the type only usually seen on *Game of Thrones*, was produced and dipped into the gigantic pile of wood that had been built that day. The Guy disintegrated quickly. There was a loud, visceral cheer when he toppled off his perch into the heart of the flames. Unlike Emily's effigy he wasn't dressed in a suit but corduroy trousers and an old Barbour jacket. Why had Emily dressed hers in a suit? An odd choice for a teenager. The bonfire blazed so strongly that Mina could feel the heat down one side of her face. She looked around at the village collected together, about a hundred figures gazing into the flames, their faces in shadow.

There was a table in the corner of the field where the smell of frying onions mingled with smoke from the fire. Mina bought herself a hot dog and, although her stomach was a knot of tension, she forced herself to swallow it, aware she'd need the calories to go to work tomorrow. She watched a group of children running around with sparklers, trying to write their names in the air. She could only remember one bonfire party that Grumps had taken her to, where she'd gorged on toffee apples and gingerbread. Her mother had refused to come but Mina had never asked for an explanation as to why she didn't like Guy Fawkes Night. Another mystery to add to the others. Yet the sounds and smells produced the pull of nostalgia. She longed for her mother as she stood amongst these families making their own memories.

She looked around for someone to talk to. People were either paired off or knew each other. She put her empty glass of punch down on a trestle table and slipped away unnoticed. The track back to the pub took her past the large manor house. There was no lighting so she switched on the torch on her phone to guide herself over the stony ground. The house was in darkness except for an upstairs window where a lamp burnt. A figure passed in front of the window reminding Mina of Sadler and the conversation they'd had about a mad woman in the attic the first time they'd met. The welcome sight of The Nettle Inn bathed in light lifted her spirits and, as Mina pushed the door open, she saw that all the tables were full so she headed to the bar where Emily was pouring a glass of beer.

'Oh, it's you. Been up to the bonfire?' A group of men were sitting on stools to one side and they turned to look at her.

'It's quite a sight. I thought you'd be there.'

'I was there for the start, then I nipped back. It's a busy evening for us here too. What can I get you?'

'Just a Diet Coke.'

Emily handed her a bottle and an empty glass and took her money. Mina pulled up a stool the other side of the bar to the men, one of whom was looking at her with unashamed curiosity. 'You from the village?' he shouted to her across the bar.

She shook her head. 'Bampton.' He was a short man in his fifties with what remained of his fair hair cropped short. 'Not far.'

'Far enough,' he muttered.

'My mum used to come here a fair bit, though. You might have known her, Hilary Kemp.'

The man looked confused and shook his head.

'Can I show you a picture of her?' She slid the photo of her mother over the bar towards him.

The man shook his head again. 'Never seen her before, love.'

Mina passed over the other photo. 'These were her friends.'

The man stared at it for a moment and pointed at the girl on the left. 'What was her name?' He angled the photo into the light. 'She was a teenager when I was a young lad. I can't remember her name. Began with a G.'

'I thought it might have been Valerie Hallows?'

'Hallows. That's it. I remember now. Her family are from Hallows Hill. Weren't you friendly with her?' Mina looked up in surprise and saw he was directing his question to Emily Fenn.

Emily flushed and moved to serve a customer.

'I went up there looking for someone called Catherine. She visited my mother in hospital.'

The man laughed. 'You won't have got much of a welcome. It's a close knit world up there. Can I see the photo again?'

He studied the image. 'It's taken in the churchyard. You can see the old yew tree behind it.'

'You mean the stonework's the church.'

'That's right. Em?' He turned but Emily had left the bar and headed off into the kitchen.

'The churchyard? That's a funny place to take a picture of girls in tennis whites.'

'There used to be a court in the field next to the graves. It's all overgrown now but I played on it myself.'

'So why not take a photo there rather than go into the churchyard?'

'Why don't you ask Emily?'

'You think she might know some of the girls?'

'Know the girls?' The man grinned and pointed with a grubby finger to the fourth girl. 'She'll know who that one is.'

The girl had wavy fair hair that looked thin and lank. She was slim but with large hips and short legs. The type that might run to fat later in life. Mina squinted at her features and made the connection. Emily was taking over two plates of food to one of the far tables. Despite the impression of strength she gave, her shoulders were hunched from years of running a busy pub. Behind the dumpy frame and stooped posture, however, Mina could see she had the same shape as the girl in the photo.

'Do you know—' She wanted to ask the man about the other three girls but he'd disappeared off towards the toilets. His group of friends were finishing their drinks and talking about picking their kids up from the bonfire. Mina waited for a few minutes but the man never reappeared and his friends dispersed.

Emily came back to the bar and shouted something at her assistant. The blonde girl nodded and Emily disappeared out of the front door.

Mina turned over the photo and looked once more at the figures. Four of the five girls identified. Valerie, Ingrid Neale from the big house, Emily who'd claimed she'd never heard of Mina's mother, and Nell Colley who had been writing a memoir. It wasn't much and Mina wondered where this journey was taking her. Was it helping, digging into the past, or was it making her grief worse? Mina looked around her.

'Is Emily coming back?'

The blonde girl shook her head. 'Not for a couple of hours. She's going to help with the clearing up of the bonfire.'

'She said she had too much to do here.'

The girl shrugged. 'We can manage.'

Mina finished her drink and went up to her room. On the landing, she saw, illuminated by a car's headlights, the figure of Emily hurrying away from the pub towards the manor house. With her head down, she had the air of a woman with a purpose in mind. Emily, supposedly occupied with the busy pub, had disappeared after overhearing the discussion of the photo. Mina looked around her, wondering if she should stay. Emily was hiding something. Mina thought of the deserted canal boat and of her childhood home and felt faint with longing. She couldn't return to either home yet. She sat on the bed and put her head in her hands.

46

Sadler, sitting opposite Llewellyn, was shocked to discover that his boss, for once, appeared to be at a loss for words. As Sadler handed him the papers, Llewellyn took off his jacket and rolled up his shirt sleeves, clearing his throat.

'I've not had to do this for years. I was still in uniform when I was last involved in an exhumation. I remember it played on my mind for years afterwards. The white tent, the lights, the machine going in. There's nothing natural about digging up the dead.'

Sadler shifted in his chair. 'I think you might be the only serving policeman who's been involved in an official exhumation. I've looked back through the records and the last was in 1983, which is probably the one you attended. We've asked a specialist firm to get involved in the removal of the body. Our own personnel won't be doing the digging. You don't have to be there.'

'Oh I'll be there all right. My staff will be there coordinating and observing. They're not doing this by themselves. Is there no other way?'

'I don't think so. I've spent the weekend thinking about it and today sorting out the mechanics. I just need your go ahead. We have a link between Hilary Kemp whose death is being treated as suspicious and now both Ingrid Neale and

Nell Colley whose deaths were being, if not investigated, then scrutinised by Connie and Dahl.'

'I see they've confirmed the evidence of diamorphine hydrochloride in the saline drip bag.'

Sadler nodded. 'It's a soluble form of morphine.'

'Is it definite that they'd find the drug in Nell Colley's body if she was given an overdose?'

'Bill says it should be possible to identify raised levels that would constitute a lethal concentration of the drug.'

'What about the other possible victim, Ingrid Neale? Who ordered her cremation?'

'Her family, who say it was stated in Ingrid's will.'

Llewellyn sighed. 'Which leaves us with Nell Colley. You don't think we should have picked it up before?'

'I don't think, in this instance, that there was anything to raise our suspicions. But now we have a link between Hilary Kemp and Nell Colley. Given Ingrid Neale's cremation, we might never be able to fully investigate her death.'

Llewellyn rubbed his face with his large hands. 'What do the family say about Nell's exhumation?'

'There's no family, just a neighbour who benefits from the will. She's naturally shocked and was initially resistant to the exhumation but it was put to her in terms that the coroner had ordered it.'

'Not much she could do then. Think it's significant that she objected?'

'There could be a genuine reason.'

'Letting sleeping dogs lie, I suppose. Who'll be there?'

'The team: me, Connie, Dahl.'

'Not Matthews?'

'She worked the weekend.'

Llewellyn grunted. 'She's not in a bad mood, is she? She couldn't honestly have expected to take charge of a complex investigation like this.'

'She can take credit for us initially focusing on Nell Colley. I might have been inclined to sign off the file. Everything was done by the book.'

'Well, Matthews certainly does that. You need one copper like that but hopefully not all of them, otherwise a boring place it would be. Anyone else going to be there?'

'Bill Shields. If we had a suspect, we'd need the defence pathologist there too. It's not relevant as we're still in the dark. Bill will be overseeing the medical aspect of the exhumation.'

Llewellyn looked at his watch. 'What time did you say tomorrow?'

'Eight a.m.'

Llewellyn nodded. 'I'll be there.' He leant forward and picked up a report. 'There's something else I wanted to talk to you about.'

'Sir?'

'Don't look so concerned. We made three arrests last night in relation to a spate of burglaries. Caught two of them red handed. A mother and son, would you believe it? The little lad's ten, nearly eleven. The mother was caught lifting him up ready to climb inside an open bathroom window. The boy must be a contortionist despite his age as, according to the arresting officer, it didn't look like even a cat could get into the space.'

'Who was the third?'

'The mother's partner keeping a watch out in the street.

One of the neighbours spotted him and called us out. A pretty good result all round, really. It'll look good on our statistics. The public seems to think we write off burglaries.'

'You mean we don't?'

'Yes, ha ha, thank you, Sadler. Anyway, the reason I'm mentioning it is I believe your mother's address is on the list. Same modus operandi – a small window, although it appears they were disturbed before anything was taken. You can let her know that the culprits have been caught.'

'I'll do that.'

Llewellyn looked up at the catch in Sadler's voice. 'Everything all right?'

'Yes, of course, someone just walked over my grave, that's all.'

*

On his way home from work, Sadler stopped by at his mother's house. A figure was bending over in the front garden planting spring bulbs in the border with the help of a dibber. Sadler had strong memories of Ginnie doing the same over the years in a different garden. As a boy he had crouched down to help her, solemnly handing her each individual bulb, taking his time whether to select a crocus, narcissus or grape hyacinth for the chosen spot. Once, when he was a teenager, he had come home unexpectedly from school, sent home because he had forgotten his cricket whites, and had found his mother in the kitchen, crying. When he'd asked what was wrong, she'd been brusque, retrieving his clothes from the basket and running a hot iron over them.

He'd mentioned the incident later to Camilla, who'd muttered something about the change and, confused, he'd not mentioned it again. Mina straightened her back and came face to face with him.

They looked at each other in astonishment and Sadler noticed that Mina's hands were shaking as she brushed a coil of hair from her face. 'What are you doing here?' she asked and her eyes went to the car he'd parked next to the wall. 'Are you following me?'

Sadler took in her tired face, flushed not only from the planting but from the strain of recent events. 'My mother lives here.'

'But a Camilla Stevens called me.' Mina looked stricken, embarrassed after their weekend meeting.

'That's my sister. This is my mother's house. Ginnie Sadler.'

Mina groaned. 'I'd actually make a crap detective then.'

He held his hand out to her and she took it, unashamed of the crumbling soil on her fingers. 'I didn't realise it was your mother. Camilla didn't mention it.'

'No reason why she would. I should have made the connection. There can't be that many gardeners working in Bampton.'

'There's just me at this time of year. The other guy broke his foot over the summer fixing a drystone wall.'

Sadler stared at her for a moment, taking in her wan face and tired eyes. 'I don't suppose it matters.' He looked at his watch. 'Is Mum in?'

'I think so. I haven't seen her at all. Camilla showed me the shed, although I have my own tools and I can see what needs doing. I found the spring bulbs and am planting as I clear the weeds.'

'She's not even brought you a cup of tea?'

Mina put her hand behind her back and stretched, letting the vertebrae click in relief. 'Not to worry. Perhaps she doesn't welcome the help. I always have my own flask anyway.'

Sadler frowned towards the house. 'I'll check she's okay.'

Mina turned back to the bulbs, swirling them in the bucket with her hands, her own version of Sadler's boyhood random selection. Sadler used his key to enter the door.

'Mum?' He looked to the left and saw Ginnie standing watching Mina at work. 'Is everything all right?'

Ginnie looked as if she was in a trance. 'Who is she?'

'The gardener? She's called Mina. Camilla asked her to give you a hand.'

'Yes, but who *is* she?'

Sadler joined his mother at the window and watched as Mina, unaware of the scrutiny, carried on with her planting.

'She's called Mina and her company goes by the name of The Land Girl. Haven't you been out to talk to her yet? I'm sure she'll do whatever tasks you ask of her.'

'It's hard seeing your garden in someone else's hands.'

'I can understand that.'

'Do you know her last name?'

'It's Kemp. Why? Is it important?'

Ginnie turned away from the window. 'You see a lot of people around Bampton. I thought I recognised her, that's all.' For the first time she focused on her son. 'Why are you here? Is everything all right?'

'I was checking on you.' He looked at his mother but she had moved back to the window and was watching Mina. 'If you're concerned about your safety after the break-in, I wanted to let you know that we've made some arrests. They were breaking and entering through tiny windows so they were almost certainly responsible for your incident.'

'It was random?' She looked across at him. 'I wasn't targeted?'

'Only targeted in as much as you'd left a window open. Are you sure everything is all right?'

Ginnie hesitated for a moment. 'Everything's fine.'

Sadler thought of the tea dance notice. Could he mention that? His mother's naturally pale skin was even whiter than normal. He found he couldn't articulate the words. Instead he focused on the tangible. 'When Camilla was tidying up while you were in hospital, she found something.'

Ginnie whirled around and stared at him. 'What? What did she find?'

The distance that had always lain between him and his mother had widened over the years. As their eyes met, Ginnie almost as tall as Sadler, he was surprised to feel the prickle of fear. He shook it away.

'There was a jumper with blood on it. Camilla didn't know whether to mention it to you.'

'Oh that. I had a nosebleed before I called the ambulance. It was heavy so I took off my top and used it to mop it up. She should have asked me.'

'Everything else is all right?'

But his mother had turned back towards the window and was once more watching Mina.

'Everything's fine,' she murmured, continuing her vigil.

47

When Mina had finished in the garden, she lugged her tools back to the van and took a long swig from the water bottle she kept on the passenger seat. Aware of her full bladder, she looked briefly to the house. Should she knock and ask to use the toilet? Perhaps Sadler's mother was more ill than he'd mentioned, for the elderly woman had made no move to come and see the results of Mina's hard work. She hesitated for a moment, and then slid into the van and started the engine.

At St Bertram's she nipped into the toilets and then hung around in the foyer waiting for Catherine to finish her shift. At half three, the girl came out of the lift wearing not her school uniform but an old-fashioned dress in a pale lemon fabric spattered with mauve polka dots. Dressed so unsuitably for the season, she'd draped her grey school cardigan around her shoulders to keep herself warm and was clutching the collar to her chin. She spotted Mina straight away, hesitated for a moment, and then made her way to the desk and pulled her badge over her head.

'I'm sorry about Mrs Kemp.' She refused to look at Mina, instead scratching her name on a clipboard, her signature fat and childlike. 'I got your message from Gerry. It was nice of you to let us know.'

'I'm sorry I missed you at the farm.'

The girl made a face, still not looking at Mina. 'I have to go.'

'I just want to talk about what she said when you last spoke to Mum.'

The girl scrunched up her eyes. 'She wasn't making much sense. I was frightened.'

'Frightened? It was you who came up to me and told me about the Cutting.'

'Oh that.' The girl sounded bored but the words had a fake weariness to them.

'I've been having a think. It might be to do with the railway, down near the Topley Trail. Did she mention anything else about trains?'

'She didn't say anything about a railway. She talked to me about the drowned village. You know, over at Derwent.' The girl didn't want to speak to her, desperate to get away, her eyes darting from side to side.

'The drowned village? What did she say?'

'Not much. She just wanted to talk about the village that was drowned. I don't know why.'

'And you're sure you didn't see her on the day she died?'

The girl shook her head.

'Did you try?'

'No! Why are you asking me about this?'

'Who's Valerie Hallows?'

Catherine looked furious. 'My grandmother. She died before I was born. A long time ago. Why are you asking me this?'

'Gerry said you were very interested in your family history.'

Catherine recoiled. 'That's nothing to do with you. I'm doing some research, that's all. We're an old family. Up there is my land and my heritage. I'm interested in what happened to my family. There are those who want to help and those who don't.'

'Who's helping you?'

'I'm not talking to you.' Catherine raised her voice and the woman in charge of the reception desk came over towards them.

'Is everything all right, Cathy?'

'I'm just talking to Catherine about her visiting my mother before she died.'

The woman looked from Catherine to Mina. 'Is there a problem?'

'She's asking me about my grandmother. That's not got anything to do with her.'

'Why don't you go home, Cathy, unless this lady has anything else to ask you?'

Catherine scuttled off, leaving behind the scent of cheap perfume. Mina turned to the woman. 'Isn't she a bit young to be volunteering for this? Surely she must see patients who are very ill?'

'Cathy likes doing the work and the patients like her. We get very good feedback from them. We've others from her year group that don't go down so well.' The woman hesitated. 'Catherine is a little . . .'

'What?'

'Immature, I think. She lives up on a farm in Hallows Hill. Just her and her mother. The father's long gone.'

'Gone away?'

'No, sorry, I meant he died. I didn't put it very well, did I? The Hallows have been up there farming for generations. The farm keeps getting passed down to sons who don't want it. It'll be Catherine's next but she doesn't look the farming type to me.'

'She's very thin.'

'Oh, I think she's robust enough physically, but she has, well, these obsessions of hers. I get the impression the mother's not around much. According to Catherine, her mother has a job that takes her out and about.'

'Obsessions about what?'

'Oh nothing. She just gets a bee in her bonnet about things. Never mind that. Look at me standing here gossiping and there's someone over there looking lost. I'd better leave you to it.'

The woman bustled off and Mina, at a loss, turned to go.

'She's obsessed with the railway.'

Mina looked around to see the source of the voice and spotted a large girl in a school uniform. Unlike Catherine, she hadn't changed but had stuffed her blazer into a thin rucksack.

'You mean Catherine?' Mina walked over to the girl and looked at her name tag. Noelle, no surname. 'You go to the same school?'

'Bampton Grammar, yes. We have to do loads outside school, though. It's all part of contributing to society. Only, Catherine does what she wants.'

'What do you mean?'

'We're supposed to keep our school uniforms on during the daytime but Catherine couldn't wait to get changed today. It's just one example. And she's always down at the old railway exploring. That's weird too. There's nothing to see.'

'How do you know she's always there?'

Noelle looked down at her feet. 'I live at the bottom end of Bampton. She passes our house, a lot. We're the last row before you get on the Topley Trail at that entrance. She gets the bus to Cold Eaton, not from outside school but from the one near us by the trail. I watch her sometimes and she's always coming from the direction of the old railway.'

'How long has this been happening?'

Noelle looked confused. 'I don't know. I gradually noticed that Cathy kept walking past the house. I'm sorry about your mum. Catherine told me. She liked her.'

'That's okay.' Mina turned to go.

'She was so upset she had to go home. I think she liked visiting your mum.'

Mina stopped. 'What do you mean go home? When was this?'

'On Wednesday. She came back down to sign out. We were supposed to finish at half three, the same time as school, but Cathy came down half an hour earlier and said she was upset because one of her patients had died.'

'How did you know it was my mum?'

Noelle thought for a moment. 'She must have said. She said the name or something. I knew it was Mrs Kemp, I remember her from the library too when I was small.'

'Cathy knew my mum had died on Wednesday?'

'That's right. It's not a problem, is it?'

Then why didn't she say when I just talked to her? thought Mina. *Why go through the charade of thanking me for coming to see her?*

'How did she look? I mean, was she okay when she heard about my mum?'

'I told you, she was upset. She couldn't wait to go home.'

*

In her grief, nothing made any sense. Mina and her mother had been close. Their different personalities hadn't prevented the bond between them growing and blossoming as Mina became an adult. Hilary, however, clearly had valued her privacy and what Mina had thought to be an aspect of her mother's personality was now potentially something else. Mina in the middle of her heartache was trying to uncover something that had been deliberately left in the past.

Hilary's words were coming back to haunt her and she felt adrift in her grief. She knew about plants and the colour of soil. And how the seasons melded into one another and each was as eagerly awaited as the next. She was innocent in the ways of deceit and mistrust and her head pounded at the strands that weren't unravelling. The police were investigating the death of her mother, Emily Fenn had lied about knowing the Valerie in the photos, and now the police were taking an interest in that long disbanded group of friends.

Mina had a slight advantage over the police but it felt like a millstone. They were unaware of Hilary's admission, if it was that, of killing Valerie, and of Catherine's reference to the Cutting. That embankment must be important because her mother had always avoided the railway and had refused to venture near the walking trail. The man at the steam railway had warned Mina about the Cutting. Strange tales including one of a naked man. Remembering the note left on her wind-screen, Mina thought of the little fingers clasping at the pen in the foyer. Not the same handwriting surely, and yet the scrape of pen on paper had brought to mind the note.

Instead of going to the car park further along the trail, Mina drove to Cutting Lane and pulled up at the bridge. She tucked her van into a verge and folded in the wing mirrors. It was deathly eerie. Not foggy but the air heavy with mois-ture, which gave the autumn vegetation a swampy sheen. She changed into her gardening boots, which were heavy soled with thick treads that could tackle the most boggy of terrain. She set off up the steep slope; a rail had been put against the steps and she hung onto it to steady herself on the mossy path. As she reached the top, she was nearly spun off her feet by a man rushing past her carting a small child.

'Dadeeee! Don't want to go yet. Back to the trains. Whoo whoo. Where's the choo choo? Whoo whoo.' The child was screaming with delight and the man stopped briefly to adjust the child in his arms.

'Stop it, Archie.'

The child ignored him. 'Whoo whoo.'

The man's mobile phone rang and, as Mina stood at the top of the Cutting, she could hear the conversation across the clear air.

'Where the hell are you?' A woman's furious voice. 'I said take him out for an hour not all afternoon. It's nearly dark.'

'We were delayed. Something happened. I thought I saw a girl in the tunnel but I was mistaken. I had to go back and . . . well . . . go back and look.'

'Look for what?'

'Not now. I'll tell you when I get home. This place gives me the creeps. I thought I saw a girl go into the tunnel but she never came out. I need to get us out of here.'

Mina shifted around to get a good look at the man. He was aware of her scrutiny and turned his back on her and continued down the hill out of earshot. He finished the call and began to run, hunched over the little boy, as if protecting him from rain although the sky was clear. Mina squinted after him. Why was he running? Perhaps he was late for something. When he reached a little white car on the side of the road, he took a moment to strap the child into the back seat and drove off at speed.

Mina watched the car take the corner and disappear from sight, and then looked back at the tunnel. What had he been running from?

PART THREE

Valerie

48

Monday, 15 December 1947

The little girl watched as her mother rocked the crying baby on her shoulder, holding tight to his sturdy legs as his bawls echoed around the valley. With her other hand, she clasped the sleeve of her daughter's coat, aware that the little girl was desperately trying to wriggle away. She'd put extra clothes on them both. The baby was wearing a thick cable cardigan knitted by her aunt in Llangollen. In his temper, he pulled at the fat buttons, his face puce with the effort. The girl was wearing her winter coat, which was already too small for her. Spindly arms poked out from the sleeves like pipe cleaners, a large expanse of flesh between the hem and the start of the woollen mittens. Never mind, it kept her warm enough today. She knew how cold this valley got. The intuitive knowledge of a child of these parts. Derwent valley held a chill that would take more than the winter sun and unseasonal drought to dissipate. The girl looked up at her mother, who had spotted a movement and become unnaturally still, watching transfixed as the men went about their business at the base of the church spire, tiny figures at the bottom of the valley.

'Will it be loud?' the girl whispered. 'Will it go boom?'

'It'll go more than boom,' said the stranger next to her, his rough Derbyshire accent made thicker by the Woodbine hanging out of his mouth. 'That'll give the babby something to cry about.'

The girl ignored him but her mother jiggled the child harder, trying to dampen the screams.

They'd been held back at the top of the valley, a disparate group of people forming a wall on the hill's crest. Not once did the men below look up. Many of the crowd were sightseers, here after reading an article about the church's demolition in the local newspapers. The rest knew this valley inside out. News of the dynamiting had spread around the invisible network winding through the Peaks. When the appointed day had come, people had downed tools, called in sick and bunked off school to see the act with their own eyes.

'It's a terrible shame,' her mother commented to an elderly woman. She took in the water that usually covered the church spire, left intact when the village was drowned. The water had retreated during the hot summer and, not being replenished, was still lapping around its base. The valley looked parched. A dry winter is worse than a dry summer. 'We'll be telling this tale to our grandchildren.'

'Not me.' The elderly woman caught the little girl's eye. 'The money gave us a fresh start. I'm settled where I am and I'm not going to rake over old coals. The past is finished.'

'You're here, though.'

The elderly woman didn't turn but her eyes behind her glasses filled with tears. 'Best forgotten,' she repeated.

'They'll ask anyway.' Her mother surveyed the valley. 'Don't you think?' There was a hint of a plea in her voice.

'This won't be forgotten. They say the bells have gone to Chelmorton and Cold Eaton and the pews to one of them churches in Bampton. They'll make a new history.'

The other woman was silent and the mother was compelled to continue. 'And what about the school kids standing over there? They'll remember. The fact they're here means they know about the old village. They'll remember it when it's their grandchildren who are drinking water that's come from this reservoir.'

She pointed towards a group of children, most of whom the girl recognised from the drowned village. Some of those families had been entwined for generations, father going to school with mother, grandparents working in the fields, ancestors coming together in times of sickness, blight and strife. Now they were scattered around the Peaks, making a new life in new communities. Some welcomed. Some not.

There was a shout from below and the group fell silent. She felt her mother put her hands over her ears as the roar echoed through the valley. She looked up for reassurance and saw that her mother was smiling. 'We'll remember, won't we? And we'll tell. This is a story that will be carried down the generations.'

The older woman shrugged and turned back to the cloud of smoke and debris.

49

Monday, 6 November 2017

Mayfield huffed into the room, her hips knocking a paper tray flying. 'It never rains but it pours. And what's more, the heavens always open when I'm about to go home.'

Connie looked out of the large window of the CID room, which showed a darkened sky but no rain on the window. 'It's clear out I think.'

Mayfield rolled her eyes. 'I wasn't talking about the weather. I was referring to this bloody job. Why do we always have an emergency at six o'clock in the evening?'

'What's happened?'

'We've just had news of a fatal collision on the Matlock road. At least one fatality.'

'Not again. Some idiot overtaking?'

'A car shot out of the side road into the path of an articulated lorry. The driver says he didn't even have time to brake. There's a child involved, apparently.'

'Oh no, how awful. It's Accident Investigation's job, though. What do they want CID for?'

'They don't, but because I was dawdling by the control room inspector listening to the news of the incident, I hadn't handed over to the duty officer. Which is when the incident log came in from uniforms. We've got a missing vulnerable person.'

Connie looked at her watch. 'Great.'

'Exactly. I'm supposed to be going to my singing class tonight.'

'I didn't know you could sing.'

'I can't, which is why I'm going to classes. It's a new group that's been set up. A choir for those who can't read music. We sing modern stuff: songs from the shows, Elvis . . .'

'Elvis is modern?'

'You know what I mean.'

There was a short silence. 'Who *is* the next duty officer?' asked Connie.

'Vinnie, but I think he was hoping for a quiet night. His wife's in hospital due to have her first. They're inducing it any day now.'

Connie held out her hand. 'Give it to me. I'll take it then hand over to Vinnie.'

'You sure?'

Connie was reading the incident. 'Fourteen-year-old girl hasn't come home from school.' Connie looked at her watch again. 'It's only quarter past six. You're having a laugh, aren't you? She's probably drinking cider in one of the local parks.' Connie looked again at the log. Catherine Hallows. 'Shit.'

'What?'

'Didn't you read the name of the missing person?'

'No. Why?' Mayfield leant closer. 'Oh no.'

Connie scanned the rest of the report. Aged fourteen, about five feet two with dark hair and blue eyes. Last seen wearing yellow polka dot dress.

'What does the mother say?' Mayfield sat down in her chair, clearly glad to take the weight off her feet.

'She's called a couple of her daughter's friends and they haven't seen her since the morning's lessons which she attended. Afterwards, she went to the hospital to do a couple of hours of patient support, which she apparently completed. She's not been seen since she left around 3.30 p.m.'

'That's still only a couple of hours missing. You want to leave it a bit?'

Connie looked down at the piece of paper. 'Of course not. Shit, I knew I should have interviewed her at the weekend.'

'It's possible she's bunked off somewhere. Fourteen's one of those funny ages. You're partly still a child and yet you're almost an adult.'

'She's a vulnerable person who isn't where she should be.'

'I know that but it's a bit odd. The mother's saying that the girl wanders around the countryside. Talks about being connected to her ancestors and yet she calls the police the minute she doesn't arrive home on time.'

'She usually gets a bus to Cold Eaton and either walks up the hill to the house or her mother picks her up. She wasn't on her regular bus or the two after that.' Connie sighed. 'I need to speak to the mother.'

'Do you think her disappearance might be connected to the Hilary Kemp case?'

'She was a person of interest and we were due to interview her so it's possible. I'll head out to the farm now. The uniforms have conducted an initial search of the house, which hasn't revealed anything untoward. It doesn't look like she's hiding in the farm. Where's Dahl?'

Mayfield looked at her watch. 'Gone for the night. Do you know what, I think I might have worked out why he needs to leave early.'

Connie closed down the computer and picked up her handbag. 'Never mind about that. I'd better go and see Lorna Hallows.'

*

Sadler opened the door to Nell Colley's house. The dusk meant he could slip through the entrance without attracting the attention of Nell's neighbour. They would be committing one of the worst atrocities on the body of Nell tomorrow morning. Removing it from the earth where she'd been laid to rest. Thankfully, her time out of her grave would be quick. By tomorrow evening she would be back in her resting place. The body would give up some secrets but not all and Sadler wanted to see the house for himself.

Connie and Dahl had done a good job of clearing the space of any evidence. Sadler began in the bedroom, a place where most people often kept their secrets, but found nothing. He moved to the two spare rooms, barren spaces with none of the junk people usually deposit in unused bedrooms. He made his way downstairs and into the dining room. A low G Plan sideboard held crockery and old silver cutlery. In the drawers, tablecloths and starched linen napkins were lined up neatly. Sadler slid his hands inside but found nothing untoward.

A bang on the door made him jump and he went to open it. A small thin woman stood uncertainly on the doorstep.

'Are you the police? I saw the lights on.'

'I am.' Sadler reached into his pocket but the woman had backed away.

'I was just checking. Have you . . .'

'It's tomorrow.'

Janet looked down. 'I'll say a prayer for her tonight.'

'That would be a good thing to do.'

Emboldened, the woman looked up. 'I always say that even if you don't think it does any good, it can't do any harm.'

'I suppose not.'

'Were you looking for something?'

'I wanted to see if I could find anything about the memoir Nell was writing.'

'You don't think that has anything to do with anything?'

'I don't know.'

'Now I think about it, I'm pretty sure she didn't have a laptop. I remember asking her if my grandson could borrow one and she said she'd never got on with computers when she was working. She must have intended to write it by hand.'

'You're sure she never talked about it?'

'Only in the vaguest terms. She was definitely doing research. I'm sure she said.' Janet looked around her. 'I'm not sure what about.'

'At the library?'

'No. She wouldn't go there. She refused, I've no idea why. She took a few bus trips, though. Said they were research trips. She was very secretive about it.'

'Research trips to where?'

'She never said. All I know was she caught the bus. She was looking at the timetables when I called round.'

As Janet moved away, Sadler shut the door and rifled

through the telephone desk next to the doorway. Nothing there. He moved through to the kitchen and saw a letter rack hanging on a wall. Two bus timetables were sitting in the top bracket. He pulled them down. One was for Cold Eaton and the other for Ladybower reservoir. The Cold Eaton one he flicked through and put it back in the rack. The Ladybower timetable was thicker and, as Sadler unfolded it, he saw that it had been bulked out by two used envelopes set on top of each other. Both had, on one side, Nell's home address and stamps that had been inked at the Bampton sorting office. Local correspondence, although what the envelopes had once contained was impossible to tell as both were empty. It was the reverse side of them that was the revelation, the white paper covered with tiny writing. Sadler took them over to the kitchen table and put them side by side.

The first envelope contained a list of seemingly random words, Nell trying to get her thoughts straight. Sadler scanned through the items. *School, Cold Eaton, yew tree, promise, Valerie, the Neales, Ladybower, tunnel, after.* The final word had three dashes underlining it. Some of the references were easy to guess, others not. The Neales presumably meant Monica and her sister Ingrid if she was referring to her childhood.

Sadler turned his attention to the other envelope. It was A5 in size and had been folded in half to cover the writing scrawled on the back. Here, Nell had made a start on a narrative of sorts. Squinting in the poor kitchen light, Sadler deciphered the tiny words.

It's hard to know where to begin and I've spent a long time getting my thoughts in order. I have to start, though, as the intervals between my attacks are beginning to shorten. I've realised that you can go at any time. Ingrid's death showed me that at least.

Now I see that I must start at Cold Eaton because what came before it – school, making friendships – was nothing compared to how we were in the village. I've just come back from a trip there and it hasn't changed at all. The pub had the same sign hanging with the clipper ship in full sail now faded with age and exposure to the elements. The old house still stands at the top of the hill, unkempt as ever. I walked to the house and no further. The former railway line I couldn't face nor did I get beyond the entrance to the churchyard. I can rely on my memory for those parts of the narrative. I'll have to. Some things are too hard to revisit. One good thing did come from the trip, though. I saw the one who came up with the idea of the punishment and I told her I was going to write this. She didn't like the idea at all.

The narrative stopped. Sadler went back to the letter rack and searched through the contents but nothing else was to be found. He picked up the two envelopes and stared at them again. Nell had told someone in Cold Eaton she was writing her memoir and 'she' hadn't liked it. He bundled up the letters and placed them back into the Ladybower timetable. Ladybower. The name was also on Nell's list. What was the significance of the reservoir?

50

It would be her last night at The Nettle Inn. Mina couldn't face the obfuscation of Emily and the others at the bar this evening. People told you nothing but kept an eye on your movements and she was sick of it. She found the top end of Cutting Lane blocked off when she left the bridge and the young traffic cop ordered her to reverse back down the lane, forcing her into a long detour along country roads that deposited her in the heart of Bampton. She parked and slipped into the minimarket next to the town's main square. It was a small shop with just five aisles, a strip of which was dedicated to alcohol. She picked up a bottle of red, found a half-decent-looking baguette and some Derbyshire cheese, light coloured with fine veins of blue.

At six o'clock, the dark had fallen and the lights dotted around the square gave off an amber glow. As she approached the van, someone was peering into her driver's window. She coughed loudly and the figure stood up and walked quickly away. Mina opened the van and checked the back seats before getting inside. She locked the door and sat for a moment, her heart thumping. A potential thief checking if she'd left something of value inside the van? Possibly, or perhaps the author of the note left on her windscreen at the Cutting. When her heart had slowed to a steadier pace, she drove out of Bampton and towards Cold Eaton. As she turned left off the main road towards the isolated village, the car behind her also indicated and followed her.

I'm spooked. Ignore it, she cautioned herself. She drove carefully down the meandering road and was relieved when she saw the light on in the window of the house on the outskirts of the village. She drove faster towards the safety of the pub and, instead of using the car park to the side, pulled up outside the front door as she had seen other patrons do. The car behind her drove past without the driver looking at her. This was odd in its own way for surely human curiosity would have impelled you to look at the car you'd just driven behind, even it was only to see if they were someone from the village. Mina sat for a moment and then crawled up the hill after the car. The village ended at the old manor house but the vehicle was nowhere to be seen. With a sigh, Mina reversed and drove back to The Nettle Inn reflecting on her paranoia.

The pub was empty except for a couple eating at one of the corner tables. Emily wasn't anywhere to be seen so Mina scribbled a note to her to say she wouldn't need a table reserving this evening. She made the steep climb up to her room as her knees groaned in protest. Light was seeping from a door immediately at the top of the stairs. The Nettle Inn had a new guest. As the board squeaked under her foot, the door opened a fraction and shut again. Mina was left with the impression that she'd been studied and assessed.

As she went into her room, she saw that a note had been thrust under the door. She unfolded the slip of paper.

LEAVE VALERIE ALONE.

Mina turned the note over. There was nothing else; it was just a piece of paper ripped out of a notepad. She folded the note, put it in her back pocket, and went downstairs. Emily was back behind the bar, totting up a round of drinks on the till.

'Has anyone been up to my room today?'

Emily flushed. 'I made up your bed and gave it a quick dust. Why?'

'Was there a note on the floor when you went in?'

'I didn't see anything. What note?'

'Someone's put a note under the door. I wondered if it was you.'

'Me? A note about what?'

'It doesn't matter.'

Mina climbed up the stairs once more and paused outside the room at the top. Gathering her courage, she gave a sharp rap on the door. There was no answer. She tried it again, louder this time. Again no answer. She turned the handle but the door was locked. With a baffled glance at the door, Mina moved to go back to her room as the timer on the hallway light bulb switched off and she was plunged into darkness. She swore under her breath and fumbled around for the light switch. *It's a health and safety risk*, she thought. *Like the rest of the bloody building.*

The next thing she knew, Emily was standing over her while a paramedic was putting an oxygen mask over her face.

'Wha—'

'You're back with us. How are you feeling, Mina?' The paramedic's voice was muffled in her ringing ears. 'I'm giving you some oxygen. Can you hear me?'

Mina nodded and looked up at him in puzzlement. He understood the unspoken question.

'It looks like you tripped coming up the stairs and you've landed awkwardly on the landing. There doesn't seem to be much damage. Have you fainted in the past?'

Mina shook her head.

'You should have put the light on at the bottom.' Emily sounded annoyed rather than concerned.

The paramedic frowned. 'How's the head, Mina?'

'All right.' She pulled at the mask. 'I just need to sleep it off.'

'I don't think so. I want you to take a trip down to St Bertram's. You okay with that?'

'Do I have to?' Memories of her mother's last days came flooding back. 'I'd rather stay here.'

'You've had a fall. I'd rather someone looked at you. We'll take you down in the ambulance and you can call a friend to bring you back. Okay? Do you want to try to stand?'

Gingerly he helped her up, aided by a female colleague who appeared out of the shadows. As she stood she felt a rush of blood to her head. She was still wearing her coat, so she checked her pockets. Her phone and purse were still there. She turned to Emily.

'Where did you find me?'

'I told you, on the landing sprawled outside your door. You must have tripped on the last stairs. I'll have to put up a sign telling residents to switch the light on at the bottom. Once you get to the top you've got to cross to the other side of the landing to find the switch.'

But I made it that far, thought Mina. *I knocked on the door opposite and fumbled around for the switch at the top of the landing, not on the last stairs.*

'What about the person in the room at the top of the stairs? Didn't they hear anything?'

'What person?' Emily looked sharply at Mina. 'That room's empty. They all are.'

'I thought . . . I thought there was someone staying there tonight.'

Emily shook her head. 'There's no one staying here but you.'

Mina stared at Emily in dismay. *She's lying.* She turned to the paramedic. 'I'll go with you.'

51

On the way out of the station, Connie counted the number of cigarettes left in the packet in her handbag. Five. Theoretically, given she was limiting herself to ten fags a day, those five should last her through the evening. However, she had the habitual smoker's fear of running out and waking up in the morning, desperate for a puff. On the way to Lorna Hallows's house, she called at a shop and bought herself a packet.

It was one of those places, once so common to rural England, that was gradually disappearing. It was part florist, part fruit shop and also served as a corner shop for odds and ends that local residents might need. Two elderly women sat chatting behind the counter and, over in one corner, a young woman breast-fed a child. The women recognised Connie and one of them reached up for her usual brand of cigarettes.

'Am I that predictable?'

'We were just saying that we hadn't seen you since, oh, Wednesday.'

'I'm cutting down.'

'I've heard that before,' the other woman cackled, ringing up the price on the till. 'You're not going up Cold Eaton way, are you?'

Connie looked up in surprise. 'Near there. Why? Oh, you've heard about the accident?'

'It's a bad one, apparently. A guy with a kid in the back. One's dead but we don't know which.'

Connie winced. 'I'm not going that far.'

'A lorry driver told us. They're passing the message along their radios to avoid the road.'

Connie looked out of the window at the clear evening. 'It's okay now but people drive too fast when it's foggy.'

'That road is a devil and I've heard it wasn't the lorry driver's fault. The car just came out of a side road, they say.'

Who says? thought Connie as she picked up her fags and left the shop.

Hallows Farm was as remote as you can get in the Peak District without being completely off grid. The road that led up to the farm from Cold Eaton was barely more than a track with a few passing places. Switching on her main beam, she came to a sign, mottled with age with the name of the farm just discernible. The driveway looked uninviting and, concerned about her car's suspension, Connie parked next to the gate. She took her torch out of the boot and set off down the bumpy track. Connie reflected that she would need to revise her opinion of a neurotic mother, for surely this wasn't a place that a woman fretful about personal security would choose to live. The farm was pitch black in the night and the remoteness of the cottage must be a severe hindrance to an active teenager's social life.

As she neared the house, a light came on, illuminating a woman who was standing by the front door with a large black Labrador sitting by her feet. She was wearing green corduroy trousers, flared around her ankles over trainers. A black and white checked shirt was tucked into her waist, part of it spilling

283

out. She had obviously dressed in a hurry and looked forlorn as she watched Connie approach, shielding her eyes from the glare of the torch.

'Have you found her?'

Connie shook her head. 'Not yet but we're looking. I've come to ask you a few more questions.'

She walked over to the woman and held out her warrant card. Lorna Hallows didn't look at it.

'I felt stupid when I called but that was a couple of hours ago when it was still light-ish. Now the darkness has fallen I've lost all my confidence. She definitely left the hospital and headed out towards the bus stop. After that, it's a blank. Look, come in.'

Connie followed the woman through the front door, which led straight onto a long living room. An open fire was burning and the heat of the room was such a contrast to the outside temperature that Connie could feel her skin begin to itch.

'Is Catherine's father around?'

'He died.' There was a note of finality in the woman's voice. Subject closed.

'What about other relatives?'

'There's only me and Catherine. She sometimes goes in to say hello to Gerry and Maureen in the house at the top. They've not seen her since earlier in the week.'

'You've not managed to speak to the school at all? They may be able to give some pointers as to where she might be.'

Lorna crossed to the fire and poked one of the logs with a stick. 'No one's answering the school telephone and there isn't an emergency number to call. I rang one of her friends, Abby, who said that she saw Catherine this morning and that was it.'

'She goes to Bampton Grammar? She's happy there?'

Lorna kept her back turned away from Connie. 'I suppose so. She's a quiet girl. Everything goes on in her head, she doesn't let much out. In year eight she was bullied and I had to go into the school and sort it out. I thought they kept an eye out for these things but clearly not.'

'The issue was resolved?'

'One of the girls was expelled. That's how bad it was. She's certainly not getting bullied any longer.'

'You're sure about that?'

'As sure as I can be. I have meetings once a term with her class teacher. It was the school's suggestion after her history. They've not spotted anything and Catherine does appear happier.'

'She's never come home late before?'

'She, well, she does like to disappear but that's mainly at weekends. I never know where she goes, she just takes herself off.'

'What about after school?'

'She's never this late into Cold Eaton because if she misses her normal bus, there's only two others after and that's it for the night. There's no way of her getting home.'

'The bus drops her—'

'Outside The Nettle Inn. She sometimes walks from there. I'll meet her when I can but I work so it's not always possible. Emily Fenn gave her a key to one of the rooms upstairs in the pub to do her homework but she rarely uses it. You know what kids are like.' Lorna looked up. 'She tends to walk home when I'm not around. She takes the path past where the gallows once stood.'

Connie took a deep breath. 'Okay, so what about this evening?'

'I finished earlier than expected so went to wait for the bus. I just missed it so I assumed Catherine had started walking and I drove up here to wait for her. She should have been home by about four thirty at the latest. Maybe five.'

'You called the police at six. You didn't wait long.'

'I went to see Gerry at the end of the lane and he'd not seen her and neither had Emily at the pub. There's nowhere else for her to go. I rang the station number for advice and they sent a car straight away. Did you know they searched the house and out the back?'

'You'd be surprised how many teenagers we find hiding in their houses.'

'Isn't there anything else you can do? It's been hours now.'

'I think we need to think about the sequence of events assuming Catherine got the bus as far as Cold Eaton. The patrol cars are looking out for her in Bampton. When you're not giving her a lift, Catherine takes the old path from Cold Eaton to here. I should walk the route just to see if she's had an accident.'

Lorna opened a packet of cigarettes and, with shaking hands, offered one to Connie. Reluctantly, Connie shook her head. 'I've walked the path twice tonight. There's nothing there. It's the first thing I thought of. What else? I feel helpless just waiting here.'

'I also need to contact the bus company.'

'The drivers should recognise Catherine. I tried to call but no one is answering the phone there. The only place I managed to speak to was the hospital and she clocked off her shift there at half three as usual.'

'Does she have a mobile?'

'That's switched off, which is normal for her. She's not a typical teenager. I usually have to persuade her to turn the bloody thing on. The only thing she uses it for is to search the internet.'

'What about a boyfriend?'

'She doesn't have one. It's not a problem if she did. I appreciate I'm only her mother but I've not spotted anything.'

'Was there trouble at home?'

Lorna looked up, hurt in her eyes. 'There's only her and me and we're close. I can't even remember the last argument I had with her.'

'She's fourteen.'

'Yes, but a young fourteen if you know what I mean. She likes books, sitting on the computer, walking around here . . .'

'She didn't say anything to you before she left for school this morning?'

'All I can remember is saying goodbye and shutting the door. That's it.'

Connie looked at her watch. The girl had only been missing for a few hours but, at fourteen, she was a vulnerable child with no history of absconding.

'Can I see her room?'

Connie followed Lorna up a steep, narrow flight of stairs that led onto a small landing. Catherine's bedroom was painted in a light purple with thin gauzy curtains matching the colour of the walls. The walls were bare, no pictures of pop groups or film stars. A narrow bed was pressed up against the window. No bedside table, only a floor lamp. Connie opened the white chest of drawers and rifled through the contents. Just clothes and childish underwear, no bras. There was a small desk in the alcove and the single drawer held a variety of coloured pencils and flowery notebooks. Connie flicked through them. All were blank.

'There's not much to see, is there?'

'Not much,' agreed Connie, looking at her watch. 'It's been a long day, is there any chance of a cup of tea?'

With the girl's mother out of the room, Connie slid her hand behind drawers, looked under the bed and searched for other hiding places where a girl might store her possessions. She found nothing. She picked up a photo of a small teenager with dark hair, standing with her back to a tree. The girl had none of the confidence Connie associated with the teenagers who streamed out of the gates of Bampton Grammar. She was looking into the camera, her expression uncertain although she was trying to smile. Perhaps this fragility would have made her a magnet for bullies.

Lorna reappeared with the tea. Connie showed her the photo. 'Is this Catherine?'

'Yes. It was taken over the summer on holiday. There's a similar one downstairs which I gave to the first police who came.'

'This photo, is it a good likeness?'

'I'd say so. Did you find anything?'

'What do you mean?'

'I could hear you opening drawers when I was downstairs. So, did you find anything?'

Connie shook her head. Unashamed. 'Nothing at all.'

'Where do you think she is?'

'I don't know. Teenagers often disappear for short periods

of time. I know I did once when I was fifteen. I took a train into Manchester and stayed out until two in the morning. I then had to phone my mum for a lift home.'

'Catherine's not like that.'

'Are you sure? I don't mean she's gone into town. I mean she could have been persuaded by a friend to go somewhere. Let me see what I can do.'

Using the torch on her phone, Connie picked her way carefully through the potholes to the top of the track. She slid in front of the steering wheel and groped for her fags. She checked both pockets of her coat but could find nothing then delved into her handbag. *Bloody hell. Don't tell me they've dropped out of my pocket.* She opened the car door and went back towards the house checking on the ground. Something glinted under the kitchen window but it was a rusting dog bowl.

Connie knocked on the door but it went unanswered. She peeped through the kitchen window and saw Lorna emerge from a room at the back with a basket of washing. She untied a rope at the side of the Aga and the airer sitting above it gradually lowered. As she watched, the woman pegged the first garment onto the wooden slats and Connie watched the blue dress billow from the wooden rack. She changed her mind about knocking on the door and made her way back up the track thinking, her cigarettes forgotten. The nurse's uniform now drying in the kitchen meant Lorna was possibly implicated in the case of Hilary Kemp. Connie switched on the engine and made her way back to the station to work through the night.

52

The next morning, Mina's head still ached, a dull throb at the back of her skull. The codeine she'd ingested was only touching the outer fringes of the pain and had induced a lassitude she was trying to shake off. An x-ray in the hospital confirmed that no permanent damage had been done to either her head or ankle and they'd discharged her after a night's observation on a general ward. Back at The Nettle Inn, she was still unsteady on her feet. She put a thick sock on over the bandage and support sleeve given to her at the hospital and eased her foot into her boots, leaving the zip at the back undone and the laces loosely tied.

On the landing, she stopped outside the door at the top of the stairs and flung it open. It was empty, the bed bare, unmade for visitors. Across the room, Mina could hear a commotion coming from the gravelled area outside the pub. She crossed the chilled room and looked out of the window. The car park was half full, not tourist cars but local vehicles: Land Rovers, farm trucks and even a tractor parked in the corner. A group of people were huddled together, talking and gesticulating. Another noise permeated the room, the sound of a woman sobbing. Mina went back into the corridor and closed the door behind her. Hobbling down the stairs, she made her way to the breakfast table. The bar was full, the mood subdued and Monica Neale was sitting at a table, weeping into a towel.

Mina looked around, trying to fathom what had gone on. Amongst the huddle of people standing about, Mina recognised Harry Neale. She caught his eye and he came over to her.

'It's a terrible business.'

'What's happened?'

'There's been an accident on the Matlock road. Monica's cousin, Patrick Kersey, is dead and his young son is in hospital in intensive care. His injuries are serious. They're not sure if he'll pull through.'

'Jesus.' Mina looked across at Monica who continued to sob into the towel. 'Do they know what happened?'

'It seems it was Patrick's fault. He pulled out from a side road straight into the path of a truck. He was going so fast, they don't think he slowed to give way at all. The driver's in a state. He says there was nothing he could have done.'

'The poor man. There was a funny mist when I was out yesterday. Patchy, so sometimes it was clear as a bell and then you were engulfed in it. Perhaps he couldn't see the end of the road.'

Harry looked unconvinced. 'We all know the roads around here. And what it's like to drive in fog. The first rule is to slow down. What the hell was he thinking of?'

'That's a bit harsh.'

'Is it? Well, maybe I'm sick of hearing of accidents along that stretch of road. Last year it was a couple of guys who came out of this pub worse for wear, although Emily usually looks out for that sort of thing. They drove out of Cold Eaton down the Matlock road and an hour later they had both been thrown out of the car and were lying in a field. They hadn't even hit anything. No one knows how they ended up there.'

'They can't have been wearing their seatbelts.'

He shot her a look. 'They clearly weren't wearing them but what did they collide with to throw them clear of the car?'

'I don't know.' Mina's voice sounded small and Harry relented.

'I'm sorry, I'm taking it out on you. Don't mind me.' He looked at the still weeping Monica. 'The Kerseys are relatives. It's hit Monica hard. Anything with family always does.'

He went to his wife and, left alone, Mina found the collective grief of the people in the pub overwhelming. Her throbbing head was a constant reminder that someone here had attacked her and the sadness pouring out of Monica was too much to witness. She needed to get out of the building and leave Cold Eaton.

'It's a bad time around here at the moment,' she heard one man say. 'I passed Bampton church on my way down here and it's full of police.'

'You think something's happened there?'

'They had diggers there.'

'Digging?' There was a silence as the other man digested the information. 'What the fuck were they digging for?'

'It was an exhumation, wasn't it? There are rumours about something going on at St Bertram's. I bet it's to do with that.'

In shock, Mina moved to the door, van keys in hand. Sadler was clearly widening the investigation into her mother's death and he'd said nothing to her. At the entrance to the pub, she halted at a familiar term. Cutting. They were talking about the Cutting. She looked towards the group and caught the eye of one of the farmers, his muddy wellingtons dropping clods of dirt over the floor. 'Did the accident happen up by the Cutting?'

He shook his head. 'Not by the Cutting. The other end of the road. The car shot out of Cutting Lane onto the Matlock road. It's a bloody dangerous stretch at the best of times. We've had plenty of accidents over the years.'

Mina thought back to the previous day. 'How old was the son? The one who's in hospital?'

The farmer shrugged. 'I don't know. Two maybe or three. A toddler. Why?'

'I think I might have seen them up at the bridge. They passed me as they were going down the embankment on foot. Yesterday evening.'

The farmer turned towards the weeping woman. 'Monica,' he raised his voice. 'This young lady saw Patrick and Archie at the Cutting yesterday. He must have taken the boy for a walk along the path.'

Monica stared at Mina and stood up. Harry put his arm around his wife and pulled her towards him. For a moment, before she turned towards her husband, Mina caught a glimpse of the malevolence in her expression and the look chilled her.

53

It's only in films that exhumations happen at night. In reality, they take place whenever they can get all the personnel assembled and close off the churchyard to avoid distressing other mourners. Eight o'clock in the morning was the pathologist, Bill Shield's favoured time. He could remove the body from the earth, take it to the hospital where his staff were waiting and do the post mortem that morning. Nell Colley would be back in the ground by nightfall.

The preparation had been meticulous. The company outsourced by the police was experienced and efficient. They had covered each of the surrounding graves with a plastic shroud, a type of bubble wrap that gave the landscape the aura of a film set. Over the grave being exhumed, a tent had been erected and a large light was shining to help the diggers. Behind him, Sadler could see a huddle of police officers in high visibility vests stopping any visitors to the site and moving on the gawkers who had begun to gather.

Connie was standing next to him looking green.

'It doesn't look like any press have got wind of this yet.'

'With any luck we'll be finished before they realise what's going on.' Sadler looked down at her. 'Are you all right?'

'My mum's buried over there.'

She nodded to the far end of the churchyard where a patch

was reserved for cremations. Sadler swore slightly under his breath. 'Why the hell didn't you say so?'

'Because I wanted to be here. I worked late last night on this and I'm not missing out on anything.'

'There won't be anything to see. Go back to the station and find out the latest on Catherine Hallows. She was still missing an hour ago but that might have changed. Who's looking into her mother's employer?'

'Matthews. It shouldn't take long.'

'St Bertram's is a large hospital. She could be attached to any department.'

'Then why didn't she say? Why didn't she tell me Catherine was volunteering at her place of work?'

Sadler sighed. 'Can we please wait and see? You have to wear uniforms in nursing homes or if you're a district nurse. I want to see what Lorna Hallows's job is before we jump to any conclusions.'

Dahl, also in a high vis vest, came out of the tent. 'We're about to lift the coffin out of the ground. Do you want to come in?'

Sadler shook his head and stayed next to Connie. He could see Llewellyn's tall form near the tent's entrance, checking all his personnel were okay. He also saw the figure of a woman he didn't recognise, dressed in a heavy overcoat.

'Who's she?' he asked Connie.

Connie looked over. 'She's the priest.'

'Who asked her to be here?'

Connie turned to him. 'It's her churchyard, she probably wanted to attend.'

A van backed in towards the entrance of the tent. Both

Sadler and Connie looked on transfixed. 'The remains must be above ground.'

They watched as the coffin was put into the back of the van under the watchful eye of Bill Shields.

'That's that then.' Sadler turned away. 'Don't go to the post mortem, Connie. Dahl can be present. Later today, I want to show you something I found at Nell's house, some notes and a short extract. She'd definitely told someone she was writing the book.'

'Do you know who?'

'That's the problem. I only know that it was a woman in Cold Eaton.' He looked to see Connie's reaction but she was frowning towards the entrance to the churchyard.

'What's Mina Kemp doing here?' she said.

Sadler looked across and saw Mina gesticulating to one of the police officers. 'I'll go and see.'

He made his way across the damp grass to her. She stopped arguing with the police officer and turned to him to watch his approach.

'Whose body are you exhuming?'

Sadler sighed. 'How did you find out about it?'

'At The Nettle Inn at Cold Eaton. They're gathered there to talk about an accident that took place on the Matlock road. It involves a local family but someone also mentioned that there were police at Bampton churchyard.'

'I need you to go, Mina.' He blocked her view of the tent and she made no effort to move past him.

'Who is it?'

'I can't tell you.'

'Is it connected to Mum's death?'

'I can't tell you that, either.'

'Please.'

He looked down at her. Worry lines creased her face, fading into something darker. 'Look, I can't tell you anything. Why don't you go back to work, Mina?' He looked at her closely. A faint bruise was forming high up in her cheekbone that she hadn't attempted to cover with make-up. 'Are you all right?'

'I think someone decked me last night.'

'You think? What do you mean?'

'I was going to my room at the pub and the next thing I remember is waking up on the floor. They're saying I fell but I'm pretty sure someone hit me over the head.'

Sadler felt a wave of anger. 'I want you to go home. Not to The Nettle Inn and not to the boat. I'd feel happier if you were in your house.' He looked around him. 'I'm short of staff but I can get a uniformed officer to accompany you if it would make you feel safer.'

'I'll feel safer on the boat. If I shout, someone will hear. In my house I'm on my own.'

'The boat then, but don't open the door unless you recognise the voice and feel safe.'

'Who are you exhuming?'

He whispered, 'I can't say.'

'Will you come and see me? On my boat. The *Evening Star* down at Bampton wharf. I've got something to tell you.'

'About your mother?'

She nodded. 'I think I might know what it's all about. The bare bones of it at least.'

'I'll come later this morning. You haven't seen Catherine Hallows, have you?'

'Catherine? Only yesterday. Oh no, she's not missing, is she?' Mina looked over to the retreating hearse. 'Will you come and see me as soon as you can?'

54

Susan Barr came out of the hairdressers with her hateful hair teased into the curls that would no doubt drop in the coming rain. She should have put her foot down when she was fifteen and refused that perm her mum had insisted she have to cheer herself up. It had started a lifetime battle between her and her mousy hair. First the curls then the blonde dye. Nothing brassy, her father wouldn't have stood for that, but something to lighten her spirits along with her mood. Susan had long ago forgotten what her hair originally looked like. 'Mousy' she would tell her grandchildren but surely it would now be grey or even white. And still these weekly visits to the hairdresser every Tuesday to style her hair into this rigid helmet.

She bought a local newspaper and took it into the Aroma café. She enjoyed the young buzz of the place and the no nonsense attitude of the servers. Over her steaming coffee she flicked through the pages of the paper, going first to the letters of complaint, which always made her laugh. The decades she'd spent away from Bampton had been a godsend. She'd seen that there was a life outside Derbyshire, that there were other ways of looking at life and she'd encouraged this attitude in her own children. There's no one way of doing things she'd preached to them as children and, perhaps, hopefully, they were passing this maxim on to their own children. The people who wrote in to the *Bampton Chronicle* had clearly never left the confines of this town. Phrases such as 'This country is going to the dogs' or 'It's not how it used to be' abounded and the minutiae of the supposed decline of Bampton was picked over in excruciating detail.

Having satisfied herself with the continued narrow-mindedness of the paper's correspondents, Susan turned to the front pages. The top story was about a man killed and a child in intensive care after he drove out of a side road and into the path of a lorry. The lorry driver, to whom no blame was being attached, was in hospital with minor injuries. He hadn't been going fast but a six-axle articulated wagon will cause a massive amount of damage even at slow speeds.

Susan read on. The newspaper had tried to speak to the mother, which showed the insensitivity of some people. The poor woman must have been devastated. A relative, though, had revealed that the mother had spoken to her husband minutes before the accident and had described him as being in an 'agitated state' before driving away from the former railway line.

The coffee soured in Susan's mouth and she had to resist the temptation to spit the bitter liquid back in her cup. Instead, she forced it down and picked up the paper to read the article again. There was nothing else that gave any indication what the man had been agitated about. Patrick Kersey had been driving down Cutting Lane after a walk on the former railway line. At the end of the road, instead of slowing down, he'd driven into the path of a lorry. His wife had spoken to him moments before the crash and he had been agitated. Agitated? What about?

Susan pushed her coffee cup aside and went to the counter.

'Do you still have those maps of Bampton that you used to give out to the students?'

The Greek woman shook her head. 'I stopped doing them. Prices have gone up and I need to make cuts somewhere. I'd rather it wasn't the food and drink.'

'It doesn't matter. Don't worry.' Susan turned.

'Hold on. I might still have one out the back. Do you want me to look?' The woman moved away from the counter and disappeared through a door. She returned with a slightly stained map bearing a photo of Bampton's main square.

'I don't know why the tourist office doesn't give us free ones. I had to get these printed at my own expense. Anyway, you have it.'

'I just want to look at something.' Susan walked back to her table and spread out the map in front of her. She looked to the east of the town and oriented herself by finding her childhood home. With a finger she traced the path she had once trod confidently from her house to school. She followed the route as it neared the railway line until she came to the spot where it crossed over the track. It had a name, she'd not known it at the time. 'Over the bridge' if she was going to refer to it at all, but here it was on the map. Cutting Embankment and Road leading away from the bridge towards the Matlock road. Cutting Lane. It was from here that the man had fled with his child.

From what?

55

Connie looked up as Matthews walked towards her desk looking dejected. Her colleague had a sheen of sweat on her face and the skin around her eyes was stretched pale white. With Sadler preoccupied with the exhumation, Matthews was leading the search for Catherine Hallows and it seemed to be taking it out of her. Connie, still feeling queasy from the exhumation, was glad to get back to the office. Glad to be excused from the PM. Pleased to be in the land of the living, or missing, rather than the dead.

'Any news?'

Matthews shook her head and flopped down opposite Connie. 'Nothing. There have been no positive sightings of Catherine Hallows for nineteen hours. We're reinterviewing Catherine's friends. They were questioned by uniforms last night and said they hadn't seen her at all yesterday after the morning's lessons. After which, she went to the hospital. I'm going to speak to the Super about bringing in a specialist search team.'

'You think she might still be at her mother's house?'

'I'm going to cover all bases. If she's definitely not there, I want it confirmed. I don't want anyone saying I missed anything.'

All officers had a description of Catherine and those carrying PDAs had been sent the snap identical to the one Connie had seen yesterday evening. There had been no sightings of a girl in a polka dot dress.

Connie reached out her hand and briefly touched Matthews. 'We've done everything right so far. Have you found out where Lorna Hallows works?'

'I spoke to Mrs Hallows this morning. She was surprisingly calm. I'm not sure I'd be as composed if my daughter was missing. She's a district nurse. She never goes to Bampton hospital in a professional capacity.'

Matthews's phone rang and Connie shamelessly listened to the conversation, which consisted of a series of grunts from Matthews. As the receiver went down, she banged her head on the desk.

'What's the matter?'

'Mayfield's gone into labour.'

'Great!' Connie's smile fell when she saw Matthews's face. 'That's good, isn't it?'

'It means we're one person down. I'll definitely need to speak to Llewellyn about resources. I'm going to head up there now.'

Matthews disappeared, holding the door for a large man who looked briefly around the office before making his way to her desk. On his sleeve she could see 'Road Police Unit' printed in large letters.

'DC Childs?'

'That's me.' *Bloody hell, the guy was huge. He must be about six feet five. How come I've never spotted him before?* thought Connie. 'How are things?'

'Not good, to be honest. Did you hear about the accident coming out of Cutting Lane?'

Connie grimaced. 'Yes. How's the little boy?'

'Critical according to the last update but the injuries aren't life changing, if you get my drift. We're going to have to look again at the traffic calming at that stretch.'

'The car didn't stop at the junction. The lorry driver could have been doing thirty and it still would have been a nasty accident.'

'I know and that's the reason I'm here. I've just interviewed the wife of Patrick Kersey who was killed. The thing is, the mother's in a state but she was able to give us an accurate description of the last few minutes before the car crashed. Patrick had apparently taken Archie for a walk down the Topley Trail and was rushing away from the scene because he'd seen a girl walk into the tunnel at the top of Cutting Lane and she hadn't come out.'

Connie stared at the man, telling her brain to ignore the fact that he was completely fanciable. 'Did he give a description?'

'Only that she was about fourteen. He used the term "schoolgirl".'

'What the— Why didn't he call us or look for the girl? Why'd he go haring off in his car?'

'According to Jenny Kersey he was completely spooked by what he'd seen and wanted to get them both home. He was acting like he'd seen a ghost.'

Connie looked around the office. 'We're short of personnel today. I'll have to go and look by myself.'

He smiled at her. 'I'll take you down to the spot if you like.'

*

In the car he introduced himself as Sergeant Morgan.

'Don't you have a first name? Or do you keep it quiet, like Morse?'

He kept his eyes on the road and laughed. 'Morgan is my first name.'

Connie looked out of the window. 'Sergeant Morgan. That's a funny way to introduce yourself.'

'Standard procedure.'

She turned to him. 'Standard procedure? It bloody isn't. It's standard to give your rank and last name.'

'I just did.'

'What is your first name?'

'Morgan.'

'So you introduced yourself as Sergeant Morgan. Rank and first name. What's your last name?'

'Morgan.'

Connie swore.

He relented. 'My parents, in their infinite wisdom, gave me the same first name as my last. My name's Morgan Morgan.'

Connie snorted with laughter. 'It's not.'

'I'm afraid so.'

'But weren't you teased at school?'

'Nope. My birthday is in September. I was the eldest in my class and built like a brick shithouse. Never been bullied in my life.'

'But you can't even shorten Morgan to anything. You're Morgan Morgan.'

'I know. I'm not bothered, to be honest. No one takes the piss out of me I can assure you.'

I bet they don't, thought Connie.

She expected to see police tape or at least some evidence of the accident but the road was clear. 'There's nothing to see.'

He glanced at her. 'We reopened the stretch at six this morning. The emphasis is on getting traffic moving again, even when there's a fatality.' He slowed down and pointed at the road leading onto the carriageway. 'That's where the car came out into the path of the lorry. Road conditions were fine but visibility was poor. He didn't stop to meet the junction.'

Morgan turned down Cutting Lane, a narrow winding road that just allowed two cars to pass. The road climbed and then levelled out as they neared a large brick bridge. Morgan pulled into the side of the road and pointed to it. 'Welcome to the Cutting.'

56

Mina, unable to settle, spent the morning on the deck of the boat wrapped in one of her mother's ancient blankets. Her canoe, unused for days, needed checking over and then taking out along one of her usual routes. The problem was that Mina had lost her confidence since her fall. In her confusion, she couldn't decide if she was safer here than at The Nettle Inn. She was now doubting whether she had been attacked at the top of the stairs at all. Perhaps Emily was right and she had merely tripped in the darkness. Away from Cold Eaton, the village didn't seem as menacing as it had that morning and now it was the boat that was making her jittery. Her foot was throbbing from her short walk to the churchyard, although the accumulation of painkillers made the ache appear reassuringly distant. Here on deck she could at least hear and smell the water around her and also, if she was being honest, keep watch on who was approaching the boat. She was relieved when Sadler arrived, parking his car next to her van.

He looked at the lettering on the boat's stern. 'The *Evening Star*. It's a good name. Better than some of the supposedly witty ones you see on the boats going up and down this stretch. I saw one the other day called *Cirrhosis of the River*.'

Mina got up, wincing as she put down her foot. 'You like

the canal? It's not to everyone's taste. People thought Mum had gone mad when she decided to live here.'

'I live on it. The other side of Bampton. In a house, though. One of the old workers' cottages.'

'Ah, the posh bit.' She regretted it as soon as she said it and glanced across at him. He was touching the lettering on the side of the boat.

'Did you know the evening star is another name for Venus?'

'The goddess, you mean?'

'No, the planet. It's how it's referred to after sunset.'

'Funny. I never knew.' She looked at him. 'Mum never said why she called the boat that. I can't remember the boat's original name but Mum changed it.'

'It's the brightest star in the sky. I often see it myself over the Peaks. Perhaps your mother used to look up at it too. Can I come on board?'

'Of course. Sorry.' Mina was aware of the flush spreading up her cheeks. 'I should have invited you but my brain has turned to mush. I think it's all the painkillers I've been taking.'

Sadler took in the deck chair and blanket. 'You're watching for someone?'

'I'm not sure if I just fell at the pub. There was someone in the room next to mine. I'm sure of it, but Emily, the owner of the pub, said it was empty. When I came to, lying there on the landing, I thought I'd been pushed. The trouble is the distance of time has made me doubt myself.' She watched him turn away and look down the canal towards the village that held all the secrets.

'I might make a trip out to Cold Eaton myself. I wouldn't

mind having a look at the place.' Sadler moved around the boat. 'There's nowhere for anyone to hide here. You should be safe enough.'

He looked across at her, concerned, and Mina dropped her eyes. 'Let's go inside.'

He followed her down into the cabin and shut the door behind him. In the dim light she told him the story of her mother's recognition of Valerie and the revelation that she had not only thought Valerie was dead, but that she had killed her.

'Do you believe her? The story that she told you. Did it ring true?'

I hate myself, thought Mina, *but I have to answer this truth-fully.* She looked him in the eyes. 'Yes. I believed her. I think at the time she told me that she believed that she'd killed Valerie. But, when she was perfectly lucid, she was sure she hadn't.'

'So let's start from the assumption that your mother was involved in an act that, at the time, she believed ended up in the death of Valerie, even though she later realised this couldn't have happened. What was your mother like?'

'Hilary was cool, bookish and self-contained. She chose a profession that allowed her to immerse herself in her passion. Completely different to me.'

'You mean the gardening?'

'Yes, and Hilary was the first to recognise it. She gave me the little patch of garden at the front of the house that I filled over the years with bedding plants, gaudy pots, spiky shrubs. It just grew and grew and it even featured in the local paper when I was fifteen. People would slow down outside the front garden and look at the display. Mum even once caught a neighbour pinching plants.'

'You say she was self-contained. She never talked about her childhood?'

'No, but my grandfather was around so it's not like her past was closed to me. She never referred to the past, though. Her childhood, schooldays, her relationship with my father. She wasn't prepared to discuss anything.'

'The fact that she never referred to the past might also be indicative of a trauma. When your mum was a teenager she was possibly involved in something that harmed Valerie. From what you say, it probably wasn't deliberate but she'd mistakenly believed that Valerie was dead.'

'So you think she didn't kill Valerie? But Valerie's dead, I've seen the grave, so who did she see at the hospital? She didn't have any visitors apart from Catherine Hallows. Unless someone from another ward came to visit her.'

Sadler had his eyes on her. 'When your mum said she saw Valerie did she see Valerie as she is now or as she was?'

'What do you mean?'

'If she saw her childhood friend then Valerie would be your mother's age, in her seventies. If she saw Valerie as she remembered her, bearing in mind you say she hadn't seen her since she was a child, then Valerie would look like a teenager.'

'You think she was hallucinating? That's what the nurses said.'

Sadler sighed. 'She might have been but there are other reasons why Valerie might look as she did. The first possibility is that Valerie is alive and Hilary was shocked that Valerie had grown old as she thought Valerie was dead.'

'That would mean Valerie had made it into her private room and I'm pretty sure that she had no visitors.'

'The second possibility is that she saw Valerie as she remembered her as a teenager or a young woman. Valerie Hallows had a son who had a daughter.'

Mina's mind cleared. 'Of course. She saw Catherine and thought it was Valerie, her grandmother. Of course. How stupid of me. But how does that help? Valerie died in 1963. Mum was at university by then. She specifically told me she hadn't seen Valerie since school. She can't have been involved in Valerie's death at all.'

'There may have been an incident before that. I don't think it's coincidence that Catherine was in Hilary's room. She says she saw Hilary in the corridor and decided to visit her. That's not enough of a reason for Catherine to stray from the ward that she's been assigned to and seek out Hilary. She wanted something else from your mother.'

'What?'

'I hope it was to talk to her. However, I can't discount the possibility it was to do your mother harm. The problem is, I don't know why.' Sadler kept his eyes steadily on Mina. 'Do you?'

57

'Jesus. It's a bit grim. People actually choose to walk here?'

Morgan smirked. 'The Peak District can be divided into those who like to walk through its dramatic if unforgiving scenery and those who prefer to sit on their arses ignoring the landscape around them. The latter is made up of locals, teenagers and, it seems, ninety per cent of my colleagues.'

'You like the outdoors then?'

'It's better than sitting indoors watching episodes of Jeremy Kyle when I'm not on shift.'

'You walk or cycle?'

He looked down at her. 'Both. Shall we go?'

They ignored the steps up the steep embankment, pushing instead through a narrow gap in the hedgerow.

'This isn't an official entrance onto the path, which is why it has no parking nearby. It looks like this hedge entrance has been used a few times, though. I suggest we walk through the tunnel in the direction that Catherine is likely to have taken and see if we can see anything.'

Connie looked around. 'We're hardly likely to have been the first ones through this morning. If there was anything obvious someone would have notified us.'

'But we need to take a look.'

'How will we know we're going in the right direction?

Patrick never said which way the girl was going.'

'She'll most likely have come from the direction of Bampton, walking away from the hospital where she was volunteering. It's unlikely she will have approached the tunnel from the opposite direction.'

They had reached the path. Near the tunnel was a wooden bench where an elderly couple were eating sandwiches and drinking coffee from a flask.

'I know this place. I've jogged this far in the past. I didn't know it was called the Cutting, though. What a horrible name.' Connie braced herself as she was nearly knocked over by a gust of wind. 'Good God, it's a wind trap.'

Morgan winced as pieces of grit bounced off his cheek. 'We might as well do what we came for. It won't be windy in the tunnel.'

They made their way towards the tunnel down a path made of compacted grit and sand. It was narrower than Connie remembered; it could only have carried a single rail line. On either side of the track there was a small verge and, as the incline increased, a steep embankment led down to houses below.

'We really need to be combing through all the shrubbery down there if we're looking for a body.'

Morgan had his eyes on the approaching tunnel. 'It'll be quite a search. Let's see what we can find in the tunnel. Look up there.' Connie followed his gaze. 'So we assume that Patrick and Archie Kersey were standing on top of the tunnel as they watched the girl go in.'

'They wouldn't be that easy for Catherine, if it was her, to spot. You have to look up and crane your neck to get a view of the path at the top.'

'Okay. I'll take your word for it. You're about the height of a fourteen year old.'

'Thanks very much.'

'The point is that they can't be seen. On the other hand, if you're looking down you're going to see a girl approach from quite a distance.'

'But will you see them go into the tunnel?'

Morgan looked up. 'I think I'd better go up there and take a look. I'm not sure how tall Patrick Kersey was but let's assume he was also of average height for a man. I'll crouch down a bit.'

Connie tracked Morgan's retreating form until he stepped out of view. 'I'm at the top of the bridge. Can you see me?'

'No,' she shouted up. 'Can you hear me?'

'I can hear and see you. Carry on walking and stop when I tell you to. I want to see how long you stay in my sight.'

Connie carried on walking.

'STOP. Where are you?'

'Virtually at the mouth of the tunnel.' She looked up and could see nothing until she saw Morgan climb onto the fence and lean over at her.

'If you were attacked outside the tunnel it would have to be right at the entrance.'

The picnicking couple looked at them in alarm, gathered up their things and hurried off.

'Yes,' she shouted back at Morgan.

'The verge on both sides of you is flat leading to the brick wall of the tunnel. There's nowhere to conceal someone. Okay, now I want you to walk down the tunnel and come out the other side. I want to see how long Patrick might have waited until he realised that the girl hadn't come out the other side.'

'Do I have to?'

'What?!'

'Do I have to go down the tunnel?'

'Why, are you scared?' As he leant over, she could see that he was grinning down at her.

Connie couldn't have articulated the dread that she felt at the thought of entering the long tunnel where she could hear the wind echoing around its cavernous interior. Morgan was taunting her so she took a deep breath and plunged into the tunnel. Inside the air grew stiller and colder and was tinged with a smell she sought to identify. Death? She wasn't sure. Small strips of lighting illuminated her way and she stayed in the centre of the path. She pulled out her mobile phone and, switching on the torch function, tried to see into the sides. Even with the weak light she could see there was nowhere to hide a body.

As she reached the end of the tunnel, as the aperture grew wider, she could feel her heartbeat becoming more regular. She came out into the open and couldn't ever remember being so pleased as a gust of air swept over her.

'Stop!' Morgan called out. Connie halted. 'I can see you now. Where are you in relation to the opening of the tunnel?'

'It's just behind me.'

'Hold on.' Morgan came running down the other side of the embankment and, after reaching her, he took off his hat and wiped a hand through his hair. He put his hat back on and looked around him. 'You were through the tunnel in three minutes. Let's say Patrick waited up to about ten minutes but,

315

at some point, he must have realised you weren't coming out. So we need to look inside the tunnel.'

'Bloody hell, Morgan. I've just walked through it. It's not that wide and the sides are made of brick. There's no one in there.' Connie hesitated, remembering a smell that she had tried to push away as she walked the path. 'Only . . .'

'Only what?'

'There is this odd smell, but I might have been imagining it. That place certainly gives me the creeps.'

'Let me see. We should have brought a torch. I've one in the car.'

'We can go back and get it if we spot something. Let's get this over and done with.'

Together they walked back down the path Connie had just taken. Morgan was looking around him with interest, feeling the walls with his fingertips. 'Whether it's Catherine who came into this tunnel or not, it's still odd that a girl entered a tunnel and didn't come out.'

'You think there might be a secret door? Like in Scooby Doo.'

'Hardly secret. Perhaps a ventilation shaft or something. Do you know anything about railway tunnels?'

'Oh yes. I'm a trainspotter in my spare time.'

He ignored her sarcasm and carried on feeling the walls. When they reached the opening at the other side, he nodded in the direction of the car. 'Can you get the torch? It's on the back seat.'

Connie huffed off furious. What a wild goose chase. Apart from the place giving her the creeps there was nothing to suggest anything untoward. She retrieved the torch and made her way back to Morgan. He was about halfway down the tunnel, still looking around him. She shone the beam up into the ceiling and down the walls.

'It all looks okay.'

'Yes, but you were right about the smell. It's not decomposition you can smell, though, it's fresh air.'

'Fresh air? It smells rank in here.'

Morgan shook his head. 'It smells like all tunnels, a bit earthy, that's all – but I can also smell a clearer air which is stronger as you get into the middle. Can you give me the torch?' She passed it to him and he shone it slowly around the walls of the tunnel. 'Look up.'

Connie followed his gaze.

'Can you see?' He made a circle with the beam just above his head so that she could see a small bulge in the brickwork. 'It's a ventilation shaft. It's wide enough for a grown man to get in there as they were used for maintenance. Maybe not as big as me, but certainly an adult.'

'But it's shut off.'

'There'll be a door that opens to one side.' He moved the beam. 'See that iron rung? You'll turn it and it opens. You then sidestep through to the shaft. We need to take a look.'

'I'm not going in there.'

'There's no need. We can see from the top.'

Morgan switched off the torch and she followed him out of the tunnel and back up the embankment. He looked around him.

'If it's a ventilation shaft it's got to come out somewhere.'

Connie puffed as she climbed the hill. In the distance she could see the housing estate that had been built on the outskirts of Bampton in the fifties and added to over the decades so it was now residential sprawl. In front of her was knee-high brackish undergrowth.

'You can't go poking around in there. Look at the state of it. You won't be sure of your footing. If the ventilation shaft comes out there and it's not covered, you could go plunging into the tunnel.'

'I'll tread carefully.'

Connie sighed. 'You're heavier than me. I'll go and you hang onto my arm.'

Morgan searched around on the floor and found a thick branch snapped off after recent winds. 'Use this. Poke it in the ground in front of you, and as long as it hits rock you can walk in front of you.'

Doing as he said, Connie gingerly stepped through the undergrowth, using the stick to guide her. She went deeper into the thicket, aware that Morgan was following closely behind. 'I'm following in your footsteps, just keep going.'

'This is ridiculous. I can see that this undergrowth hasn't been walked on for years. It's up to my knees.'

'Carry on. We're looking for the shaft's entrance.'

As Connie pushed the branch into the ground, it buckled and twisted in her hand. 'What the fu—'

'Are you okay?'

'Oh my God, Morgan.' She stepped back so that he could take a closer look.

58

'What happened? If it was that simple then I wouldn't have wasted all this time. I only have three leads. The first two are Cold Eaton and the Cutting. That place is definitely significant, not least because my mother was always disparaging about the Topley Trail even though, the Cutting aside, it's a beautiful path. She avoided the place for a reason that I'm sure is to do with the mystery. The other clue is a photo I have of a group of friends. It was a long time ago. People are dead and those left aren't talking about the past.'

Mina was sitting on a small, straight-backed sofa covered in a thin olive cord material. It suited the boat, and her. Sadler, whose girlfriends had been a type, glamorous and unavailable, forced himself to recognise his attraction to a woman with whom he wasn't able to anchor any previous experience. Not only was she physically different from the past women in his life but she was like no one else he had met. She emphasised the differences between her and Hilary and yet Mina had her mother's composure and self-sufficiency.

'Connie mentioned that you had a picture of Hilary and her friends.'

'It's important to you because of the presence of Ingrid and Nell. For me, it's a dead end. I know what Valerie looks like and that Valerie is no longer alive.'

'You're sure?'

'Monica Neale confirmed it. I've seen the grave in the churchyard and Monica pointed out Valerie to me in the photo.'

'Does Catherine look like Valerie?'

Mina screwed up her eyes trying to remember. 'I think so. Not in the face perhaps, more in the build. Small and slight with the same slightly wavy hair. Not like my wiry curls. I think there's a resemblance.'

'Very often it's not just looks that are handed down in families but gestures and mannerisms. When Catherine visited your mother in the ward it may have been something about her that triggered the memory. We might never know.'

Sadler hesitated. Mina, watching him closely, spotted it. 'There's something else?'

'Another member of Catherine's family is a nurse. Does the name Lorna Hallows mean anything?'

Mina shook her head. 'No, but surely she has got to be a stronger suspect if you think my mother's drip was tampered with. I met Catherine. A young girl wouldn't do that.'

'She might. I'm afraid I'm not as confident of the innocence of children as you are.'

'There's definitely a link to Cold Eaton across the generations. My mother had friends there. Emily whose family owned the pub, Ingrid in the manor house and Valerie up above the village on Hallows Hill. It's why I went to stay in the pub. To find the girls.'

'And when you say across the generations, you mean Catherine Hallows who still lives above the village and visited your mother in hospital?'

'Yes, exactly. It's horrifying to even contemplate it. I thought she cared about Mum. She even brought Mum some flowers. Red campion, the type you find alongside railways and canals.' Mina frowned.

'Are you sure Catherine left your mum the flowers?'

'No, I'm not, I just think it was her. No one else visited Mum. You don't think Catherine could have visited Ingrid and Nell too?'

'I'm not sure. She was in school when Nell died, according to her teacher. Ingrid, I'm pretty sure, died of natural causes but she was the catalyst for everything that happened. I'm fairly certain of that. Your mother seeing Valerie in the hospital didn't start this chain of deaths. It had already begun with the death of Ingrid and Nell's determination to bring to light an old event.' Mina, he thought, looked relieved. The days of searching must have been a heavy weight to bear alongside her grief. It was time to take the burden off her. 'You mentioned that the photo was your clue. You think that something might have happened amongst the group of girls?'

'It's the photo itself that first gave me the idea. The girls have an air of privilege. Well, there's nothing really surprising about that. But there's something else too. An almost, I don't know, sense of something not quite right.'

'Can I see the photo?'

'Of course.'

She handed him the image and his eyes immediately went to the girl standing in the middle of the group. As he focused on the tall girl with the long, fair hair, he could hear Mina talking over his shoulder.

'So, on the left is Valerie. You can see she *is* small and thin like Catherine. You might be right about Hilary mistaking Catherine for her grandmother as a child. Next is Ingrid who I never met but she does look like her sister, Monica. Next to her in the middle is a girl I don't know. Then there's Emily Fenn. She's really changed and put on loads of weight but she still lives in the village in the pub. The last girl is Nell. Her neighbour identified her in this photo.'

Mina, as if noticing that her words weren't getting any reaction, trailed off. 'Is everything all right?'

'Emily Fenn is still alive and hasn't mentioned any attacks or feeling unsafe?'

'No. Nothing. What's the matter? You've seen something in the photo, haven't you? Tell me what it is.'

Sadler continued to stare at the image. 'You haven't been able to find out the identity of the middle girl?'

'Monica Neale was playing it cool and Emily won't even look at the photo. She personifies everything that's odd about that place. She claimed never to have heard of Valerie when it was obvious she had because she even appears in the photo. When I was showing it around the pub the other day she just walked off as if she wasn't interested, but when I went upstairs, I saw out of the window that she had her coat on and was heading up to the big house where Harry and Monica Neale live.'

'Your mother was behind the camera?'

'I assume so.'

'Can I have the photo, Mina? It's evidence.'

'I was supposed to scan a copy for Connie but, after the accident, it slipped my mind. She called my mobile late last night, probably to chase it up. Perhaps I should go back to

Emily and ask her who the girl is, although she's unlikely to tell me.'

'There's no need to give it to Emily. I know who she is.'

She looked at him in shock. 'You do?'

He didn't reply but turned over the photo. 'GIVEN. What does that mean?'

'Nell's neighbour thinks it's the girls' initials mixed up so that it makes a recognisable word. It adds to the air of mystery. You can feel it, can't you? The odd atmosphere in the photo. It's not just me.'

'No, Mina. It's not only you. It's definitely there.' He looked up at her, aware of her face near his. 'Will you trust me with this?'

'You're going to take the photo? It's all I have of the girls.'

'I'll keep it safe, I promise. Do you want to take a picture with your phone for safekeeping? I need the original. It's important.'

He watched as she angled her phone and copied the image, more competently than Connie must have done. She checked the quality of the photo she'd taken and nodded. 'This will be okay.'

'I don't want you to go to work today or, in fact, for the rest of the week. Are you able to do that financially?'

'It's autumn so I always make provision for it being a bit slack. What will I do instead?'

'I want you to stay away from all your clients and I mean all of them. Instead, will you go through your mum's things and see if you can find any more photos of the girls? Or anything from your mum's childhood.'

'There's hardly anything to search. What am I looking for?'

Sadler willed himself to be calm. 'Did your mother ever mention anything about tea dances?'

'Tea dances? I can assure you that wasn't her thing at all. She was built like me. I hardly ever saw her in a dress. What have tea dances got to do with this?'

'I need you to trust me. I know it's difficult but will you do that?'

'And what will you do with the photo?'

Sadler looked at the GIVEN girls and took a deep breath. 'I need to do some digging of my own.'

59

Sadler stepped off the boat, leaving Mina despondent. He touched the pocket in his jacket where he had placed the photo and dropped his eyes to hers, puzzled and questioning. He did another round of the boat, checking her window fastenings before his eyes fell on the canoe.

'Do you use it?'

'All the time, before Mum died. I'm not sure I feel up to it at the moment.'

'Go for a paddle, Mina. This boat is safe. If you come back and notice anything odd, don't go aboard. Go and sit with one of your neighbours. For the moment, you're as safe here as anywhere and you have people nearby.' He nodded at Anna who was swabbing down the deck, her stiff back suggesting an awareness of what was happening on the next boat. 'Exercise conquers fear and uncertainty. Take my word for it. You've met my assistant, Connie, haven't you? She'd agree with me.'

'I don't think she likes me.'

He smiled and said nothing, climbing onto the towpath and towards his car.

After he had driven off, Mina massaged her aching foot and flexed it for a moment. She looked down at the canoe and made a decision. Anna had stopped mopping and was leaning on the handle, looking across at Mina.

'Is everything all right? There's not been any trouble, has there?'

'Why do you ask?'

'It's probably none of my business but I saw your visitor and he had an air of authority about him.'

Mina looked at Anna's kind face. 'I had a fall where I was staying. Nothing to worry about. I'm wondering whether to get the canoe out.'

'I think it'll do you the world of good.'

Feeling fragile, Mina put on her flotation jacket before dropping into the canoe. Its open hull meant she could still move her legs and as the brackish smell from the close water wafted towards her she could feel some of the tension begin to dissipate. None of her old routes appealed. What was the point of a morning or evening routine if the day had coalesced into a confused blur? Instead she struck out towards Step Bridge and pushed on through it, enjoying the plunge into the darkness and the rush of cold air as she paddled. She kept up the pace, passing out of Bampton, away from the *Evening Star*, away from Cold Eaton, away from the Cutting. Walkers along the parallel path thinned out and disappeared while Mina's throbbing head began to clear.

Feeling her arms, unused to the exercise, begin to tire, she kept her eyes on the large building in the distance, a huge factory-like edifice split in two by a clock tower. Derelict, Grade II listed apparently, it stood as a monument to a time when buildings were constructed to contain as well as impress. Mina couldn't remember what the building's original use was but the relic from the Victorian era sent a chill down her spine and her mood plummeted. She turned the canoe around early and, with a plan formulating, headed back to the *Evening Star*.

*

The railway office was empty except for the miserable-looking man she had encountered the last time. What had his sister called him? Something short. Tom? Jim? He was drinking a cup of coffee from one of their manky cups and flicking through a railway magazine. 'The train's not running today.' He didn't even bother to look up at her.

'It's you I wanted to talk to actually. I came here before and your sister made me a cup of tea. We talked about the Cutting.'

'Oh aye. I remember.' He stopped flicking through the magazine and stared at the page featuring a large photo of a steam engine. 'What's it you want?'

'Have you heard about the latest accident?'

'The one near the Cutting. I heard. Is that why you're here?'

'You said it was a strange place and you're right.'

He finally looked up at her. 'You've been there?'

'I went there recently and I wanted to ask you a few more questions. Are you all right with that?'

Jim shrugged and pushed the magazine away. 'There's not much I'm going to be able to tell you.'

'When I came here last time, you spoke about a man who'd been seen without any clothes. Do you remember?'

'Aye, I remember.'

'The thing is, I was wondering if any girls ever got into danger near the Cutting.'

Jim stood up. 'I don't remember anything like that. Just that me and Jean were warned about going near the place because of the naked man.'

'When you say naked man, do you mean some kind of flasher?'

'I'm not sure it were that and I never heard of a child actually being molested. There was talk of a man with no clothes on being spotted there. This was when I was a nipper.'

'In the fifties?'

'I don't know exactly. I was a young lad in short trousers, so about then.'

'You don't know who it was?'

'They never found him. My dad occasionally used to go out looking for the man with a paraffin lamp. The rumour was he'd hang about near the Cutting around dusk. So my dad would head off down there to try to catch him.'

'But he didn't.'

'No. But even when we were growing up, we were warned to stay away from the Cutting and we did.' He tipped his tea into the sink. 'Is that all?'

Mina turned to go. 'I suppose so. It's such a strange tale.' *And I don't understand,* she thought, *why a naked man could be significant.*

60

Wednesday, 6 November 1957

Valerie waited in the stillness, fighting the claustrophobia that was sending her brain freewheeling into the darkness. In her fear, she was aware of the irrationality of worrying about how she'd explain her hair. She could feel a patch where the girl had grabbed it and pulled out a clump. Who had that been? Not Hilary. She'd spotted a flicker of compassion in Hilary's eyes before the girl had turned away and let her friends take over. No. Not Hilary. Ingrid, probably. Of all of them, it was Ingrid who hated her the most. Ingrid of the bad skin and the smell of the ammonia she put on her spots to get rid of them.

Valerie tentatively touched her head, found the tender spot and winced. The pain stopped her brain from free fall and slowed, for a moment, her racing heart. It wasn't quite blackness. Almost but not quite. The way down was blocked to her. One of the first things she'd done was to use her feet against the door but it was shut. Impossible to open from the inside. She was pinned to the rung of the ladder until someone found her. If anyone found her. Would someone tell? Would Hilary tell? They couldn't leave her to die.

Minutes passed. Or was it hours? On her perilous perch,

Valerie panicked, beating her feet against the door. Once, she heard a train whoosh through the tunnel and then another. She would die in this dank tomb. She twisted her body so her back was to the wall and grasped the ladder with her small hands. *I have to see what's at the top.*

The iron ladder was surprisingly easy to climb. Rough grooves were carved into the rungs, giving traction for her stockinged feet, her shoes discarded at the bottom of the shaft. Up she went, light as a feather, and the air grew cooler but fresher. And lighter. She climbed until she could go no further and met more metal. This time a hatched grate. Her fingers slipped between the spaces, feeling the cold air, and she pushed and pushed. It wasn't locked. It was just too heavy for her to lift. She braced herself against the wall of the tunnel and tried again; the iron lifted a crack and fell again.

Shoots of bramble poked through the grating scratching her hands.

'Can anyone hear me?' Her voice was faint. She licked her cracked lips and tried again. 'Is anyone there?'

She could hear a rustling in the undergrowth. A fox curious of the intruder probably. She saw a shadow darken the opening and she was aware of the grate being lifted effortlessly and a rush of cold air on her face. She tried to climb further but fear and fatigue meant she nearly slipped back down into the abyss. A pair of strong hands lifted her up by the arm and carried her away from the hateful shaft and out of the undergrowth.

The man placed her down on the grass. As her eyes cleared, Valerie looked up at her rescuer, desperate to give her thanks and saw, with a start, that he was naked.

61

Tuesday, 7 November 2017

Sadler sat in his office with his head in his hands looking down at the photo. He'd pulled down the blinds, a signal to the few members of his team in the Detective Room that he wasn't to be disturbed. The five girls were from an age long gone. A time of stronger class distinctions. Where you were segregated into schools according to your ability at the age of eleven and that distinction stuck for the rest of your education. These girls had all been bright. No late starters here. And amongst them, his mother Ginnie. Sadler turned over the photo and looked at the word on the back. GIVEN. He frowned and looked closer.

His phone rang and he picked it up. A voice he didn't recognise staffing reception.

'I've got a lady by the name of Susan Barr here. She says it's important. To do with the crash on the Matlock road.'

'Can't you direct her to whoever's investigating that?'

'She says she thinks she might have information about the missing girl.'

'Take a statement then.'

'I tried but it's a complicated story going back to the fifties and—'

'The fifties? I'll come down and get her.'

Sadler opened his door. Only Matthews was left at her desk. 'Where is everyone?'

'Dahl's attending the PM. He's not back yet. Connie's disappeared somewhere. Mayfield's in labour.'

'Fine. Can you wait in my office? There's someone who wants to speak to me about the missing girl and I want a word afterwards.'

Sadler didn't miss the spark of apprehension in Matthews's eye. He went down into the reception, and sitting on one of the hard plastic chairs was a woman wearing a short coat with a scarf unsuccessfully covering what looked like recently permed hair.

'Ms Barr.'

'I feel a fool but I had to come.'

'Do you want to come into my office? You'll be more comfortable there.'

Matthews, notepad at the ready, was already sitting in the chair Connie normally preferred. She pulled out a chair for Susan who sat down in relief. 'You're going to think I'm completely potty but I read about the accident in the newspaper and I had to tell someone. It seems so daft as it's a story that goes back to when I was a teenager.'

We all have them, thought Sadler. *A moment in time when your life takes one direction when it might have gone a different way.* Camilla had once confided to him that, before she drifted off to sleep, she thought of the baby who had died only a few hours old and how life would be with a young teenage daughter.

Connie had surely had hers in the last case when she'd

threatened to resign and spent days languishing in her flat until she'd been spurred to resurrect her career. Surely she too, occasionally, stopped to think what parallel life she might lead outside the force.

The woman sitting in front of him was telling a story of when the lives of six teenagers, seven if you included Susan Barr, had changed irretrievably. It was a simple enough tale. Six schoolgirls had entered the tunnel at Cutting Lane and only five had emerged. The sixth, who surely must be Valerie, had . . . what? Come to harm, certainly.

'How meticulously did you look in the tunnel?'

Susan Barr looked uncomfortable. 'I went down one side of the tunnel then back along the other. There was lighting. Not brilliant but I could see enough.'

'Did you look in the ventilation shaft?'

She stared at him in shock. 'The ventilation shaft?'

'Most tunnels have them, especially the longer ones. It's somewhere for the fumes to escape.'

'I never saw anything.'

'It can be quite high up or, if it was lower down, there will have been a door that was kept locked. It's possible one of the girls knew how to open it.'

'Can you check?'

'I think we're going to need to. And you think it might have happened again?'

'It was in the newspaper. A man and a boy in the car hurrying away from the Cutting. It says the source was from the police.'

'We can double-check. It's helpful that you've told us of this.'

'What do you think happened to the girl?'

Sadler's thoughts were on Catherine Hallows and he misunderstood the question. 'We're doing everything we can to find Catherine.'

But Susan was obsessed by an event that had taken place sixty years earlier. 'I mean to the girl in the fifties. What do you think happened to her?'

'You didn't recognise any of the girls you saw?'

Susan shook her head. 'They were about my age but they were at the grammar school. I didn't know any of them.'

'Hilary Kemp?'

'No.'

'Nell Colley? Ingrid Neale?'

Susan shook her head. Sadler opened his notebook. 'I have a few more names. Emily Fenn?'

Susan shook her head.

'A girl named Valerie Hallows?'

Again a shake of her head.

Sadler took a deep breath. 'Ginnie Sadler?'

Matthews turned to him but Susan was shaking her head once more. 'These names mean nothing to me. I told you I didn't recognise them.'

Sadler pushed the photo towards the woman. 'Do you think these could be the girls?'

Susan looked like she was in shock. 'Good God. These girls have inhabited my nightmares for sixty years but I'd swear it was them.'

'You don't recognise any of the girls individually?'

'No, but it does look like them.'

Sadler shut his notebook. 'Leave it with me. We need, in the first instance, to find Catherine Hallows and check she's safe.

Then—'

'Yes?' She looked at them eagerly. 'Do you think that you'll be able to find out what went on in the tunnel?'

'I'm going to try.'

Matthews took Susan back to reception then returned to the office and shut the door behind her.

'Sit down, Matthews.'

She did so, looking resigned.

'I need some help.'

It wasn't what she'd expected. Her head shot up. 'What do you mean, help?'

'I've got a conflict of interest in this case that I've only recently discovered. I need to speak to Superintendent Llewellyn and my mother in that order.'

'You think she was one of the girls in the tunnel? You mentioned her name just then.'

Sadler swivelled the photo to Matthews and pointed at a tall figure with long fair hair. 'This is my mother.'

Matthews looked at a loss for words. 'How do you want me to help?'

'I need to do everything by the book. I don't want any of my personal connections seeping into the case. I want to talk to my mother first, assuming Llewellyn is happy for me to do so. She needs to tell me what she knows about what happened in that tunnel. Afterwards, I want you to take over the case.'

'Me?' Sadler thought he saw the glint of tears.

'You're the best person for making sure everything is done properly.'

Matthews nodded and was about to reply when the door

opened without a knock. It was a young uniformed constable. 'Sir. They've found a girl near the Cutting. Initial identification suggests it's Catherine Hallows.'

'Is she—'

'She's alive but suffering from exposure and in a critical condition. She's in the hospital now.'

'Who found her?'

'Connie and a member of the traffic division. Goes by the name of Morgan.'

So here we are, thought Sadler. *All paths lead to the Cutting.*

62

There were three people behind the desk at the library, none of whom Mina recognised and each engrossed in their tasks. She went over to the noticeboard and checked that the replacement card was there. She found it tucked away on the bottom left of the board, the message written in Joseph's neat capital letters. She moved it to the centre of the board and approached the desk.

'How far do your local papers go back?'

The group looked at each other. 'Hold on.' One woman opened a drawer and took out a file, flicking through the pages.

'Okay, we have the *Bampton Express*, which goes back to 1971.' She looked up hopefully.

'Anything else?'

'That's the only paper that's still going. We also hold the records for the *Bampton Mercury* between 1951 and 1967. I guess it must have shut down around then.'

'They're on computer?'

'Everything's been transferred to microfilm but we also have physical copies of some records. Do you want me to check?'

'Would you? Fingers crossed it's the actual newspapers. I'm not sure if I'll cope with microfilm.'

'Oh, don't worry too much about that. It's easy to use. We need to go downstairs to the reference section.'

The room was partially underground. The full length windows that illuminated the ground floor extended into the lower room and, as Mina looked up, she could see feet walking past on the pavement above. It was a long, narrow room, lined with books with a table stretching down its length dotted with reading lamps. At the far end was a row of computer terminals.

'Let's have a look.' The woman traced her finger along a shelf of outsized books. 'Here we are. You're in luck. We have the paper copies of the *Bampton Mercury*. What year were you looking for?'

'I don't know, exactly. Sometime in the nineteen fifties. Can you leave me to look through?'

At the retreating sound of the clip of heels on the parquet floor, Mina pulled out 1956. Hilary would have been fourteen then. A little young, perhaps, but already at Bampton Grammar. The *Mercury* had been a weekly broadsheet and, as she flicked through, Mina began to get a sense of how the paper was laid out. Local news on the front page, national headlines on pages two and three and then back to local news. Letters to the editor took up a whole page in the centre of the paper and local and national sporting achievements jostled for space at the back.

She made her focus the local news, editorial and readers' letters. It took her over two hours to get through 1956. In 1957 there was talk about one of the stations on the Bampton line shutting because of poor usage. This was a good ten years before Beeching. Already the railway was

338

proving to be uneconomic. Responses were muted. One reader worried how he would get to Skegness for his annual holiday, and another, who was a nurse in Sheffield, said she'd have to give up a job and take a lower paid one in Bampton. There was no mention of a naked man. The summer of 1957 was a heatwave and Mina found a photo of the train from Bampton station packed with holidaymakers during the wakes weeks, the traditional holidays in the Peaks. Mina heaved the bound volume back onto the shelf and took down the book labelled September to December 1957. There, amongst the readers' letters, she found what she was looking for.

Sir, it has come to our attention that a man, divested of any clothing whatsoever, was spotted in the environs of Cutting Lane on the evening of 12 September. Residents of Bampton are advised to take appropriate action to protect their women and children.

Good God. It sounded like the writer had swallowed a bowl of marbles. Why such convoluted language? It was clearly the style of writing required by the paper even though ordinary residents of the town must have read it. She continued to turn the pages. The next entry came on 10 October, not in the form of a letter but a short article. It reported that the man had been seen by a number of walkers in the fields around the top of the bridge. He'd made no attempt to approach anyone and had continued on his chosen path without looking at those who had spotted him. He had, however, been completely naked.

The naked man. One of the witnesses had been an eleven-year-old girl with her brother aged around four. Mina

339

thought of Jim and Jean. Had it been them? Jim had been suitably vague but the ages might fit. He said he'd been in short trousers. A young lad. What was interesting was that the man hadn't approached the children but had kept on his intended path. If he was a predator, surely he would have tried to engage the children in some way. Adults had also spotted him. He'd not tried to hide himself, instead walking on his chosen path.

It wasn't the image of a predator that entered Mina's head but of the 'Naked Rambler' she had seen a news item about on TV. He simply liked to walk without any clothes. Was this the same person? In the back of her mind she was trying to remember something. A naked man walking. It wasn't related to present time. At some point, someone else she had talked to other than Jim had referred to a man and clothes or lack of them. Who had it been? The image of Emily Fenn popped into her head and a man without his clothes she had mentioned when Mina was studying the figure of the Guy.

63

'She's only just alive. We've not been able to speak to her yet.' The ICU unit was at the back of the hospital, away from the incident room and the interviews that Sadler's team were painstakingly conducting. Connie was waiting for him outside the entrance to the unit, slumped like a ragdoll on a chair although his appearance seemed to revive her.

'The mother's with her?' asked Sadler, taking the seat next to her.

'She hasn't left her side. We'd already talked to her before we found Catherine. Your guess was correct this morning. She does work as a district nurse. She's not connected to the hospital at all. Interesting you thought of that.'

'Catherine said to the volunteer leader that her mother was always out and about, which doesn't sound like the phrase you'd use about someone going to and from a place of work. I guessed she'd have a role in the community.'

'The thing is, I talked to Lorna about her job while she was sitting next to Catherine. She visits people in their homes. She's never heard of Nell Colley or Hilary Kemp but she did say she deals with a lot of elderly patients in the course of her work.' Connie stood up and massaged her calf. 'I think I pulled a muscle up on the railway bridge.'

'You believed her?'

'She appeared to be telling the truth. She was curious why I was asking, of course, but distracted by her worry over Catherine. She also told me she's in demand because she took an extra qualification that allows her to prescribe drugs as part of her work.'

'Has she been missing any diamorphine?'

'I couldn't ask her that. She has a seriously ill daughter. I'd already pushed my luck in terms of informal questions. We'll need to interview her tomorrow.'

'We also need to know if Catherine had access to any drugs.'

'Yes.' Connie looked down at him and made a face. 'Not a pleasant thought, is it?'

'It's not. You found Catherine at the top of the escarpment? At the Cutting?'

'It looks like she'd been in the ventilation shaft and got into difficulties. She managed to climb out but injured herself in doing so.'

'Inside the ventilation shaft? You think she accessed it from the tunnel below?'

'According to the witness, Patrick Kersey, the man who was killed yesterday in the car accident, he saw the girl entering the tunnel and not emerging. So, yes, we think she accessed it from below.'

'Voluntarily?'

'We're not going to be sure about this until we speak to her.'

'Are all her injuries consistent with attempts to escape from the shaft?'

Connie shook her head. 'I don't know. One of the paramedics thought he could detect the smell of morphine. It has the scent of vinegar, apparently. But we found her at the top of the shaft. She couldn't have climbed that ladder if she was drugged.'

'She'd been missing nearly twenty-four hours. She may have looked for a way out when the effects of the drug wore off.' Sadler looked up as a doctor came towards them but passed without stopping. 'I've been speaking to a witness, Susan Barr, about an event that happened sixty years ago.'

Connie stared at him, puzzled. 'It's relevant to now?'

'I'm pretty sure it's the start of the case. I think that ventilation chimney was used in an attack by a group of schoolgirls in the fifties.'

'You think that's what Nell Colley was going to write about?'

'I think it was a pivotal point in all the girls' lives. I've been thinking about group dynamics on the way here. I remember studying it as part of my inspector's exams. How normality becomes distorted when you belong to a gang. I suspect Nell was part of a group of girls who may well have had a set of rituals to create a sense of belonging. It's a fascinating subject. Rules are created to ensure the group is paramount over individuals. If someone transgresses them, a form of punishment is dished out.'

'So the book would have been about teenage friendship and an act that they had committed to protect it. From what?'

'I don't know.'

'What happened to the girl who went missing in the tunnel?'

'I don't know that either. I've been talking to Mina, who's been following the same trail after her mother hinted at what had happened. The victim, Valerie Hallows, appears to have died in her early twenties. She was Catherine's grandmother.'

'An interesting enough story for a book?'

'Perhaps it was intended to be an act of atonement for what happened.'

Connie stretched out. 'This could be it. The link between everything. Nell Colley decides to write a book about the attack and one of the original girls decides to stop her.'

'That would tally with the extract I found on the envelope but—'

'Why kill the other girls? Good question. I don't know. It's not a nice story but hardly earth-shattering.'

'Catherine must know some of the answers.'

'Which is why we need to speak to her urgently. Are you staying here?'

'I think I'd better. When she comes around, *if* she comes around, she'll be able to give us more information.' Connie paused. 'She's our main suspect, isn't she?'

Sadler hesitated. 'I think she is our prime suspect for killing Hilary Kemp. I'm not so sure about Nell Colley.'

'Catherine was at school that morning and was marked in the register as present. We checked when we spoke to the school this morning. Catherine's been missing lessons and we know she was at the hospital when Hilary died. Nell will be harder to prove if the teacher was right.'

'Can the teacher remember her being there?'

'No, but she's pretty sure that if she marked Catherine as present then she will have been. The school register is a legal document, apparently.' Connie shifted slightly. 'I think there's someone behind Catherine.'

'I agree, but if Catherine administered the diamorphine into Hilary's drip, she's going to be facing a murder charge even if she's a minor.'

Connie swallowed and nodded. 'There's got to be mitigating circumstances, though. She's being manipulated by someone.' Sadler could feel the anger in his colleague at the thought of a vulnerable minor being manipulated into committing an act that would have devastating consequences for the girl's life.

'I agree and I'm going to get to the bottom of it whatever the personal cost.'

Connie twisted in her seat, alert at his change in tone. 'What do you mean personal cost?'

'The photo that Mina Kemp showed you. How closely did you look at it?'

'It showed a group of girls in tennis clothes. I didn't look at it closely at all.'

'Two of the girls were Ingrid Neale and Nell Colley, both now dead. The third was Valerie Hallows who died in 1963 apparently by her own hand.'

'And the other two?'

'One of them is Emily Fenn who owns the pub in Cold Eaton and the other . . .' Sadler hesitated, 'is my mother.'

Connie stared at him. 'What?'

'I know. I've just told Matthews and she's been primed to take over the case from me after I've seen Llewellyn.'

'Sadler,' Connie hissed. 'These women are in danger. What the hell are you doing here? You need to go and see your mother as soon as possible.'

'There is a possibility that I have to confront that my mother may be the murderer.'

345

Connie stared at him. 'You mean she was at the hospital? Of course, you said she was sick.' Connie's mind was working. 'Your mother? You don't surely—'

'No, I don't. But I'd be a fool not to consider the possibility. I can't talk to my mother on my own. Will you come with me tomorrow?'

'Bloody hell, Sadler. Why not tonight?'

'Because I need to do this properly, which means speaking to Llewellyn first. Will you come with me?'

'Of course I will. But if you don't mind me saying . . .'

'What?'

'You're a bit bloody calm about all this.'

*

Camilla looked alarmed when she spotted him outside her house. Sadler's nephews danced around him as he got out of the car but she took one look at her brother's face and shooed them inside.

'Is everything all right? It's not Mum?'

'Not what you think. Can we have a chat on our own?'

Camilla went into the living room and turned on the TV. 'Sam? What was the film that you wanted to watch last week?'

Sam appeared, looking wary. '*Iron Man*, but Dad's got to watch it with us as it's a 12A certificate. Ben might be scared.'

'Can I trust you to fast forward if Ben gets frightened?'

The delighted Sam snatched the handset off his mother and scrolled through the recordings to find the channel. Camilla followed Sadler into the kitchen and shut the door behind her. 'What's happened?'

346

'Mum's involved in the case I've been investigating. The murder of a patient at St Bertam's.'

'Involved? Involved in what way?'

'I'm not sure.'

'But when you say involved, you don't mean *involved*.' Camilla stared at him in horror.

'I don't know.'

'Francis!'

'I've missed so many clues. Mina, the victim's daughter, saying her mother refused to talk about Topley Trail, for instance. Remember Mum was the same. Refused to take us to the railway museum even though I went through a phase of loving trains as a boy.'

'What? Don't be daft, Francis. It just wasn't her thing. You know what Mum liked to do with us. Visit churches, walk in the hills with a picnic squashed in her rucksack. Trains weren't part of it.'

'No, but she loved walking and yet we never went anywhere near that path. When I spoke to Mina, so many things she told me about her own mother echoed with ours.'

'Like what?'

'Refusing to talk about school, avoiding the railway line, wary of intimate friendships. I know Mum has loads of friends but how many does she know really well, confidantes?'

'I think you've got this wrong.'

'Remember that leaflet about the tea dance that you found? Can you remember anything else about it?'

'I'm not sure. It was a date in June. I remember it was odd that there was no address written on it, which made it difficult to place. You think it's important?'

'I do but I can't for the life of me think how.'

'How's Mum involved in your case?'

'She was part of a group of girls where something catastrophic happened. It appears to have blighted all their lives.'

'Mum's life hasn't been blighted. She's led a full and interesting life. We've talked about it before. She hasn't led a blighted life.'

'No. No, she hasn't. You're right. Camilla. You're the person I needed to see. I'm nearly there but not quite.'

64

The Nettle Inn was closed when Mina got there the next morning. Curtains were drawn across the small windows and the car park was empty. The leaves that Mina had meticulously swept the previous week had been replaced by a new fall, which was swirling over the tarmac. Mina walked around to the side door and opened it. Emily was sitting in the seat that Monica had wept in the previous day. She too looked like she'd been crying.

'You're not staying?'

Mina shook her head. 'I'm better off back in town.'

Emily stood up. 'Cold Eaton's not for everyone. It's hard when you're new to the village. You stand out. Not everyone likes it.'

'You mean me?'

'Not just you. It's always been like this.' Emily turned off the lights to the room. 'I'm shutting the pub today in respect for the Kerseys. I'm not going to take any more residents either. The rooms are closed for the winter.'

'Who was in that middle room when I had my accident?'

Emily shook her head. 'I wasn't lying to you. The room was empty.'

'It was locked when I tried the handle before I hit my head.'

'Locked? But the only other person who has a key is Catherine Hallows. I gave it to her months ago so she could

349

do her homework in peace when the weather's bad and she wants to wait for her mother to give her a lift up to Hallows Hill.'

'Catherine? It can't have been her in that room. Catherine's missing and has been for a couple of days. Who might she have given the key to?'

'I . . .' Emily pressed her lips together. 'I don't know.'

'Who did you tell about the photo I had?'

'I told no one.' Emily was a poor liar and, in despair, Mina snapped.

'I saw you hurrying up to the Neales'. Did you tell them?'

'Perhaps. I think I said something.'

Mina stood up. 'I don't know what you did to Valerie but I know it ruined her life. You're not going to tell me what went on. So don't. Keep your secrets. But I've come here to warn you. Nell's dead, Ingrid is dead and my mum's gone. Have you thought about that?'

'Ingrid Neale was sick. I helped Monica nurse her. You told me your mother was ill. I don't know anything about Nell Colley.'

'What about you? Are *you* feeling okay?'

'Me?' Emily looked at her in astonishment. 'I have nothing to be scared of.'

'I wouldn't be so sure about that. I want the name of the naked man.'

Emily looked away.

'You know who I mean. When we were talking about the figure of the Guy you bring down every year for bonfire night, you mentioned that there was someone around here who didn't like to wear clothes.'

350

'Oh him.' Emily laughed. 'What the hell has he got to do with anything? If you want to know, when we were teenagers, a young lad in the village began to renounce all his worldly goods. You'd see him walking around the fields when he thought no one was looking. Naturism, isn't it? Must have been bloody cold up here.'

'But he made it into the paper? People thought he was a pervert.'

'Malcolm Cox a pervert?' Emily laughed. 'He's just a law unto himself. By the time the sixties came along he had his clothes back on.'

'Malcolm Cox? You mean the man who lives up from the church?'

'That's the one. He's well known around here. He inherited the cottage from his parents and has settled down. He has his clothes on these days.'

'He's not dangerous?'

'He's a loner but he's all right, really. He went through a romantic phase as a teenager, that's all.'

'You never saw him down by the Cutting?'

Emily's face fell. 'I'd stay away from that place if I were you.'

Mina kept her eyes on her. 'You're not sorry for what you did? Whatever you did in that tunnel, you don't regret it?'

Emily stared at her, defiant. 'You don't understand. You don't know what it was like then. Why don't you just leave it be?'

'It's not finished. Whatever it was, it resulted in a death.'

'Death? No one died.'

'Valerie died. After the Cutting, she died after having that baby of hers. By her own hand, Harry Neale told me.'

'What baby?'

'Harry Neale told me Valerie Hallows died after having the baby. She took her own life.'

Emily was staring at her. Her eyes shrouded with decades of secrets. 'So that's how it is, is it? You've gone down the wrong track, lovey. That's all I'm saying. You took a wrong turn. Ask Malcolm Cox.'

65

'This is the end of the investigation for me.'

Sadler sat in the passenger seat of Connie's car watching, through the swishing windscreen wipers, the front door of his mother's house. He remembered helping Ginnie to paint it years ago when she'd moved in. She'd chosen a pale mustard colour although he and Camilla had protested it wasn't practical in the Derbyshire weather. They had given in to her, though. Glossed the half-paned door of the fifties semi so that it shone against the black tiled step.

Connie, her hands on the steering wheel, turned in her seat. 'Don't say that. It's not the first time something personal has encroached on an investigation. It's what happens around here. One of the coppers looking for Catherine this week said he was distantly related to the family.'

'This is my mother. Whatever happens from now on will be for someone else to decide.'

'Matthews?'

Sadler shrugged. 'Why not? She's a safe pair of hands and I've primed her to take over if Llewellyn agrees.'

'Is she okay with you talking to your mother first?'

'I didn't really give her much choice.'

They'd picked up Dahl from the station. Sadler had been resigned. 'He might as well come with us. I'd like him to wait outside while I speak to my mother but he can come.'

Dahl, to his credit, had asked no questions on the way over and was sitting in the back seat, silently listening to their conversation.

'Did you speak to Llewellyn?' asked Connie.

'I went to his house late last night. I got his permission to talk to Ginnie. Depending on how this conversation goes, I might see him later and ask for some voluntary leave. I need to stay away from the rest of the investigation.'

'We're not going to do a formal interview, are we, when we speak to Ginnie?' Dahl's disembodied voice came from the back of the car. 'When we find who doctored Hilary Kemp's drip, the CPS will do their nut if there are any blurring of professional boundaries.'

'We're going to interview her as a potential witness. Informally.'

They continued to stare at the door. Connie sounded near to tears. 'She can't have killed Hilary Kemp. She was sick in hospital with cardiac problems.'

'I don't think my mother's a murderer but I suspect she knows a significant amount about what happened in 1957. I want to know what. I also want to find out why there was a break-in at her house.'

'When you went to see Mina yesterday, couldn't she give you any more information?'

'Mina's searches have always been in relation to finding Valerie. Once she had done that, she realised her mother couldn't have killed Valerie Hallows despite supposedly seeing her in hospital.'

'Valerie Hallows?' Dahl leant forward.

'Yes, exactly, Catherine's grandmother. Why are you looking at me like that?'

'That's not right. The Hallows have lived on that farm at the top of the hill for generations.'

'I know.'

'So where does Derwent village come into it?'

'Derwent?'

'Hilary was rambling on about the drowned village and when one of the hospital porters asked about it she mentioned Valerie. Valerie must have come from the drowned village.'

Sadler turned in his seat and stared at Dahl. 'Say that again.'

'Valerie came from the drowned village—'

'Look.' Connie pointed as the yellow front door opened and shut. Ginnie was still pulling on her coat as she shut the door behind her. It was a newish fawn raincoat that Sadler couldn't remember seeing before. She buttoned it up to her neck and belted it tightly but her head had no protection from the downpour and she hunched her shoulders as she left the front garden.

'Will she be all right?' Connie sounded concerned. 'She has heart problems.'

'We need to follow her.'

'I'll do it.' Dahl had opened the door. 'I'll call you, Sadler, if she goes away from the road so you can pick up the trail again.'

Connie switched on the engine, letting it idle for the moment. As Ginnie reached the bottom of the road and took a left, she engaged the car and set off after her.

'She's not going to be looking around her in this rain, is she?' asked Connie.

'She's not looking anywhere at all.'

'Where do you think she's going? She's clearly heading somewhere specific. She can't get to Cold Eaton on foot, can she?'

'She can get to the Cutting, though, can't she? Susan Barr told me she used to take the path from the Cutting to the new housing estate. That's this one.'

'This? This isn't a new development.'

'They were new houses once upon a time, though, weren't they? If Susan is right, she'll head towards the end of the fifties houses before where the estate was extended in the seventies.'

Connie drove past Ginnie and pulled in opposite a gap between two houses, one in the fifties terrace similar to Ginnie's and the other a newer bungalow. Between them was a green public footpath sign pointing down the gap. Neither of them turned their heads as Ginnie swished past them and disappeared up the path. Sadler stared after her. Dahl came over to them and opened the door, sending shards of rain into the car.

'I think you should go, Connie. If she turns and sees me following her, she might change her mind. You're smaller and, er, obviously a woman. I'll drive.'

Connie slid out of the car and Sadler reached over to her. 'We'll meet you at the Cutting. Keep your distance. It must be where she's going. It'll take you about fifteen minutes to walk there. We'll park somewhere out of sight. I'm calling Camilla to meet us there.'

*

The rain hit Connie as soon as she left the car. She hurried down the path, ignoring the water sliding down her neck, and slowed slightly when she saw Ginnie climbing over a stile.

She sheltered under a tree and watched the tall figure cross the field towards the raised bank that demarked the old railway line. When she had turned again and was walking alongside a drystone wall, Connie hurried after her, snagging her trousers on the stile, her shoes seeping with water as she squelched across the field.

When she met the Topley Trail, the ground turned compact and she began to trudge after Ginnie. A few cyclists hissed past her, making her feel less alone. There was a slight bend in the tracks and the Cutting came into view. Connie tracked the old path until she reached the Cutting and saw, with a lurch, a figure standing against the skyline.

'Shit.' Ginnie might not be able to see Connie trailing in her wake but the figure would easily spot her. Connie moved off the path and got out her mobile. Sadler answered on the first ring.

'We've got a problem. There's someone there waiting for Ginnie on the top of the Cutting.'

'We're on our way. You'll get there as quick as us on foot.'

'But they'll see me as soon as I leave this path.'

'Go through the tunnel and walk up the embankment from the other side. They won't be looking behind them.' Sadler was firm but Connie could detect a quake in his voice. 'Do it quickly and protect them both.'

66

Mina found Malcolm Cox sitting on the bench outside his garden in the same position as the previous week. His only concession to the chill was that he had swapped his khaki shorts for a pair of old corduroy trousers. He watched her approach and moved up along the bench.

'It doesn't look like you've come to do the hedge.'

She took the place next to him and regarded the church opposite, more visible than the previous visit after the tall beech trees had shed their leaves. 'You were the naked man who used to roam the fields, weren't you?'

He grunted in amusement. 'The Peaks have always been a bit alternative but I think it was a first for here.'

'You were a naturist?'

'We all have strange ideas when we're younger. Mine was naturism. I was into the writings of George Bernard Shaw. Have you read any of his books?' He turned to her and, in his hopeful expression, Mina saw a glimpse of the younger man.

She shook her head. 'Sorry. I'm here because I need your help. Can I show you something?' She handed him her phone and enlarged the photo of the girls so they filled the screen. 'I guess you recognise some of the girls here. Can you tell me what happened in the Cutting?'

'It were 1957. I'll never forget the year because I'd just turned

358

twenty-one. I'd finished university, had money in my pocket and I was in full bloom of taking my clothes off. I used to wait until it was getting dark. I didn't want to frighten anyone.'

'You made it into the paper.'

'I got a sense people weren't happy with it. I used to avoid where others might see me but my land adjoins the Cutting so I was entitled to go there.'

'Even though there was a railway line?'

'One train an hour, each way. We all knew the times. Well, on this November day, I saw this girl in the grey uniform of Bampton Grammar. You should have seen how the kids dressed in those days. None of this shabby stuff you get these days with their hems hanging down, either that or their skirts hoiked up to their armpits. No, all the girls looked neat as a pin. But not this one when she came out of the rabbit hole.'

'Rabbit hole?'

'The shaft that leads down into the tunnel.'

'How did she look?'

'She smelt bad. That's what I remember. I think she'd been to the toilet on herself. She also . . .' He glanced across at Mina. 'She couldn't speak so I took her back here. I held her by the arm and she kept falling over like she'd lost the use of her legs. So I had to prop her up but she'd fall again.'

'You didn't recognise her?'

'No, and I couldn't get a word out of her to get her home. She told me her name was Valerie. So I took her back here and the first thing she did was take all her clothes off.'

'What?' Mina's voice was full of disbelief.

'Not in front of me or anything. No, she went to the front room, the nice one that my mother used to keep as a parlour, and I gave her a blanket. I took her clothes and I burnt them on the fire. She dressed herself in the clothes I gave her, a pair of tweed trousers and a flannel shirt. Funnily enough they fitted her.'

'Did she say anything?'

'I got dressed and put her in the back of the tractor. She hardly spoke the whole time, just said her name was Valerie, and pointed the way home. Her parents opened the door and took her off me. I told them where I found her and they shut the door. No time for me. They looked at me as if it were me that attacked her. Bampton lot. They're funny buggers there.'

'But, hold on. I thought Valerie lived in Hallows. That's where everyone has been telling me Valerie Hallows lived. Up on the farm at Hallows Hill.'

'You mean Grace Hallows in the photo? What's she got to do with it? Why would I go up to Hallows Farm?'

'Grace Hallows. Who's she?'

'Buried in the churchyard.'

'Valerie Grace Hallows.'

'That's it.'

'She's Valerie!'

'She wasn't called Valerie. She went by her middle name, Grace.' He pointed at the image on Mina's phone. 'That's Valerie.'

67

Friday, 9 May 1958

The Peak District Pauper Lunatic Asylum had been renamed, after much debate, the Margaret Drake Hospital for the Mentally Insane. Margaret Drake was a wealthy benefactor, still living, who had donated a large sum of money to bring the huge Victorian building into the twentieth century. Rumours swirled of a mentally deficient brother locked up in an institution in Scotland but no one was sure of this. The Derbyshire hospital now boasted a heated swimming pool, refurbished tennis courts in the garden and the once shabby ballroom had been refitted to look like the one at the tower in Blackpool. However, the tall clock tower in the middle of the building continued to brood over the patients. A place where time stood still but inmates were reminded of life's passage by the arms of a clock that had continued to move for two centuries.

A radiogram had been set up on one side of the room, over-seen by a male nurse, an elderly gent who preferred the music of Acker Bilk, or Billy Acker, as he renamed him, to the more modern swing music or, God forbid, Elvis Presley. The taffeta in Valerie's underskirt stood out stiffly from her body and the starched lace rustled against her stockings as she walked. She was aware of eyes swinging to watch her progress, and dropping when she met their stares with one of her frowns. A row of men idled on the other side of the room, many of them smoking, giving the impression of coiled anger. She walked past them, avoiding the row of chairs where she could sit waiting for a partner, and, instead, sat down at one of the small round tables and reached for a fairy cake. It was a delicate thing, the butter icing deliciously sweet in her mouth.

'It's all right for you, you're so tall.' Melanie, a recent arrival at the house, looked enviously at the cakes.

'I'm like a beanpole. I'd rather have your curves.' She didn't sound convincing even to her own ears.

'No you wouldn't. You can eat what you like. I can feel my bottom getting bigger just looking at that cake stand.'

Valerie smiled and reached for another. 'It's better than dancing.'

'The foxtrot not to your taste?'

'Not when you're taller than most of your partners.'

'Oh well, perhaps they'll start playing rock and roll. That'd be progress.' She eyed Valerie. 'It's not that bad here, is it?'

'I'm not so sure about that.' Valerie looked down. 'What treatment are you going to have?'

'I don't know yet. Why?'

Valerie thought about the ECT. The cold metal trolleys that she was strapped to, making feeble jokes with the other patients. The subsequent blinding headaches and upset stomachs. She also remembered the crushing routine. Making beds, washing, playing cards. She turned to Melanie.

'The nurses are nice. And the grounds. You can walk in the gardens. Get some fresh air.'

'I heard that there was film night. I don't want anything too scary. Maybe Cary Grant.'

'Probably. I'm not into films.'

'I simply need a rest. My nerves were shot. The doctor suggested here. I'd heard about the dances and the art classes. It seemed like a good idea.'

'You had a choice?' asked Valerie.

'Well, no. When I couldn't stop crying one day, they sent me here. But I don't mind. It's not like they never let you out. I mean, you're leaving soon, aren't you?'

'Next week.'

'Well. There you are. You must be feeling better.'

'Yes, I must be.'

'Will you have to carry on with treatment? Take the medicine?'

Valerie thought of the small white pills. Some good, some not. 'It depends.' *Never*, she thought. *I'm never taking one of those tablets again in my life.*

'My mam told me to think of it like a fresh start. When I leave, I'm not going to tell anyone where I've been. Certainly not a man. You know what they're like.' Melanie gave Valerie a sideways look. 'Best not mentioned.'

'I'm not going to tell anyone at all.' The vehemence in Valerie's voice surprised them both.

'Well, no. New start and all that.'

'Valerie's going to be left behind. I've decided to use my middle name when I leave here.'

'Ooh that's a good idea. I'd like to do that, except my middle name's Gladys and that's ever so old-fashioned these days. It's worse than Melanie. I would if I could, though. What about you? What's yours?'

Valerie looked at a man approaching the table and took another cake. 'Virginia. My middle name is Virginia. I'm going to be Ginnie.'

68

Wednesday, 8 November 2017

As Connie sped towards the figures, she lost sight of which one was Ginnie. They were both tall, wearing long coats that covered them like shrouds. Standing on the brow of the hill, they faced each other. Fragments of conversation came across the air to her as she puffed towards them, glad of the recent bouts of running she'd forced her idle body to endure. One of the figures turned at the sound of Connie's approach, the shock on her face turning to fury.

'Who's this? Who've you brought with you?'

Ginnie turned to Connie, her eyes calm. 'I think it might be over.'

'Over?'

Monica launched herself at Ginnie, who lifted her arms to defend herself, her limbs taking the force of the blows. Connie saw in horror that one of the sleeves of Ginnie's raincoat showed a slash of red. She hauled Monica away from Ginnie, forcing the knife from her hand, and pushed the squirming figure onto the ground. Putting her knee on Monica's back as she applied the handcuffs, she turned the body, partly so her captive wouldn't suffocate but mainly so she could take a closer look at the woman in whose eyes she'd spotted the gleam of the fanatic.

Ginnie had taken off the mac and was wrapping it around her arm, blood mingling with the soft mist of rain that had begun to fall causing a pink stream to drop to the ground and mix with the earth.

'Are you okay?'

Ginnie nodded and Connie turned to wave at the figures running up the Cutting from the road below.

Sadler made it first and ran towards his mother, taking off his jacket. Dahl hauled the still wriggling Monica to her feet.

'Be careful.' She was too late. Dahl got an eyeful of Monica's spit and, as she felt her tension dissipate, Connie was seized with the desire to laugh.

'I'll take her down to the car.' Dahl looked at Sadler. 'Does your mother need an ambulance?'

'Please.'

'I'll call it.' Connie took out her mobile.

'No, Francis. Please. I'm all right.'

'You've been—'

'No!' Ginnie's vehemence shocked them all and even the retreating Dahl looked back briefly. 'I have some bandages at home. Let me wrap up the wounds with them. If I can't staunch the blood, then we can go to hospital. Will you take me home?'

At Sadler's nod, Connie put her mobile away. 'I ought to go with Dahl. I don't think Monica will make an easy passenger.'

'Take her to the station and call a doctor. I want a preliminary physical and mental health assessment after she's charged.'

Connie looked at the pair. 'What about you two?'

366

Sadler nodded to the car that had just drawn up to his. 'Camilla's here.'

*

Ginnie's house was freezing as usual and Sadler went to the control panel and overrode the settings. The radiators sprang to life as Camilla helped her mother into a chair. Sadler found the first aid kit and applied TCP to Ginnie's slashes. Ginnie was right about her injuries; the blade had only skimmed the skin. She winced at the sting from the antiseptic but allowed her son to minister to her.

'You're lucky she didn't kill you. She managed it with Nell Colley.'

Ginnie closed her eyes briefly. 'Monica was always slightly unstable but she'd not have taken me, or, for that fact, Emily Fenn. We're both made of stronger stuff.' She looked up at her son. 'You know.'

'Yes, I know.'

'Know what?' Camilla sat in the chair opposite and looked pale. 'What's going on?'

'I'll tell you in a minute but, before I start, just tell me. How did you discover I was Valerie?'

Sadler held out his hand and briefly touched his mother's shoulder. 'The drowning.'

'The drowning?' Ginnie smiled. 'Of course. If it's got to be something that gave me away, I'm glad it's that.'

Sadler moved across to the sofa and sat down. 'You were from Derwent village. Camilla and I were brought up on the story you told us. How the village had been drowned to make

367

way for the Ladybower reservoir and your family moved to Bampton. A few years later, you went to see the demolition of the church spire that during dry seasons would reveal itself.'

Camilla said nothing, her eyes on her brother.

'You talked about it a lot to us and as children we were entranced. So much so that we never really noticed that you never spoke about your school days.'

'She went to Bampton Grammar,' said Camilla. 'When I went there, I knew it was Mum's old school.'

'But that's about it. That's all we did know.'

'Mum was always busy, out and about.'

'She was. She's always had a huge group of friends and has always made friends easily. Some of the friends we do know are from when we were young but why are there no school contemporaries amongst them?'

Camilla turned to her mother. 'Mum?'

Camilla held out Ginnie's arm as Sadler applied gauze to the cuts and began to wrap around a crepe bandage, ignoring the fact the use-by date was ten years old. 'I've always avoided gangs, tribes, in whatever I do. The minute a group gets cliquey, I leave. I prefer dealing with people on an individual level.'

'But it wasn't always like that, was it?'

'No, it wasn't. At Bampton Grammar there were six of us in the same year who went around together. Me and five friends. We gravitated towards the village where two of the girls lived. Emily Fenn, whose grandfather ran the pub, and Ingrid Neale who lived in the manor house. The Neales have been there for generations.'

'And Grace Hallows lived on nearby Hallows Farm.'

'Grace,' Ginnie smiled, lost in thought. 'I'd quite forgotten about Grace.'

'It's caused a lot of confusion. Sharing the same first name. Valerie Grace in her case and Valerie Virginia in yours.'

'It's only in novels where people aren't allowed to have the same name. I was known as Valerie. Grace, whose mother had aspirations of grandeur, preferred to call her daughter by her second name. It was considered the posh thing to do.'

'I don't understand what this has to do with anything. Is it to do with the tea dance leaflet that I found in your bed?' Camilla took the bandage off Sadler and kneeled at her mother's feet to secure the ends.

'The tea dance comes later. There were six of us. The three I've already mentioned – Emily, Ingrid and Grace. The other two came from Bampton like me, Hilary and Nell.'

'What about Monica?'

'Monica was three years younger than us. A baby, or so I thought. And yet Monica's love of the railway meant that she knew about the tunnel shaft and the way in.'

Camilla looked up. 'What happened?'

'I can piece together a lot of it. I can start the story if you want,' said Sadler.

Ginnie shook her head. 'No. I'll tell it. It started one November. The six of us were walking along the railway track and when we were inside the tunnel, the girls shoved me into the ventilation shaft. Six of us walked into the tunnel and only five came out. I was left inside.'

'My God. How long were you in there for?' Camilla looked horrified.

'A few hours. Five, six. It's difficult to tell as it was getting dark. I managed to climb the ladder, though, and I reached the top. A man found me and took me home to my parents.'

'A stupid joke.' Camilla was outraged. 'A stupid childish prank.'

Ginnie shook her head. 'It was nothing of the sort. It was premeditated and done out of spite and hate.'

'Why? Why would they hate you?'

'Because,' Ginnie looked at her daughter, 'I was young, naive and fell in love with the wrong man.'

69

'But I don't understand. That's Valerie.' Mina, her head pounding with confusion, took the phone from Malcolm and pointed at the girl on the left of the photo, small and thin like her granddaughter.

'That's Grace Hallows. Lived up on Hallows Farm and buried in the churchyard over there.'

'Then who's this Valerie?' A tall girl with long blonde hair and a confident half-smile. Mina remembered Sadler's shock at seeing the photo. *Oh no*, she thought, and felt her hands begin to shake.

'She lived down in Bampton. That's where I took her home. Away from the spite of this village. They were evil, them girls.'

'They were young and stupid.' Mina's voice cracked.

'You been in that tunnel?' Mina nodded. 'Fancy yourself stuck inside there in the dark, do you?'

'No.' Mina was in tears. 'It was a cruel and horrible thing to do.'

'Now you're talking sense. I know what it's like. You see it with the animals. One takes the lead and the others follow suit. It was like that there.'

'Who was the ringleader?'

Malcolm shrugged. 'I don't care. Makes no difference. It

wasn't that lass they shoved up the shaft. And not one of them sorry, I bet.'

'Hold on.' Mina felt a well of grief rise up inside her. 'My mother was sorry. She spent her life being sorry. It's what she asked me to do. Find Valerie and check she was all right.'

'She's not going to be all right, is she? I heard she were in a mental home for a while.'

'You didn't check to see if she was okay afterwards?'

'Me? Wasn't me who put her in the chimney. I did my bit, which is more than anyone else.'

'I've made a complete mess of things.'

'Aye.' He contemplated his garden. 'Was it Emily who sent you up here?'

'Yes, although I can't imagine what she thinks of me.'

'Emily's not so bad. She was good friends with your mam before it all happened. I expect she was sorry to hear your mam died but no one to tell. That's the trouble with up here. No one talks about anything but we know the ins and outs of lives. Go back and see her.'

*

Emily was waiting for her as she descended the hill, a stout figure still with the old-fashioned pinny tied at the waist, her shoulders stooped. Was the well-built girl with the high-necked cardigan buttoned at the top still discernible? Perhaps, by the way she held her head to one side.

'I feel such a fool.' Mina had reached Emily, who nodded.

'We were all fools. Come inside.'

Emily led Mina across to a room at the back, through a

door marked 'Private'.

'My grandfather used to call it the parlour and the name's stuck, although most people wouldn't know what one was these days anyway.'

The square room was simply furnished but the pieces were good quality and fresh flowers scented the room.

Emily sat down heavily in the armchair and handed Mina a black and white photo. She looked tired, the landlady's face finally showing her age. 'I've been wanting to give this to you since we met but it never seemed the right moment. It's from before. Before everything. It was taken on our first day in the fourth form.'

Mina studied the photo. Two girls sitting at their desks. Hilary slightly behind a young Emily. Both were wearing a crisp white short-sleeved blouse and a checked skirt. Innocent eyed, their expressions held none of the hauteur of the following summer.

'What happened?'

Emily grimaced. 'Adolescence. You just want to fit in, don't you? You follow the crowd. Even your mum, though she was cleverer than all of us.'

'What about Valerie? What did she do?'

'She was part of the gang but she kept her distance. She wasn't originally from around here. She came from much further up, the old village drowned by the Ladybower reservoir. Did you know?'

Mina shook her head. 'But I've been chasing after the wrong Valerie. I thought it was Valerie who lived up at Hallows Farm.'

'Grace? She was one of us, all right. Her mother had ideas above her station despite living on that rackety old farm. She went by her second name.'

'But my grandfather said that Valerie was dead. The timings would fit with Grace's death.'

'I think that was me. I sent your grandfather Grace's death notice with a short note saying to let Hilary know. It announced the death of Valerie Grace Hallows. Hilary was away at university at the time. Your granddad must have told her that Valerie was dead and not shown her the actual notice.'

'But Mum thought you'd killed her.'

Emily looked down, twisting her hands in her apron. 'After what we did to Valerie, she ended up getting hospitalised. I knew she wasn't dead. I'd occasionally see her around Bampton. She'd avert her eyes, or I did, but I knew Valerie was still alive.'

'Why didn't Mum see her?'

Emily made a face. 'I don't know. Hilary worked in the library and I certainly avoided the place. Maybe their paths never crossed either, although that would be strange. I think, perhaps, as your mother declined, her fears blurred into each other.'

'What was she like? The real Valerie, I mean?'

'She was different. More developed. We didn't think anything of it until one day Ingrid saw her walking down one of the lanes holding hands with Mr Neale.'

'Harry Neale?'

Emily gave her a withering look. 'Not Harry Neale. The girls' father. Tom Neale. He spoilt the two girls rotten, Ingrid and Monica, and they adored him too. Ingrid couldn't believe it. She could hardly speak when she came down to tell me. She stood there white as a sheet just out in the back yard and told me she'd seen Valerie holding hands with her own father.'

'And it was true?'

'I guess so.'

'You asked Valerie?'

'What was the point? She would hardly have said yes, would she?'

'Perhaps it was innocent.'

'Oh, I think it was innocent enough. The distance of time has given me that at least. Ingrid saw them holding hands and she and her sister spied on their father for a few days. That's all they saw. A bit of kissing and hand holding.' Emily paused. 'That was enough.'

'But if you say Mum just went along with it, who were the ringleaders?'

Emily stared at her in astonishment. 'Ingrid and Monica of course. Ingrid because she was the apple of her dad's eye. Monica, well, Monica's always been a bit different. Odd.'

'Different? How do you mean?'

Emily looked down. 'I'm glad it's all going to come out. I heard about the book and I was glad. I wouldn't have minded. Ingrid would but she wasn't around to say anything, was she? But Monica. Well, Monica is still here and she wouldn't have liked the idea of the memoir at all.'

70

'Tom Neale. Such an innocuous name and, in many respects, an ordinary man. It could have been a footnote in our history except for those girls.'

'Tom Neale was the father of Ingrid and Monica?'

'He was a gentleman. A kind, ordinary person who was interested in the world around him. I was always a little bit different. I came from a different part of the Peaks and he was fascinated about the drowning of Derwent village. He asked me to come into his study and tell me all about it.'

Camilla made a face. 'It sounds a bit predatory to me.'

Ginnie paled. Annoyed. 'It wasn't. After all these years, I still remember his kindness.'

'You had an affair.' Camilla went over to the sofa and sat next to her mother. 'That's not so terrible.'

'No. It's not so bad, is it? It was innocent and non-sexual. But jealousy is a terrible thing to behold. Have you ever seen it in its full force?'

Camilla shook her head. Sadler, feeling his temples ache, nodded. His mother glanced across at him.

'When did you realise the girls had discovered your relationship?' asked Sadler.

'I stopped being invited along to the group gatherings in the churchyard. I spied on one of the meetings and heard mention of a punishment but I thought it would be something mean and childish, not terrifying. I thought I'd die in the tunnel, walled up like some medieval bride. Somehow, though, I managed to get myself to the top of the shaft and a man found me.' Ginnie looked like she wanted to say something and then changed her mind. 'He took me back to my parents.'

'What did you say to them?' asked Sadler.

'I didn't speak for a month. They had no idea what happened to me. I was examined by our family doctor. They assumed I'd been attacked and he recommended a spell in the Margaret Drake.'

Camilla looked in astonishment at her brother. 'The ment . . . psychiatric hospital? I know the building. It's derelict now, a huge stone pile with a clock tower in the middle of it.'

'It looked grimmer outside than it actually was. Away from the acute ward, we were treated decently.'

'The therapy worked?'

'It wasn't called therapy then. We were *treated* and it wasn't nice. It did, however, get me speaking again.'

'And you told them what happened?'

'Never. I didn't tell anyone at all.'

'Didn't anyone ask?'

'Who's to ask me? I was sent to the hospital because I wasn't talking. They were focused on finding a cure for that. They knew it was a psychological problem and so they treated me for shock and depression. The tea dance was part of that.'

'They had *tea dances*! You mean with sandwiches and cake.'

Ginnie threw her head back and laughed. 'Yes. It sounds

377

ridiculous now but there you have it. On a Friday, tea and cake and a foxtrot or whatever.'

'You kept the leaflet?'

'It was like an itch that I wanted to scratch every so often. Then I saw Hilary in hospital and I retrieved it from my shoe-box where I keep my odds and ends. A reminder from the past. It's so long ago. The sting does go from trauma. People don't always tell you that but it doesn't hurt forever.'

'But you hid it in your bed.'

'I had this nosebleed that wouldn't stop and I had to hide it quickly. You found it?'

Camilla nodded.

'I shoved it under my sheets. I couldn't get my nosebleed to stop, my heart began to race and the next thing I was in hospital.'

'You had a CT scan, didn't you?' Sadler thought his mother looked tired but at peace. The past held no terrors for her. 'To check the position of your pacemaker. I should have realised. That's where you saw Hilary. She saw the adult Valerie and she recognised you.'

Ginnie nodded. 'I knew she worked in the library, which is why I avoided the place. I saw her a couple of times over the years. Once in the supermarket so I hurried away. Another time at the old baths. I was swimming and she passed me in the pool.'

'She didn't recognise you those times?'

'I don't think so. I had long hair as a teenager. Long and fair, my mother used to call me Rapunzel. I cut it short when I left the hospital and then I was grey by the time I was thirty. I changed and I wasn't sorry, either.'

378

'How did she recognise you in hospital?' asked Camilla.

'Our glances met and I saw the look of recognition in her eyes. I was in a wheelchair and I looked across at a patient lying on a bed. She was obviously very ill. Our eyes met and, well, we knew each other. It was as simple as that.'

It was the question Sadler had wanted to ask from the beginning. 'Did Dad know about the attack?'

Ginnie shook her head. 'No one except my mum and dad.'

'And Tom Neale?' asked Camilla. 'Did you see him again?'

'Don't you understand?' Ginnie looked angry. 'I saw no one else again. I went away to boarding school after leaving hospital and didn't come back until I'd finished university. We never went near Cold Eaton.'

Sadler sighed and stood up. 'I think I need to make us some tea.'

As he listened to the kettle boil, Sadler could hear the murmur of voices from the living room. Camilla had always been closer to their mother than he and it seemed that this revelation wouldn't dent that intimacy. A movement behind him and Camilla was standing in the doorway.

'I don't blame her for not telling us. It doesn't matter, does it?'

'No.' Sadler poured the water into the pot.

'That woman you arrested, Monica. Was Mum in danger from her?'

'Monica was desperate to protect her family's reputation and for the act of violence to remain secret. It was only Nell and, to a certain extent, Hilary's daughter Mina who were interested in revealing what had happened in 1957. Everyone else was happy to let it lie. Mum was never any threat to Monica.'

'So what about what I just saw up at the Cutting?'

'Mum saw Mina in the garden and heard about the exhumation of Nell Colley through one of her friends. It's all anyone's been talking about in Bampton. She got in touch with Monica to see what was going on. It was a stupid idea. Monica is prepared to defend her family honour and the part she played in the attack on Mum to the bitter end.'

Camilla grimaced. 'You know what? I may not have as many friends as Mum but I think if that's the form female friendship takes, I'll stick with my books.'

71

In Emily's parlour, the lit fire warmed the room. The building was silent, centuries of secrets absorbed into its walls. Tomorrow it would be filled with farmers fresh from the fields, stopping in for a quick half before returning to their tractors. For the moment, it was just the two of them. Emily was studying the note left on Mina's van at the Cutting. The writing was now barely legible, the ink smudged from being carried around in Mina's rucksack, its soft edges seeping into the still damp paper.

'It's not Monica's handwriting. She writes like me, the old-fashioned way. You found it on your van?'

Mina nodded. 'It was tucked under the wiper. I saw someone watching me from the bridge but I couldn't make out who it was. Not tall, though, someone around my height.'

Emily looked at the fire that glowed in the grate. Malcolm's wood was drying out, it seemed, a strong flame emitting welcome heat. 'Shall I?'

Mina nodded and Emily threw the note onto the flames. 'We look after ourselves here in the village.'

'Is that why you lied to me when I first showed you the photo? You said you didn't recognise it.'

'I never thought . . . I never realised the extent of the damage. I just saw a girl wafting a photo around that dredged up all these memories. You looked like your mum and you knew our ways. Did you know it was my father who told your mum that logs needed to be stacked in a circle to keep them dry?'

Mina shook her head. 'I thought it was common knowledge.'

'It was the way you said it. It could have been my father speaking. I thought you'd come to rake up the past and, instead, the past had already come to us.'

'Who was it who came up with the punishment for Valerie?'

'I don't even remember. Ingrid, I think. Monica, possibly. It was she who discovered the ventilation tunnel. She knew how to prise open the door just a fraction so that no one would notice that it was ajar.'

'Monica.' Mina gazed into the flames, thinking.

'We were all culpable, though. Remember the figure of the Guy?'

'Of course. I could hardly forget.'

'You said it was like a voodoo doll. I modelled it on Tom Neale. Showed it to the girls, except Valerie of course, and they loved it. Even your mum.'

'God.'

'We were young and I've come to my own peace with the past. I'm sorry your mum's last moments prevented her from doing so.'

'She asked me to find Valerie and I've at least done that.'

'What will you do now?'

Mina shrugged. 'Go back to the house or maybe the boat. I can see why Mum liked living there.

'Go back to the boat, then, and carry on. That's all you can do.'

Mina studied Emily. 'The detective, Sadler, he took the photo. He recognised the real Valerie.'

Emily looked up. 'What's he like?'

Mina, embarrassed, shifted in her seat. 'Tall, good looking, intelligent, cool.'

Emily snorted. 'You might as well be describing Valerie.'

'He'll talk to her. The truth will come out.'

Emily nodded. 'Good.'

72

'So we never had a Shipman in our midst.' Llewellyn sat back in the chair he'd dragged from the Detective Room into Sadler's office. He stretched out his long legs, wincing in pain as the muscles relaxed. 'For a moment I thought Bampton would earn its place in history for the wrong reasons.'

'We've had our fair share of horrible crimes.' A new case had already landed on Sadler's desk. A tip-off about drugs being sold out of one of the houses on the new estate to the east of Bampton. Something to get his teeth into. Nothing to do with his family.

'Oh, don't get me wrong. We're no different from any other small town. It's just a Shipman-style murderer would have brought us the prurient and the macabre. I'd rather people came here for the puddings and scenic walks.'

'The press have hardly shown any interest at all. The comms team have had a quiet two weeks even if we haven't.'

'I didn't like the exhumation.' Llewellyn massaged his calf. 'I'm getting old. I *feel* old. The only consolation is that it served its purpose. Toxicology identified raised levels of morphine in Nell Colley's liver.'

'We also have a confession. Monica Neale has admitted administering an injection to Nell during a visit to her house to prevent her writing her memoirs. Nell made a fatal mistake when she met Monica during her trip out to Cold Eaton and told her of her plans.'

'Why didn't she just write the bloody thing?' Tiredness had made Llewellyn irritable.

'She'd started it, even if it was merely rough notes on an envelope. I think Nell had been prevaricating about writing the book for years. Ingrid Neale's death cleared her mind. Now was the time for the truth to come out. Our histories take time to unknot. It's not simply a case of putting pen to paper.'

'An affair with a married man long dead. A childish prank gone wrong. It was all history. Who would have cared?'

'Monica cared. She's been charged, of course, but she's been sent to a secure psychiatric unit pending a mental health assessment. It will be for the courts to decide her culpability in the killings.'

Llewellyn sighed and stood up. 'Catherine Hallows is still in a coma and it's not looking good. If she recovers, she'll be charged with the killing of Hilary Kemp.'

'Incited by Monica, but still . . . What does Catherine's mother say about everything?'

'Lorna is adamant Catherine didn't have access to her drugs but I'm not so sure. The team are going through Lorna's prescriptions and drug stocks at the moment. The paperwork hasn't really been kept up to date so I suspect we're going to discover that this is how Catherine accessed the diamorphine.'

'Then Lorna may well be looking at charges too. Have you updated Hilary Kemp's daughter?'

'I'm going there now.' Sadler hoped that the flush that he could feel forming under his skin wasn't visible. Llewellyn, however, was no fool.

'She's an attractive woman.' He looked under his eyebrows at Sadler. 'You know the rules, though. No fraternising with witnesses. Say your bit and leave.'

Sadler, embarrassed, said nothing.

'Of course.' Llewellyn turned to go. 'In a year or so, given that she really was only a peripheral witness, who knows what might happen. Just be careful. You know the rules and you're best when you stick to them. Others . . .' Llewellyn looked out to where Connie was laughing with a uniformed officer. 'Is that Morgan Morgan over there?'

Sadler looked confused. 'Who? That's never his name.'

'It is. His family is Welsh like mine. Unlike my father, however, his didn't pause to think how a name like that would sound to the English.' Llewellyn peered through the glass. 'He seems to be getting on very well with Connie.'

*

'Are you going on a date with Morgan?'

Connie looked at Dahl in surprise. 'Not on your life. You wouldn't know but I had a disastrous affair with your predecessor.'

'I'd heard.'

'Oh, great. I thought it was old news by now. Who told you?'

Dahl grinned at her. 'I heard it while I was in Glossop.'

Connie stared at him, her hands on her hips. 'Oh that's brilliant. My sex life made it to the outer reaches of Derbyshire. That's the reason I'm keeping work and my private life separate from now on.'

'Morgan definitely fancies you. He asked me if you were single. Well, not quite as obvious as that. He asked if you lived alone.'

'*Did* he?' Connie couldn't keep a note of satisfaction out of her voice. 'Well, if you meet any nice men who look like Morgan but aren't coppers, send them my way. Hold on.' Connie picked up the ringing phone on her desk and listened to the message.

'Shit.' She fumbled in her handbag looking for her mobile.

'What's the matter?'

'That was reception. Mayfield's been trying to call me. She had her baby at three o'clock this morning.'

'Brilliant. What was it?'

'A girl, apparently. Is that what she wanted? I don't remember asking.'

'I doubt she minded. Should we have a drink to celebrate later?'

'What do you mean later? After work or much later, say, nine o'clock?'

'Ah, that.' Dahl looked embarrassed. 'You've probably noticed I have to leave early some nights.'

Some? thought Connie. 'Never spotted a thing.'

'You're a crap liar. How about after work I take you to meet someone?'

'Great.' Connie cheered up. 'I'd love to meet your mother.'

*

The low autumn sun glinted off the gold trim of the *Evening Star*. There were more plants than Sadler remembered seeing before, pots grouped together in a profusion of greenery but carefully chosen so that there was nothing left trailing that might trip the unwary. Arranged by someone who knew what they were doing.

'What do you think?' Mina's voice behind him made him jump. She was wearing knee-length denim shorts, probably cut down from an old pair of jeans, and a thin jumper.

'Aren't you cold?'

'I'm freezing but I was in the water earlier in waterproofs looking at the underside of the boat. Don't come near me as I must smell rank.'

'Is there a problem?'

'I wanted to check before winter comes, that's all. I don't fancy doing any repairs in the snow.'

'You're moving in then?'

'I've got the house on with a letting agent. I'm not burning any bridges but, for the moment, I'm going to live on the boat.'

'Reconnect with your mother?'

'Do you know what, I don't think that's likely. Whatever I learnt, it hasn't made me know her any better.'

'You don't resent her?'

Mina brushed past him and stepped onto the boat. 'I don't want one incident defining her life, just as I don't want how she died to overshadow who she was. She was more than that. More than the person who decided to play a stupid childish trick in 1957. She led a happy life, of sorts, until she got sick.'

'She never forgot, though, did she?'

'No, she didn't, and neither did Ginnie.'

'No.' Sadler looked down. 'It's odd how we have a shared

history, isn't it? I only made the connection at the end. Derwent village. It was one of the few things that Mum would talk about. She loved to speak of the village under the reservoir and of how she had seen the church spire blown up. If I'd known all along that Valerie was from Derwent, I might have made the connection.'

'Lucky for me you did in the end.' She paused as Sadler held out something. 'Those again. What are they?'

'Red campion. The flowers are faded. I thought you'd recognise them.'

'Who really left them for my mother?'

'Probably Catherine. She wasn't all bad. That's what I want to say. She cared enough to give your mother some flowers. You need to know people are more complicated than just good or bad. I learnt that from my mother at an early age. I never realised she was speaking from experience.'

'How is she?'

'Ginnie? My mother is a survivor.'

'That much is obvious. She doesn't hate me?'

'Hate you? Of course she doesn't. My mother had a past before me. Us children always think our parents' lives start when we were born. Ginnie had a love affair, a traumatic incident and a hospital stay and she decided not to tell anyone. I think I admire her all the more for it.'

'That's good.'

'That I admire her?'

'No, that she doesn't hate me.' She was smiling at him, embarrassed and defiant.

'No, Mina. She doesn't hate you. Can I come on board?'

Acknowledgements

Thanks, as ever, to my agent Kirsty McLachlan at David Godwin Associates and to all at Faber, especially Louisa Joyner, Libby Marshall, Sophie Portas and Richard Fortey.

Thanks to all the bookshops that support my novels, especially those which I've visited over the years. Libraries have also been very supportive and I had a wonderful autumn tour in 2017. Thanks to everyone who came along to hear me speak about my books. It's always lovely to get out and about and meet readers.

Thanks to bloggers, reviewers, friends and relatives who have read and promoted my books and to my fellow Petrona judges.

Special thanks, as ever, to my cousin Pete Westlake for his ongoing patience with my police questions. Also to Tony Butler, to whom *The Shrouded Path* is dedicated, who has done so much to check my work for errors. He and his wife Judith are a continued support.

Thanks to all my family, including my father who sends copies of my books far and wide. And special love and thanks to my husband, Andy, who is a constant source of encouragement.